HOUDINI VS. RASPUTIN

C. Michael Forsyth

Published by Freedom's Hammer Productions
Greenville, SC
http://freedomshammer.com

Publisher's Note: This is a work of fiction. Except for historical figures, the characters are a product of the author's imagination. Any other names or resemblance to actual people is completely coincidental.

ISBN 978-0-9884780-6-0
Library of Congress Control Number 2018956219

This book is dedicated to my son,
playmate and creative partner Brett Forsyth,
who has taught me to value the imagination.

ACKNOWLEDGEMENTS

First and foremost, I must credit William Kalush and Larry Slocum, from whose book *The Secret Life of Houdini* I first learned of the magician's trip to Russia. The book provided invaluable details about the tricks he performed there. Robert K. Massie's classic book *Nicholas and Alexandra* contained a treasure trove of information about the Tsar's household. I could not have depicted Rasputin accurately without the books *Rasputin, Rascal Master* by Jane Oakley, *The Rasputin File* by Edvard Radzinsky, *Rasputin, the Untold Story* by Joseph T. Fuhrmann and *Rasputin, The Man Behind the Myth* by Patte Barham and Maria Rasputin (the mystic's daughter).

Much thanks also to John Cox, whose website *Wild About Harry* offered vital details about Bess and Harry Houdini's private lives. My beta readers Jordan Auslander, Bob Lind, Sean Brodrick, J.E. Franklin, and Marc Allan Gunnells gave me extraordinarily helpful suggestions, as did members of my writing group, the Greenville chapter of the South Carolina Writers Association. I appreciate the dedication of my proofreader Tricia Drammeh. And, as always, my wife Kaye Christopher has my eternal gratitude for all her unwavering support.

CHAPTER ONE

A Safe on Wheels

1903

"You will find Siberia exceptionally inhospitable this time of year, Mr. Houdini," said Chief Lebedoeff, director of the Okhrana, Russia's secret police. He smiled wolfishly at the magician standing before him, clad only in boxer shorts.

"Well, I'm used to lousy weather. I did a three-month engagement in London and I can tell you, it rained every day," the handcuffed escape artist wisecracked. The truth, though, was that the Moscow air was already pricking his bare chest like knitting needles.

Lebedoeff grimaced, peeved that the American was so hard to intimidate. He snapped his fingers and two burly guards began to wrap chains around the escape artist's legs.

"We'll see how amusing you find all this as you lie naked in the Siberian Transport Cell for the twenty-one-day trip," he sneered. "You'll have plenty of time to reconsider the wisdom of challenging the Russian people and their protector, the Okhrana."

Loud clangs rang out in the courtyard of Butyrskaya Prison as the guards clamped shackles to Harry Houdini's ankles. Surrounded by six of the chief's men, the Handcuff King faced the dreaded Transport Cell, a safe on wheels used to ship dangerous criminals and rabble-rousing enemies of the state to imprisonment in the ice-enshrouded wasteland. It stood in the corner of the courtyard, ready to be hauled off by a pair of draft horses.

"Oh, I may not be lying there as long as you think," Houdini said with a grin. The magician's wife, Bess, wearing a fur coat and bonnet, stepped forward.

"Good luck, my dearest," she said, reaching to embrace him.

Lebedoeff slipped between them, wagging his index finger.

"Tut, tut, tut. I'm afraid you must wait to show your affection until your husband returns from his trip," he said with a self-satisfied smirk. "You see, I have heard about your little trick of passing a key to him as you kiss."

"But surely, you will allow our good luck kiss," she protested. "It's our tradition."

"I am sure it is—which is precisely why it will not take place today."

The chief was now absolutely certain that Houdini had no key or lock-picking tools on his person. Moments earlier, he had ordered the magician to strip to the waist, and had his men run their hands through his bushy hair, then meticulously check his ears, mouth, nostrils, armpits and between his outstretched fingers.

Satisfied that the upper body was free from devices, he bade the American empty his pockets, and Houdini turned them inside out to prove they contained nothing. The escape artist then had to strip down to his briefs. The men had pried apart the American's toes and inspected the bottom of his feet.

To the magician's dismay, although not surprise, Lebedoeff ordered him to drop his undershorts and lie spread-eagled face down on an examination table. Two officers held him down while a third probed his rectum.

"Hey, we just met," Houdini, unperturbed, had remarked to the guards. "I expected flowers first, at least." The search had turned up nothing.

Now, after intercepting the kiss, the secret police chief knew he'd thwarted the only possible way his foe could hope to smuggle a means of escape into the Transport Cell. Bess frowned, plainly distraught.

"It's all right, sweetheart," Houdini assured her. "We'll have breakfast at that cute café by the Moskva River, just like I promised. And Chief Lebedoeff will pick up the check, right?"

"If, as you claimed you can, you escape within an hour— which I sincerely doubt," Lebedoeff returned. He snapped his fingers again and another guard hurried forward, holding a set of heavy chains and four padlocks. "After the wagon is locked, we will secure the outer bolt with these."

"Hold on. That's not fair, chief," Houdini argued. "We agreed that you wouldn't use any extra locks; the wagon would be exactly as it is for any criminal getting sent to Siberia."

"Shall I inform these gentlemen of the press that you have been defeated by the Siberian Transport Cell before you even set foot in it?" replied the official, gesturing to four reporters and a photographer who stood on a reviewing stand nearby.

"No, I'll carry out my part of the bargain," Houdini relented. "Even if changing the rules midstream is a dirty trick in my book."

"Place our American guest in the Transport Cell," Lebedoeff commanded.

The guards swung the massive iron door open, picked up the shackled magician and dumped him in the back of the escape-proof carriage.

Houdini looked around the cell, which was entirely lined with zinc sheeting. A trickle of light poured between the bars of the door's tiny window. The door's outer handles were thirty-six inches below the window. *That's farther than any man could reach unless he was part orangutan,* Houdini thought.

Lebedoeff personally locked the door and, for good measure, secured the handles with the chains and padlocks. Then he pressed his pale, narrow face up against the window and held up the key.

"One more thing, Mr. Houdini. It is my duty to inform you that this key is incapable of unlocking the door. The nearest key that can do so is in the possession of the warden of the prison in Siberia."

"Why, you dirty—" Houdini cried, bashing his shoulder against the door.

"*Dos vidaniya,*" Lebedoeff said with a merry salute, sliding the window shut. The Russian chuckled wickedly and strutted from the vehicle. He nodded to the driver, who whipped the draft horses and cried for them to go.

"I thought that clown would never leave," Houdini said to himself. "Time to get out of this paddy wagon."

Houdini now stretched out his hand and grinned at the one little thing the Russians had overlooked in all their meticulous probing: a sixth finger on his right hand, which contained the tiny tools he needed to escape. He had kept the false finger in his right trouser pocket while his upper body was searched. While turning his pockets inside out, he'd donned the flesh-colored appendage. After he dropped his pants, the searchers had been too busy exploring his nether region to take a second look at his hands.

Lucky for me no one's in the habit of counting fingers, he thought. Houdini pulled off the false finger and plucked out a lockpick. It took just under ten seconds for the celebrated Handcuff King to free himself from the cuffs and leg irons. Now to escape the Transport Cell itself—which Houdini intended to do, not just within an hour, but before it even left the courtyard.

The previous day, Houdini and his assistant Franz Kukol had been permitted to inspect the Siberian Transport Cell, while the chief of the Okhrana watched them like a hawk. Although the wagon was the most formidable of its kind they'd ever laid eyes on, it hadn't taken long to spot its one vulnerability: the bottom of the carriage. Mumbling to himself, with a tape measure in hand, Houdini had made a huge production of inspecting the door lock and calculating the distance from it to the window. All that was to divert attention from Franz, who "accidentally" dropped a matchbook, giving him a chance to scrutinize the underside. Sure enough, there were eight wooden slats beneath the body of the cell, mounted on ridges.

Houdini rapidly hatched his escape plan. He wasn't going to try to defeat the door lock or climb through the window. He would slice through the zinc sheeting of the floor, saw through the narrow strips of wood holding the slats in place and escape from under the vehicle. That task required two additional tools: a miniature, serrated tin-cutter and a high saw—a coil of wire with saw teeth, devised by brain surgeons to cut through the cranium.

Kneeling, he used the metal cutter to slice a two-foot section of the zinc floor at the corner of the carriage. He carefully peeled back the metal. His ambitious plan was to leave the Russians clueless about how he'd managed the escape. With the high saw, he began to cut through one of the strips of wood that held the boards in place. Slicing through two of them would be enough to slide two slats out of the way and squeeze through.

The plan depended on split-second timing. Houdini would have to drop out of the bottom of the moving "safe," roll clear of the back wheel and crawl to cover just as the Siberian Transport Cell stopped behind a monument to Tsar Alexander III that stood in the courtyard.

A distraction at the critical moment was needed, of course. As the carriage neared the bronze statue of the monarch astride a mount, Bess began to weep and clutched the chief of the secret police by the lapels of his coat.

"My husband will be ruined if you allow him to be taken to Siberia," Bess protested. "He'll be the laughingstock of Europe, and we still have so many engagements left on the Continent. The debts we've incurred to finance this trip are enormous."

The woman's hysterics drew the attention of the Russian officers, as well as dignitaries who stood on a reviewing stand a few yards away, along with reporters from the *Vedomosti*, the nation's oldest and most prestigious newspaper.

"Mr. Houdini should have thought of all that before he so arrogantly issued his challenge," Lebedoeff declared, loud enough for all to hear. He was plainly enjoying her discomfort.

"Perhaps we can arrange something?" Bess whispered.

Lebedoeff gave a reptilian smile, the kind the serpent might have given Eve. He was on familiar turf now; bribes were the grease that kept the great Russian Empire running smoothly.

"A donation to the officers' retirement fund would certainly be appreciated," he said. "And I would be happy to accept it personally. Do you have a figure in mind?"

"Perhaps fifty rubles?" Houdini's wife offered tentatively.

"I would suggest one hundred rubles."

Bess bit her lip, appearing to mull over the exorbitant demand.

Inside the Siberian Transport Cell, Houdini finished sawing through the strip that held one slat, then slid the board out of place. But as he began to cut the second strip, the carriage rocked and the high saw slipped out of his hand. He watched with horror as it sailed out of reach and landed in the snow.

Of all the rotten luck! Houdini thought. He could reach the instrument, but that would mean his arm would be exposed to the onlookers. *Up to you now, Bess.*

Thirty feet away, Bess watched the carriage approach the statue.

"Perhaps eighty rubles," she suggested to the chief of the Okhrana.

"You are in no position to negotiate, madam," he replied.

"Very well."

Lebedoeff flicked his woolen-gloved finger upward and shouted, "Stop!" The driver reined the horses and the carriage stopped, obscured by the monument.

Houdini felt the jolt, his cue to drop out of the bottom of the carriage. But now they were behind schedule, and his only hope was to use the tiny tin-cutter—never meant for such a job—to finish sawing through the wood.

Bess, for God's sake, please stall that joker a little longer, he thought. He sawed furiously.

"So, this is how the great Houdini has defeated the police departments of the world, escaping from one jail after another," Lebedoeff pontificated. "I'd always suspected that it could only be accomplished with fraud and bribery. It's a bit of a disservice to the common man to give him the illusion that a man can escape from anything, isn't it?"

"That is a damnable lie!" Bess shrieked, and all heads turned to her. She began to sob. Peeking between her fingers, she looked for any sign of her husband sneaking out from behind the statue.

Taken aback by her outburst, Lebedoeff gently took her arm.

"Please, madam, compose yourself," he said in a hushed voice. "Such situations as this demand discretion."

At this moment, Houdini pushed the second board out of the way and squeezed his way to the ground. Lying on his back, he reached back and pulled the zinc flooring back into place, then slid the wooden boards into position on the ridges.

Seemingly inconsolable, Bess continued to sob and rant. By now, all eyes were on her.

"It is because we are Americans, isn't it?" she cried. "You hate us all!"

"Be reasonable, madam," Lebedoeff said, reaching for her. She smacked his hand out of the way. Over his shoulder, Bess saw Houdini darting from behind the monument to the nearest building.

"You are quite right," she told the chief, sniffling. "Forgive me for that display of weakness. I will wait for my husband to prove himself."

Lebedoeff's face fell. "Now, let's not be too hasty," he told her. The head of the Okhrana could feel those rubles slipping through his fingers.

"No," Bess said firmly. "Let the challenge go on, for better or worse."

"Very well!" Lebedoeff snarled. He yelled to the driver, "Move your behind!" As the observers returned their gazes to the carriage, it continued down the path and through the prison gates—the driver unaware that his sole charge was no longer inside.

Lebedoeff turned to his officers. "Attention!"

The six guards jumped into place and stood abreast, shoulders back and chests puffed out.

"You are all to be commended for being so keen-eyed and diligent," their leader said, pacing before them. "You have helped preserve the dignity of Mother Russia. Each of you will receive a special—"

He was interrupted by a pink-cheeked young officer who came scampering across the snow.

"He's here, he's here!" he hollered.

"Who's here?" Lebedoeff growled in annoyance.

The young officer pointed to the administration building, where Houdini stood in the doorway waving, a blanket over his shoulders and a steaming bowl in his hand.

"Your man here was kind enough to offer me a cup of borscht," Houdini yelled to the head of the Okhrana. "Never had beet soup before. It's nearly as good as my ma's chicken soup and that's saying a lot."

Lebedoeff stumbled back in shock and had to grip the arm of one of his men to remain upright.

***

Moments later, Houdini and Franz faced Lebedoeff inside the prison office, a grim room crowded with lateral files overflowing with the arrest records of labor organizers, student protesters, anarchists and other troublemakers. Layers of wanted posters were taped to the walls, some yellowed with age. As Houdini sat spooning out the last drops of his soup, Lebedoeff paced back and forth, glowering.

Franz extracted a sheet of paper from his briefcase.

"Sir, this is a paper verifying that Mr. Houdini escaped from the Siberian Transport Cell," he said hesitantly. "If you don't mind, it requires your signature."

"After that, we can all go to that café and have coffee—on you," Houdini said, placing the empty bowl on a desk. "Maybe I'll sample one of your famous pirozhkis and, of course, the tea cakes." He stood and clapped the Russian on the shoulder. "No hard feelings?"

The chief looked down at the paper, which bore an illustration of Houdini chained and handcuffed in the Siberian Transport Cell. A bold heading proclaimed, "Houdini Escapes Russian Death Wagon." Soldiers in comically oversized fur Cossack hats and waist-length mustaches pointed bayonets at the wagon from all sides.

Lebedoeff ripped the paper in two, then in quarters and flung the pieces to the floor. Houdini realized he'd pushed the chief too far. The guy was already steamed at being licked by an upstart and cheated out of a hefty bribe. He wouldn't put up with being mocked in the newspapers.

"I will not sign my name to any document that disparages the Tsar's security forces," the Russian snapped. He spun on his boot to march out.

"Now hold on, buster. A deal is a deal!" Houdini exclaimed. He zipped around the desk to block the Okhrana chief's way. *How I'd like to clobber this pompous jerk!*

"Stand aside, unless you want to be truly arrested, here and now." Lebedoeff's Arctic-ice eyes left no doubt that he was serious. Houdini stepped out of the way, bowed and waved him out with mock reverence. Lebedoeff stomped off with the sullen fury of a bully defeated in a schoolyard fistfight.

"Well, it looks like I'm paying for lunch, Franz," Houdini groaned.

Bess, who'd been speaking to the reporters outside, entered.

"That barbarian must be the rudest man on Earth," she declared. "He practically bowled me over as he yelled in my face. He's got to be joking about the letter, right?"

"Oh, he isn't as funny as he looks," Houdini said, dispirited. "The double-crossing son of a bitch won't verify the escape."

Franz picked up the torn bits of paper. "It doesn't matter, boss. Those Russian reporters saw it all."

"Yes," said Bess, brightening. "They're begging you to come out to be photographed."

Houdini sighed. "Let's get it over with."

"Not so fast, dear. Your hair's a mess." She took a brush from her handbag and fussed over him, returning it to a semblance of order.

"This tour is turning into a mess," her husband mumbled.

A regal voice came from behind them. "Perhaps I can be of assistance."

They all turned to see a gentleman with a flowing, snow-white mustache and a chest full of medals approach from the doorway. Houdini recognized him as one of the dignitaries who'd been on the reviewing stand, although they hadn't been introduced.

"I was quite impressed with your performance, and I think the person I represent would be too," the newcomer said with great dignity. "My signature will carry as much weight as Chief Lebedoeff's—more, I should think."

The elderly gent's authoritative manner demanded attention. His English was impeccable, Houdini noticed. He seemed like the kind of guy who could speak a half- dozen languages fluently.

"And you are ...?" Houdini said, raising an eyebrow.

"Count Vladimir Fredericks at your service," the official said. "I am Chief Minister of the Imperial Court. The Tsar has heard of your exploits and wanted me to see you perform firsthand. After what I witnessed today, I have no doubt that he and the Tsarina Alexandra would very much like to see you perform. Can you appear at the Kremlin Palace in a week's time? The Imperial Family is having a small gathering."

Jackpot! Houdini thought. He looked at Bess and she beamed.

"Tell His Supreme Majesty we'll be there!"

As soon as the old man left, Houdini asked a reporter if the guy was the real deal. Sure enough, Count Vladimir, a Finnish nobleman by birth, was the master of court life and impresario of all ceremonies. He bestowed all medals and arbitrated all disputes.

"Do you know what this means?" the magician asked Bess, picking her up and spinning her around. "If we knock the Tsar's socks off, it'll be international news. Every royal house in Europe will pay through the nose to see us!"

CHAPTER TWO

The Black Peril

The Grand Kremlin Palace was the Tsar's residence while in Moscow. Sprawling over five square miles, it boasted seven hundred rooms and nine churches, most notably a cathedral with a looming bell tower. The Houdinis were to perform in one of five reception halls, Georgievesky Hall, a grand room with sweeping arches and dazzling chandeliers.

As Franz finished setting up, Bess changed into her costume in an adjacent room. She'd designed the glitzy outfit herself, with padding to complement her slight, elfin figure. Count Vladimir Fredericks introduced the magician to the twenty-four guests of honor, who were beginning to drift into the hall.

Growing up among New York immigrants, Bess had picked up some Russian. Houdini had been born in Hungary, and his mother spoke Hungarian, Italian, Spanish, French and German. He'd taught himself Russian and became fluent for the tour. Of course, most of the educated class knew English, and they used it tonight for the Houdinis' benefit.

Houdini bowed as he greeted the Tsar's sister the Grand Duchess Olga, and his mother, the stern-faced Dowager Empress Maria Feodorovna. He was next introduced to a man of about twenty-two in humble student attire just shy of shabby, in sharp contrast to the finery of the hoi polloi. At a glance, you could tell it was the only suit he'd ever owned.

"This young man is the poet Illya Volkov, one of our country's most promising writers," Count Vladimir said. "He will honor us with a reading as part of the evening's entertainment."

The poet had a mop of straw-colored hair that fell to his eyebrows, and dark, deep-set eyes, soulful as a basset hound's. Count Vladimir looked about.

"The Tsar and Tsarina will be here momentarily and I should prepare," he said. "Volkov, would you be so kind as to carry on the introductions?"

"Of course, Your Illustrious Highness."

When the Chief Minister of the Imperial Court was out of earshot, the poet pulled Houdini closer and glanced around furtively.

"If you outwitted the secret police, you can't be all bad," he said with a mischievous twinkle in his eyes. "You should teach the trick to some of the less gifted."

"Aren't they all villains?"

The poet laughed. "Apparently, you've never heard the Russian saying, 'All the good men are in prison.'"

"You're not some kind of radical, are you?"

Even before setting sail from America, Houdini had heard about the unrest in Russia: anarchists planting bombs to assassinate officials; workers and students marching through the streets, demanding reforms—not to mention the frequent pogroms in which mobs murdered hundreds of Jews.

Illya shrugged. "I am neutral in politics. I'm an artist. But the country is on a razor's edge. On one side, greatness. On the other ..."

Before the poet could elaborate, another young man swaggered up to them, holding a champagne glass. He was exquisitely handsome, slim and impeccably coiffed, decked out in a tux and tails.

"Greetings, Volkov!" he addressed the poet.

"Harry Houdini, may I present Prince Felix Yusupov the Younger," said Illya.

The aristocrat gave Houdini's hand a firm shake, but his sweet, heavy cologne reminded the escape artist of the showgirls on Coney Island.

"I trust you have something amusing in store," Yusupov said, taking a sip from his glass. "We've seen more than our share of fortune tellers, mystics and mediums. It's all become a bit tiresome."

"I'll try my best."

"See that you do." Yusupov was smiling, but Houdini didn't like his tone. The guy oozed idleness and privilege.

"You'd better do as Yusupov says," Illya advised, placing a hand on the aristocrat's forearm. "He has his very own dungeon."

"Not every home has one of those," noted the magician.

"My friend is taking poetic license, and who has more the right," Yusupov explained. "One of my palaces, in Moscow, was built over the site of a hunting lodge of Ivan the Terrible, who was quite the aficionado of falconry. As well, of course, of torture and execution. When my palace was being built, they uncovered underground chambers with all manner of grisly instruments of torture, and skeletons still chained to the walls. Needless to say, all that has been cleared out."

"Why? I can't think of a better way to deal with rude houseguests," jested Illya.

Yusupov spotted the Grand Duchess Olga beckoning him from across the hall, through a flurry of bejeweled women in evening gowns and generals in uniforms festooned with medals.

"Excuse me. I am being summoned. Remember what I said, Mr. Houdini. Nothing old hat."

As he strutted off, Houdini turned to Illya. "Full of himself even for a prince, isn't he?"

"He has plenty of reason to hold his head high," the poet replied. "Yusupov is the wealthiest man in all of Russia, except for the Tsar—perhaps. He inherited a fortune of twenty-one million rubles, invested in land, palaces, jewels and, in his St. Petersburg palace, one of the world's most valuable private art collections. Four Rembrandts and counting, I understand."

Next, Illya brought Houdini over to the Grand Duke Nikolai Nikolaevich, cousin of the Tsar, who was escorting a pair of women dressed in black. Nikolaevich, a six-foot-six giant with blazing blue eyes, wore a beard trimmed to an intimidating point. His barrel chest was adorned with medals, and a dagger hung from his belt. The nobleman exuded the fierce energy of an Iron Age warrior-chief. Compared to Yusupov, his grip was overbearingly masculine.

"I bet you could crack walnuts with those mitts," Houdini joked.

Nikolaevich chuckled, clearly pleased.

"I've found that bending steel rods each morning is an excellent means to increase the strength in one's hands and forearms," he said in a robust voice as deep as any bass in a barbershop quartet. The nobleman gestured toward the women.

"My wife, the Grand Duchess Stana, and her sister, the Grand Duchess Militsa."

Stana and Militsa advanced in lockstep like Siamese twins and presented their hands to kiss. Militsa's narrow face was extraordinarily pale and she had the prominent, hawkish nose of a bird of prey. But her dominating features were penetrating black eyes that shone like pearls.

"So, you are the magician of whom we have heard so much," she said, as Houdini kissed her hand. "Are you a follower of Zarathustra?"

Houdini shook his head. He was an avid student of the history of magic, each year accumulating what he hoped would one day become a vast collection of books on the subject, but the name of the ancient Persian mystic was only vaguely familiar to him.

"In the wooded mountains of Montenegro where I was born, the ancient pagan ways survive. We even have sorcerers who speak to the dead," Militsa intoned in the mesmerizing manner of a Delphic oracle. "I know that the supernatural is real—as does anyone familiar with the miracles of the great elders of the Russian Orthodox Church. I have devoted much of my life to the study of mysticism. Modern theophysicists such as Madame Blavatsky, of course, but in particular the mysteries of the prophet Zarathustra, who taught the magic of the Persians. I have steeped myself in his teachings—in the original language—and I have learned what true magic is: both a science and a religion, the worship of forgotten gods."

"Well, it sure sounds like you could teach me a thing or two about magic," Houdini said. "Suddenly, I feel like an amateur."

She smiled, although she seemed to recognize that he was patronizing her.

"You've come here to dazzle the court with your mysteries," she said. "Would you share with me what you have planned?"

Oh, you bet I can, Houdini thought. *I have your number, sister.*

"Well, we'll do the mind-reading act," he told her. "Some card tricks and the East Indian Needle Trick. The Metamorphosis, of course, that's always a big hit. You'll enjoy that, I promise."

"And your grand finale?"

"Well, it has to be ... grand. The bell tower of the Kremlin's main cathedral. I thought of making it ring on cue."

Militsa laughed. It was a rather harsh and cruel laugh that reminded Houdini of a raven's caw.

"That bell hasn't rung in over one hundred years," she said. "I imagine the rope to ring it has rotted to dust."

"Yes, I found that out, which is exactly why I thought it would be such a neat trick to surprise the Tsar and his guests by having it mysteriously peal," Houdini explained. "But it was just too difficult. So, I have another mystery in mind."

"You have me intrigued. I look forward to seeing this marvel."

The magician bowed as the grand duke marched off, with the sisters drifting close behind, black gowns trailing, reminding Houdini of Dracula's brides. When they were a safe distance away, he turned to Illya.

"Well, those two ladies are odd ducks. What's their story?"

"Ah, the Montenegrin sisters," said Illya. "They are known as the Black Princesses."

"Because of their black hair or because they dress in black?"

"Both ... or perhaps their black hearts. Another nickname wags have for them is The Black Peril."

"Sound like real charmers."

"It was Militsa who introduced the Tsarina Alexandra to spiritualism, séances, tarot cards and all that other hocus-pocus," the poet revealed. "No offense meant."

"None taken."

A footman passed, bearing an hors-d'oeuvres tray, from which each man snagged a cracker topped with cream cheese, caviar and radish.

"Thanks to Militsa, a never-ending procession of clairvoyants, fortune-tellers and holy fools have traipsed through the palace to advise the Imperial Family," Illya continued while nibbling the treat. "Let's see ... there was Matrona, the Barefoot Prophetess, who spoke in tongues and needed another simpleton to translate. Peter the Hunchback. And now, there's the esteemed 'psychic healer' Monsieur Philippe. You'll meet him in a moment. Perhaps it's only jealousy, but more than one courtier told me he has an unhealthy influence over the Tsarina, and through her, of course, the Tsar."

"She's a fascinating woman, though, this Militsa," Houdini mused, as he polished off his cracker. "Taught herself Persian even?"

"I've been to her palace. Every day is like Halloween: summoning the dead, prayers over the bones of saints, spooks making tables rise. Enough to make your hair stand on end."

"She doesn't scare me," Houdini said with a laugh. "Halloween is my favorite day of the year. Heck, if I play my cards right, I might land a gig at her next shindig."

Bess came from the dressing room in the showgirl outfit she wore as the magician's assistant. It showed off her legs, used to good advantage when the audience had to be distracted.

"Do I look all right?" She turned her back for Houdini to inspect the buttons.

"You look better than all right," her husband said, taking care of one button she'd missed. "You put these dames with their fancy jewelry to shame." He would have patted her backside if they weren't in a reception hall full of swells. The writer took Bess's hand.

"Illya Volkov," he said, bowing.

"Illya's a poet," Houdini told his wife. "Everyone says he's terrific."

The young man waved away the compliment. "I'll be torturing you with a recitation shortly."

A trumpet blared, and the Imperial Couple marched arm and arm into the ballroom, accompanied by Count Vladimir. The Tsar wore a white uniform bedecked with medals, with a sash and sword. The Tsarina Alexandra floated gracefully toward the Houdinis, tall and willowy, dressed in a white silk gown embroidered in silver and blue. She wore diamonds in her hair and pearls at her throat, with purple amethysts on a corsage.

Houdini bowed before them. Bess curtseyed. They'd performed for enough royalty by now that she could do it without looking like a shy Catholic schoolgirl.

The Tsar beamed. "I haven't seen a magician in years," he revealed with boyish enthusiasm. He turned to the Tsarina and added apologetically, "I mean a stage magician, of course, Alix."

The emperor had warm, dark eyes and a gentle face. Houdini had pictured a severe autocrat, a man who would send troops charging into battle with no qualms and order a rebellion put down with cannon fire. Tsar Nicholas reminded him of the proprietor of an English country inn.

"It is a pleasure to meet you, Mr. Houdini," Alexandra said, offering her hand for him to kiss. "It is not often that we have visitors from your country. It must be exciting to live in such a wild land, full of red Indians and cowboys." The granddaughter of Queen Victoria, she spoke with a distinct British accent.

Houdini noticed a slightly swollen belly that suggested she was pregnant. Her complexion was fair, her hair a reddish gold, her eyes a dark blue. As she moved her head, the diamond earrings flashed all the colors of the rainbow. There was a sense of nervousness about her, like a prey animal.

"More Italian immigrants than Indians now, Your Imperial Majesty, but it is a great, growing country," Houdini told her.

"This is a special night, the feast of Saint Ammon the Egyptian," Alexandra said. "I imagine there must be a good deal of supernatural energy in the air. Will that help?"

"Assuredly, Your Imperial Majesty."

The empress was a knockout, no doubt. But her naïve questions made him doubt she had the common sense God gave a rabbit to keep it from wandering into a wolf den. The Tsarina gestured to a pair coming up behind them. A plump woman with a puffy, moon-shaped face was on the arm of a short, stocky man with drooping eyelids and a twirled mustache that made him look like a villain in the funny pages. He wore the uniform of an imperial military doctor, complete with gold epaulets.

"My lady-in-waiting, Anna Vyrubova, and our spiritual advisor Monsieur Philippe," Alexandra said. "I'll leave you with them, Mr. Houdini. I imagine you and our trusted friend will have a great deal to talk about."

"Indeed, madam. I hope you enjoy the show," Houdini said, bowing again as the Imperial Couple moved on.

Vyrubova informed them gravely, "Monsieur Philippe has been indispensable to the crown. It is he who is responsible for Her Imperial Majesty Alexandra now carrying a male heir."

Monsieur Philippe gave a modest bow.

"You Frenchmen are known for romance, but that surprises me," Houdini said. Bess elbowed the magician in the side, and Illya bit his fist to stifle laughter.

"You've made the child a boy? May I ask how you achieved this miracle?" Houdini asked.

"I employed a combination of hermetic medicine, astronomy, psychurgy and some of the more arcane transcendental arts," the spiritual advisor explained.

"Psychurgy?"

"It is rather like the molding of clay, except that instead of a potter's hands, the power of the mind and will shapes the evolution of the embryo," Monsieur Philippe elaborated, his hands shaping an invisible baby in the air. "The woman's fervent prayers are needed too, of course. Faith is an important component."

Houdini nodded with understanding, as if a mechanic had matter-of-factly explained how a diesel engine worked.

Well, in a few months, Philippe's talent as a psychic sculptor will be put to the test, he thought. *The odds aren't bad, really: fifty-fifty. If the baby is a boy, these suckers will take it as proof that his cockamamie theories are correct. If a girl pops out, he'll come up with another mouthful of malarkey to explain it.*

"When Bess and I are ready for our first ankle-biter, I'll have to look you up," he said.

"I would be honored, sir," Monsieur Philippe replied with another bow, and the duo moved on.

Bess rolled her eyes. "That wasn't very funny. Some of us have been trying to have a baby, not to mention any names."

"This Philippe, is he a doctor?" Houdini asked Illya.

"Not one I'd trust to treat a mosquito bite, though I think he has some kind of 'honorary' degree from somewhere," the poet chuckled. "He was a fairly decent butcher back in France, I hear."

"Why is it so important for the Tsarina to have a son?" Bess asked. "Doesn't she have four girls already who can inherit the throne if she doesn't?"

"Even a Tsar wants a boy to play catch with," Houdini suggested. "Or shoot pheasants with more likely." *Or peasants,* he added mentally.

"It is a bit more than that, Mr. Houdini," Illya explained. "No woman can inherit the Russian throne."

"But wasn't there a Catherine the Great?" Bess asked.

"Catherine's son Paul wasn't much fond of her ways," the young writer went on. "As soon as he became emperor, he passed a law changing the rule of succession forever."

Count Vladimir announced that the festivities were to begin. The Imperial Couple took their seats in ornate chairs decorated with the coat of arms of the Romanov family: a two-headed eagle and the mounted figure of St. George slaying the dragon. The closest members of the royal family took their seats beside them, with other aristocrats, government officials and courtiers radiating outward according to rank.

A sixteen-piece orchestra performed selections from Rimsky-Korsakov and Tchaikovsky, then a troupe of players enacted a scene from Chekov's *The Seagull*. It was all top notch, but Houdini started to get restless, itching for his turn in the spotlight. Just before Houdini went on, Illya was called up to the front.

There was no sign of the flippancy he had exhibited while gossiping about the courtiers. The young man stood stiffly, like a schoolboy preparing to read the Gettysburg Address in front of squirming classmates and beneath the stern gaze of a schoolmarm. As the words tumbled out, he delivered them with growing passion:

"They say our native land is cold,
Yet face we the winds with faces bold.
Yes, our teeth chatter and grind,
As we trample snows and blizzards blind.
We march as one and not alone,
And each calls this frozen earth his own."

The poem continued in that vein for several more stanzas, with business about reindeer dashing through glistening snows, the northern lights, Kodiak bears and so on, but Houdini's attention wandered. For the thousandth time, he rehearsed his act in his mind, visualizing every detail. He was confident that he and Bess had everything down pat, but there was always a chance something could go awry.

If I blow this and wind up with egg on my face, I'll be a laughingstock in Europe, and when it hits the papers back home, there too, he thought. Fear of public humiliation mixed with anticipation of triumph energized the magician to the point that he could barely sit still any longer.

Illya, too, was getting wound up, his gestures becoming more animated as he reached the finale:

"Underneath a golden sun,
Battles lost and battles won,
On this ancient holy ground,
Echoes of their courage sound,
The heroes of our country stand.
My Russia, mother, native land."

Regardless of the cynicism that Illya had displayed regarding court life, Houdini had no doubt that the young man bore a genuine love of country. The crowd rewarded the poet with a torrent of applause.

The Tsar himself stood and clapped with an enthusiasm that approached religious fervor.

"Bravo," exclaimed Nicholas. "You have captured the essence of patriotism."

"A lesson some of our politicians need to be taught," whispered Prince Felix Yusupov, who sat beside Houdini.

"What do you mean?" the magician asked.

"Those fools who want to form a duma, a sort of parliament, and make the Tsar forsake his God-given role as father to the people. Share the rule with bourgeois factory owners, lawyers and professors, some without a parcel of land—even a burial plot—to their names."

The American was about to make a case for democracy when Count Vladimir signaled to him to come forward.

"And now I have the honor of introducing the great Harry Houdini, renowned throughout the world as the greatest master of self-extrication and magic who has ever lived."

Houdini and Bess made their way to the front.

"It is my great privilege to perform before the Imperial Family and these distinguished guests," the escape artist said. "May I present my wife Bess, who will assist me." They bowed, hand in hand.

Houdini launched into some simple sleight of hand, then confounded the audience with the East Indian Needle Trick, in which he appeared to swallow seventy-five needles and twenty yards of thread, then regurgitate it all in a string of threaded needles. He built his way up to the mind-reading act.

"We will now demonstrate the mystery of second sight," he announced. "For this, I will need the participation of some of you in attendance. Bess?"

His wife crossed the room and took up a position by the stained-glass windows. From his breast pocket, Houdini withdrew a black handkerchief.

"Grand Duke Serbius, would you kindly blindfold Mrs. Houdini?" the magician called to a good-natured guest to whom he'd been introduced earlier.

The dapper nobleman obliged, although he did so with some difficulty. The blindfold slipped a few times before he got in place and knotted behind her head.

"Good thing this is an audience, not a firing squad," Houdini wisecracked. Polite laughter followed. The line was guaranteed to get belly laughs in America, but he supposed that might be because firing squads were mustered less frequently in the U.S. than in Russia.

"Now, please gently turn her so she faces the window."

Serbius spun Bess so that—had she been able to see—she would be looking out at the snow-blanketed courtyard. Houdini strode to where the Imperial Couple were seated and knelt before the Tsarina.

"Your Imperial Majesty, I ask you now to think of a number between one and 1,000."

Alexandra took nearly a minute to think of a number, presumably considering several choices.

"Do you have it?" Houdini asked patiently. She nodded with great solemnity, those marvelous diamond earrings sparkling as she bobbed her head.

"Whisper it into my ear, and into the ear of The Tsar," the magician instructed the empress as he knelt beside her.

The Tsarina leaned over and whispered in her husband's ear, then into Houdini's. Her breath on the tiny hairs behind his ear was gentle as a baby's, and he caught a whiff of her fragrance, which he recognized as rose with a hint of green tea.

"Now, I must ask for total silence in the room," he announced in a stentorian tone. "Your Imperial Majesty, please picture that number in your head. Clear all other thoughts from your mind and concentrate. Bess will try to reach out to your mind."

Alexandra closed her eyes. He could see the space between her perfect eyebrows knit as she concentrated, as if she were working out a calculus problem in her head. After a moment, Houdini stood.

"Now, Bess, please quickly tell us the number that you see."

Bess hesitated for dramatic effect. Then she blurted out, "I see ... 749."

The Tsar gasped.

"Tsar Nicholas, has my assistant correctly identified the number?" Houdini asked.

The Imperial Couple cried excitedly in unison, "Yes. Yes, that is it."

Houdini repeated the trick with the Tsar and several other guests. Everyone wanted a go, either to experience the miraculous or to disprove it. Those who hoped for the latter were sorely disappointed. Each time, Bess guessed the correct number. Alexandra turned to Monsieur Philippe, who sat in a place of honor directly behind her.

"How is such a thing possible?" she asked in childlike wonder.

"It is achieved through thought transference," the Frenchman informed her matter-of-factly. "I've seen this kind of demonstration put on many times. Each of us has the capacity innately. It is a matter of practice."

He seemed to be barely repressing a yawn as he said it, Houdini observed. *You insufferable blowhard! Okay, let's see you play down our next little number.*

"With your permission, Your Imperial Majesties, we will perform a mystery known as the Metamorphosis," he announced. "We first introduced it while performing with Welsh Brothers Circus in 1895 and it has gained us some notoriety. Prince Felix Yusupov, would you kindly assist us?"

Tickled to be included, the young aristocrat approached as Houdini passed him a short rope and turned his back.

"Kindly tie my hands, Your Highness."

It appeared that Yusupov didn't spend much time tying farm gates shut. His knot seemed more suited for a bow atop a Christmas gift than securing a prisoner. However, he made up for it by adding multiple square knots. Houdini turned to face the audience.

"Bess, the sack, please."

Bess displayed a large black bag before the audience, shaking it like a bullfighter waving a cape and turning it inside out to demonstrate it was perfectly sound. Then she placed it over her husband's head. The bag fell to his ankles, leaving only his shoes exposed. She pulled a cord securing the bottom of the bag and knotted it. Bess guided her husband to a large chest. She opened it, and Houdini nimbly stepped inside. He hunched down, then she closed the lid and locked it with a heavy padlock.

"Prince Felix, would you be kind enough to place the key in your pocket?" she asked, placing the key in Yusupov's hand.

Slowly and theatrically, the aristocrat placed it in the breast pocket of his dinner jacket and patted it.

"You'll have to give me a hug to get it from me," he whispered. Bess ignored the flirtation, keeping a smile frozen on her face, and turned to the Tsar.

"Your Supreme Majesty, may we have use of your sword?"

The Tsar placed his hand on the jewel-encrusted hilt of the ceremonial sword, then hesitated. It had never served in a practice bout, let alone a battle. There wasn't a ding in the blade or even a smudge marring it, because a servant had polished it less than two hours before.

"You won't damage it, will you?" the monarch asked almost timidly.

"I assure you we will not," the magician's wife replied.

He stood, drew the saber and handed it to Bess. As he leaned forward, scrutinizing the scene for any skullduggery, she pushed the sword through the latch of the chest. It was now plainly impossible for the lid to open even if Houdini miraculously unlocked the padlock from the inside.

"Prince Felix?" she said, extending her hand. With a courtly smile, Yusupov helped her onto the chest.

"Thank you for your assistance," Bess said. "You may take your seat."

As she posed there, graceful as a ballerina, Franz handed her a large black sheet, which she unfolded and held aloft with her hands stretched out. The chest disappeared behind it. Franz signaled the orchestra, which began a drumroll.

"I wonder how long it will take him to get out of there?" a courtier whispered.

"I wager it will take him fifteen minutes or more," his companion guessed.

"It's a bet."

Bess suddenly tossed the curtain up, so that for a split second, she could not be seen. Three loud claps came from behind the curtain. As the sheet fluttered down, the audience gasped. For there, standing in her place, was Houdini. Out of the bag, his hands free.

Mystified members of the audience mumbled, mouths agape.

"Has anyone seen my wife?" Houdini asked.

Scattered laughter. The touch of humor kept the more superstitious attendees from bolting for the door. For some kind of magic was surely at work.

"Well, let's see ..." the magician said with an easy grin. He stepped off the chest, withdrew the sword and returned it to the Tsar, who remained entranced.

"Prince Felix, the key please?" Houdini asked, extending his hand.

Yusupov stared at him blankly for a moment, in a fog of disbelief. Then he recovered and passed the magician the key.

"Excuse me," the prince said. "It's not every day one sees a wife turn into her husband." Houdini turned the lock, removed the padlock and opened the lid.

"So, there you are!"

Inside the tied bag, lay Bess. Houdini helped her to her feet and yanked off the bag. Bess stood smiling before the audience, her hands tied behind her back, just as his had been. Applause exploded in the hall, echoing off the walls. The Tsar again leaped to his feet, leading a standing ovation.

"A miracle!" he exclaimed. He turned excitedly to Monsieur Philippe. "Have you any idea how it was done?"

"Yes," echoed the Tsarina with enthusiasm that surpassed even her husband's. "Did Mr. Houdini truly perform a miracle of transubstantiation—change his form into that of his wife?"

"Teleportation," the Frenchman corrected them, looking somewhat shaken. "They use psychic abilities to dematerialize and then when they have exchanged places, they rematerialize."

"Is that also commonplace?" Illya asked with feigned innocence.

"Is our dear Monsieur Philippe correct?" Tsar Nicholas asked Houdini. "Teleportation?"

"I won't contradict him," Houdini said. "After all, he's the expert." Monsieur Philippe sank into his seat, deflated. Beside him, Militsa and Stana glared at Houdini.

"Is there more?" Grand Duke Serbius asked. "I imagine it would be hard to top that, but you've whet our appetites." The crowd murmured in agreement.

"Your Illustrious Highness, I thought I'd leave the choice of our final mystery to you and the rest of the audience," Houdini told Serbius. "Could someone bring me a paper and pen? Oh, and I'll need a top hat."

"You can have mine," Serbius said. "I'll have my man fetch it."

Moments later, the magician sat in a chair before the assembled guests, with the writing implements in hand and the hat at his feet.

"Now, I would like each of you to take a moment and imagine a feat I might perform. For example, pull a rabbit out of that hat."

"That's too easy," Illya called out.

"Tell that to the rabbit who has to wait in there," Houdini joked. "He might have claustrophobia."

Houdini pointed the tip of the pen to the Tsarina. "Let's start with you, your Imperial Majesty. Now, don't go easy on me. Choose a feat that genuinely seems quite difficult to you."

"I should like you to make roses sprout in that empty vase," Alexandra requested.

"A brilliant choice," Houdini said, much to her delight. "And you, Tsar Nicholas?"

The monarch leaned forward as an idea occurred to him, then he thought better of it. He started to speak again, then stopped.

Indecisive as Hamlet, Houdini thought.

Finally, the Tsar announced, "Well, I would like to see snow fall."

Houdini wrote on the paper. *Snow, in Moscow? Apparently, creativity isn't the Tsar's strong suit*, he thought. Houdini turned to the emperor's mother.

"And the Dowager Empress?"

Maria Feodorovna held up a crystal wine glass. "Can you turn all the wine in the room into water?"

"That's one way to spoil an evening," called a voice in the back, prompting laughter.

Houdini went around the room, calling out a guest's name and dutifully jotting down feats. As each guest tried to outdo the other in cleverness, the tasks became more outlandish and complex. He was to make a horse appear in the hall, make a cat turn into a dog, turn the white walls red. Finally, he came to Militsa. A wicked smile played on her lips.

"I should like to hear the bell of the Kremlin cathedral ring," she declared loudly.

Houdini grimaced. "Are you sure ...?"

"Quite," she said, taking great delight in watching the magician squirm.

Houdini sighed and added the suggestion. When everyone had proposed a magic trick, Houdini carefully tore the paper, separating each line of writing into a separate slip. He folded the slips and dropped them into the hat.

"Mr. Volkov, would you please take the hat and shake it vigorously?"

"Anything to advance the cause of magic," the poet said and shook the top hat as if he were throttling an enemy.

"Please present it to the Tsar," Houdini instructed. Illya knelt before the monarch.

Said Houdini, "Your Supreme Majesty, kindly reach into the hat and select a paper at random." Tsar Nicholas, who didn't have much opportunity for fun, smiled warmly as he reached into the hat. He made a show of rummaging around and then withdrew a slip of paper with a flourish.

"If you would be so good as to read it, Tsar Nicholas," said Houdini.

"You are to make the Kremlin cathedral bell ring," Nicholas announced. "I'm afraid that even your powers may find that an insurmountable challenge. That bell has not rung within the lifetime of any man now alive."

Houdini paled.

"I'm afraid you are not so lucky tonight, Mr. Houdini," Militsa said, eyes glittering.

The Tsar caught the magician's pained expression.

"Should we try another?" he asked obligingly, reaching again for the hat. Houdini shook his head somberly, as if he'd been asked to lasso the moon and tug it to earth.

"No, I will try to do it." He turned to the crowd and announced. "By midnight, the Kremlin bell will ring."

Yusupov consulted his pocket watch. "That's a half hour from now."

CHAPTER THREE

The Unmasking of Monsieur Philippe

Thirty minutes without entertainment was an eternity for many of the jaded aristocrats. Militsa was only too happy to come to the rescue.

"Your Imperial Majesties, Monsieur Philippe perhaps can provide a small diversion," she suggested. "The night is imbued with psychic energy."

The Frenchman raised his hands in protest. "This night belongs to the Houdinis. I don't wish to impose."

"Nonsense, Monsieur Philippe," Alexandra reassured him. "I have a question for the spirits. If, of course, Mr. Houdini has no objection."

All eyes turned to the magician.

"None whatsoever, Your Imperial Majesty," Houdini replied. But, balling his fists, he thought, *Of all the nerve!*

A servant rolled in a small table belonging to Monsieur Phillippe, and the crowd gathered around. He explained that he "just happened" to have brought it with him from the emperor's palace in St. Petersburg, where the spiritual advisor resided in luxury. The French psychic sat with the Imperial

Couple, who held hands and looked up at him expectantly, as if receiving marital counsel from a priest. In the middle of the table was a spirit board, similar to the Ouija boards rising in popularity among devotees of the occult in America. A small, triangular iron planchette sat on the wooden board on which was printed the letters of the Russian alphabet, numbers one through ten, as well as "yes," "no," "goodbye," and a variety of cryptic symbols.

"Tonight, we shall reach out to the spirits," Monsieur Philippe announced. "For this, we will need absolute silence in the room."

"Dim the lights, please," Militsa said. A servant pushed a lever on the wall, and the chandeliers dimmed. From a drawer in the table, Monsieur Philippe removed a crystal ball the size of a softball and held it before Tsar Nicholas.

"Your Supreme Majesty, gaze into the mystical sphere and free your mind of all concerns."

The Tsar gazed at the orb, which captured the remnants of light in the room. Facets within it created a prism effect, and a variety of colors could be seen as Monsieur Philippe moved it closer to the ruler.

"As we have done in the past, I will count down from the number ten to one," said the spiritual advisor. "When I reach one, you will be fully open to the spirit world. Do you understand?"

"Yes."

"Ten ... nine ... eight ... seven ... six ... five ... four ... three ... two ... one."

The Tsar's face took on an otherworldly expression.

"Is someone there?" Monsieur Philippe asked softly. For a moment, nothing happened. The audience watched both the spirit board and the Tsar with rapt attention. Then the Tsar's hand stirred and the planchette moved to the word "yes."

"Spirit, tell us your name."

The planchette tediously spelled out, "A ... L ... E ... X ... A ... N ... D ... E ... R ... 2." Several guests gasped, and murmurs filled the hall.

"Who is it?" Bess asked Illya.

"It is his grandfather, Alexander II," Illya explained. "He was assassinated when the Tsar was a boy." The planchette now quickened its pace, spelling out two sentences, which Monsieur Philippe read aloud as the words formed.

"Remember ... you have been ordained ... by God to be as a ... father to the people ... Let no one deny you ... absolute rule ... or Russia will suffer ruin."

Nicholas looked like a schoolboy cowering before an overbearing headmaster.

"Yes, grandfather," he said.

The crowd murmured approvingly. Alexandra grasped Philippe's arm with a kind of desperation, like a woman afraid a lover will leave her.

"Now me, Philippe. I must know about my child."

The conjurer repeated the ritual. His efforts to put the empress into a trance were not immediately successful. She was so nervous, her bosom rose and fell rapidly.

Monsieur Philippe spoke to her soothingly, "Your Imperial Majesty, close your eyes. Let the planchette move as it wishes." The planchette truly did seem to move of its own accord, the Tsarina's delicate fingers merely passengers.

This time, the Tsar himself read the message as it was revealed: "You will ... bring forth an heir ... to the throne. The boy's name ... will be Alexei ... A child of surpassing beauty ... and in perfect health."

"Oh, Nicky!" Alexandra cried in delight and squeezed the hand of her psychic advisor in gratitude. "Thank you, Philippe." The crowd applauded.

"The lights," Militsa called. Philippe dabbed his dripping forehead with a handkerchief.

"I am a bit weak," he said. The spiritual advisor rose from his chair, then dipped as if passing out. Two alert footmen caught him.

"Forgive me, Your Imperial Majesty," he said, wheezing. "As you know, the use of my powers can be draining."

Houdini smirked. *This guy sure hits every corny note in the book.*

"I don't suppose even Mr. Houdini can surpass that," Stana said so all could hear. The performance had deeply moved the royal couple, and their jovial mood turned sober.

"He has his chance now," Yusupov said, looking up from his watch. "It's two minutes before midnight now."

Houdini turned with an uncertain look to Militsa, upon whose thin, blood-red lips a triumphant smile was evident.

"Very well," he said. "Kindly turn the lights down again."

As the servants turned down the gas lamps, the magician lit a candlestick and passed it to his wife. With Bess following him, Houdini strode to the window that overlooked the Kremlin Square. He placed one hand over his forehead and with the other, pointed at the tower, which was visible in the moonlight. The guests gathered around him as he withdrew a handkerchief from his vest pocket.

From his jacket pocket, he produced a small glass bottle filled with purple powder.

"What is it?" Stana whispered to Monsieur Philippe. The empire's official psychic shook his head, frowning. Houdini opened the bottle and sprinkled the substance on the handkerchief. Then he began waving it in arcs in the air in front of him. The purple powder sparkled in the air like fairy dust.

"Powder travel through the night, your assignation before midnight," the magician intoned. "Sent from Heaven or deepest Hell, do our bidding and ring the bell." Then, dramatically, he flung the huge windows open.

Dead silence. Only a frigid wind blew in.

Houdini turned slowly from the window, closing it, and faced the crowd, crestfallen. He heard a jumble of confused muttering and a few snickers. Count Vladimir Fredericks snapped his fingers, and in a moment, the room was fully illuminated. Militsa looked like a black widow spider that had just dined on its latest groom.

"Even the most gifted mystics' powers fail them at times," Monsieur Philippe offered comfortingly. Houdini lowered his head, and Bess took her husband's hand with the steeliness of a woman who stands by her man in the face of disgrace.

The silence was suddenly shattered by the pealing of the Kremlin cathedral bell. A hush fell over the audience. Alexandra grabbed Houdini's arm. She gazed into his eyes as if adoring a living icon.

"You are truly a miracle worker!" she cried.

Nicholas took him by the other arm. "I think that was beyond even your powers, Philippe!"

"Bravo!" Grand Duke Serbius cried, and the call was taken up by all the other guests.

Militsa elbowed Monsieur Philippe. "For the love of God, do something," she hissed in a low voice. "Something bigger!" But the spiritual advisor collapsed into a seat.

"So much psychic energy has been dispensed tonight, it might be dangerous to continue," he said weakly. "It is like the electrical energy that remains in the air after a lightning storm."

Houdini couldn't repress a smile. The charlatan didn't seem to have a handle on physics, let alone metaphysics.

However, rather than leave his rival dangling in the wind, he said magnanimously, "Monsieur Philippe is quite right. The spirits have been obliging tonight; we don't want to push our luck."

As he passed Militsa, he whispered, "Looks like luck was with me after all." Her eyes narrowed to beady pinpoints, while her lips fought off a scowl.

Monsieur Philippe bowed before Houdini.

"Your gifts are quite extraordinary," he said. "I have never seen the likes of it before." His humility seemed genuine, although whether he viewed Houdini as a superior psychic or a superior huckster, the American couldn't tell.

Militsa's look was less that of admiration than one of vampiric hunger.

"When one has such talents, one should not confine them to parlor tricks. It takes years of honing one's abilities to reach the level whereupon one can manipulate matter at a distance," she said. "Sometime I should like to discuss the paranormal with you in private."

"It would be an honor," Houdini said, taking her hand. *Those eyes are like a shark's,* he thought. *Soulless.*

A short time later, when the party ended, Houdini stood on the balcony with Tsar Nicholas, who offered him a cigar.

"Monsieur Philippe is the most gifted psychic that I have ever seen—and take my word, the Tsarina has invited many through our doors," the monarch said. "But your abilities dwarf his. May I ask, what is the source of your power? Does it come from above, from God, or from within your own soul?"

Houdini shook his head. "Your Supreme Majesty, perhaps Count Vladimir misspoke when he described our act to you," he said. "When I call myself a magician, I don't mean I'm a sorcerer. The truth is, everything I do is an illusion, purely for entertainment. I can tell that you and your wife are devout believers in the Almighty. I don't want to give you the wrong idea, that God is acting through me. It would be, well, blasphemy."

"But how, then?"

Houdini shifted uneasily. As mild-mannered as Tsar Nicholas was, Houdini knew he wasn't used to being told no. In fact, the mind-reading act was simple enough. He and Bess used a code in which a mundane word conveyed a specific number:

1 Me

2 Say

3 Now

4 Tell

5 Please

6 Speak

7 Quickly

8 Look

9 See

10 Concentrate

When Houdini had used the exact wording, "Bess, *quickly tell* the number you *see*," she knew immediately that the Tsarina had told Houdini the number 749.

As mystifying as the Metamorphosis appeared, the solution was obvious to anyone who really thought it through. The back of the seemingly solid chest had a trap panel that Houdini released from the inside, allowing him to escape.

The magician easily freed his wrists from the inexpert knot behind his back, before Bess even placed the black sack over his head. The cord Bess used to secure the sack ran through a series of metal eyelets. Houdini merely needed to pull on the rope from the inside to open the sack. As Bess raised the curtain, he exited the box. As she threw the curtain in the air, he clapped his hands and hopped atop the chest. Bess dropped down and slid into the chest through the open back panel, closing it behind her.

As Houdini joshed with the audience, Bess pulled the sack over her. Inside the sack, she used the inner loop system to pull the knot tight at the top of the bag. Then she slid into the wrist restraints, left slack by her husband.

By the time Houdini withdrew the Tsar's sword, unlocked the padlock and opened the lid, Bess was the box, in the same "inescapable" predicament he had been. Of course, being able to make the switch almost instantaneously had taken years of practice.

Making the Kremlin cathedral bell ring wasn't half as difficult. Franz had slipped out and stationed himself on the rooftop of a nearby building with an air rifle in hand, with instructions to shoot the bell precisely at midnight. As soon as Houdini's assistant saw the candle-lit handkerchief waving to confirm the order, he fired off a volley of almost silent shots, causing the age-old bell to ring.

Having identified Militsa as the guest most likely to toy with him, Houdini planted in her mind this "impossible" miracle. What seemed the most difficult part of the trick, ensuring that this feat was the one selected from the hat, was actually the easiest. When jotting down the audience suggestions, he'd simply written "Make the Kremlin cathedral bell ring" on each slip of paper!

Of course, there wasn't a snowball's chance in hell that he would reveal any of that to the Tsar.

"Your Supreme Majesty, we magicians have a code of honor. It forbids us from revealing our methods," he explained.

Tsar Nicholas nodded. Honor, duty—those were concepts he understood better than mysticism.

"The truth is, Tsar Nicholas, I've been in this game for years now, and I haven't encountered a single person I believe has supernatural powers," Houdini said.

The Tsar rubbed his jaw, puzzled. "But you've heard of what Monsieur Philippe has done, and have witnessed it with your own eyes."

Houdini hesitated. Another cardinal rule of the magicians' code was never to expose how a fellow performer's trick worked. It was pulling the rug out from under a guy's feet. But this Philippe was no colleague or even a rival in the same racket. He was a charlatan, pulling the wool over the eyes of these pious rulers.

"Your Majesty, if you can spare another moment, I want to show you something," he said.

When they returned to the grand hall, almost all the guests had departed. Monsieur Philippe was leaving alongside a servant who wheeled out the table on which the crystal ball and spirit board sat. Count Vladimir accompanied him.

"Wait one moment, sir," Houdini said. "I forgot to give you my card." He extended his hand with his calling card, but it slipped out and the card fluttered to the floor.

"Oops!"

The magician dropped to one knee beside the cart. When he stood, he held up a small device made up of a rod with a piece of metal at the end. He presented the gadget to the Tsar, who gasped in surprise as it veered in midair and the metal clung to his sword.

"Why ... it's a magnet," Nicholas exclaimed.

"Yes, a magnet," Houdini confirmed. "With a rod to move it and guide the planchette from beneath the table." As soon as Houdini had noticed the planchette was metal, not wood, the solution was obvious to him.

The Tsar turned toward Philippe in disbelief, like a child who'd just learned there was no Tooth Fairy.

"Monsieur Philippe?"

Unprepared, the psychic healer gave the most preposterous answer imaginable: "I don't know how that got there."

Houdini chose to let him off the hook. "Well, it's clear as day, isn't it? Some enemy of the crown is trying to cast doubt on Monsieur Philippe's powers."

The spiritual advisor had broken into a sweat and dabbed his forehead with his handkerchief.

"Why yes, of course," he said.

Tsar Nicholas turned to Count Vladimir. "We must get to the bottom of this. Contact Lebedoeff and have him launch an investigation."

CHAPTER FOUR

A Battle of Wills

C ount Vladimir Fredericks invited Houdini for lunch at the restaurant of the Hotel National, the newly built, luxury establishment where the magician and his wife were staying. The 202-room, 56-suite building designed by famed Russian architect Alexander Ivanov was walking distance from the Kremlin.

The count introduced Houdini to a dish called Russian Pelmeni Dumplings with minced veal wrapped in thin dough, while he himself dined on *Uzbek Plov*, a rice dish cooked with lamb, garbanzo beans and raisins.

"His Supreme Majesty wishes you to join the court as his new spiritual advisor," Count Vladimir said.

Houdini sighed. His revelations about trickery apparently hadn't sunk in.

"What about Philippe?" he asked.

Count Vladimir waved his hand dismissively. "You sowed a seed of doubt in the Tsar's mind. He ordered a physician to examine Alexandra. The doctor discovered that she is not in fact pregnant."

"But her belly ...?"

"Apparently, it is known as a 'hysterical pregnancy.' It is not altogether uncommon. A woman fixated on bearing a child becomes convinced that she is expecting and takes on many of the physical characteristics: morning sickness, even leaning back as she walks. Her Imperial Majesty is quite distraught, as you can imagine." Fredericks paused to take a sip of black tea. "Philippe maintains that her failed pregnancy is the result of weakness of faith. 'Only faith is capable of moving the mountain,' were his exact words to her. Once she suffered doubt and called the obstetrician, the miracle failed, so he says. Like Peter losing his ability to walk on water."

"I take it the Tsar was unconvinced?" said Houdini.

"Even Alexandra has lost complete confidence in Philippe's abilities."

"Well, naturally."

"What the Imperial Couple desire now is a person whose powers are genuine, in whom the empress can put her faith." Count Vladimir leaned forward and looked into Houdini's eyes meaningfully.

"Well, I certainly can't deliver on the boy-child promise either—or walk on water," Houdini cautioned him.

"The Tsar and Tsarina trust you," the Minister of the Imperial Court said earnestly. "They believe in your powers."

"I don't know ..."

"Tsar Nicholas is prepared to be quite generous. You will be afforded a monthly stipend of one thousand rubles. In addition, lodging at the Imperial Family's official residence in St. Petersburg—or if you prefer, in an apartment in the city, with servants and a coachman. You will find St. Petersburg as different from Moscow as night and day. It is a cosmopolitan city, like Paris."

The Houdinis were, in fact, scheduled to begin a month-long engagement in St. Petersburg in two weeks. But that was to be their last in Russia. He'd escaped from a jail cell in Butyrskaya Prison and delighted audiences at the Bolshoi Theater. Their European tour was coming to an end, and they were set to sail back to America. He had been looking forward to escaping this country of bleak skies and frigid weather.

"I need to discuss it with Bess," he said.

"Of course. Consider it. Is a fortnight enough?"

Houdini nodded.

***

Bess and Houdini relaxed in a lavish hotel suite where dignitaries from across Europe had slept. Houdini sat at the desk, sketching out his concept for an act. He would be buried alive in a sarcophagus, like a pharaoh. Perhaps even wrapped like a mummy. Bess lounged on the bed in a silk robe, reading a travel book.

"I've been reading about St. Petersburg," Bess said, holding up the book. "It really is as cosmopolitan as Paris."

"Yeah, but it's not America, sweetie. It would mean being tied down in Russia for at least a year, or who knows how long."

"We also would want for nothing," she persisted. "Darling, audiences are so fickle. Remember the days when we were living hand to mouth? I seem to remember a certain someone having to hop around in an ape-man costume to make ends meet. This would mean security."

Houdini held up his hands. "The best security is right here. Hands that can get out of any handcuff ever made."

"Yes, yes, I know, I've read all about it," she said impatiently. She pointed to a photo of a ball depicting cavalry officers twirling society ladies, resplendent with diamonds. "Can you imagine living that way?"

"Come on, Bess, it was neat to hobnob with those swells, but we'll never be one of them."

Bess pouted.

"Those dames in the fancy gowns and so many necklaces, it's a wonder they can lift their heads," Houdini moaned. "You really want to join that crowd?"

"It's like something out of a fairy tale," explained his Brooklyn-born spouse, holding the magazine to her bosom. "What girl doesn't dream of being a princess?"

"Just remember, come midnight Cinderella found herself riding home in a pumpkin."

Bess bowed her head. "You're right, I suppose. I'm being silly."

He sat next to her. "And there's another thing. Remember the last night we did our medium act? The look in those rubes' eyes? When that woman came up after the show with her crippled daughter and asked if we could heal her? We promised we wouldn't trifle with people's religious feelings anymore. Nicholas and Alexandra, they believe God is acting through us."

"Yes, yes, that's true, but ..."

Two brisk knocks interrupted them, and Houdini answered the door

"A message for Mr. Houdini," the bellhop said, delivering an envelope on a silver platter. As he left, the magician opened it. Houdini's eyes moved back and forth as he skimmed over the note, then he burst out laughing.

"Well, isn't this nice? An invitation to a masquerade ball held by Militsa at her palace in St. Petersburg." He began to tear it up.

"What are you doing?" Bess said, hopping to her feet.

"Are you kidding? You should have seen the look in her beady eyes when we made a fool of Philippe. You can bet they're pretty steamed I caught the charlatan with his pants down. That witch will poison us both if she has half a chance."

"She's not going to kill us in a ballroom full of people," Bess argued, putting her hands on her hips. "Please, sweetheart. What is the point in being in Europe if we stay cooped up in this hotel? I just want to have one night of romance."

One night, Houdini thought. *Maybe if she gets an up-close look at these arrogant foreign fat cats, she'll see the light.*

"Okay," he sighed, sure to make his reluctance obvious.

Bess hugged him and gave him a smooch that made the whole thing worthwhile.

Then she frowned. "Only I have nothing to wear. Not to a fancy masquerade ball."

He held up the note. "Militsa is one step ahead of you." He read aloud, 'I will be happy to personally help Mrs. Houdini select a suitable costume'"

***

The four-hundred-mile ride on the Moscow–Saint Petersburg Railway whisked them across a landscape dominated by snow-blanketed plains and fir trees.

After the trip, the Houdinis sat in a horse-drawn carriage rolling through the broad and sweeping boulevards of St.

Petersburg. It truly was a fairytale city, full of golden spires and domes rising above a seething swamp.

The metropolis had been built by Peter the Great in the seventeenth century as part of his grand scheme to westernize Russia, turning it away from the Orient. More than two hundred thousand laborers perished in the monumental effort to construct a city in the marshlands where the River Neva met the Baltic Sea. A marvel of engineering, the city straddled nineteen islands linked by bridges, with dozens of canals winding through it.

Peasants had hauled millions of tons of granite across the vast Russian plains to build the baroque palaces of the nobility that lined the Neva. The public buildings were just as grand with massive columns and ornamented windows.

Even shops were dazzling, their stucco fronts mimicking the style and colors of Italy. Through the carriage windows, Houdini and Bess saw wealthy women in furs pouring into these establishments. The ladies brushed past exiting shoppers with servants on their heels carrying bags overflowing with clothing and jewelry. Even by day, these upper-crust ladies sported diamonds to flaunt their station in life.

"You see, darling, just like in the pictures. It really is a magical place," Bess said, clutching Houdini's arm with excitement.

"You wanted to be Cinderella, you get to be Cinderella," he replied. "Just remember, not everyone in this city is a prince."

They settled into a luxurious suite at the Belmond Grand Hotel Europe, a gargantuan structure that took up an entire block of Nevsky Prospekt, the city's historic central thoroughfare. That afternoon, Bess met Militsa, as agreed, at the shop of Madame Brissac, the most famous dressmaker in St. Petersburg.

Madame Brissac had amassed a fortune creating unique gowns for the Imperial Family, the wives of tycoons, opera divas and the like. In her elegant salon, women sat on gold and blue chairs of French design, exchanging gossip, while models displayed the latest gowns from Paris. These society ladies eschewed Russian, chatting in French. Bess knew only a smattering of French. However, she was able to decipher a bit of risqué repartee between two powdered and perfumed chatterboxes.

"I hear Adaelada Vasiliev is to become engaged to Sokolov, the banker."

"And give up her lover, the cavalry officer?"

"Who said anything about giving him up?"

Bess tried on the costume Militsa had picked out for her: Esmeralda, the Gypsy girl from *The Hunchback of Notre Dame*. She looked in the mirror, captivated by how the long, curling black wig completely altered her appearance. It was charming, but the plunging neckline revealed too much, she felt, especially with the bustier thrusting her modest breasts to give her cleavage.

I look like a floozy in a burlesque show, Bess thought.

"It's a bit daring, don't you think?" She pulled the peasant blouse up a bit. "Perhaps if I wear it like this?"

Militsa tugged the garment back down further than it had been.

"It's quite the fashion amongst the young women of St. Petersburg," she assured Bess. Indeed, many of the models parading through the shop in front of clients flaunted a quantity of flesh that would have invited arrest a decade ago in America. Militsa ran her hands down her waist.

"You have a wonderful figure. It would be a shame to conceal it."

Bess blushed. The woman's fingers tracing her waist and hips felt like a spider's feet. The attention was flattering. She'd always considered her slender hips too boyish. Yet for some reason, the sudden intimacy was also a little off-putting.

"What will be your disguise?" she asked guiding Militsa's hand gently away.

"That, my dear, will be a surprise," the noblewoman said with a coy smile. She took a brush and began to shape Bess's hair. Houdini's wife found she didn't like the black-eyed fan of necromancy standing behind her. She'd grown up in a German immigrant household where the existence of witchcraft and the "evil eye" was accepted as scientific fact.

She's the sort of character who stabs you in the back and sits right back down for tea, Bess thought.

"Your husband's powers are quite remarkable," Militsa said. "Yet many a magician can be thwarted. Madame Blavatsky could not operate in a room with heavy fragrance. Cagliostro was frustrated by the presence of mirrors. Does your husband have any such obstacle?"

With her back to the noblewoman, Bess took the opportunity to scowl. *What kind of fool does she take me for? If my husband did have some kind of supernatural ability, I certainly wouldn't spill the beans to you!*

"Salt," she replied casually. "Salt weakens him. It's kind of like an allergy." Bess turned and saw Militsa's eyes sparkling with fascination.

"Yes, yes, of course, salt," the occult aficionado said, nodding thoughtfully. "An ancient counteragent against magic."

"Naturally, you have to be discreet," Bess hastened to add.

"It will be our little secret," Militsa agreed, petting her arm.

Salt was the first thing that had popped into Bess's head. *Silly, but it seems it did the trick.*

***

The following night, the Houdinis' hired coach passed through the gates of Militsa's palace on the southern bank of the Neva. Nearly as large as the Tsar's palace, the estate boasted a formal garden modeled after Versailles. As they mounted the marble staircase, footmen costumed for the occasion as Roman soldiers pulled open bronze doors engraved with the figure of Zeus.

"Walk into my parlor, said the spider to the fly," Houdini whispered to his wife.

In the ballroom, more than two hundred costumed guests swirled about to the Blue Danube waltz. Houdini recognized the Hunchback of Notre Dame, Napoleon, Julius Caesar, plus an assortment of medieval knights and ladies, cowboys and fairytale characters. Little Red Riding Hood and her wolf were on hand, along with Sleeping Beauty and Puss in Boots. Others stepped out of Greek mythology: satyrs, wood nymphs, the Minotaur. Houdini had decided to wear only a tuxedo and a white mask, an attire chosen by many of the more reserved men in attendance.

A towering Viking marched over and shook Houdini's hand, and from the iron grip, Houdini instantly recognized the Grand Duke Nikolai Nikolaevich. His wife Stana wore a Cleopatra outfit. Rather daring, it showed off her navel, from which Houdini averted his eyes. Her dark mascara, in the style of an Egyptian queen, made her black eyes look even more sinister.

"Thank you for inviting us," Houdini said. "Where is our hostess?"

Militsa glided across the floor toward them, wearing a white powdered wig and a gown in the style of the late 1700s.

"Marie Antoinette!" guessed Bess, who recognized the historical figure from a painting.

"Care for some cake?" Militsa asked, presenting her prop, a papier-mâché birthday cake. Houdini noticed red dots simulating stitches around her throat and gestured to his own.

"I don't quite ...?" he began.

"Oh, forgive my macabre sense of humor," Militsa giggled. "The poor thing was beheaded in the French Revolution."

Houdini and Bess laughed dutifully. *Come a revolution, a head like yours will be among the first heads to go*, Houdini thought.

"Hopefully, the aristocracy will fare a little better here," the escape artist said. "The guillotine's gone out of style. I think they hang people these days." He regretted the quip as soon as it came out of his mouth. The grand duke and his wife responded with sour looks.

"I'm sorry if that was out of line," Houdini added quickly.

"Think nothing of it," Militsa replied, taking Houdini by one arm and Bess by the other, and leading them into the party. "This is a night for fun. Nothing is off limits. I do hope you'll take advantage of some of our more esoteric entertainments tonight."

She gestured to the alcoves where fortune tellers were busily discerning the futures of guests by every conceivable means: palm reading, crystal balls, tea leaves, tarot cards. Some were costumed as old Gypsies; others wore the robes and cone-shaped caps of magicians or the garb of Tibetan monks.

"I have gathered here tonight the finest clairvoyants in Russia," their hostess informed them. "A medium from the Balkans is conducting a séance upstairs."

"Holding auditions?" Houdini asked.

She gave a sly smile. "After a manner of speaking. Now, enjoy yourselves." She winked at Houdini and moved on.

The bacchanalian atmosphere put Houdini on edge. Some of the women's costumes were outright scandalous. One was dressed as the Greek goddess Artemis in a tunic that scarcely covered her derrière. Another, in a flesh-colored bodysuit, came as Lady Godiva.

It looks as if, any minute, a Roman orgy is going to break out, he thought.

After a few dances with Bess, the escape artist sulked by the bar, taking tiny sips of champagne. He was close to a teetotaler even under ordinary circumstances, and something told him that tonight he'd best be on his toes. He suddenly became aware of the scent of jasmine.

"Do you not enjoy dancing, Mr. Houdini?"

He'd not noticed that a tall woman in a geisha costume and oriental mask had crept up next to him.

"I have two left feet," he offered.

"I rather doubt that. I suspect you are quite nimble. Perhaps you would find the séance more entertaining." Her high, sing-song voice was clearly not her natural one.

Houdini frowned. "Such things, talking to the dead and the like, don't they find it at odds with their religion?"

"The Orthodox Church no longer speaks to us, to the higher elements of society," she explained. "We seek enlightenment elsewhere."

"Seek sensation, don't you mean?" he parried.

"There are many ways to discover spiritual fulfillment," the mystery woman replied. She gave an enigmatic smile and took his hand. Then she turned and shuffled off in mincing steps as if her feet were bound in the traditional Japanese style. Houdini looked around then took a peek at the note she'd passed.

"The library at 10:00," it read in dainty lettering.

Houdini tucked the note in his breast pocket. Was this a proposed assignation? He'd had notes passed to him by women backstage and they always ended up in the circular file. He'd have to make sure to toss this one in the fireplace before Bess handled his suit and a row broke out.

Or was this something else? And what about that "spiritual fulfillment" claptrap? After a few minutes, as the ten o'clock hour approached, his curiosity got the better of him. Bess was being swept around the ballroom by a man in a bear costume and wouldn't miss him. Houdini slipped out. Where exactly was the library? Upstairs, he imagined. He crept up the stairs.

Houdini walked down a hall adorned with paintings of Militsa's family. All shared those black eyes, some lifeless, others glowing with fiendish intensity. From behind a door, he heard rapping on a table, followed by a voice proclaiming, "It is I, your late husband." *Earmarks of a garden variety séance*, he thought.

Next, he passed a linen closet where a meeting of the flesh rather than spirit was in progress. The door had been left slightly ajar. A hooded red robe hung from a hook, blocking Houdini's view, but from within emanated the unmistakable grunts and sighs of fornication.

"Looking for something, sir?"

Houdini turned to see a rosy-cheeked girl of about twenty-three in a maid's costume.

"Er, yes. The library."

"You want a book, sir?"

He realized now that she actually *was* a maid.

"The truth is, big social gatherings like this give me the jitters," he confessed. "A book settles my nerves."

She nodded sympathetically, leaned forward and whispered, "All those goings-on, the fortune tellers. It's not very Christian, is it?"

He also leaned in. "Exactly."

"This way, sir," the like-minded lass said.

The maid guided him through labyrinthine hallways to the library. He thanked her, then entered through the creaking door. The shelves of Militsa's library were jammed floor-to-ceiling with books whose bindings suggested great antiquity. He picked up a leather-bound tome from the ornate mahogany desk where a candle flickered.

The Methods of Cagliostro. His hostess was no dilettante, that was for sure. If she'd read one in ten of these books, she'd be a formidable authority on the occult.

Suddenly, a bookshelf pivoted silently inward, revealing a secret inner room. He caught only a glimpse of its stone-walled interior. The crimson flames of a fireplace flickered, and he took in a whiff of sulfur. Houdini put his fists on his hips and addressed the figure who entered.

"Now, look here, sister. I don't know what this is all about, but ..."

However, it wasn't the mysterious Geisha. It was Militsa. She tread toward him so silently that the eerie thought occurred to him that her feet were not touching the ground.

"So, you are not incorruptible, Mr. Houdini," she said.

Houdini blushed. "You don't think that ... Look, I'm a married man. I just was curious."

"Of course you were, my dear. Care for a glass of wine?"

He nodded. Although he needed to keep his head clear, he also wanted her to believe his guard was down. She poured wine into a crystal goblet and passed it to him.

"An '87 Bordeaux Meursault-Perrieres, from one of the finest Burgundy vineyards," she said.

Houdini took the glass and sipped it. "Well, you have my attention."

"Since you are to be the Tsar's new spiritual advisor, I thought it wise that we become acquainted."

"Word travels fast."

"The Tsarina keeps no secrets from me."

"Well, I haven't made up my mind."

"The Tsar's offer is not generous?"

"Oh, it's generous enough. But we Americans value our freedom. The idea of being beholden to one man, performing like a trained seal and unable to go when and where I please ... well, that would take some getting used to."

Militsa stepped closer to him, like a cobra slithering toward its prey.

"There is something more valuable than freedom," she said.

"I haven't heard of it."

"Power."

Her black eyes took on a disconcerting glow in the candlelight. Houdini realized he didn't like the taste of the wine at all. Salt. Just what Bess told him to expect. *Well, at least it's not poison.*

"How familiar are you with the art of hypnotism?" the noblewoman inquired.

Houdini shrugged. "I've seen hucksters do it at nickel-a-ticket shows. Make some fellow squawk like a chicken or babble like a toddler. A shill, of course."

"What if I were to tell you that it is very real? That there are practitioners who can bend even the strongest mind to their will?"

"Real as your Monsieur Philippe?"

"The trances into which he put Tsar Nicholas were quite real, I assure you," Militsa insisted. "You've heard of the Tsar's decisions to crush peasant revolts and student protests. Do you think that soft and pliable man would have acted with such an iron fist without prompting? Or have waged war against Japan? No, that marshmallow would have let the peasants overrun his palace. He was like a puppet in Philippe's hands."

"And who has been pulling Philippe's strings—you?"

"I and a group of patriotic members of the aristocracy understand the importance of projecting Imperial might. And of preventing radicals from chipping away at Imperial rule."

"Well, I'm sure you know Philippe has been given his walking papers."

She bared her teeth. "Which is exactly why you are here."

Houdini raised one eyebrow. "I get it. You want another puppeteer to get in the Tsar's head. Only I don't know a thing about hypnotism."

"It is a skill easily acquired by a man of your intelligence, I assure you. I have an entire shelf devoted to techniques developed by masters of the art over centuries."

Houdini put down his goblet beside the candlestick on the desk.

"First off, I still think the whole thing is hokum," he declared. "I don't believe a man can be made to do anything he thinks is wrong in his heart. And even if you could, it isn't right."

Militsa nodded patiently, as if he were a child babbling about an invisible friend. She was not a big believer in conscience, he gathered.

"Well, I quite understand your position. While you're here, there is someone I want you to meet." She called into the next room. "Come, say hello to Mr. Houdini."

A tall, stocky figure with a brown beard long as an Old Testament prophet's emerged from the secret room. The man was dressed in the modest gray coat of a Siberian peasant, with trousers no less shabby hanging down over coarse boots. He sported a large, pockmarked nose and weather-beaten skin, with hair parted in the middle falling to his shoulders in oily strands. His beard was equally unkempt and harbored bits of food.

"Mr. Houdini, may I present my friend, Father Grigori Rasputin," Militsa said.

The bigger man grabbed Houdini's hand and shook it vigorously. His palm was as rough as sandpaper, a peasant's hand, his fingernails long and curved inward. Beneath the nails resided so much grit, they looked black, like the claws of an ogre in a children's book. Rasputin's thick, blue, sensuous lips pulled back into a grin.

"My new friend, let us embrace as brothers," he said, and hugged Houdini. He gave off a strong odor that brought to mind a mountain goat. Houdini pulled away as quickly as civility would allow. Rasputin's gray-blue eyes, glistening like twin moons, captivated him.

"Father Grigori is a starets, a holy man," the grand duchess revealed. "I first caught sight of him sawing wood in a Kiev courtyard, and learned that he was a Siberian who had a reputation for prophecy and healing. Since I brought him to St. Petersburg, I have found that reputation to be well deserved. I've seen him make the blind to see, the lame to walk. He has even cured venereal disease."

"I'll keep that in mind," Houdini said.

Rasputin bowed humbly. "It is the Almighty who works through me."

"I must return to my duties as hostess," Militsa said, patting Houdini's forearm. "I will leave the two of you to discuss mystical matters."

The two men locked eyes and there was an awkward moment of silence.

Then Houdini said, "So, you're a … monk?"

Rasputin laughed heartily. "No, I am too given to the temptations of the flesh for such a calling. But I have studied under many monks. I walked close to four hundred miles from my home in Pokrovskoe to meet with the brothers of the monastery in Verkhoturye. That was the beginning of my spiritual journey."

Hundreds of miles in Siberia? It sounded preposterous. Yet the oddball looked sturdy enough to walk over mountains, Houdini thought. Rasputin trained those dazzling eyes on Houdini.

"You are a most extraordinary man," the Russian said. "God has chosen you to be a conduit of his power."

"I'm a showman," Houdini said in a weaker voice than he intended.

"The Tsar needs a man like you to guide him," Rasputin continued. "It is not by coincidence that you came to Russia at this time. The Supreme Being ordained it."

Houdini felt those luminescent disks orbs luring him in, and instinct told him to avert his eyes. But his ego wouldn't allow him to let some filthy Russian peasant who looked like he ought to be picking potatoes lick him in a staring contest.

"You will go to the palace, and you will find great happiness and fulfillment there," Rasputin's deep, sonorous voice intoned. That voice tugged Houdini like an undertow.

"You do wish to serve the Tsar?" Rasputin asked, only he didn't make it sound like a question.

"I haven't decided," Houdini replied. But he had decided, hadn't he?

"I think that you have decided in your heart." Rasputin smiled knowingly and tapped his own temple. "Your brain just doesn't know it yet." His pupils expanded, retracted to tiny pinpricks, then loomed large again.

My God, is he able to dilate his pupils at will? Now, Houdini couldn't tear his eyes away, try as he might.

"Your pretty wife, she loves St. Petersburg," Rasputin said pleasantly. "And you wish to please her."

"Well, perhaps. But I wear the pants in the family. And to be honest, I miss America."

"Bah, your home country can wait."

He has a point, doesn't he? What's the big rush, really?

"You want to stay here and be helpful to the Tsar," the Russian said.

"Sure, I want to be helpful to the Tsar," Houdini echoed.

He sensed the peasant's thoughts becoming his own, like unclean parasites that had slithered into his ear and skittered about his brain. Houdini realized he was in a trance and tried by force of will to break it, but he found it impossible. This man who could slip out of a straitjacket in seconds was imprisoned. The magician tried to turn away, but found his feet were frozen in place as if encased in a cement block.

CHAPTER FIVE

A Warning Bell

"Then, we agree," Rasputin said jovially. "You will accept the Tsar's offer, my son."

If this guy asked me to throw myself into the fireplace, I would, Houdini thought. Yet in a corner of his psyche, the escape artist stood free.

Fire! In his mind's eye, now, he could see his salvation.

Houdini stumbled back to Militsa's desk. He reached back and placed his palm just over the candle, so close that the flame licked his hand. Houdini winced and closed his eyes, shutting out Rasputin and his mesmerizing gaze. He turned his back on the big Siberian and clutched his hand.

"Ouch, that smarted!" he exclaimed. "That sure was clumsy of me."

"Do you need a bandage, Mr. Houdini?" Rasputin cried, stomping toward him.

"No, I'm all right. But I better make sure Bess is staying out of trouble. It was swell meeting you, Rasputin." Houdini beat a hasty retreat.

Militsa entered from the secret room, which she'd accessed from another entrance and where she'd been listening intently.

"Did it work?" she asked.

Rasputin stroked his mangy beard.

"That is a very dangerous man," he said.

A few minutes later, Bess was dancing the Vienna waltz with a man decked out as the Scarlet Pimpernel in eighteenth-century regalia, when a figure in the macabre robes and skull mask of the Red Death cut in.

"Hey, that was a little rude, bub," she protested as he swept her across the floor. "We'd only just begun."

"Pipe down and dance with me toward the door," came her husband's voice.

"Darling! Where did you get that costume?"

"There's a cheating husband who's having a fling with Little Bo Peep in the linen closet. He'll be a little ticked off when he reaches for his robe."

"Are you crazy? Are you saying you stole a guest's costume?"

"We've got to get out of here. I'll explain later."

"But I promised the Mad Hatter a dance," his wife said with a pout. She let go of her husband and used a handkerchief to dab perspiration from her cleavage.

"Time to leave Wonderland," Houdini said, offering his elbow. "For Pete's sake, just take my arm."

They fled the ballroom and walked rapidly to the front entrance. Houdini asked a footman to call for their coach. Moments later, when they saw their coachman taking his position atop the carriage, Houdini felt a rush of relief, and he and Bess hurried down the steps. He had an idea the Black Sisters would not like his revealing the content of the discussion to anyone, although he planned to keep mum about it. How far would they go to ensure his silence? He didn't want to find out.

But just as they reached the coach, a figure blocked them on the path: the Geisha.

"I don't think our hostess is ready for you to leave," she said in that odd, high-pitched voice.

"Now look, kid, I've had enough fun and games for one night," Houdini snapped. "Run along."

When she refused to stand aside, Houdini pushed past her. And as he did so, she caught his wrist. He pulled away, but her grip was surprisingly strong.

"Hey, hands off the merchandise!" Bess cried. Houdini noticed people gathering at the doorway. Stana was speaking with some urgency to two muscular footmen.

Houdini yanked again, but the Geisha's fingers didn't give. The escape artist felt an uncustomary sensation: panic. He prided himself on his physical strength. It was humiliating that a woman—attired as a subservient Japanese one, no less—could hold him prisoner. But she was doing just that, and with little effort, while wearing a victorious smile.

Acting on instinct, Houdini used his free hand to snatch the mask away. The Geisha gasped and let go, bringing her hand up to cover her face. She looked vaguely familiar, but the garish white makeup made identification impossible.

"Come on," the magician told Bess, and helped her into the carriage. As several footmen came running down the steps, Houdini thumped the roof of the coach.

"Get a move on!"

The carriage took off. Looking back through the rear window, he could see both of the Black Sisters at the doorway, along with their guards and the mysterious Geisha. Beside them, in a wide stance, was the towering Siberian peasant from whose grasp he had so narrowly escaped.

***

The Imperial Family had numerous palaces, but chose to dwell at Alexander Palace at Tsarskoe Selo, fourteen miles southwest of St. Petersburg. The palace was situated in a picturesque, manmade park—eight hundred acres of velvety green lawns; woodlands; gardens planted with exotic flowers, and artificial lakes, including one big enough for small sailboats. The grounds were studded with monuments, obelisks and triumphal arches. A tall iron fence surrounded the Imperial Park, patrolled by bearded Cossack horsemen in scarlet tunics and black fur caps.

Houdini accompanied the Tsar on a leisurely walk around the grounds on a winding path through a grove of trees, while six English collies raced friskily around the monarch. Nicholas carried a shotgun over his shoulder, a Holland & Holland Royal that was a gift from King Edward VII of Great Britain. Normally, a servant would have toted the weapon, but this discussion called for the utmost privacy.

"This is my favorite spot," the Tsar said, stopping at a pond near a pony track. He pointed to a murder of crows perched in a tree across the water. "You can always find them there at this hour."

He unslung his weapon. "Do you shoot, Mr. Houdini?"

"I don't have the nerve for it, Your Supreme Majesty," the magician replied. "Somehow I never had the heart to shoot a bird or any other critter that wasn't doing me harm."

The Tsar patted him on the shoulder. "Perhaps it's because you've been touched by the Savior."

"Maybe I'm just chicken."

"That I know you are not," Nicholas laughed. "Not a man who leaps into rivers wearing manacles."

He took a shot at a crow, nailing it dead and scattering the other birds. The dogs splashed into the water, racing to retrieve it.

"Count Vladimir Fredericks explained my offer to you?" the Tsar asked.

"Yes, Your Supreme Majesty."

"My wife, the Tsarina Alexandra, she has a very pure heart. She needs the spiritual guidance of a man of equal integrity—as do I."

"Sir, I hope I'm not out of line here, but maybe you don't need a court psychic at all," Houdini said. "I can tell you're an intelligent, highly educated man. A good man with a good heart. I bet if you just rely on your own common sense, you'll make the right decisions nine times out of ten."

The Tsar leaned his shotgun against a tree.

"Sometimes a kind heart is not enough," he said with a sigh. "You've read about the riots. I was so young when my father died in 1894, just twenty-six years old. I wasn't prepared for such responsibilities."

Twenty-six didn't seem all that tender an age to the performer. Houdini had run away from home to seek his fortune at the age of twelve.

"Well, that's the other part of it, Your Supreme Majesty," the magician said. "You don't have to make the decisions all alone. Your people can make them with you."

"You speak of a parliament, a duma? Ordinary people participating in great decisions of the country?"

Houdini nodded. "They do live in it, after all. It works darn well in America."

The Tsar pounded his fist into his hand.

"I am ordained by God to be the father of the people!" he exclaimed, betraying a flash of anger.

Houdini sighed. He had an awful presentiment of this genial fellow being beheaded like the King of France. But Tsar Nicholas's calm demeanor returned as quickly as it had fled. He clapped his guest on the back.

"It grieves me that you must return to America, but I will consider your advice. You may have left me with the most important counsel I have ever received."

While Houdini conferred with the Tsar, Bess enjoyed a private moment with the empress in her boudoir. Everything in the room was mauve: curtains, carpet, pillows, even the Hepplewhite furniture. The vases full of purple lilacs, roses and orchids, lent the room a distinctly feminine atmosphere. Her tables and shelves were lined with books, family photos, and icons made of porcelain and enamel. A painting of the Virgin Mary hung over her chaise lounge and on another wall, a photograph of Queen Victoria watched over her granddaughter, unamused. Oblivious to the splendor, Alexandra was crestfallen—behaving like a woman who'd actually miscarried.

"My dear, Bess, you have no idea what it is like," she moaned. "Philippe was my confidante, my guide. He healed me of scores of ailments. And I could share with him my deepest hopes and fears."

"Surely, you have other friends, your Imperial Majesty," Bess responded, taking her hand.

"I am not well liked. They call me 'the German woman,' as if I could choose the country of my birth," the Tsarina revealed. "They consider me a prude because I take my religion seriously, collect icons and devote myself to prayer, while they indulge in decadent parties, affairs and lewd gossip. Well, I don't want to be part of their Russia. I want to know the Russia of the peasants. The simple people who are not too proud to drop to their knees when their work in the fields is done at the end of the day, and pray to Our Lord. You and Harry are such ordinary people at heart, plain and true."

Well, that's a swell compliment, Bess thought. But something about this woman, so insecure despite her position, evoked her sympathy. Alexandra was like an injured bird.

The Tsarina squeezed Bess's hand. "Can you be my friend, Bess?"

Before Bess could answer, a rap came at the door.

"It is Monsieur Philippe, Your Imperial Majesty," a servant announced from the other side.

"Enter," Alexandra replied, glancing at Bess as if for moral support. The door opened and Monsieur Philippe appeared. In the hallway, servants stood bearing a dozen suitcases of various shapes and sizes. Bess expected the Tsarina to give the disgraced charlatan the cold shoulder, given his deception, but instead she rushed to the Frenchman and embraced him.

"Oh, Philippe, whatever will I do without you?"

"You will flourish, my dear. Your life will be more wonderful than before," he said, stroking her shoulders. "Another friend will come to you, one whose star shines far brighter than my own."

"Bless you," she said. "Still calming my nerves even now."

Monsieur Philippe took from his pocket a small silver bell and, as Bess looked on, perplexed, he placed it in Alexandra's open palm. He closed his stubby fingers over her delicate ones, encasing the bell in her hand.

"I leave you with this, Your Imperial Majesty. When you are in the presence of evil, it will ring."

CHAPTER SIX

Return to Russia

1911

Over the next eight years, Houdini's fame and fortune steadily rose. He escaped from inside an airtight, galvanized steel milk can; defeated a pair of "escape-proof" handcuffs it had taken England's top locksmith five years to engineer; learned to pilot a plane and became the first airman ever to fly one over Australia. To his fellow Americans, he was a fearless daredevil, an invincible superman. Many were even convinced he possessed paranormal abilities that he used to achieve his miraculous escapes.

His encounter with Rasputin soon ranked low among his memories; it was like a rat scuttling about in the recesses of a sub-basement. The world changed too. In New York City, which Houdini called home, automobiles had largely replaced horse-drawn carriages. High-necked collars and suffocating whalebone corsets gave way to dresses that revealed cleavage and betrayed a hint of ankle. There was even talk of giving women the vote!

Now, on the stage of the Orpheum Theater, he was rehearsing his newest and most daring escape ever, the Chinese Water Torture Cell. Suspended upside down, his feet in stocks and a steel cage around him, Houdini struggled to free himself from a water-filled cabinet. His assistant, Franz Kukol, looked on anxiously, stopwatch in hand. After what seemed an inordinate amount of time, Houdini burst from the cabinet, dripping, puffing, blowing, breathless, and collapsed on the floor.

As Franz helped him up, he checked the stopwatch.

"Two minutes and forty-five seconds, boss," he said. "That's cutting it pretty close."

"How many times do I have to tell you, Franz?" Houdini said, still catching his breath. "The longer it takes, the more suspense. I want them just about to give up hope. In fact, hire a girl to sit in the back and scream, 'He's gonna drown!'"

Franz nodded and handed him a towel. "I'll see if I can get that hat-check girl Darlene from The Billy Goat. She's a heck of a screamer."

"So I've heard," Houdini said, drying himself off. "And, say, we ought to have you on hand with an ax, and tell them you're there to save me if something goes wrong."

"That's laying it on a little thick, ain't it boss?"

Harry took the towel from around his neck and hurled it to the ground. "I'll put the damned thing in storage if we can't sell it right, I tell you."

"Now hold on, boss—"

A shout echoed through the theater, "Mr. Houdini!"

They turned to see the box office manager scurrying down the aisle.

"Mr. Houdini doesn't want anyone back here while he's rehearsing," Franz yelled, hurriedly draping a curtain over the Water Torture Cell.

"I apologize. I didn't see a thing, honest," the theater employee said. "Only this letter looks awfully important. It came all the way from Russia and it has some kind of official seal on it."

Houdini took the envelope and saw that it bore a double-headed eagle with the figure of St. George, the seal of Tsar Nicholas. He plucked out a letter penned in elegant longhand.

Dear Mr. Harry Houdini,

We hope that this letter finds you and your wife in good health. His Supreme Majesty Nicholas Romanov requests the pleasure of your company at the Palace in St. Petersburg. The ruler of Russia respects that you do not wish to be a permanent advisor to the court. The purpose is merely to entertain the Imperial Family, and the engagement would only be for four months. Please respond as soon as possible. There is some urgency in this matter."

Highest Regards,

Count Vladimir Fredericks, Chief Minister of the Imperial Court

Houdini stared at the letter, frowning. Vague memories of his run-in with Rasputin in Militsa's palace stirred.

"Holy smokes, boss, did someone die?" Franz asked, puzzled by his expression.

The magician handed the letter to his assistant, who scanned it quickly.

"What does that mean, 'urgent?'"

"Beats me."

***

It didn't take much to convince Bess to agree to the trip. She had only fond memories of their stay in Russia: the shops of St Petersburg, ballroom dancing with that cast of fairytale characters, and hobnobbing with the Tsarina herself. Houdini had never gone into detail about his unnerving encounter with Rasputin; he didn't want to spook her. She immediately began boning up on her Russian.

An ocean liner deposited them at the German port city of Hamburg. Then they rode the state railways, known as the Länderbahnen, toward Russia. Houdini sat engrossed in a Sherlock Holmes story—mysteries being among his favorite diversions—while Bess read a news item about the Romanovs in *The London Times*.

"Alexandra's wish was granted. She has a son now, and they really did name him Alexei," Bess said. "And the girls are big. The eldest is almost grown now. I can't wait to meet them. Look, they're as beautiful as their mother."

She pointed to a photograph of the family formally posed, the Imperial Couple seated and the four girls in white behind them. Young Alexei, in a sailor suit, stood beside his parents, his mother's arm wrapped protectively around him.

"They look so happy," Bess said. "Like an ordinary family."

Is that a wistful tone in her voice? Houdini wondered.

Bess no longer performed with him. For one thing, his act had become so spectacular that a costumed assistant seemed superfluous. For another, she had developed ill-defined medical issues that doctors chalked up to "hysteria," and a general jitteriness that kept her off the stage.

She'd always been superstitious. But of late, it seemed her obsessions were getting the better of her. Bess refused to enter a dressing room if she heard someone whistle inside, fearing it was cursed, and dreaded the color yellow because it was unlucky.

"Remember the time I wore a yellow costume and you nearly died in that river jump?" she argued on one occasion. Houdini had no choice but to oblige her and keep anything yellow from her sight, even an egg yolk.

But there was no doubt Bess suffered from some real physical woe. Always frail, she didn't menstruate and never had. They'd consulted a slew of physicians and none could help her. A doctor ruled out the possibility she could bear children. Most likely, some hormonal issue was involved, he said. Certainly, her body was far from curvy. She was so petite, she wore a size-one shoe. Houdini showed no sign of being bothered by her infertility. Their home in Morningside Heights was filled with pets that they considered their "children."

Petey the turtle roamed the flower beds in the backyard of the townhouse. Rudy the rabbit performed with Houdini on occasion when a young visitor demanded to see him pull a bunny out of a hat. Laura the parrot shared their bedroom and was known to repeat the magician's swear words. And, of course, there was Charlie, a small white Pomeranian given to them by the Grand Duke Serbius on their last visit to Russia in 1903.

"Believe me, a dog is more loyal to you than any kid will ever be," Houdini once told her.

Now, on the train, looking at the photos of the Tsar's brood made Bess think of their beloved menagerie.

"I do hope the maid will watch over them properly," she fretted. "Remember the time she fed the dog chocolate?"

"They'll be fine. And there's Cassie to help look after them."

Bess laughed. Cassie was the name of their imaginary child.

"I tell you, that kid is going to be president one day," Houdini joked.

Days later, when they arrived at the St. Petersburg train station, they found the place teeming with passengers dragging steamer trunks, with loved ones greeting them, amid billowing smoke and the cacophony of chatter in Russian and French. Beside them, a young woman leaped into the arms of an arriving soldier. She was built like a heifer, but ardor gave him the strength to hoist her aloft.

A uniformed man holding up a sign bearing the name Houdini caught their eyes, and they made their way to him through the mob. A fellow with remarkable strength, he lugged their bags, while a pair of footmen in blue velvet livery of the Romanovs trotted along behind.

"I am Vanya," he told them. "A truck will bring your two assistants and their gear."

Houdini had expected a car to pick them up as well, but Vanya brought them to a golden stagecoach, elaborately decorated and bearing the Imperial crest on either side. It was drawn by six white horses and accompanied by four mounted Cossacks of the Tsar's Escort. The coachman, too, was decked out in formal livery and had such a dignified bearing one might have thought he was an aristocrat himself.

As the carriage took them through the broad avenues of St. Petersburg, Bess pointed at the sights with excitement, practically bouncing in her seat.

"And imagine, I had to twist your arm for us to come here again," she commented to Houdini. "We should have been back ages ago."

About fifteen minutes into the trip, the road was blocked by traffic and the driver had to take an alternate route that took them through a decidedly less prosperous area. Factory workers trudged through the streets, leaning into the wind, in shabby coats speckled with soot, the material too thin to fully shield them from the cold. Houdini was sure there'd been poverty here on their last visit, but somehow this scene seemed more dismal.

"They don't look wildly happy, do they?" Bess noted.

"What guy does on the way to work?" He shrugged. "Take a good look at the faces of the poor schleps on the IRT subway sometime."

But she was right. When the people looked up at the carriage, there was little affection in their eyes. Except for one elderly subject who reverently removed his hat for the Imperial carriage, and a handful of boys who chased them for a block, waving, most of the downtrodden acknowledged them with sullen stares. Houdini half expected the workers to pelt the coach with tomatoes, a reaction he was familiar with from his early days in show business. The Tsar had indeed finally assented to the formation of the Duma, Houdini had read, but it seemed that the parliament had a long way to go when it came to reforms.

Tsarskoe Selo, though just outside St. Petersburg, was a world apart. The coach swept up the driveway through wrought iron gates, past armed sentries. While the palace had a substantial corps of ceremonial guards on their last visit, the security now bordered on suffocating. Besides the Cossacks who by custom guarded the Tsar, a permanent garrison of five thousand infantrymen of the Imperial Guard was now in place, with riflemen positioned on rooftops and towers. As an added layer of defense, thirty sentries patrolled the interior of the palace, stationed in vestibules, corridors, staircases and even the cellars.

"No one's going to be assassinating this Tsar anytime soon," Houdini said. "A mouse couldn't get in this place."

"Or out," Bess said, a little taken aback by all the security. "Except for you, of course, sweetheart."

A footman sprang forward to open the carriage door and helped them alight. At the palace door, two gaily attired footmen with huge orange and red ostrich plumes on their hats swung open the doors, while two others helped the couple off with their coats and hats.

"This way, sir and madam," one of the servants said. They marched behind the footman down long halls, beneath magnificent chandeliers, across oriental rugs spread on gleaming parquet floors.

Alexander Palace sprawled over one hundred rooms and boasted a staff of more than a thousand servants to trim its lawns to the precise centimeter, keep the vases stocked with freshly cut flowers, groom horses, maintain a fleet of motorcars, polish silver, serve at banquets, and dress the Romanov family.

The two-story building was divided into a center and two wings. The central structure housed chambers for state business and formal affairs. The Minster of the Imperial Court, ladies and gentlemen in waiting, and any guests had apartments in one wing. In the other was the sanctuary where the royal family had their private quarters. The footman led Houdini and his wife to their room in the guest wing.

Each room of the palace had the distinct aroma of a different type of flower. In their room, the delicate fragrance of hyacinths wafted from Ming vases. Mahogany, marble, gold and crystal everywhere the eye could see created an environment of absolute luxury.

Houdini flopped into a chair beside a multicolored stove that warmed the room and put his feet up on an ottoman.

"Not too shabby."

The canopied bed was piled high with pillows and covered with velvet sheets. Bess grabbed a bedpost, spun around it and flung herself on the bed. She rubbed a pillow against her face and sniffed the perfumed lace.

"It's grand, isn't it, darling?"

"It beats the classiest hotel we've ever been in, that's for sure."

"I should very much like for you to make love to me on this bed," she said in a mock British accent.

It was a tempting offer. Bess had been stingy with her favors in recent months. What was eating her, he had no idea.

"Hey, I'm supposed to entertain the Tsar's children this afternoon, you know," he protested, rubbing his hand over his jaw. "And I could use a shave."

Bess beckoned him with her index finger and a come-hither smile.

"Jeez, some girls just won't take no for answer," he said, unbuttoning his shirt.

***

Just under an hour later, a gold-plated telephone on the desk rang. When Houdini answered, the solemn voice of a palace telephone operator announced, "You are called to the apartments of His Supreme Majesty."

Houdini ran his palm over his chin. He'd just taken out his shaving kit, but it would have to wait.

"The key is winning over the children," he told Bess as they dressed. "If they get bored, we're licked and we'll be sent packing."

Houdini was good with children when it came to entertaining them for charity at an orphanage or hospital. But with none of their own, he and his wife didn't have much experience dealing with them one-on-one. Five against one, he thought, feeling the jitters coming on.

"We'll do just fine," Bess assured him, straightening his collar.

A servant guided them through endless marble-floored corridors to a formidable iron door. On either side towered a pair of black men, none shorter than six-foot-eight, garbed gaudily in scarlet trousers, gold-embroidered jackets, curved shoes and white turbans: a quartet of African genies.

"The Ethiopians guard the private quarters of the Imperial Family," the footman explained. "Hercules, these are the Houdinis. They have permission to enter."

Hercules, the broadest-shouldered doorman, bowed, and he and his compatriots opened the door. They made a great show of doing so, as if it could not be opened without the fortitude of Hercules' namesake.

"How are you doing, chief?" Houdini said to Hercules as he passed the Ethiopian. The colossal figure looked down at the smaller man like a lion regarding a mouse not worthy of consumption.

The servant ushered them into a reception room. Compared to the grandeur of the corridors through which they'd passed, the Romanovs' personal quarters were positively homey. The furniture was simple and family photographs hung every on every wall, save over one cabinet where a crucifix was prominently displayed. As they entered, Tsar Nicholas rose from his chair to greet them. Bess attempted a curtsey, but Alexandra caught her midway and embraced her with a motherly kiss.

"Oh, Bess, I am so glad to see you. And you, Harry. I hear that you've gained even more fame since last we met."

The Tsar had a few more grey hairs; his eyes were a bit sadder now. But his manner was just as warm as he took Houdini's hand.

"We are so grateful to you, Mr. Houdini. It's not so safe as it was to take the children out for entertainment. Only last month, an assassination attempt was made on the Grand Duke Serbius."

"The country is going mad," Alexandra fretted. "Sometimes it seems only our constant prayers are keeping Russia intact."

"Let us not exaggerate, Sunny," Nicholas scolded her gently. "Here, please, help yourself to some of the finest that our country has to offer."

The Imperial Couple guided their visitors to a small table laden with caviar, black and red, prawns, anchovies, herring and chicken bitki. Suddenly, a far door opened and a gaggle of children rushed in, jabbering excitedly.

"He's here, the magician's here!" the four girls squealed. They were followed by a stocky woman Houdini recognized as the Tsarina's lady-in-waiting Anna Vyrubova, accompanied by a younger woman.

Vyrubova now walked with a cane and hobbled after the girls. "I'm sorry, we couldn't contain them, Your Imperial Highness," she cried.

"You remember Anna Vyrubova," Alexandra said to the Houdinis. "And this is the children's nanny, Maria Vishnyakova. Girls, don't just stand there. Introduce yourselves."

The eldest girl, about sixteen, was formally dressed in a high-necked dress with a lace bodice and a sash around her waist, pinned with roses. She stepped forward and curtseyed.

"I am Olga," she said. She had chestnut blonde hair and blue eyes, set in a broad Russian face. Her cheeks flushed with excitement.

"I am Tatiana," said the next girl, who was dressed identically to her older sister. Tall, pale and slender, with rich auburn hair and grey eyes, the fourteen-year-old was the spitting image of the Tsarina.

Houdini turned to Alexandra. "I had no idea your daughters were such beautiful young ladies. The newspaper photos don't do them justice."

Olga giggled and blushed. Tatiana retained her composure.

"Continue, girls," Tatiana said sternly.

"We call her the governess because she's so bossy," said the youngest girl, out of turn. She stuck out her tongue at Tatiana.

"And who are you, young lady?" Houdini asked, stooping to meet her large blue eyes.

"She's Anastasia and she's being quite the brat for cutting in," said her older sister, a twelve-year-old with a peaches-and-cream complexion and a sturdy physique that would have suited a milkmaid. She shook Houdini's hand, then embraced Bess.

"I am Maria."

"Well, it's a pleasure to make your acquaintance, Your Imperial Highnesses," Houdini said.

To his surprise, ten-year-old Anastasia kicked him in the shin. Playfully, but with enough oomph that it smarted.

"None of that or you'll be bitten," she shouted, and laughed.

"Darling, no more of your misbehavior or you'll spend the rest of the day in your room," Tsar Nicholas said, sternly but with an undertone of affection that told Houdini he probably let the lot of them get away with murder.

"Please call us by our Christian names, or better yet our nicknames," Maria explained. "I'm called Mishka." She pointed at Anastasia. "Be careful of that little monkey; she's always pulling pranks. She can be quite naughty."

Anastasia shoved her, playfully, one might argue, but hard, and Maria returned the favor. These two girls were dressed alike, just as the older two were. A boy careened into the room and pushed between his sisters. Chasing after him came a pair of men in sailor uniforms who grabbed for him in vain. He ran right up to Houdini.

"Are you the magician?" he demanded.

"Alexei, introduce yourself properly," Alexandra said disapprovingly.

"Alexei Romanov, Tsarevich of Russia. Aren't you going to bow? I'm heir to the throne!"

Houdini clicked his heels together and saluted.

"At your service, sire."

"Mr. Houdini does not have to bow, Alexei," Nicholas explained to his son. "He is an American, not our subject."

Alexandra gestured to the sailors. "Houdini, this is Derevenko and Nagorny. They look after Alexei."

"I bet this little devil needs guards on him twenty-four hours a day," the magician said with a grin. Alexei beamed at the suggestion that he might be a dangerous character. Continued the magician, "Ladies, may I introduce my wife, Bess."

"Oh, tell us about America," Olga begged, taking Bess by the hand and sitting with her. "What do women wear? Is it true that some of the daring ones show their knees?"

"Have you ever seen an Indian?" Maria queried.

"Have you met the President?" Tatiana asked Houdini.

"Not the current one, but Teddy Roosevelt," he replied.

"I don't want to hear about fancy clothes and presidents, I want to see magic!" Alexei cried boisterously.

"I don't blame you," Houdini said. "I get bored stiff hearing women talk about bonnets and bustles. Let's get down to business."

Houdini took out a deck of cards and dazzled the Imperial Family with some of his trademark tricks, including Jumping Gemini, the Crazy Card Bend, and tossing cards and catching them boomerang style. He'd always thought close magic required more skill than large-scale stage acts. The audience was close enough to see everything—and little Alexei quite frequently interrupted the show to demand a peek at cards the magician was holding or to examine his sleeves.

Please don't let this be the one time a brat spots me palming a card, Houdini thought.

Alexandra sat in a rocking chair, knitting. Nicholas smoked his pipe and from time to time, applauded enthusiastically. The magician and his wife performed their mind-reading act, which excited the girls, especially Anastasia, who put Bess's powers fully to the test. Alexei found it less captivating.

"I want to see him get out of a straitjacket," he demanded.

"I left my straitjacket in the room. We'll have to take a crack at that tomorrow. But I brought some rope," Houdini said, taking a ball of twine out of his pocket. He borrowed scissors from their mother and cut them each a piece. "Here, tie me up."

The children encircled Houdini like cannibals descending on a captive and eagerly used their cords to bind his wrists behind his back, his ankles together and his arms around his torso. Olga and Tatiana blushed and giggled. Bess realized the sheltered teens were not accustomed to the proximity of men outside close relatives. Now they were near enough that Houdini, who prided himself on his acute sense of smell, could distinguish their perfumes: Olga wore La Rose, while Tatiana had spritzed on Jasmin de Corse.

Houdini wriggled and writhed on the floor. The amateurish knots of the children were easy to defeat. But he made a great spectacle of it, taking five minutes to extricate himself from the ropes, when he could have freed himself in half that time. After he succeeded, the children applauded and the Tsar clapped even louder.

"It's all well and good for you to get out of knots that we tied, but we're only children," Anastasia pointed out astutely. "I bet you can't untie yourselves from sailor knots."

Alexei's guardians Derevenko and Nagorny didn't have to be asked twice. They jumped at the opportunity for a manlier task than babysitting. As Houdini expected, they were quite expert at tying knots. They would have done a fine job securing any lines on a ship. However, nautical knots were never made to restrain a man, and Houdini had practiced extricating himself from every variation. When Alexei's minders were quite confident that he was inescapably bound, Houdini asked the Tsar to take out his pocket watch.

"If I can trouble you to time me, Your Supreme Majesty?"

"It would be my honor," the Tsar replied.

Within two minutes, the escape artist was a free man, displaying his hands before them.

"Bravo! More, more!" the children shouted, none more delightedly than Alexei. Alexandra shook her head.

"Now that is quite enough. Mr. Houdini has spent all morning traveling to see us. He needs his rest. You'll see him at dinner," she said, directing a look of gratitude at the magician. Alexei pouted and the girls protested noisily as the nanny and Alexei's sailors hustled them out.

"Bess, would you care to accompany me to the knitting room?" the Tsarina said. "I want to tell you all about the wonderful friend who has come into our lives, just as Monsieur Philippe prophesied."

***

Houdini returned to his room. Scratching his jaw, he remembered that he needed a shave before dinner. In his undershirt, he took out his kit and applied Pears Shaving Soap. As he reached for the straight razor, the pitter-patter of tiny feet caught his attention.

Houdini spun around. There was no one. *Christ, are there rats in the palace?* It was hard to believe. But he knew that even in the swankiest apartments in New York City, including the Dakota Building, sewer rats had a nasty habit of slithering up through drain pipes. Putting the unpleasant image out of his mind, he began carefully drawing the razor across his cheek.

This time it was a giggle.

He spun again. He marched to the closet, yanked open the door and out tumbled Anastasia. She sprawled on the floor, laughing hysterically. Houdini put his fists on his hips.

"I suppose you think that was awfully funny," he said. "What do you think you're doing in here?"

Well, at least it wasn't Olga or Tatiana, the visitor thought, repressing a shudder. *If one of the older girls had snuck into my bedroom, this engagement would've been over as soon as it began.*

"Can you really read minds?" Anastasia asked, wide-eyed.

"You just saw our act, didn't you?"

"You didn't answer my question!"

"And I won't, either. Now skedaddle."

Anastasia crossed her arms and stuck out her tongue. Ten years old or not, it wouldn't do for her to be found in his room, he knew. So, the best way to get rid of the mischievous imp was to give in.

"All right, all right, I'll show you how it's done," he said. "But you have to swear not to tell anyone. Not even your mother."

"I promise."

"A promise isn't good enough. Put your hand over your heart," Houdini commanded. The youngster complied.

"Now repeat after me," Houdini said in his sternest voice. "I swear upon my mother that I will never tell anyone the secret of Harry Houdini's mind-reading trick. I cross my heart and hope to die." Anastasia closed her eyes, repeated the words solemnly, and sealed the pledge by crossing herself.

This wasn't the first time Houdini had explained the mind-reading trick. In fact, the last time he was in Russia, he let the cat out of the bag for the wife of Grand Duke Serbius. The aristocratic lady had taken great delight in baffling her friends. She, too, took an oath of secrecy and stuck to it. It gave people a tingle to be in on a secret, he'd realized. It was like belonging to an exclusive club.

"Okay," the magician began. "Mrs. Houdini and I have a code we use, with little gestures. For example, if she turns and sees my right foot in front of the left, that means yes. If the left is in front of the right, that's a no."

Anastasia laughed and clapped her hands. "Why, of course! It's so simple."

Houdini nodded. "So simple, the audience overlooks the obvious."

"Teach me the code. Please."

"Well, there's an awful lot of it. How about we start with the alphabet today?"

And so, he taught her the signs: Wrinkling your brow, scratching your nose; brushing a stray lock of hair off your forehead, each gesture standing for a letter of the alphabet.

"Oh, wouldn't it be splendid to do it at a party?" she exclaimed. "Maria and I could pass messages without anyone knowing. If she thinks an officer at a ball is handsome, she can show me with her feet."

Houdini frowned. *Oh brother, what a mistake I've made. The little monkey will spill the beans the minute she lays eyes on her sisters.*

"Of course, I won't tell them," Anastasia hastened to add, as if she could indeed read minds.

"Well, naturally you won't. You swore, didn't you? Now, Your Imperial Imp-ness, time to beat it." To his dismay, she shook her head.

"You must show me how to untie myself," she demanded.

"Now, for Pete's sake!" But from the expression on the girl's face, he could tell that arguing wasn't going to get him anywhere. It would just keep her in his room longer. He retrieved a cord from his suitcase and turned to see that she'd put her hands behind her back.

"Let's not get ahead of ourselves," he said, gesturing for her to put her hands in front.

"But you—"

"Do you want to learn or not?"

Pouting, she put her hands in front of her. He bound her wrists in a simple square knot.

"Now, you have tiny fingers, which is very helpful," he began.

"My fingers are not tiny," she protested. "They're exactly the right size for my hands."

"Well, of course they are. I only mean that—"

A knock came at the door. *Oh, this is just grand,* the magician thought.

"I'm indisposed," he hollered.

Staccato raps hammered the door.

"Quick, under the bed," Houdini whispered. The girl didn't hesitate. She dropped to the floor and scooted under the bed. Houdini opened the door and at first saw no one. Then he looked down and saw the boy, Alexei.

"Where's Anastasia?" the little lord demanded.

"How would I know? In the nursery I'd guess," Houdini replied, holding the door only a few inches ajar. Before he could say another word, the princeling ducked under the magician's arm and sprinted into the room.

"Anastasia, I know you're in here!" he cried.

"She's not," Houdini claimed. The boy dropped to his knees, stuck an arm under the bed and seized a fistful of his sister's hair.

"Ouch, you're hurting me!" a voice came from under the bed.

"Well, that's an awful hiding place," Alexei observed, letting go.

Anastasia crawled out and pointed at Houdini. "It was his idea!"

"Now, hold on a minute—" the magician began.

"You've tied her up!" the boy said, pointing an accusatory finger at their guest.

"He's showing me how to escape," Anastasia explained. "Go on, Mr. Houdini."

Houdini sighed. *I suppose before the hour is out, the whole litter will be crowded in here.*

He showed the girl how to extricate herself, as her brother looked on impatiently. Once she was free, she marveled at her hands as if she'd never laid eyes on them before.

"Me next," Alexei demanded.

"Where I come from, kids ask for something they want," Houdini said. "Politely."

"I'm the Tsarevich. I command!"

Houdini started to put the rope back in his suitcase.

The boy hurriedly added, "But because you are our friend, I will make an exception. Please?"

Alexei had a little more trouble than his sibling getting out of the knot. Struggling to slip free, the six-year-old lost his balance and fell flat on his face, banging his side on the bedpost on the way down.

Houdini helped him to his feet. Anastasia gasped and covered her mouth.

"Oh no!"

Blood was dribbling out of the boy's nostrils and onto his shirt.

"It's just a nosebleed. I'll get a handkerchief," Houdini said, turning to look for one in the drawers. Hearing a whimper of fear, he whirled back and saw that Alexei was pale and his eyes were wide with terror.

Christ, I didn't figure him for a sissy, Houdini thought. *Too much pampering?*

To his surprise, Anastasia flung open the door and shouted at the top of her lungs, "Help! Help!" In two heartbeats, the sailors burst in.

"We've been looking all over for you, Alexei," Derevenko admonished the frightened lad, hauling him to his feet.

His partner Nagorny snapped heatedly at Houdini, "What were you thinking?"

"Keep your shirt on, sailor," the magician said, squaring off with him. "It's just a darned nosebleed."

But the look of fear on Anastasia's face told him it was something more.

CHAPTER SEVEN

The Miracle Maker

Doctor Eugene Botkin, the royal physician, stepped out of Alexei's bedroom into the hallway, where Houdini sat on a marble bench. Peering into the room, the magician caught a glimpse of Alexandra fretting over the boy, holding his hand and comforting him.

"It's all right, my dear Baby. We've sent for Our Friend," she said. Bess stood beside the empress, an arm around her shoulder.

"Were you able to do anything for the boy?" Houdini asked.

Dr. Botkin, a stout man in a blue suit, with a gold watch and chain across his substantial belly, shook his head.

"There is nothing that I can do, nor any other physician," he said, and continued down the hall. Houdini hopped up and blocked him.

"Now hold on, doc. What the heck is going on? What's wrong with that kid?"

Dr. Botkin sighed. "If you are to remain in this household and play with the children, I suppose you must understand why the gravest precautions must be taken with the Tsarevich. What I am about to tell you is a state secret. You must swear yourself to secrecy."

Just as Anastasia had done a short time before, Houdini took the vow.

"The Tsarevich suffers from hemophilia," Dr. Botkin informed him somberly.

"I beg your pardon?"

"It is a disease of the blood. When you or I cut ourselves, the blood clots at the wound, sealing it. A scab forms and healing begins. But when a hemophiliac is injured, the bleeding continues. And in this situation, it was not only the nose. When he struck the bedpost, this might have caused internal bleeding, and that is far more dangerous—potentially deadly."

"Oh, no! Is it contagious?"

Dr. Botkin shook his head. "It's a hereditary disease. It has cropped up in several other descendants of Queen Victoria, including Prince Leopold."

Houdini thought of mischievous little Anastasia, and the thought of her facing such a lethal disease hit him like a load of bricks.

"His sisters too?"

"Only the males in a family inherit the disease, for reasons science does not know."

Houdini groaned and raked his hand through his bushy hair. "If that poor kid suffered one iota of harm on account of me ..."

"You had no way of knowing," Dr. Botkin pointed out. "It was our fault for not telling you, even though we knew you would be spending time with the children. Alexei is a rambunctious child despite his illness, perhaps in rebellion against the cocoon in which the family must keep him. But do not worry. Someone has already been summoned to take care of him, someone whose remedy has never failed."

"A specialist?"

Dr. Botkin shook his head. "A slew of doctors have treated Alexei without success: oxygen, hydrogen peroxide, bone marrow, aspirin—which only worsened the condition—and even snake venom. The Tsarina considers them all quacks. She puts her faith in her spiritual advisor. You may have heard of him."

Houdini doubted that. "What's his name?"

"His name is Rasputin."

***

Rasputin strode down the hall, accompanied by Anna Vyrubova, who hobbled beside him on her cane as she struggled to keep up with his long stride. *He's moved up in the world,* Houdini thought as the taller man approached. His rough peasant shirt had been exchanged for a brilliant red silk blouse embroidered with flowers. Black velvet trousers and soft kid boots replaced the mud-splattered, weather-beaten leather. Where previously a strip of dog-chewed leather around his waist had served as a belt, there now was a silken cord. From his neck hung a gold cross studded with jewels.

Those gems must have cost a fortune, Houdini thought.

When Rasputin saw Houdini, he broke into a broad smile and embraced him. Houdini recoiled, but the Siberian lifted the smaller man off his feet.

"You are here to bring sunshine into the life of the Tsarevich," Rasputin declared. "This is excellent."

"I see you've done well for yourself," Houdini replied, pointing to the cross, which hung from a silver chain

Rasputin smiled and bowed humbly. "A gift from the Tsarina for my small services." He ran his fingers—now clean, but still sharp and claw-like—over his chest in a strangely sensual gesture. "This shirt she embroidered herself."

"I've heard about your service. What exactly is it you do?"

Rasputin's eyes probed Houdini's like prison searchlights, but Houdini knew by now to avert his own.

"Come, let me show you," Rasputin said, putting an arm around the magician's shoulder and leading him into the boy's room. Alexandra rose to her feet, ran to Rasputin and kissed his hand.

"Praise the Lord that you were near!"

"Do not worry, Mama," he said.

The Imperial Couple were considered the father and mother of the nation, Houdini knew, but Rasputin's bold familiarity startled him.

Closer now to Alexei, Houdini was alarmed to see that the boy, in a blue bathrobe, was pale as chalk. Curled up in the fetal position under the blanket, he writhed in pain. The sight amplified Houdini's guilt. He felt as if he'd kicked the poor tyke down a flight of stairs. Alexandra looked at Houdini like he was a skunk that had slinked into the bedchamber. Before she could object to his presence, Rasputin interceded.

"I asked that my friend witness this," he told the empress.

Alexandra frowned, but Alexei let out another awful groan, and she returned her full attention to her son. The sailor Derevenko sat on the other side, patting the boy's forehead with a damp cloth. Rasputin knelt between the Tsarina and the stricken youngster.

"Close your eyes and pray, Mama. And you as well, Mr. Houdini and Alexei's loyal guardians, but silently."

Houdini bowed his head, and it would seem to a casual observer that he had shut his eyes like the others, but seeing through apparently closed eyes was a skill he used for many a trick. The room was silent and took on the atmosphere of a church, with candles flickering about the room and all the observers mouthing silent prayers. Rasputin took the boy's small hand in his huge, leathery ones.

"Look at me, Alexei," he commanded gently. The boy, whose eyes had been clenched closed, opened them and gazed up at the holy man.

"My sweet boy, you must not allow fear to overcome you. You have nothing to fear, for the Lord is with you. He is now taking away your pain. You feel nothing but tranquility, as if you are sailing across a peaceful lake."

The deep voice was soothing. No, far beyond that. Houdini himself felt a strange calm coming over him. And he could see that the others were stock still, as if frozen in a photograph. Alexei stopped writhing about and lay in bed peacefully. The trickle of blood from his nostrils ceased to flow, like a river suddenly dammed. After a moment, he turned to his mother.

"Don't weep, Mother. I am feeling better," he said.

She embraced the boy, then stood and threw her arms about Rasputin's broad shoulders.

"Bless you, bless you!"

Rasputin turned to Houdini and smiled beneficently.

***

By that evening, order had been restored to the household. While Alexei remained in bed, regaining his strength, the other children joined the Houdinis and the Imperial Couple— as well as Rasputin—for dinner. The room boasted tall windows framed by red velvet drapes trimmed in gold braid, and a lush carpet so deep, Bess almost tripped when one of her heels caught in it. A fine damask tablecloth covered the dining table upon which sat plates of china bearing the royal crest. At each place, there were goblets crested in gold. Behind each of the velour chairs hovered a footman in blue livery and white gloves, who doted on the diner before him, bringing course after course and whisking off plates the instant the guest finished one.

Over dinner, Rasputin regaled them with stories of his Siberian hometown of Pokrovskoe, using a variety of voices to dramatize the foolish exploits of drunkards, triumphs of practical jokers, and the misbehavior of barnyard animals. Some smacked of tall tales to the magician, but the Imperial Couple did not display the slightest hint of skepticism. The children hung on the holy man's every word. Houdini realized that to the Romanovs, the "real Russia" was as exotic and semi-mythical as America. He seethed at how Rasputin grabbed all the attention, leaving him in the role of an ignorant tourist.

Rasputin spoke only his native tongue; Russian was the only language he knew. He ate with his hands, brutishly, pieces of food accumulating in his shaggy beard. But if his lack of proper table manners offended the Imperial Couple, it didn't show.

"Tell Mr. Houdini about the horse thief," Anastasia coaxed the family's spiritual advisor. The other children pestered Rasputin until he relented and launched into what was apparently an oft-told tale.

"I used to play with the children of Pokrovskoe and quarreled with them, had fistfights with them like any other boy. I was a bit of a rascal. Yet I never dared to pilfer the smallest thing," he said. "You see, I believed that everyone would at once know that I had stolen something, because whenever one of my comrades stole, I myself was aware of it.

Even when he had committed the theft far away and hidden the object he had taken, I could always envision the object behind him.

"Once, when I was sick in bed, some townsmen came to my father, who was headman of the village, about a stolen horse. Most of them believed it was one of the *brodyagi*, wanderers who passed through the village. I awoke from my sickbed and pointed to the richest and most respected men in the village, declaring that he was the culprit. The man denied this vehemently. My father was, of course, angry and embarrassed. But the townsmen became suspicious and followed the rich man to his backyard. They watched from the shadows and there, sure enough, they spotted the horse. As was the custom of the day, the thief was beaten within an inch of his life."

"Isn't that astonishing?" Alexandra asked the Houdinis.

"A real humdinger," the magician agreed.

Yes, he thought, *if a single word of that yarn is true.* Still, as loony as it sounded, he had to admit that what had transpired in Alexei's room—a boy brought back from death's door apparently through Rasputin's sheer force of will—defied science. Houdini felt a tinge of jealousy toward Rasputin. This man who, without any education and only native ability, not only could steal the limelight, but might conceivably be capable of *real* magic!

CHAPTER EIGHT

The Mystic's Invitation

After dinner, Olga and Tatiana each took one of Bess's arms and said giddily, "Come, Bess, you must see our rooms." The visitor glanced at her husband, who nodded in approval.

"But straightaway afterward, come to my boudoir," Alexandra called to Bess as all the girls carted her away.

The Tsar clapped his knees. "While your wife is occupied, I must show you my library," he said to Houdini. "I understand you are quite the collector of books."

"It's one of my biggest vices, Tsar Nicholas."

The girls' room was unexpectedly Spartan, Bess found. They slept on hard camp beds without pillows, and the furniture was simple lemonwood. A stenciled frieze of pink roses and bronze butterflies adorned the wallpaper. At each child's bedside, rested Bibles and prayer books. *Like novices in a convent*, Bess thought.

The girls changed into their nightdresses, and they knelt beside their beds as Rasputin sat in a rocking chair, leading them in prayer:

"Enlighten mine eyes, O Christ, lest at any time I sleep unto death, lest at any time mine enemy say, 'I have prevailed against him.'

Glory be to the Father and to the Son and to the Holy Spirit ..."

The girls' eyes were closed, their faces tilted upward. Kneeling so close to Rasputin's feet, they seemed to be making their supplication to him rather than the Almighty, Bess thought. The mystic was gently caressing the hair of the oldest girl Olga, who was nearest to him. Through her nightgown, ripening breasts were visible, and her parted pink lips invited a kiss. The tableau made Bess uneasy, but there was no trace of a leer on Rasputin's face.

"... Be my soul's helper, O God, for I pass through the midst of many snares. Deliver me out of them and save me, O Good One, for Thou art the lover of Mankind. Both now and forever, unto the ages of ages. Amen."

Rasputin kissed the top of Olga's head. She and the others hugged him and climbed into their beds—except Anastasia, who decided she was a rabbit and began hopping up and down. The holy man caught her on the fourth descent, carried the joyfully squealing child to her bed and tucked her in.

The children begged to be told stories before going to sleep and Rasputin, after much protest, complied. He told them the tale of the Legless Rider, of the Evil Witch Baba Yaga, of the Hijacked Horse. As Rasputin entertained the children, their nanny Maria Vishnyakova stood folding towels beside Bess.

"Does he always spend so much time in the children's quarters?" Bess asked casually.

"The children adore him."

"Yes, I can see they are completely at ease with him," the American woman acknowledged. Rasputin emanated gentleness and warmth. He seemed far from the sinister sorcerer her husband had described. Still, maternal instinct caused Bess to remain until the girls finally told Rasputin good night. They left together down the hallway.

"The children admire you," she complimented him.

"I am not like the priests they have met," the mystic explained. "They know that I am just a simple peasant."

"We all know you're something much more than that."

"If that is what you wish to believe," he said and bowed. Abruptly, he placed his hand on her shoulder.

"Are you quite happy in your marriage?" he asked. Nonplussed by his sudden forwardness, Bess took a few seconds to answer.

"Happy, why yes, of course," she replied. "We've been married seventeen years." She became aware that they were alone in the corridor. The nanny was still in the nursery straightening up.

"Your husband is a remarkable man," the mystic noted.

"Yes, he is. One of the most remarkable in the world." It sounded as if she were trying to convince herself, she realized. Rasputin's gaze was so penetrating, Bess felt that it would be impossible to lie to him.

"You are quite a remarkable woman too, although others don't see it," Rasputin said, patting her forearm affectionately.

"Me?" She blushed.

"You sometimes feel like a satellite to him, a moon around his star, almost invisible."

Bess didn't respond. She couldn't; she was lost in those magnetic eyes. It was as though he could see her naked. No, more than that, straight to her bones.

"You were a performer once yourself?" the spiritual advisor pressed on.

"I sang a little with a trio called the Floral Sisters. But we weren't very good."

"Oh, but you were."

As he said it, she realized it was true. Her confidence in her talent returned. She echoed him. "We were good. One of the best at the time, actually."

The nursemaid emerged from the room and as she caught up with them, the holy man broke off his inquisition.

"You must come to my apartment where I hold meetings with some of the faithful," he told Bess.

"Your followers?"

He laughed heartily. "I have no followers. I call them my Little Ladies. We pray together; we ask for guidance in learning the Lord's plan for us."

"That sounds so wonderful," Bess said.

"We will see you there," Rasputin said, glancing at the approaching nanny.

She extended her hand to shake, but he kissed it instead. A part of Bess found those slobbering lips repugnant, yet their touch sent a tremor rushing through her.

CHAPTER NINE

The Jeweled Box

The Tsar's vast library of glass-fronted bookcases was full of tomes carefully arranged by subject and language, with Russian, French, English and German books bound in fine Moroccan leather.

"Once a month, our librarian provides me with twenty books selected from among the best in the various nations," the Tsar revealed to Houdini.

The magician whistled, marveling at the collection. When he'd purchased his New York townhouse, it had taken three moving vans to transport all his books. However, this library dwarfed his storehouse of learning. He ran his hands along the books and one caught his eye.

"*War and Peace*," he read, opening the cover. "Signed by Tolstoy."

"Feel free to take it," offered Russia's ruler.

"I couldn't."

"It's yours. Please, I insist."

Houdini admired the precious first edition, then glanced over and saw the Tsar thumbing through a book in German, illustrated with dragons and fairies.

"Fairytales?" the magician asked.

"I shall read this to the children tomorrow evening—after your entertainment, of course."

"You read to the children?"

"Almost nightly."

Loving as my own father, Houdini thought. *Yet, haven't the older girls outgrown magic beanstalks and elves? Every father wants to protect his children from the outside world, but there's something to be said for a dose of reality. On the other hand, it might not be a bad idea for those girls to know there were big bad wolves out there.*

When Bess reached Alexandra's room, she found the Tsarina propped up on pillows on a chaise lounge, reading aloud a tearful letter from a friend whose engagement had just collapsed. At her feet lay a small Scotch terrier. The room was still mauve, but now it was crammed floor to ceiling with crucifixes and other religious images. Forged from tin, iron or gold, icons of saints sat on every desk, shelf, windowsill, countertop and in even the smallest nook, some obviously the handiwork of artisans, others crudely fashioned by peasants.

"You spoke with Father Grigori?" Alexandra asked enthusiastically.

"He is an incredible man," Bess replied. "I've never met anyone quite like him."

"His powers are vast and deep. He radiates the power of the Supreme Being."

"Still ... I wonder," Bess began cautiously. "Is it a good idea to have such an unusual character in a, well, intimate position with the family? With your children?"

Alexandra sat up and gestured for Bess to sit beside her.

"You know of my son's condition?"

"Yes, Harry told me."

"There is no more exquisite torture than watching helplessly as your beloved child suffers from extreme pain," the Tsarina explained. "Do you know that the royal family of Spain puts their hemophilic sons in padded suits and pads the trees when they go out to play?"

Bess shook her head, trying to picture it.

"Before the Almighty brought Father Grigori to us, I would pray for relief for Alexei for hours in this bedroom, or in the chapel in the crypt of Fedorovski Sobor," Alexandra continued. "I pleaded by the light of oil lamps for the life of my son, kneeling until my knees were chafed. Father Grigori has given him health, and nothing is more important."

"Yes, of course."

"And he has eased my own illnesses. Until he came, I spent many a day in bed, suffering shortness of breath, gasping, my lips turned blue. Excruciating headaches, swollen limbs, blotches that appeared on my skin."

"What was wrong?"

"The foolish doctors called it 'progressive hysteria,'" Alexandra scoffed. "Other crackpots called it 'psychomania.' All colorful ways of saying the problem was my own mind."

"And Rasputin, he's able to give you relief from these ailments?"

"Yes. And more than that, he has brought peace to my soul. Only when I am in his presence am I able to rest. Spiritual bliss comes only when Father Grigori, my teacher and mentor, is sitting next to me and I am kissing his hands and resting my head on his blessed shoulders."

Bess looked about the room, as much a shrine as sleeping quarters.

"Do you truly believe he can cure any ailment?" she asked.

"Yes. If your faith is strong enough." Alexandra looked at her with concern. "My dear, you're not ill, are you?"

Bess laughed. "No, I'm fit as a fiddle."

The thought of a figure who could calm frazzled nerves and cure female conditions with a few simple words appealed to her—and frightened her at the same time.

When Bess returned to the bedroom, her husband was reading by the fireplace.

"You should see the Tsar's library," Houdini said, holding up the formidably thick book. "*War and Peace*, signed by the author. A gift from Nicholas. It'll look pretty good next to the Twains."

Bess, slowly undressing, did not respond. She had a faraway look in her eyes, he noticed.

"You sure spent a long time with the girls," Houdini observed.

"Well, I spoke with Alexandra afterward. And Father Grigori."

"Who?"

"Rasputin."

Houdini put down the book. "You spoke with Rasputin. Alone?"

"For just a minute."

"He didn't try to put the whammy on you with his eyes, did he?"

"Of course he didn't. And what's the big idea, buster? I thought you were the one who didn't believe in 'the evil eye.'"

"I don't. But evil is another story. The guy is an oddball, isn't he?"

"You can say that again." Bess turned her back. "Help me with my brassiere strap, will you?"

He stood behind her and began to unhook the undergarment, which had only recently come into fashion.

"Do you think he really has mystical powers?" she asked. "That what he did with Alexei was beyond the normal?"

Houdini's brow furrowed. "I don't know," he admitted reluctantly. *Could it be merely hypnosis, perhaps causing blood vessels to contract? Or is it something more?*

***

The next morning, Houdini entertained the children for two hours in Alexei's playroom. It was a boy's paradise, full of marvelous toys: electric trains; battalions of tin soldiers; a model of Moscow accurate to the finest detail and populated by miniature people; a fleet of ships ranging from Spanish galleons to submarines; a replica of a mine, featuring an elevator that took miners up and down; functioning factories, complete with doll workers who went to work at the touch of a button. The Tsar's son proudly demonstrated all these to his American guest, but then sighed mournfully.

"What I really want is a bicycle," Alexei said. "But Mother won't let me have one. She says it's too dangerous."

Now, Houdini got it. By deluging the boy with such gizmos, his parents hoped to make him forget the many games he was forbidden to play.

"Your mother is right," Houdini said.

"You do dangerous things all the time, Mr. Houdini," the six-year-old argued.

"Well, you see, I'm not an important person," the magician explained patiently. "I'm a regular Joe. You have an important job to do one day, to be Tsar."

That seemed to mollify the boy. Houdini, never ashamed to borrow ideas from his competitors, used what he'd learned from Rasputin to win over the children. He let the boy play horsey on his back and told the children about his escapes, his life in the circus and adventures around the world. They were impressed that he ran away at an early age.

"I should like to run away like you and join the circus," Anastasia announced. "No one would ever have to know who I was. It could be a secret. I'd be up on the flying trapeze."

"I would be a magician's assistant," Tatiana said with a wistful glance at Houdini.

"I would be a clown," Alexei declared. "Maria, throw your handkerchief on the ground. I'll show you how I can slip on a banana peel."

"Whoa, no you don't," Houdini said, making a traffic officer's stop gesture. "No practicing your pratfalls on my watch."

Houdini showed them how to do card tricks, and then the older girls performed for the magician and his wife on the piano while Alexei accompanied them on the balalaika. The children introduced Houdini to their many pets, including a spaniel named Joy and a performing donkey with a repertoire of tricks. He could rear up, kneel, or roll over on command. Houdini and Bess, in turn, told the kids about their own menagerie.

"I discovered our fox terrier Bobby in a butcher's shop," Bess told them. "His owner was treating him horribly, so I bought him on the spot. Mr. Houdini trained him to get out of a pair of miniature handcuffs and even a straitjacket, and billed him as 'Bobby the Handcuff King.'"

At 11:00, the children's French tutor Pierre Gilliard arrived. A genteel fellow in a stiff collar, twirled mustache and goatee, he announced that it was time for their lessons. Alexei practically had to be hauled off by force.

When Houdini and his wife returned to their room, the magician hugged Bess with glee.

"Between the two of us, we've got those kids eating out of our hands," he declared. *Let Rasputin do all the hocus pocus he wants on Alexei,* Houdini thought. *He works his side of the street, I work mine and we can all get along ... maybe.*

***

Bess was eager to walk the streets of St. Petersburg, and Houdini obligingly took her to town. A chauffeur transported them in a freshly waxed 1910 Delaunay Bellville, one of twenty-one vehicles in the Imperial Personal Garage, each with its own driver. The escape artist's wife chose as her first stop the shop of the fabled jeweler Peter Carl Faberge, practically running between its baroque columns and through the door like a child on her first visit to a candy store.

Russia's elite zealously patronized Faberge. His handiwork adorned society matrons and debutantes alike, at wedding receptions, birthdays and other galas. Bess joined the throng of women oohing and ahhing over the items on display: necklaces, brooches, cufflinks, clocks, and tiny, exquisitely detailed flowers, parasols, animals and human figurines.

"Anything you want, Bess," Houdini told her, hovering close behind. He thought, *something's been eating her the last few months, but what wife's little worries can't be solved with the right piece of jewelry? Now it's just a matter of finding the perfect thing.*

Faberge quickly greeted them. In a sharp suit and without a single hair out of place, he stood ramrod straight. He placed in Bess's hand a miniature mounted Cossack fashioned of translucent blue enamel, encrusted with tiny diamonds.

"A gift, courtesy of the Tsar," the proprietor said. "And for you, Mr. Houdini, I am honored to present this." It was a jade figurine of the magician trapped in a gold cage that fit in the palm of Houdini's hand.

"The honor is mine," Houdini said.

"Just like yourself, the figure can ..."

Before Faberge could finish his sentence, the cage popped open and Houdini removed his miniscule double.

"... escape by means of this hidden button?" Houdini finished Faberge's sentence.

The jeweler gave a tight smile. He was clearly more comfortable as a purveyor of marvels than an observer. However, as he saw the magician eyeing one of the famous Faberge eggs on display in a glass case, he brightened.

"Would you like to see how the eggs are made?"

"Would I ever!" responded Houdini. He figured he could afford a moment away from Bess, who was busy inspecting an inch-high emerald unicorn.

"Mind if I check out the workshop?" he asked her. "I'll be right back and we'll pick out something swell for you."

"Go on, go on," she said, shooing him away.

Faberge reserved his finest work for the Imperial Family. Each year, his craftsmen prepared an Imperial Easter Egg.

Beyond their beauty, the master jeweler's ingenuity was manifested by the surprises within each one. One opened to reveal a basket of wildflowers made with chalcedony petals and gold leaves. Another popped open on the hour and a jeweled rooster arose, crowed and flapped its wings.

In the workroom, eleven men hunched over desks, jeweler's magnifying lamps on their heads, each utterly absorbed in his own project and oblivious to the world.

"Igor, show Mr. Houdini our latest creation," the proprietor called to one of the employees.

A skeletally gaunt, somber man, Igor looked up like a resurrected corpse unwillingly summoned from its final resting place. With obvious reluctance, he stood and presented a blue-green and yellow egg, topped by the golden double-headed eagle. Inlays of silver tracks crossed what appeared to be a map of Russia.

"That is the route of the Trans-Siberian Railway," Faberge explained. "You can remove the top by ..."

Houdini touched the crest, opening the egg. Inside was a scale model of a train, a perfect replica made of gold and platinum, with a gleaming ruby for the headlight.

"Holy ..."

"Turn the key," Faberge said, his eyes twinkling. The magician obliged, and the miniscule locomotive began to move in a little circle. Houdini whistled.

"It's pure genius, he marveled.

"Thank you," the jeweler replied, beaming. "Praise from a man of your ingenuity is welcome indeed."

Igor wore a sullen expression that Houdini instantly recognized. It was a resentfulness he'd seen in men whose genius was stifled or overlooked. The magician had learned to show appreciation to the inventors of devices that made his elaborate escapes and mysteries possible, even if their contribution could never be public knowledge. He patted Igor on the shoulder.

"And you have terrific craftsmen on your team," he said. "Can't imagine how long this must have taken."

Houdini noticed a small box on the workman's desk and reached for it.

"What's this going to be?"

The thin man pushed his hand away. It wasn't precisely a slap, but perilously close.

"Don't touch that!"

"Igor!" Faberge cried sharply. "Forgive me, Mr. Houdini. Igor is very proprietary of his work, as are many of my craftsmen." He added sternly, "He sometimes forgets that he is not the owner of this establishment."

"I apologize, sir," Igor said. "It's extremely delicate."

"Don't worry about it," the magician said, although he saw no remorse in the craftsman's eyes.

"It is to be a snuff box," Faberge explained. "It was commissioned by the Grand Duke Nikolai Nikolaevich. It is far from complete, because the mechanism—"

"Excuse me, sir," said a front-desk clerk who had poked his head in the workroom door. "Mr. Houdini, there are two gentlemen outside who wish to speak with you."

That was a surprise. They must have been sent by the palace, Houdini reasoned. No reporter or fan could know they were here. He found Bess, who was intently studying a butterfly pendant, and let her know he was stepping out for a moment. On the bustling street, he saw a bulky man in nondescript clothes, with a nose that looked like it been broken more than once.

"Let me guess, you want an autograph," the famed escape artist said pleasantly, although the big lug looked more likely to be an aficionado of boxing than sleight of hand.

Another huge figure bumped into him from behind. It wasn't so unusual to be jostled in a crowded city—after all, Houdini lived in Manhattan. He didn't give it a second thought ... until he felt a hard object poking his ribs.

A gun!

CHAPTER TEN

The Conspirators

"**Y**ou will come with us, yes?" the broken-nosed man said politely.

"Wait a minute, there must be some mistake," Houdini protested.

"I do not think so."

The duo hustled him into the backseat of an automobile, a no-frills black 1909 Puzyrev that made a Ford Model T look ostentatious. He fit snuggly between the pair. The driver, blessed with a neck as thick as a bull's, stepped on the gas and the vehicle took off.

"You hooligans better think twice about this," Houdini warned them. "I'm a personal guest of the Tsar. Knock this off or you'll be headed for Siberia so fast—"

The goon with the gun pocketed the weapon, while Broken Nose drew handcuffs from his coat.

"It's no good trying to kidnap me, if that's what you've got in mind," Houdini railed. "Do you dopes have any idea who I am?"

"We know who you are, Mr. Harry Houdini."

"Well, then you know that there's no place you can stick me I can't escape from."

"Put out your hands, please," Broken Nose said with infuriating politeness.

Houdini stuck out his wrists. Then he whipped them out of the way, grabbed the man's wrist and elbowed him in the throat. His captors scrambled for him but he slipped around them like an eel. With both feet, he kicked the rear window and it shattered. The goons reached for Houdini as he shot out the window. But it was impossible to stop him—because the two Russians had somehow ended up handcuffed together!

Houdini hauled himself onto the roof and stood like a surfer as the car swerved through traffic, avoiding carriages, wagons, bicycles and other automobiles.

"Stop the car, you idiot," Broken Nose shouted to the driver. As he hit the brakes, Houdini hopped onto the side of a wagon headed the other direction. Clinging to the rails by his fingertips, he saw that it was filled to the brim with crates, chairs, lamps, paintings and even a grand piano.

The magician inched gingerly along the side of the mover's wagon and narrowly avoided being raked off by a carriage headed in the opposite direction. Houdini finally reached the front and climbed in beside the driver. The man turned to him, eyes widening with fright.

"Are you r-r-robbing me?" he stammered. "Do you want me to raise my hands?"

"Keep them on the reins, you ninny," Houdini shot back. "And get me to the nearest police station."

"The headquarters of the Okhrana is a few blocks away," the driver stammered. "Will that do?"

"Well, step on it!"

***

Houdini hopped from the wagon and darted toward the headquarters of the secret-police headquarters, a forbidding four-story structure with tiny windows. Looking over his shoulder, he could see the car of the would-be kidnappers wending its way through traffic. He dashed up the stairs and past a pair of startled officers.

"I need to speak to Chief Lebedoeff," he demanded as he reached the front desk.

"Lebedoeff is no longer in office," a young desk officer replied. "Mr. Dzhunkovsky is in charge now. Do you have an appointment?"

"I am Harry Houdini and I'm a personal guest of the Tsar."

"Houdini, the magician?"

A second desk officer looked up from his newspaper. "Are you going to escape from one of our cells?" he asked eagerly.

"Not unless I'm put under arrest. Someone just tried to kidnap me."

The young officer escorted him up a marble stairway to an office door bearing a bronze nameplate engraved Vladimir Dzhunkovsky, Director of State Security. The officer knocked with some timidity.

"I have Mr. Houdini here, sir," he called.

"Come in," a sharp voice barked. When the magician entered, he saw four men in the room, three seated with their backs turned, facing a desk. The fourth stood from behind the desk, wearing a uniform, thick mustache and a severe expression.

"What took so long? Where are Lopitan and Migunov?" demanded the boss.

"I don't know, Chief Dzhunkovsky," the young officer said in a quavering voice. "Mr. Houdini ran in a few moments ago."

"What?" Dzhunkovsky cried, staring at Houdini. "You mean my officers didn't bring you here?"

"No. A couple of roughnecks tried to kidnap me," the escape artist explained. "I gave them the slip and came straight here."

"Those men were my officers!"

"Gee, if they'd only told me, I wouldn't have put up a fight."

Befuddled, the chief stroked his mustache, then said, "I am Vladimir Dzhunkovsky, Deputy Minister of the Interior and Director of the Okhrana. I apologize for bringing you this way, rather than contacting you at the palace, but this is a delicate matter and secrecy is of the utmost importance."

"If I'd known that, I wouldn't have stood on top of a car in the middle of traffic," Harry replied with a slight chuckle. "Well, I guess no one recognized me."

The other men had risen from their chairs, and Houdini recognized one of them.

"Count Vladimir Fredericks!" Houdini shook the old man's hand energetically.

"It's good to see you again," said the Minister of the Imperial Court, who'd first invited Houdini to perform before the Tsar. "I've been in Moscow."

A man with a receding hairline and Van Dyke goatee introduced himself.

"I am Prime Minister Pyotr Stolypin," he said. The official in turn introduced Houdini to Archbishop Theophan, confessor of Nicholas and Alexandra. He wore the dark robes and head garb of an Orthodox Church official.

"It's an honor to meet all of you," Houdini said. "But I have a feeling you don't want autographs. What's this all about?"

Stolypin gestured for Houdini to sit. "You have met Rasputin, I assume."

Houdini nodded. The mere mention of the mystic's name made him queasy.

"Have you had the opportunity to form an opinion of him?" the Prime Minister asked.

Houdini scrutinized the faces of the men around him and knew he could be frank.

"I think he's a louse."

Stolypin chuckled. "Good. Then we needn't waste time convincing you. Many are persuaded by his religious rhetoric and his supposed miracles. They genuinely believe him to be a second Christ incarnate who can do no wrong."

"I've seen his type before," Houdini snorted. "On the circuit. Faith healers pulling the wool over the eyes of rubes in their revival tents."

The new chief of the secret police nodded.

"I served Russia for seven years in the prisons, and saw a hundred Rasputins," Dzhunkovsky said. "Men who make the sign of the cross one moment, and then in the next, take you by the throat and strangle you, while wearing the same blissful smile."

"So, he really is a wolf in sheep's clothing?" asked Houdini.

"More dangerous than any wolf that ever stalked the Ural Mountains," Prime Minister Stolypin replied, nodding solemnly. "You understand why, don't you?"

Houdini shook his head, frowning. "I can't say I do. The fellow does give me the willies, but people everywhere want to believe in something. You should see the crowds in the waiting rooms of mediums in the States hoping to hear one word from their relatives on the other side."

"The problem is that the Tsarina is his most ardent follower and the most blind," Dzhunkovsky explained.

"I suppose that's to be expected," offered Houdini. "After all, he seems to be able to help her son, somehow."

"Yes. Through whatever strange powers he has, it appears that he has kept the hemophilia at bay," the Prime Minister said. "But the boy Alexei's survival has come at a terrible price. Alexandra is completely in Rasputin's thrall, and through her, so is the Tsar. She believes Rasputin's power to safeguard her son, and therefore Russia itself, is absolute. So, she has bestowed on him immeasurable power. Certainly, more than I have as Prime Minister. What he says, she takes as gospel, and she in turn has the Tsar wrapped around her finger. In recent months, Rasputin has had a say in every appointment in the highest echelon of government.

"Royalty, bankers, businessmen seek him out that they may be granted an appointment to a position at the court, or the government or armed services. Members of high society on the verge of financial ruin or public scandal beg him for the Tsar's protection. From the highest born to the lowliest factory worker, they kneel before Rasputin for every manner of favor.

"You can see them standing for hours at lines outside his apartment building to plead for a letter from Rasputin to take to the Tsarina. Tycoons offering wads of money. Highborn women offering their virtue. All this for those precious scraps of paper on which are scrawled a simple message to the Tsar in an almost illegible hand. 'My Dear and Valued Friend, do this for me, signed Grigori.'"

The thought of that monster holding such power put a chill up Houdini's spine.

"Hasn't anyone warned the Tsarina that Rasputin is no good?" he asked, turning to Archbishop Theophan.

"In her mind, Rasputin is a saint, persecuted by the slander of the faithless," said the church official. "She has made him her spiritual guide and refuge, her mediator with God. The empress sees anyone who criticizes Rasputin as a force of darkness trying to obscure the light. Enemies of 'Our Friend' are quickly given the boot."

"It's that conniving witch Militsa who controls him, isn't it?" Houdini asked.

Prime Minister Stolypin shook his head. "She introduced Rasputin to the Tsarina, true. But we believe that even she has lost control over him. His thirst for power is unquenchable. And he will be the ruination of Russia. For you see, many of the common people see through him. There are rumors of his drunken brawls and debauchery. Beyond drinking until the wee hours, he is a lecher who has seduced dozens of women, from scullery maids to princesses."

The archbishop gripped the cross that hung from his neck, as if a protective charm was needed when speaking about Rasputin.

"Rasputin is like Janus, the two-faced god," he said grimly. "To the Imperial Family, he exhibits the face of a humble holy man. But by night, he shows the face of a bestial degenerate. The country is indignant that such a man is welcome under the Tsar's roof. A dark specter has placed himself between the throne and nation."

Stolypin stood up and walked to the window, looking out onto the crowded street.

"So, now you see it, Mr. Houdini," he said. "This false prophet Rasputin, the Tsarina and Nicholas II in descending order of authority. Completely topsy-turvy." The Prime Minister turned from the window and looked directly at

Houdini. "The only way to disable this diabolical engine is to take out its battery."

"What is it that you are asking me do?" Houdini asked. "I'm no assassin."

"To unmask this charlatan so that even the Imperial Family can see his true face," the Okhrana director Dzhunkovsky explained. "You revealed Monsieur Philippe to be a fraud. We hope that you can do the same for Rasputin. You must break his spell over the Tsarina, or the nation will fall into ruin. Revolution, blood in the streets—and I am being quite literal."

Houdini scratched his jaw, dubious. "I don't know. He may really have some kind of power. You should have seen him restore Alexei to health. Just by holding his hand and mumbling a few prayers. I'm not superstitious, but, well, some things are mysterious even to me."

Stolypin and Dzhunkovsky traded glances and the Prime Minister nodded, giving the other the go-ahead.

"If you fail to expose Rasputin's supposed powers as fraudulent, there is another way you can bring him down," the chief of Okhrana said. "Find incontrovertible proof of his debauchery."

"If he's really so reckless, well then surely you can assign cops to follow him," Houdini suggested. "Undercover boys."

"And we have. There are men outside his home in St. Petersburg; men stationed in his hometown in Siberia, which he occasionally visits; spies who follow him to his haunts. He always manages to elude them. There is no doubt that many a society lady has fallen for his dubious charms, but these liaisons take place in his private quarters, to which we have no access. I must also admit that officers are reluctant to turn over what evidence they do gather. Every Russian knows that to oppose Rasputin is to court a one-way journey to Siberia. You, as a foreigner, are not so shackled."

The chief of the secret police paused as if reluctant to continue. "And there is one more reason our men are not up to the job. They fear Rasputin. They fear his strange powers. It's said that he can possess a man's mind and make him do horrible things. You yourself are a man of extraordinary gifts, and we have learned that you were able to resist him."

"So that's why ..."

"Yes, that is why I prevailed upon the Imperial Couple to invite you to return to Russia," Count Vladimir Fredericks interjected.

Houdini shook his head in disbelief, trying to wrap his mind around their proposal.

"When you say 'incontrovertible proof,' a letter, you mean?" he asked.

"The so-called 'Father' is practically illiterate," said Dzhunkovsky. "No, what we have in mind is photographic evidence."

He took from his desk what appeared to be an old-fashioned pocket watch and handed it to Houdini. Nothing out of the ordinary about it, except that upon closer examination, Houdini noticed that it was inordinately thick.

"A camera?" he guessed.

Dzhunkovsky nodded. "A subminiature camera, developed by the Swedish designer Magnus Niéll." He removed the windup knob at the top, revealing a tiny lens.

"The camera is operated by rotating a lever at the bottom, right here. The film is in a small cartridge and it is capable of taking twenty-five exposures."

The subminiature camera came with a viewfinder clipped onto the shaft of the lens, the Okhrana chief revealed. It could be adjusted into two positions.

"This allows you to use the camera horizontally or vertically," he explained.

"It's pretty neat," acknowledged Houdini, a lover of gadgets. He turned the watch over and saw HH engraved on the back. "I see you thought of everything. But I imagine this rapscallion does most of his debauching at night?"

Dzhunkovsky handed him an open box containing six small, peculiarly shaped bulbs.

"They are called miniature flashbulbs," the security director explained. "A new invention developed in Germany. Instead of lighting magnesium powder in the open air, they are closed lamps that contain a magnesium filament along with oxygen gas. You throw down this bulb and for a second, there is light. If you catch him in the act, we can provide the Tsar with indisputable evidence that he is nothing but a lecherous rogue."

Houdini felt a tingle of excitement at the thought of an adventure that rivaled *The Prisoner of Zenda*. Moreover, the prospect of sticking it to Rasputin held its own allure. But he was a practical man, and the conspirators' scheme seemed to have so many holes in it, he knew it was born of desperation.

"I don't know a thing about St. Petersburg," he pointed out. "I couldn't find the local cathouse any more than I could tell you where to find a rickshaw repair shop in Peking."

Dzhunkovsky rang a bell on his desk, and when a clerk appeared, he ordered, "Send in Officer Stolypin."

A moment later, a big bear of a man with magnificent muttonchops and dressed in an ordinary police uniform entered the office.

"This is my cousin Boris," said the Prime Minister. "He will assist you. I trust him not only because of our kinship, but because he has proven his knowledge of the city, as well as resourcefulness and discretion. He is equipped with a camera too."

The big policeman shook Houdini's hand.

"It is an honor to meet you, sir," he said. "I've read of your exploits. You've agreed to help, then?"

The Prime Minister looked at the magician intently.

"Will you?" he asked.

"As an American, I suppose I don't really have a dog in this fight," Houdini said. "But it sure can't be right to let an entire nation descend into chaos if it can be helped. I can't promise you results, but I'll do my best."

"That is all we can ask," said the Prime Minister.

CHAPTER ELEVEN

The Bacchae

That evening, the Tsar invited the Houdinis to share his box at the ornate blue and gold Mariinksy Theater as the National Imperial Ballet Company performed *The Bacchae*, starring the great Mikhail Fokin. Nijinsky had fallen out of favor a short time earlier, after he wore unusually revealing tights in a production of *Giselle*. The Tsar's mother was so appalled that she rose, glared at the dancer with homicidal fury and stormed off. Poor Nijinsky was given the ax in short order.

As Bess and Houdini learned from the program notes, the dance was based on the ancient Greek tragedy by Euripides. It tells the story Dionysus—the god of wine, religious ecstasy, and fertility—who returns in human form to his birthplace in Thebes, to punish the insolent city-state for refusing to allow people to offer him sacrifices.

The kingdom's ruler, Pentheus, fears that the social order is threatened by the incarnate god, who draws female citizens into the forested mountainside to indulge in rites highlighted by chaotic dance. King Pentheus ventures into the woods to see the forbidden rituals for himself, hoping to destroy the cult and bring down Dionysus.

The legendary Anna Pavlova danced the lead female role, playing the king's mother Agave, who is driven mad and transformed into Dionysus' most fanatical follower. However, a stunning young ballerina who played the leader of the bacchants stole the spotlight. Her hair was flaming red, her legs long and lean, her buttocks deliciously taut and high, displayed by a flesh-colored costume that simulated nudity. Her breasts seemed to ache for touch. When in the throes of religious ecstasy, she thrashed around with the abandon of a tigress in heat.

Houdini leaned forward, using opera glasses for a better look.

"Her name is Natasha Stepanova," the Tsar whispered, noting the magician's interest.

"She sure is something."

Bess elbowed her husband. "I guess I need to invest in a pair of tights."

"You know I only have eyes for you, sweetie," Houdini replied, putting his arm around her.

"Yeah, yeah," Bess said, shaking his arm off with mock anger. "They've invented something called the frying pan, you know."

At the climax, Dionysus ordered his female followers to attack the ruler, who had disguised himself as a woman to spy upon them. With rolling eyes and the ferociousness of sharks in a feeding frenzy, the bacchants swarmed over Pentheus and dragged him to the ground. As he fell, Pentheus reached out for his mother's face, pleading for her to recognize him. But Agave and her fellow devotees of Dionysus tore him to pieces.

At the curtain call, Houdini applauded as loudly as anyone, but the performance rattled the escape artist, who found the women's wildness unnerving. He'd been rooting for poor Pentheus.

"I don't get why the guy had to die that way," he remarked to Bess in a petulant tone. "Wasn't he the hero?"

"There's nothing to be sore about," she replied, taking his arm. "It's only a show."

When they returned to the palace later that evening, Houdini set about preparing for tonight's secret jaunt.

Houdini fancied himself something of a master of disguise. He'd learned to use prosthetics to convincingly portray a wild man in the circus. To spy on his competitors, he'd sometimes adopt the guise of an old man. Once, in such a guise, Houdini snuck into a theater where a rival magician was badmouthing him on stage. Houdini rose from the audience and berated the "lousy phony." Now, he used spirit gum to apply a false beard and whiskers. Because he expected a rough crowd, he used wax and ink to create a scar under his eye.

Boris had told him that one of Rasputin's favorite haunts was a bar called The Samarkand, where he'd often cavort with Gypsies until the wee hours. The magician made arrangements with Boris to meet him there at midnight. Houdini warned the policeman that he'd be difficult to spot.

"You won't recognize me either, sir," the beefy Russian cop had promised.

Fat chance, Houdini thought. *As if that big bruiser wouldn't stand out in any crowd!*

Now, as he donned scruffy clothes he'd picked up from a street vendor, the real obstacle was trying to get out of his bedroom in the palace.

"Darling, I don't like this cockamamie scheme one bit," Bess fumed. "Who knows what this Rasputin is capable of? Why do you think you owe these men anything?"

"All I'm going to do tonight is observe him in his natural habitat and ask a few questions," Houdini assured her as he wriggled into pants that had been haphazardly patched.

"You know it's not so smart to fool with an animal in its natural habitat," Bess noted, putting her fists on her hips. "Ask a few questions of the wrong person and in the wrong accent, and you could get shot. "

"You're right, of course, sweetie," Houdini said. "You watch over me like a mother hen. I'll be careful, I promise. Now, will you give me a hand with these boots?"

The Tsar had put the driver at Houdini's disposal. At close to 11:00 p.m., the escape artist took a ride into the city and to the sketchy neighborhood where The Samarkand was located. Houdini found the bar packed with a mix of scarred and bearded ruffians who looked like a pirate crew on shore leave. At the largest and most crowded table, Rasputin sat, surrounded by an entourage. These cronies were particularly unsavory, including one who actually wore an eyepatch.

"More vodka, more vodka!" Rasputin yelled. "Let it flow that these fine men may have their fill."

A Gypsy band, made up of men with seven-stringed guitars and tambourines, filled the bar with music, while a dozen dancers romped in a circle clapping. The raucous crowd cheered them on, none more enthusiastically than Rasputin, who roared his approval and stomped his boot in rhythm. Despite having been forewarned of Rasputin's duality, Houdini was stunned. This was an entirely different man from the pious faith healer who had hovered over the ailing Tsarevich.

The disguised magician took his place at a table next to the least lethal-looking patrons. One sported a full black beard and thick eyebrows to match; another had a face nicked with battle scars and stubble that looked as rough as sandpaper. Sharing the table were two younger men who appeared to be companions, one capped and bespectacled, the other with a mop of yellow hair. Houdini sat in an empty chair between the two pairs. The escape artist scanned the crowded bar, but saw no sign of Boris. Unless he was a true master of disguise, he must not have arrived. Only one patron approached the policeman's bulk, a hooded figure brooding over a mug in the corner, but the man wore a peg leg eaten away in places by rot.

Rasputin slapped the ample buttocks of a passing barmaid, roaring with laughter as she blushed and clutched his lingering hand. She tried to wiggle free from his leathery paws, but he swung the blonde server into his lap, deftly taking the mug she toted and tossing down a swig. The Siberian buried his nose into her cleavage and breathed in her scent.

"Here is the true heaven, my friends," Rasputin cried.

"Starets, I am engaged," the girl protested.

"But I'm in love with you," he declared. Then he laughed and dropped her on the floor. His cohorts chortled as she scrambled to her feet and made her getaway, both hands guarding her bottom. The Gypsies danced, clapped and swirled about the room.

The yellow-haired young man gestured to the dancers with a mug overflowing with foam.

"They worship the Black Virgin, you know," the young man confided in Houdini, elbowing him. "But in India, she's known as Kali, the Hindu goddess of destruction."

His bespectacled companion pounded his glass on the table. "Damn you, Volkov. No wonder no one comes to see your plays. You take the fun out of everything! So what if they're heathens? They're the only source of joy a common man can afford these days."

Now, Houdini recognized the first speaker as Illya Volkov, the poet who had performed that night at the Kremlin Palace. Though a decade had passed, he'd changed little. His dark eyes looked even more mournful, but he retained his boyish appearance. Houdini could swear he still wore the same coat, now worn and patched. Perhaps his brand of poetry had fallen out of favor. He wrote plays now too, apparently.

The Gypsies' music blended elements of the dozens of lands through which the nomadic people had passed: India, Egypt, Spain, Russia. It had a chaotic quality, an effect amplified by the frenetic dance. In contrast to the joyful expressions of the dancers, the lyrics of the song were quite dismal.

"The lightning strikes
And lashes homes
And floods wash
All has passed, has blown away,
Nevermore to return.
There is nothing left behind,
Only sadness and woe.
So, while you breathe,
Drink and dance
And live and live and live."

Rasputin, hooting boisterously and egging the Gypsies on, could no longer restrain himself. He leaped to his feet and joined the circle, tromping the wooden floor with such vigor the sound could be heard, like gunshots, over the music. Displaying agility surprising for such a large man, he squatted low to the floor, kicking out his legs in the iconic Russian *kazatsky* dance. Rasputin blazed with raw energy, his eyes aglow. Houdini felt a rush of envy for this man who could express love of life with total abandon, who could throw off the shackles of polite society at the drop of a hat.

The Siberian began to yank nearby onlookers from their chairs to join him on the dance floor, including a small group of men in business attire letting off steam after work.

"Hop, hop, hop!" he roared. "Get those elephant feet of yours off the floor." As Rasputin spun past the table where Houdini sat, he grabbed his shoulder with such force, the magician felt as if he could have been lifted up like a toy soldier.

"Don't think I haven't seen you sitting there, sourpuss!" Rasputin bellowed. "No one sits tonight."

Houdini hesitated, but realized that refusing would draw attention to himself. He put down his glass and stood face-to-face with the mystic. Rasputin grinned and for a moment, Houdini thought the jig was up. Yet it was impossible to believe that Rasputin could see through both his drunken haze and the magician's elaborate disguise. A Gypsy girl with a low-cut bodice that gave a tantalizing glimpse of her areolas moved aside to admit Houdini to the circle.

The dancers, now numbering thirteen, circled the room, spinning faster and faster. Houdini, who seldom drank, felt the room spinning as well. His gorge was rising, and he pictured his brain sloshing around in a sea of alcohol. He wanted to stop and sit down, but it was as if he were on a malfunctioning merry-go-round and if he attempted to step off, centrifugal force would send him flying into oblivion.

Just when he was about to puke, the music stopped abruptly.

"You dance like an Englishman!" Rasputin told him. "Stiff as a board. But then I love the English!" He clapped Houdini on the back as the American stumbled on unsteady legs to his seat.

"You don't get out much," Illya observed, good-naturedly. "Or are you more accustomed to the waltz?"

The music picked up again. Houdini, fit as he was, was out of breath, but incredibly, Rasputin pranced on, arm in arm with two Gypsy girls, one voluptuous with breasts like ripe honeydew melons spilling halfway out of her blouse, the other slender-hipped but with fire in her eyes that proclaimed she could satisfy any man's desire.

The black-bearded drinker at Houdini's table said in a gravelly voice, "He'll have one of those two bent over in a room upstairs before the night's over."

"Both, more likely," his stubbly-faced companion mumbled.

"He's had his way with so many," Illya's bespectacled friend added in a tone that was in equal parts prudish disapproval and envy. "Not just Gypsy sluts either. Actresses, opera singers, the wives of the captains of industry."

"Let's not leave out dancers, Andropov," the writer responded. "It's said the good father now counts Natasha Stepanova among his conquests."

Houdini recognized the name of the ballerina who had so entranced him.

"Why would any decent woman stoop to messing about with that dirty fellow?" he asked in a raspy, disguised voice.

"Dirt goes a long way with society women," Illya mused. "They get tired of those perfumed aristocrats and buttoned-up cavalry officers. They're intrigued by the thought of being saddled up by a peasant with dirt under his fingernails, and ridden into the sunset."

"And then, of course, there are those rumors about his manhood," the bearded patron pointed out, holding his hands apart. "It's said to be thirteen inches when fully sprung."

Houdini laughed. "That's not a penis, that's a halibut." Remembering his mission, he went on, "Where does he carry out all these supposed trysts?"

The scarred brute leaned in, gesturing to the others to join him in a huddle.

"My brother is the driver for the owner of the Orlov Automobile Factory," he said conspiratorially. "He takes the rich bastard's wife to the Coachman's Banya every Thursday morning at about noon. Every time, he sees Rasputin arriving at the bathhouse a few minutes afterward. And the 'monk' always leaves a few minutes after she does. Quite a coincidence, wouldn't you say?"

"Now we know how the ladies contend with the grime issue," Illya observed.

"Doubtless he cleanses their souls there," his friend Andropov said with a bitterness that suggested he had little luck with ladies himself.

Rasputin, meanwhile, was imploring the Gypsies to sing louder, bellowing, "Your voices lack timbre. Don't you have a bass in the group?"

The band leader shook his head sheepishly.

"He's sick with the flu," he replied.

"You fools should have brought him, and I would have cured him," the faith healer said with a mighty laugh. He looked around the room and spotted a stout man with a barrel chest, in bourgeois attire. He was surrounded by friends, but Rasputin zeroed in on him as if they were invisible.

"You, what's your name?" Rasputin demanded.

"It is Koslov—I, I mean, Kokovstov, sir," the big man stammered.

The Siberian hauled him to his feet. "You look like you can make a lot of noise. Show these roaming rascals what a real

Russian can do." As if herding an ox into a corral, he shoved poor Kokovstov over to the band.

Rasputin's assessment proved correct. When the burly man contributed his booming bass, the band sounded much better. When the song finished, the crowd applauded, thumping their mugs on their tables in approval. No one clapped more enthusiastically than Rasputin. He fell into his seat and pulled the man down beside him.

"You are a good fellow," he announced loudly. "I will make you Prime Minister."

Kokovstov grinned weakly, as if he couldn't quite tell if the besotted holy man was joking.

"There are many more qualified than I," he pointed out.

"You think I can't do it?" Rasputin shouted, seeming to take offense. "The Imperial Couple dance to the tune I choose, just like these Gypsy fools." He tugged on his black silken shirt. "The Tsarina made this for me with her own hands."

The scarred brute beside Houdini sneered and said in a low voice, "I'd bet my horse she's done more than that for him."

His chum toasted him in agreement. "He's mounted her like a Siberian stallion, you can be sure of that. She and that fat pig Anna Vyrubova, together I'm sure, piled up like cordwood."

The brute guffawed. "You know they say those two ..." He wagged his tongue between two fingers, mimicking cunnilingus in a way that suggested it might not be his forte, but nonetheless conveyed the message.

"That's enough," Illya said, slamming down his mug. "You're speaking of the Tsarina."

The scarred man ignored him. He said louder, "What I hear is that he's slid that giant tool of his into the daughters too, from the pretty one with the big tits right down the line. A bit young for my liking, but as they say, old enough to bleed, old enough to butcher."

Houdini snatched the bigmouth's lapels before even realizing he'd done it.

"Take that back," he snarled. "You don't have to bring the kids into it."

"You should not defend the Imperial Family," the young man in glasses scolded Houdini. "They are the chief of all the parasites."

Illya leaped to his feet. "I'll defend the honor of any woman," he shouted, swaying a bit. "You Bolsheviks go too far, Andropov!"

Equally incensed, Andropov stood too, pushing his glasses back on his nose. "Are you criticizing the Bolsheviks now? We are the country's only hope."

Rasputin rose as well, somehow aware of the ruckus, although how he could have heard any of the argument over the din, Houdini couldn't imagine. Rasputin pointed a long, accusatory finger at the bickering patrons at Houdini's table.

"Did you hear? These louts insulted the Tsarina."

He hurled a vodka bottle at the scarred brute. It whirled through the air, spewing out alcohol, and crashed into the man's skull. A lesser fellow might have fallen unconscious, but the brute smiled like this was a nightly occurrence and he'd been spoiling for a brawl. He jumped up, grabbed his oaken chair and sent it flying at the Siberian, as if it were made of balsa wood. With startling reflexes for a large man three sheets to the wind, Rasputin hopped out of the way and the chair smashed into a startled drinking companion, knocking him over like a bowling pin.

With the ferocity of wolves unleashed, Rasputin's companions fell on the four men. The Gypsy band waded into the fray, clobbering brawlers with their guitars, and in a matter of seconds, the entire tavern was a roiling sea of flying fists and tumbling bodies. Music was replaced by curses, screams, breaking glass and the sound of knuckles colliding with cheeks, chests and bellies.

Houdini, who had boxed as an amateur in his youth, held his own, knocking to the floor a succession of Rasputin's cronies who leaped at him. One grizzled, six-foot-four Gypsy with the build of a prizefighter charged the magician, sticking out a wickedly sharp dagger. As the thug lunged, Houdini pitched himself backward and skidded under the table. Houdini's attacker crouched down and followed, but the nimble magician escaped his grasp. Houdini sprang to his feet and kicked out a table leg. The massive oak table top crashed down on the lummox, who groaned in agony before collapsing.

Pleased with himself for executing the maneuver as if it had been choreographed for a stage fight, Houdini grinned and stepped back—right into the arms of a pair of Gypsies. A guitarist put him in a chokehold while a scrawny tambourine player with an unexpectedly potent punch pummeled his abdomen. The magician lifted both feet and kicked with the force of a kangaroo. The little man flew away like a paper doll caught up in a gust of wind. Grappling with Houdini, the bigger Gypsy was joined by two more. Grabbing the American by his ankles and underarms, the trio hoisted him and tossed him through the window.

CHAPTER TWELVE

The Bathing Beauty

Houdini landed face down in a mound of snow the color of charcoal, shards of glass scattered around him. As he crawled to his knees, the tavern door burst open and four Gypsies poured out. The big fellow he had crushed with the table was alive and well. He charged, wielding the table leg as a club.

Surrounded, Houdini tried to shield his face as fists pounded him and booted feet drove into his gut, groin and head. He bit an ankle and plunged his finger into an eye socket, but there were too many of them. His adversaries piled on like linebackers sacking a quarterback—then recoiled as the magician rose, slicing the air with a piece of the broken glass. Blood spattered in all directions from faces and arms. The victims screamed obscenities.

One was preparing for a second charge when a huge hand rendered bear-like by a fur glove grabbed him by the back of his collar, hoisted him into the air and flung him away.

With a mighty right hook, Houdini's rescuer sent another attacker airborne. As he did so, his hood fell off, revealing Boris's face. He had been the patron with the peg leg—a false one as now became apparent when he used it to bash another thug into a state of unconsciousness. The two ruffians he'd tossed into the snow scrambled to their feet and fled.

Houdini was grateful to have been saved from the beating of his life, if not worse, but miffed that he'd failed to spot Boris. Somehow, despite his bulk, the policeman had been less conspicuous than the master of deception himself. The cop helped Houdini to his feet.

"That was good timing, Boris," Houdini said, picking up the false beard that had fallen off in the struggle. "Thanks."

"Are you all right, Mr. Houdini?"

"I'll survive. And Harry is fine," he said, patting his savior's shoulder.

Another voice came from nearby. "Harry Houdini, the escape artist?"

Houdini turned to see Illya hunched over a few yards away, holding a handkerchief over a bloody nose.

"I knew your accent was American!" the poet exclaimed. "What were you doing in that wretched place? There's a battle royal there every other night."

"Well, I don't want it getting around that I go to dives like that. I've got a reputation to protect."

Illya's wry smile suggested that he didn't find this explanation entirely convincing.

"Well, you seemed curious about the great Rasputin," he said. "Do you hope to pick up magic tricks from him?"

"Looks like I could pick up some drinking lessons from him."

The writer laughed. "I better check on Andropov. He's not much of a fighter, regardless of how much practice he's had trading blows over politics. And he's helpless when his glasses get broken." Illya pointed down the darkened street to his friend, who was currently heading straight for a lamp post.

"Well, it was swell seeing you again, Volkov," Houdini said, sticking out his hand.

Illya shook it. "If you ever want to know more about Rasputin, come find me at 12 Kuznechny Pereulok Street. It's not much, and I share it with that fellow, but the fire is warm."

Swaying, the still-tipsy poet hurried off after Andropov.

"So, we've plenty of bruises and nothing to show for it," Boris said to Houdini in a disappointed tone.

"That's where you're wrong, big guy," Houdini replied with a grin. "I think I know what my next stop will be. The Coachman's Banya."

***

When Bess saw the purplish bruises on her husband's face, she punched him in the arm with displeasure.

"Ouch! Don't you think I've taken enough licks for the night?" he yelped.

"Just what you deserve for brawling in a saloon like a twenty-year-old sailor," she said. "Come to the bathroom."

As they crossed the room, she helped him off with his clothes. She noticed for the first time that there were yellow stripes on the cheap shirt he'd bought on the street for his disguise.

"Well, there's the problem right there. This is what you get for wearing yellow!" Bess pulled off the shirt and threw it in the garbage pail. "Rotten luck, every time."

She sat Houdini on the commode and gently began to clean the scratches with the cotton balls and iodine from their first aid kit. They never traveled without it, and Bess was well-accustomed to patching her husband up after one of his acts went awry.

"Well, that's the end of your investigation," she said emphatically.

"Like heck it is," Houdini growled. "This creep Rasputin has really got under my skin, and I've found out exactly where I can expose him for the phony he is."

"Another bar? Or a wrestling ring?"

"No, this place is a lot safer. A bathhouse. Word is he frequents it every Thursday at the same time. To meet a woman. I can catch him in the act with the camera."

Skepticism was written all over her face and he put his hand on her shoulder reassuringly.

"Sweetie, there's no danger except maybe sweat stains," the magician assured his wife.

"And slipping on soap, I suppose. At least take Franz with you."

"Oh no, I'm not getting him mixed up in this. Let him keep coming up with tricks and gags to keep the children occupied."

Bess put down the medical kit and scrutinized her husband's cheeks and forehead. He healed at an astounding rate and she knew that by morning the swelling would be gone, with just a few scratches to explain away. She pointed to them.

"How will you explain those to Alexandra and the children?"

"I'll say I was rehearsing a difficult escape."

Bess had to admit it was plausible. "I need to put you to bed," she said, leading him by the hand. She helped him out of the rest of the battle-torn costume and tucked him in under a sumptuous quilted comforter. Houdini sank into a mattress that must have cost half a flock of geese their feathers.

Just when he'd nearly dozed off, Bess shook his arm.

"There's another way we can get the goods on Rasputin," she began cautiously. He cocked an eyebrow.

"Suppose I were to drop by his apartment where he holds his gatherings with his Little Ladies," Bess suggested.

"Step right into his lair?" He sat up, jolted to alertness.

"There will be more than a dozen ladies there," she quickly added. "I can speak to them, draw them out. You know how women gossip."

"I'm not sure it's safe," her husband replied, dubious.

"That from a man with half a dozen bruises on him. You have a lot of nerve!"

He couldn't deny that the plan had potential. Something incriminating about the boozing sex fiend was sure to crop up. Houdini sighed and nodded.

"You have to promise me one thing, though," he insisted. "You won't be in the room alone with Rasputin, not for a minute."

"Of course not, dear. I wouldn't be caught dead."

He kissed her cheek. "Just be careful."

"Says the guy with the shiner."

***

Built around 1850, the Coachmen's Banya, also known as the Yamskie, was St. Petersburg's premier bathhouse, where Russians came to steam away their ailments and stress. Socialites traded gossip and businessmen cut deals there, the way relationships are forged on golf courses across America. Great thinkers and literary luminaries such as Dostoyevsky frequented it, and it was rumored that the notorious Bolshevik rabble-rouser Lenin held clandestine meetings amid clouds of steam. The facility offered rooms for families as well as private steam rooms for individuals or married couples. The rules forbade singles of the opposite sex from sharing a private room, but the proprietors turned a blind eye to illicit liaisons.

Houdini, who had phoned that morning to reserve a private room, entered the front office of the bathhouse, where he was greeted by a tiny clerk with a preposterously oversized walrus mustache. The pipsqueak accepted the famed magician's payment and handed him a robe, towel, slippers and, surprisingly, a felt hat.

"What's this for?" the American asked.

"To keep your head from overheating." Then the clerk held up a short, leafy branch. "Would you care for a venik massage before you steam? It is quite good for the blood circulation and metabolism." He whipped Houdini's forearm to demonstrate.

The magician yanked his hand away. *Getting hit by a switch like some hick kid getting a licking from Pappy in the woodshed? Thanks, but no thanks.*

"No, but there is something you can do for me," he told the clerk. "When Rasputin shows up, come get me." He handed the clerk three rubles. The little fellow looked at him quizzically, then nodded. He rang a bell and a curly-haired attendant no more than fifteen years old scurried to the front.

"Pavel, show Mr. Houdini to Number Eight," the clerk said.

The youth escorted Houdini to a locker room, where the magician removed his clothes folded them neatly and put them in a locker. He placed the pocket-watch camera on top for easy access. When the little clerk came to alert him, he wanted to be at the door of Rasputin's steam room armed and ready to catch him *flagrante delicto*.

After rinsing off in a shower and donning the bathrobe, he followed the attendant through an atrium with majestic marble columns that reminded him of Roman baths he'd seen in paintings. In this area known as a *predbannik*, visitors relaxed before a steam bath to drink herbal tea or take a break from the intense heat to socialize. Nine or ten men and women sat chatting on benches at a long table, while three men floated leisurely about a pool in the middle of the atrium, unabashedly displaying their paunches and fuzzy backs.

Pavel opened the door to the Number Eight steam room and out gushed a cloud as hot as exhaust from a factory smokestack. Houdini recoiled.

"Number Eight is our most popular among our international guests," the attendant informed him. "The steam is more visible, for those who've enjoyed the experience of a Turkish bath."

Or enjoyed a stint in hell, thought Houdini, hardly able to see through the rolling clouds.

Houdini saw no coals. Adjacent to the banya was a little room where a firebox generated steam, Pavel explained. The steam was piped into Number Eight through a grate.

"Just how hot does it get in there?" Houdini asked the attendant.

"We can make it as high as ninety-three degrees, sir."

"I'm sure it's hotter than that right now."

"I was speaking in Celsius, sir."

Houdini quickly did the math in his head. "That's almost two hundred degrees. I'm not a lobster!"

The attendant pointed to a small private pool fed by a pipe from which a continuous stream of water poured.

"You can cool off any time in there."

That was small comfort for the escape artist, who had half a mind to bolt and get his money back. But, restraining a grimace, he thanked the boy.

"I'd tip you if I had trousers on," he said. "I'll take care of you after ... Pavel, is it?"

"Of course, sir."

He entered and the door shut behind him with a clang. Groping through the mist, Houdini made his way to one of the wooden benches that surrounded the pool. He doffed the bathrobe and wrapped the towel about his waist. The newest patron of the bathhouse placed the small mat on the hot wood to protect his skin, then plopped down.

I better get used to it, he thought. *Rasputin might be late for his little tryst.* As clouds of steam swirled around the magician, he closed his eyes. Sooner or later, the clerk would knock on that door. He'd retrieve the sub-miniature camera from the locker and burst in on that hulking degenerate and his upper-class floozy. He pictured the look of dismay on the so-called holy man's face and smiled, as the remnants of the aches from his beating by the Gypsies began to dissipate. Houdini sank into a relaxed state that approached a stupor.

Was it a sound that aroused Houdini, or the sweet, seductive aroma of floral perfume? Suddenly, he became aware that he was not alone. Houdini's eyelids shot open. For a moment, he saw no one, then the mist parted, revealing a woman wrapped in a towel on the far side of the room. Startled, as if she'd materialized by magic, he recoiled, covering his eyes.

"Jeez, ma'am, I'm so sorry. I must be in the wrong room."

"Just the opposite," she said calmly. "Aren't you happy to see me? I thought you enjoyed my performance."

He stole a glance between his fingers. It was Natasha Stepanova, the ballerina. Up close, she was even more stunning, with porcelain skin and cheekbones Michelangelo might have chiseled. She reached back to loosen her dancer's ponytail and shook out red hair that cascaded down, circling her face like flames.

"Hey, what's this all about?" he demanded.

"You and I are going to enjoy a pleasant conversation." Her voice was husky, her tone sardonic. "Do you know that the tradition of the banya is almost one thousand years old? There's a colorful story about it that concerns Princess Olga's revenge for the murder of her husband by a tribe known as the Drevlians.

"The leader of the Drevlians asked the widow for her hand in marriage and she invited him to her castle. When the murderer arrived with his men, Olga commanded her servants to draw a bath for them and said, 'Wash yourselves before you come to me.' The Drevlians entered. Then Olga locked the door behind them and ordered her servants to set the building on fire. At first, the guests enjoyed the hot water. But, as you can well imagine, there were no nuptials. That early bathhouse evolved into this one, which I think you'll agree is a good deal more pleasurable."

"A ballerina and an armchair historian. You're a prize, all right," Houdini growled. So, he'd been set up. The clerk must have warned Rasputin the moment Houdini called. The same dirty trick he'd intended to pull on Rasputin was about to be turned on him. Securing the towel as tightly as any straitjacket, he hurried to the door and pulled the handle once, then yanked again as hard as he could. It didn't give.

"Hey, hey," he called, rapping on the metal. "Pavel! Attendant!"

"They'll come in about ten minutes with a camera and tripod," she informed him. His clothes were in the locker along with his own camera and the set of lock picks that he always carried.

"Now, be a good boy and sit down," the dancer said like a patient nanny.

There was a tiny window in the door. But even if he broke it, his arm couldn't reach the handle on the other side. He looked around the room, at the ceiling, at the vents, looking for an avenue of escape.

"Please don't excite yourself. I promise, it won't be long," Natasha said, twirling a lock of hair around her finger. "Just enough time for those who saw you come in to believe you to have ... enjoyed yourself here."

The heat was beginning to get to him. He sat on the edge of the pool, his legs dangling in the water. He kicked them back and forth in frustration.

"So, you're one of Rasputin's playthings, eh?" he spat bitterly. "A pretty girl like you rolling in the hay with that old goat. Why, you ought to be ashamed of yourself!"

"Now, speak respectfully. I could scream, you know, and make it look much worse."

"You know he's a phony, right? You don't strike me as dopey enough to fall for his saint act."

She smiled slyly. "No, I'm not as blind as his other adoring ladies. He arranged for me a position in the Imperial Ballet. Do you have any idea how difficult that is when your parents had no money for dance instructors, and you received your training in a hole in the wall above a shoemaker?"

"Can't be as difficult as getting the stench of that filthy peasant off your body," Houdini snarled. "I don't think there's enough steam in hell to do that trick."

Fury blazed in her eyes for a split-second, then subsided.

"You judge me," she said. "You must truly be pure of heart."

She stood up abruptly and dropped the towel, revealing a body that rivaled Aphrodite in perfection. Houdini gasped. As casually as if she were nude in her own boudoir, Natasha stepped into the pool. Her breasts, just under the waterline, were full and the nipples stood up, pointing at him like spear tips.

And I thought Rasputin's eyes were hypnotic!

"Cat got your tongue, Mr. Houdini?" the ballerina said, her own tongue flickering across her lips. "We don't need to talk. How else might we pass the time?"

"Now look, sister—"

"It would be a shame to let this opportunity pass you by, Mr. Houdini. Such opportunities don't come often—or do I flatter myself?"

"Not on your life, sweetheart. I've never cheated on my wife and I'm not about to start with one of Rasputin's leftovers."

That insult would have dealt a knockout blow to most women, but this hussy must have taken quite a few verbal punches, because she acknowledged it merely with a tiny smirk.

"When the attendants and photographer burst in through the door and find us together, they will reach the same conclusion whether you make love to me or not," she pointed out. "Since you will be publicly disgraced anyway, you might as well take home a consolation prize."

"And you're not worried about your own reputation?"

"I have a friend who will see that my name is not in the paper, only that a member of the Imperial Ballet Company was the object of Houdini's lecherous misbehavior." She leaned back against the side of the pool with her arms outstretched and yawned. "Such a scandal! Tut, tut, tut!"

Houdini had never socked a woman, but boy, was he tempted to knock her block off.

She turned away from him. "At least do me the favor of stroking my back with the venik branch. It's right there."

The magician sighed. With the towel still wrapped around his waist, Houdini climbed the steps down into the pool. The cold came as a relief, but his foot hurt when he stepped on the large drain through which water circulated out. Obedient as the bath servant of a sultaness, he took the branch and began to apply gentle strokes between her shoulder blades. What man would not be lost in the perfection of that spot?

"You do that very well," she murmured with a hint of a moan. "But a little harder, please."

After less than thirty seconds, he stopped. Natasha assumed that he had given in to temptation and braced herself for masculine hands to grab her milk-white shoulders. But to her surprise, he didn't touch her. She began to turn.

"You really don't make a habit of this, do you?" the dancer teased him.

"Don't look," Houdini said with a groan.

"Oh, are you ... out of sorts?" she said, then giggled. "Soak for a moment, relax, gather your thoughts."

Natasha rose from the water with feline grace and climbed the steps, hips swaying, her taut dancer's derriere made pink by the heat like a spanked child's.

"The steam relaxes the muscles," the temptress said. She put her hand on her hip like a teacup and leaned slowly to the left then right, then the left again. "Mr. Alistratov, my first dance instructor—and my first lover—always said the banya is an excellent place to stretch. I'm sure that to escape from straitjackets, flexibility is quite important, am I not right, Mr. Houdini?"

He did not respond. Too transfixed, she imagined. She bent slowly forward and touched her toes.

"This stretch loosens the hamstrings," Natasha purred. She held the position a moment, then bobbed up and down a few times. It was hard to believe the magician could restrain himself from leaping from the bath. She never had to go to such lengths to win a gentleman's heart. The husbands of St. Petersburg usually needed only a whiff of her perfume to surrender. It wounded her pride that she had to present herself like a lonesome alley cat.

Well, perhaps my display has rendered him speechless, the dancer thought. She turned—and to her amazement, saw that the magician had vanished!

The clerk and the attendant Pavel burst through the door a moment later with the photographer in tow, along with a half-dozen curious patrons elbowing each other out of the way for a glimpse of what promised to be the liveliest entertainment in St. Petersburg that morning.

"Where the devil is he?" the little clerk demanded, the tips of his mustache flying up in shock.

Natasha Stepanova, now in a robe, pointed to a drain at the bottom of the pool. The grate had been removed, exposing an opening barely eighteen inches wide.

"I wouldn't have thought a cat could squeeze through that pipe," the photographer marveled.

"He'd have to hold his breath and swim twenty feet," the clerk said. "It's impossible."

The siren gave a wry smile, unable to conceal her admiration. "It is not impossible. He is Houdini."

"Our Friend will not be happy about this," the pint-sized clerk fretted, tugging on his mustache. "He will not be happy at all."

CHAPTER THIRTEEN

The Lion's Den

While Houdini executed his narrow escape from the bathhouse—and from public humiliation—Bess embarked on her mission to infiltrate Rasputin's inner circle. His apartment at Number 64 Gorokhovaya Ulitsa lay off the beaten path in the western quarter of the city, located one block from Fontanka Canal. Visitors accessed the five-story brick building through a small, paved courtyard.

Rasputin's apartment was on the third floor, and a line of petitioners stretched down the flights of stairs, into the front courtyard, down the sidewalk and around the corner. The streets were lined with the swank automobiles of the wealthy: Peugeots, Bugattis and one brilliant blue Rolls Royce Silver Ghost on which twelve layers of paint had been lavished, its interior furnished with walnut, the finest leather and plush velvet carpets. A dozen uniformed officers kept the line orderly, while stationed at the doorway stood guard a trio of enormous, stony-faced bruisers who, Bess suspected, were henchmen of Rasputin's.

People from all walks of life came to seek the blessings of the holy man, to bring him gifts and plead for miracles and favors. Bankers, bishops, officers, society women and famed actresses stood in the queue in between peasants who had traveled hundreds of miles. Fortunately, Bess didn't have to wait. She was escorted in by Anna Vyrubova, Rasputin's go-between with the Tsarina, principal disciple, and chief organizer of his prayer circle.

Together, they bypassed upper-crust women bedecked in chinchilla coats and feathered bonnets, as well as peasants in sheepskin crusted with soil. Indigent and indulged alike, the petitioners parted like the Red Sea for Vyrubova and her American companion, some of the faithful bowing in respect. Vyrubova, nose raised, ignored them, but clearly basked in the adulation.

"The rich and the poor, they are all equal before God and Father Grigori," she proclaimed as they climbed the steps. "This is the one place in Russia where there is democracy."

Rasputin's neighbors included a seamstress and a masseuse, and Bess could tell they'd been cooking. Thick clouds of cabbage soup intermingled with the odors of rancid goat cheese, leather, and sheepskin coats, plus the sweat of people packing the stairwell, to produce a foul aroma. It was like the sulfurous stench one might expect outside hell's gates, Bess thought.

She was relieved when they finally reached the third floor. As they approached Rasputin's door, the third man in line—a businessman in an expensive fur coat and cap—seized Vyrubova's forearm.

"When is he coming? I've got to get back to the bank," he said in the caustic tone of a boss used to subordinates snapping to attention.

"When he comes, he comes," Vyrubova said imperiously. "Now stand aside and be silent—unless you wish to go to the back of the line." She glared at the gentleman's hand, and he withdrew it as quickly as if it had been bitten by a viper.

"I meant no offense, madam," he said, removing his hat and bowing.

The plump woman refused to acknowledge the belated subservience. She knocked and the door was opened by an attractive woman in an apron.

"Mrs. Houdini, this is Dunya, Father Grigori's housekeeper," Vyrubova said.

Dunya curtseyed, but Bess detected a slight wince at the word "housekeeper" that suggested that she might be a bit more than that.

The chief disciple led Bess into a drawing room that was crowded with eleven of his other female devotees, all finely dressed. They were showing off for each other the gifts they'd brought for their master: baskets of cheese and wine; jewel-encrusted icons; handmade gloves, boots and scarves.

"I do hope he likes this," one woman said, holding up a porcelain statue of St. Mary. "I spent twenty rubles on it."

Another held up a woolen scarf. "It took me a week to knit this, but it's far from perfect," she fretted with a furrowed brow.

Bess joined the Little Ladies in one of the chairs that encircled the room. Anna Vyrubova first introduced her to Akilina Laptinskaya, a Ukrainian with a broad face and broader rear end. Akilina served the two women tea, leading the magician's wife to think that she, too, was a servant. However, Vyrubova told Bess that she was a trained nurse and former nun.

"God has blessed Father Grigori with the strength of a horse," Akilina said. "But sometimes he wakes with a terrible headache after an evening out, and I treat him with old Ukrainian remedies."

"For hangovers, you mean?" Bess asked.

Akilina turned uneasily to Vyrubova, upon whose fleshy face a frown appeared. Bess realized she'd made a faux pas. Their master's drinking bouts were apparently not a subject for casual conversation. Nevertheless, Anna Vyrubova nodded at the nurse, signaling her to proceed.

"Perhaps," Akilina admitted. "And, of course, I give Father Grigori massages when his muscles ache or his joints are stiff from the cold. He has shown me what pure love is. He is a great man."

One by one, as the Little Ladies sipped tea, they introduced themselves and related the tales of how they came to join the holy man's entourage. Naturally, Anna Vyrubova, whose dumpy figure, fat neck and plain features set her apart from the prettier, highborn ladies, spoke first.

"When I was younger, I fell deeply in love," she began. "Father Grigori predicted that my marriage was doomed to fail. Somehow, he knew my choice was a poor one. But I was inexperienced in matters of the heart and went ahead despite his warning. On the night of my wedding, the starets' prophesy was fulfilled. Either my husband was a latent homosexual, or perhaps it was the drink or the excitement of the night that rendered him impotent. He poured vodka, glass after glass, to give him courage.

"At last, with no concern for my feelings or the sanctity of the moment, the drunken boor tried to rape me—although his mental capacities exceeded his physical ones and I remained a virgin. I was so overcome by shock and mortification, I refused his further advances. This so enraged him that he pounced on me and beat me as he shouted obscenities. I never wanted to see him again. I have vowed to have nothing more to do with husbands or marriage. To my dying day, I shall remain pure in body."

"How terrible for you," Bess said, patting the other woman's hand. It was the polar opposite to her own wedding night, following a whirlwind romance of less than two weeks. Harry had been so sweet and gentle. She offered Vyrubova a handkerchief, for it seemed she was on the verge of tears. The Tsarina's lady-in-waiting waved the handkerchief away.

"I have found my own true purpose, as companion to the Tsarina," the chief disciple said. "Many in court think I am not glamorous enough, too fat and plain and uneducated in the latest fashions. They say, 'The empress needs a more suitable lady-in-waiting.' But it is I who brings Father Grigori when he is needed. Sometimes we meet in my own cottage on the palace grounds for his sessions with her." Bess caught a fanatical gleam in Anna's eyes as she continued, "At those times, it is as if the Tsarina, Father Grigori and I are one."

"She does seem to rely on him," Bess observed.

"As do I, utterly. Not long ago, I suffered a terrible carriage accident. I must walk with this," she said, holding up her cane. "Only my prayer sessions with the starets spare me from pain."

Next to speak was Munya Golovina, a young, timid thing with pale blue eyes. She related how she had been betrothed to Prince Nicholas Yusupov, Felix's elder brother, and deeply in love. But days before the wedding, a message arrived that her fiancé had been killed in a duel—defending the honor of a beauty with whom he'd been having an affair.

"It was not so much the shock of his death, but the knowledge of his infidelity that devastated me," she confided. "I turned from the world to a spiritual life, and this led me to Father Grigori."

Next came Princess Shakhovskaya, a striking beauty with dark eyes who had abandoned her husband and children to follow Rasputin, then Barbara Uexkuell, a prominent socialite.

Elena Dzhanumova was the wife of a wealthy merchant, one of the mere handful of males that followed Rasputin openly.

"Many husbands become jealous of our relationship with Father Grigori, but mine has the maturity to accept it," she said.

Akilina, the Ukrainian former nun, claimed that Rasputin had rescued her from demonic possession at the Convent of St. Piton.

"I was in the grip of this demon for weeks, writhing about, a deep masculine voice issuing from my lips," she recalled, eyes full of pain at the memory. "The prayers of my sister nuns, the abbess herself, and the priest she summoned were in vain. Finally, the abbess called for Rasputin, whose reputation for healing was well known. Although I had attacked anyone who entered my room, Father Grigori came in without fear. He knelt beside me and commanded the evil spirit, 'I order you to be silent.' With his hands, he forced me to look into his eyes as he prayed.

"A strange peace came over me. The power of God surged through that man into me. Within a week after my recovery, I left the order to follow Father Grigori on the path to spiritual fulfillment."

Khioniya Berlatskaya spoke next. Her devotion to Rasputin had proved too much for her husband, an army lieutenant who was shattered by rumors of her adultery and committed suicide. Vera Zhukovskaya, a young writer, had experimented with cocaine, opium and hallucinogenic plants. Her quest for the exotic and sensational had once gone as far as Satanism, but even the devil himself couldn't compete with Rasputin.

Olga Lokhtina, a pretty blonde in the latest dress from Paris, proudly informed Bess that she'd been Rasputin's earliest adherent in St. Petersburg. The wife of a minor nobleman who let the starets stay in their home, Lokhtina gave the then-illiterate Siberian lessons in reading and writing. But it wasn't long before she was the pupil and he the master, the housewife clinging to his every word. Bess had the distinct impression that she had slept with Rasputin and was not the least bit ashamed of it.

"My husband has threatened to throw me out unless I agree to have nothing more to do with Father Grigori, but of course I have refused," Lokhtina said. "I would rather sleep at the feet of that blessed man and kiss his feet than dwell in a palace without him."

After each told her story, the women expounded on Rasputin's mystical powers, speaking of their master in hushed tones of reverence and adoration.

"On the night he was born, a meteor streaked through the sky," Munya revealed, eyes wide. "It was taken by the villagers as an omen of a great supernatural occurrence."

"Do you know that when he was a boy, he could calm and heal his father's farm animals?" Akilina told Bess. "Once, at the breakfast table, his father told the family that one of his horses had gone lame and would have to be put down. Grigori got up from the table, went to the stable, placed the horse's lame leg in his hand and touched the tendon. He said firmly, 'You are better.' And sure enough, the tendon was healed. He patted the horse and sent it trotting into the pasture. His father was at first very afraid because he thought it must be the work of the devil. But soon it became Grigori's chore on the farm to keep all the animals well."

It sounded utterly fantastic, yet Bess could picture the scene vividly. The women treated her to one such anecdote after another, until she was immersed in the world of the miracle worker.

A door behind Bess burst open and Rasputin strode in. The healer of man and beast wore a long black caftan, traditional coat of a Russian peasant, and a woolen cap that he tossed with unerring aim onto a hat rack. A back staircase that exited onto a side street allowed the mystic to enter and leave the house unobserved by the mob outside.

"Every day, the line of oafs gets longer," he cried, and it was impossible to tell whether it was disgust or boastfulness in his voice.

Bess could not help herself from a sudden intake of breath. She'd forgotten how tall he was, how full of masculine energy, like a dark star to which everything gravitated. The women rushed to hug him, jostling each other for a chance to kiss his hand. Bess stood patiently waiting to be acknowledged, with her hands clasped in front of her like a fig leaf. She felt her heart racing and her legs wobbling. After pecking each woman on the cheek—or, in the case of the younger women, the mouth—Rasputin marched through the drawing room to Bess. She extended her hand formally.

"You gave me permission to visit, Father," she reminded him.

Ignoring her hand, Rasputin embraced her, lifting the slightly built woman off the ground as if she were a child.

"In Russia, we hug." He stomped around the room holding her. "Look, Mr. Houdini has brought us a gift from America."

She gently pushed him away and struggled unsuccessfully to get her feet back on the ground.

"You are a tiny one," he said, chuckling, finally returning her to terra firma. "I will call you my little malchik."

Bess involuntarily covered her slight bosom in dismay. She must have mistranslated the word. "Little boy?"

"Don't worry," chuckled Akilina. "He has a nickname for each of us. Anna's is Owl. Mine is Mare, because I have the spirit of a filly."

"It is because you have a bottom like a mare," Rasputin said with a laugh, smacking it. "In my hometown of Pokrovskoe, the stallions battle to mount a rump like that."

Bess expected the socialites to gasp and clutch their pearls, as prissy American ladies of a corresponding social set undoubtedly would, but they tittered in delight. Only Akilina ventured to cry "Father!" in mock offense. Bess suddenly had a rush of dread that the faith healer might "lay hands on" her in such an indecent manner too.

"It's been a pleasure, but I must go," she said.

"You must stay," he returned. He said it warmly, not as an order, and yet Bess felt compelled to oblige. She returned to her seat.

"People have been lining up since early morning," Vyrubova said.

Rasputin sighed. "I will see visitors for two hours and not a single minute more. My belly is empty."

And so, one by one, the petitioners were admitted to kneel before the holy man and plead their cases. No one was foolish enough to come empty-handed. Each brought a gift, as an ancient might bring a sacrifice to his local god. A bottle of wine, a basket of roses, embroidered silk shirts, a Persian carpet. One elderly peasant brought a live chicken, which Rasputin accepted with greater appreciation than he had shown any other gift.

Rasputin devoted his full attention to each visitor, nodding, stroking his beard and asking pertinent questions. Bess marveled at how genuine his concern appeared. When one impoverished peasant's tale of woe moved him, he unhesitatingly took a bag of gold he'd just received and placed it in the hands of the poor petitioner. Many sought relief from pain and sickness. He laid his hand on their bowed heads and prayed in a comforting baritone. Invariably, they appeared to have been healed. Weeping tears of gratitude, they kissed the mystic's hand, then moved out of the way for the next supplicant.

Whether or not his powers were genuine, Bess was uncertain, but his concern surely was real. *My husband is wrong,* she thought. *There is another side to this man. He's not a monster.*

Rasputin spent more time on petitioners with farm soil beneath their fingernails than those with manicures. The pampered rich he scolded for their decadence and impiety. He made them bow and scrape and plead, and only then did he grudgingly agree to help them win a favor from the Tsarina. He would provide the petitioner with a slip of paper with a simple message scrawled upon it and with a little cross on the top of the page.

Bess was not sure if two hours had elapsed, but she noticed that Rasputin became restless, his foot tapping the floor, his hands rubbing his thighs. A mild-mannered, balding man sat beside the holy man, pouring out his heart about his failing marriage.

"What is more, I fear that my wife is unfaithful to me," he whimpered. "Friends report to me that they have seen a younger man squiring her about restaurants and brazenly walking hand in hand through the Hermitage Museum."

"Do you expect me to make your pecker hard for you? A young bull gets the heifer," Rasputin growled with sudden venom. "And besides, who are you to complain of philandering, when you rub yourself against that girl in your shop every time you pass?"

The cuckold's eyes widened with disbelief. "How could you ...?"

Rasputin shot to his feet as if propelled from his chair by an invisible spring. "Enough. Begone, you rascal."

"But starets ..." the man pleaded, falling to his knees before the mystic.

"Begone!" Rasputin roared, kicking him in the flank. Red-faced, the visitor fled, hat in hand.

Vyrubova rushed to Rasputin's side. He was shaking in what Bess initially thought was a fit of rage, but now appeared more like a child in the throes of a seizure, or a Pentecostal overtaken by the Holy Spirit. A half dozen of the women surrounded him.

The queen bee of the nest marched to the door and shouted out, "The Father will see no more petitioners today." There came in response moans of disappointment and murmurs of protests.

"We must have a prayer session," Rasputin said hoarsely, still swaying.

"First, you need to eat, Father," Olga Lokhtina said. "You are fatigued."

They repaired to the dining room. It was lit by a bronze chandelier and the massive table was set for fourteen. A bulky dresser full of crockery took up most of one wall. The other walls were decorated by a portrait of the Tsar and paintings of rustic scenes: peasants plowing fields, a troika pulled through the snow by sturdy steeds. The Little Ladies sat, with Rasputin at the head like the father of a family, in a kingly high-backed chair.

Dunya and Akilina served the others, sweeping out of the kitchen bearing platters of sturgeon, black bread, boiled eggs, biscuits, and glass bowls full of fruit, jam and other delicacies. They reverently set them before their master.

After Rasputin shoveled large helpings of each dish onto his plate, the women served themselves from the platters as they were passed around. He delivered a brief grace, then attacked the meal. The Siberian scooped up the food with his hands like a famished vagabond and, without pausing to wipe his fingers, intermittently petted the thighs of the women in the coveted seats beside him, Munya and Elena. Bess was astounded by the enormity of his appetite. It was like watching a bear prepare for hibernation.

Only when the starets was well into his meal did the women begin to eat, always watchful for signs he might need service. They chattered quietly amongst themselves but broke away from their conversation anytime Rasputin grunted that he needed something. The women doted over the mystic, taking turns fetching wine as he needed it, and taking the opportunity to stroke his head or kiss his cheek. He was at once their beloved father and pampered child, Bess realized.

They cooed with delight any time Rasputin deigned to comment positively on a dish one had prepared, and they looked crushed by shame when he hinted the cook had fallen short.

"The sturgeon is well seasoned, but nothing like the ones my brother and I used to catch in the river near our home," he said, licking his fingers. Olga Lokhtina, who had invested hours of loving care into the meal, bowed her head, crestfallen, her eyes brimming with tears. Rasputin fell silent, and for a moment Bess thought he, too, might burst into tears.

Vera Zhukovskaya, seated beside Bess, whispered to her, "His brother drowned, you know, when they were only boys, and Father Grigori almost went down with him."

Rasputin could not possibly have heard the hushed conversation, yet turned and set his gaze on Bess as if he had.

"I know that it is my destiny to perish that way, to sink beneath the rushing water and join poor Misha," he said with quiet resignation. The Little Ladies on either side stroked his hands soothingly, and soon he was back to gorging himself.

When the mystic was finally done, he let out an exuberant belch. The women hurried to clear his several plates, piled high with fish bones and other remains of the meal he'd massacred.

"Now let us rejoice with a hymn," he announced. All together, they sang:

"Let my prayers arise in thy sight as incense,
And let the lifting of my hands be an evening sacrifice.
Lord, I have called to thee, hear me.
Attend to the voice of my prayer as I beseech Thee,
Set a guard over my mouth, O Lord,
Keep watch around the door of my lips."

They sang with the unity of a Greek chorus, the women's voices a pleasant mix of sopranos and altos, with Rasputin's rich baritone always rumbling beneath like an underground brook.

In America, he could make a fortune singing in concert halls, Bess thought.

While Dunya and Akilina began washing the dishes, the others returned to the living room. They took their seats in a semi-circle about Rasputin's chair, which he occupied with the dignity of a medieval pope. Munya and Khioniya Berlatskaya assumed positions of honor at his feet and looked up adoringly as the starets launched into a homily.

"How is brutalized man, with his beastly habits, to begin living a life that is pleasing to God?" he asked. "How is he to climb up out of the pit of sin? How is he to find the path that leads from our cesspool into the fresh air and the light of God? Have no doubt. There is such a path and I shall show it to you."

The content of the sermon wasn't very different from the ones Bess had heard from a Catholic priest as a girl. But that voice was so soothing it filled her with serenity. Such was her tranquility that she fell into a state that combined obliviousness to her surroundings with absolute concentration on the speaker.

He spoke with dramatic gestures as well, often pointing to Heaven for emphasis or weaving his hands through the air like a sorcerer casting a spell. Rasputin's eyes were never still. They passed like spotlights from follower to follower. As they fell on each woman, her eyes became moist. When Munya's turn came, she placed her hand over her heart.

Like adolescent girls swooning over a stage actor, Bess thought with some amusement. And yet when those brilliant eyes fell on hers, she was no less overtaken. Gazing into them was like tumbling into the ocean and finding it not cold at all, but rather like a bath of milk and honey. He smiled warmly at her, a gaze pregnant with affection.

After about twenty minutes, the man of the cloth abruptly stopped.

Hoarsely, he demanded, "Bring me some wine!"

Two of the women hopped to their feet, competing to return with a bottle first. There came a knock at the door and Dunya rose to answer it. As Rasputin put the bottle to his lips and drained it, she returned from the door.

"Father Grigori, there is a visitor whom I think you might wish to see," she said with an odd expression.

"Who is it? Haven't I seen enough riff-raff for the day?" he growled.

"It is Sophia Volynskaya."

"Who?"

"The wife of that Jewish banker who was convicted of forgery and embezzlement," Anna Vyrubova explained with a bit of a sneer. "No doubt she is seeking a pardon for him."

Rasputin drummed his fingers on the arm of his chair.

"Let me see her," he decided.

Dunya led in a young, fashionably dressed woman. She was a paragon of Semitic beauty, dark-eyed with an aquiline nose and arching black eyebrows. Her ravishing looks catapulted into the stratosphere when she removed her hat and endless curls of raven hair spilled out. She wore a high-collared blouse, but that did nothing to hide the impressive swell of her bosom. The comely creature knelt at Rasputin's feet.

"Sir, I need your help. My husband faces ruin and years of imprisonment."

Rasputin placed his hand on her head.

"We must pray privately about this matter," he declared. He stood and helped her to her feet. "Come, my child. Anna, lead the prayer circle until I return."

Bess looked about at the Little Ladies to gauge their reactions. She detected more than a modicum of jealousy on their faces toward the fetching young woman whom Rasputin led by the hand through a door and into his bedroom. The door slammed shut behind the pair and there was an awkward silence in the parlor.

"Come, Dunya, I will assist you in the kitchen," Munya announced, rising.

"I'll help," Bess said.

"Please, you are our guest," protested Anna Vyrubova.

"I'd like to think I'm one of you now," said Bess.

Vyrubova gave a smile that Houdini's wife found a bit too crocodilian for her liking. The leader of the prayer circle bade her fellow disciples hold hands and as they bowed their heads, she told them to open their prayer books. They behaved reverently as Vyrubova led them in prayer, but Bess had no doubt they were just marking time until their mentor returned.

In the kitchen, Dunya, Akilina and Munya washed platters and dishes, passing them to Bess to dry. The mundane chore restored the American visitor to a more normal state of mind. While she worshipped with the other women, swaying with the hymn and then listening transfixed to Rasputin, it was as if she had been lulled half to sleep.

What happened to me? she wondered. She was frightened, yet part of her yearned to dip into those dark, magical waters again. She suddenly remembered a friend named Dot who had experimented with opium. Dot said she was "scared silly" at losing the ability to think straight, but couldn't resist the urge to return to the opium den within a week.

Bess was jerked from her reverie when a red-haired beauty glided into the room.

"Is there any food left or have you vixens finished it all?" the woman asked in a gay, mocking voice. She looked oddly familiar to Bess.

"I'll fix a plate for you," Dunya said. "But you oughtn't to be late for prayers and expect a feast."

"I was doing a little service for the Father," the ravishing redhead responded. "Remember?"

Dunya gave a quick, uneasy glance at Bess, then said, "This is the famous dancer Natasha Stepanova of the Imperial Ballet Company."

"Yes, my husband and I enjoyed your performance," said Bess, extending her hand, then realizing it was wet, withdrew it.

"One day I hope to enjoy your husband's performance," Natasha replied.

Is it my imagination or did she just smirk?" thought Bess. *Perhaps she's just one of those people whose resting face is sardonic.* Bess hadn't much cared for the way Houdini had gawked at the dancer like a schoolboy catching a glimpse of his teacher's ankle for the first time, but that wasn't the girl's fault. She struggled against instant dislike.

"Where is Father Grigori?" Natasha asked, plucking an apple from a bowl and sinking her teeth into it.

"He is with Sophia Volynskaya, wife of that crooked banker, praying with her," Munya replied.

"Yes, I'm certain she is on her knees this very moment."

Again with the smirk. This double entendre didn't escape Bess, and she found herself resenting the insinuation. She preferred to believe that the desperate wife was now confessing the error of her ways and receiving counsel from Rasputin. But what was really happening behind closed doors? Lurid images crept into her mind and she tried to banish them.

"Come, keep me company," Natasha said to Bess as Dunya handed her a plate of food that apparently had been set aside for her. She and Bess returned to the dining room.

The ballerina pecked at her food with a delicacy that equaled her grace on stage, in stark contrast to her master's boar-like onslaught. Bess asked politely about the ballet, and Natasha treated her to a series of anecdotes featuring touchy-feely instructors and bombastic impresarios, the peccadillos of prima donnas and the superstitions of famous dancers like Nijinsky who prayed to an icon of St. Vitus before going on stage.

"The producer Sergei Diaghilev has such a superstitious dread of crossing the ocean that he refuses to travel with us on overseas tours," she revealed with a merry laugh.

In turn, the dancer probed Bess for details about life with the legendary magician, whether they had children and what their home looked like. The questions were not impertinent, as Rasputin's had been, but she didn't feel very much like sharing such intimacies with a stranger, especially one who—Bess was beginning to suspect—was a card-carrying floozy. As soon as she could, she changed the subject to Rasputin.

"The women have told me about his miracles," she said. "Have you seen any?"

Natasha laughed. "It was a miracle that he arranged for my position in the company. Without him, eventually I'd have ended up one of those sad souls who teach ballet to untalented brats, I suppose."

Or shaking your fanny in the Folies Bergère, Bess thought.

"Akilina claims he drove a demon from her," she said.

"Yes," Natasha replied, washing down her bread with wine. "Well, there are also rumors that he took advantage of poor Sister Akilina during the time he spent in her cell. Perhaps that is what she needed to clear her head. They say it is thirteen inches, you know?"

"What is?"

Natasha held her forearm straight out.

"Oh!" Bess blushed, trying not to picture it. *She must be exaggerating!*

Natasha continued, "There is an odd mole near the root. Ugly perhaps, but it adds a unique sensation for the woman ... or I've heard."

Bess suddenly felt hot. She knew she was as red in the face as if she was being treated to her first lecture on the birds and the bees, and she hated this impudent girl for provoking the blush. She quickly changed the subject.

"Father Grigori's followers—admirers—all have such interesting histories."

The ballerina smiled. "Anna Vyrubova told you the one about the prophecy of marital doom, I imagine."

"Yes, and that dreadful story about how her husband mistreated her."

"Well, there are two sides to every story, aren't there?" Natasha pointed out, one corner of her lips turning up in that now-familiar smirk. "A woman might resist her husband on her wedding night and choose to remain a virgin for a variety of reasons."

"I can't think of one."

Natasha grinned enigmatically. "Perhaps when you and she spend more time together, it will occur to you."

As Bess mulled over the irritatingly vague statement, Natasha completed her meal and they joined the others.

Vyrubova greeted the ballerina with an embrace. "I am so delighted that you are able to join us. Did you have a productive morning?"

"There was a rather surprising turn of events," Natasha replied. "I'll tell you all about it later. You'll find the whole story amusing, I'm sure."

They took their seats and the reading of psalms continued. About ten minutes later, Sophia Volynskaya emerged from Rasputin's bedroom. Her face was flushed and her blouse misbuttoned. In a shaking hand, the embezzler's wife clutched a note like the one Bess had seen in the hands of other petitioners. Sophia walked stiffly, like an equestrian who'd spent too long in the saddle.

"Will you stay for the closing prayers?" Vyrubova asked genially, as if she saw nothing amiss. The raven-haired young woman shook her head—shuddering, it seemed to Bess—and as if she could not bear to remain in the flat one minute more, hurried out.

Rasputin walked out of the inner room with a bouncy gait, radiating joy. Whatever weariness had beset him earlier had departed; he was recharged. As if, like that Transylvanian prince of darkness, he had drawn life from the distraught wife and into himself.

"Now, before we part, let us all thank the Almighty for bringing us together today," he told them buoyantly.

They held hands once more, Vyrubova beside Bess. As the newcomer felt Anna's moist, plump fingers squeezing her own, it dawned on her what the ballerina had meant. Performing on Coney Island, she had heard a rumor about a can-can girl with such leanings—which she chalked up mostly to jealous gossip. At the time, such a possibility neither fascinated nor repulsed her. But the idea of this squat, homely cripple having such thoughts about her, wanting to place her lips on hers and do God only knew what else …

As Rasputin recited the closing prayer, Bess's unpleasant musings about his lead disciple scattered away like ashes in the wind and she found herself again swept along in the river of his words.

CHAPTER FOURTEEN

The Damsel in Distress

Houdini sat shivering in front of the coal stove in the writer Illya Volkov's apartment, still huddled in his coat. He'd managed to retrieve his clothes and the pocket watch from the bathhouse before making his getaway, but hadn't had time to dry off.

Illya wiped tears of laughter from his eyes as the magician finished his sorry tale of the incident at the Coachman's Banya.

"You're a better man than I, Houdini, and than half the men in St. Petersburg," Illya chuckled. "Many a stock trader has tried to sweet talk Natasha Stepanova out of her tights in vain. Yet there she was, ready to practice her most acrobatic moves, and you didn't partake."

"I'm glad I've been able to provide you with your entertainment for the afternoon," Houdini replied grumpily. "Now, will you kindly tell me who this person is who can supposedly give me the goods on Rasputin? He made a monkey of me and I'm itching to get even."

"His former best friend and now his most hated enemy, Brother Iliodor," the poet revealed. "When Rasputin first surfaced in St. Petersburg, Iliodor was a novice monk. He was Rasputin's greatest advocate and introduced him to powerful

184 |C. Michael Forsyth

churchmen. A very upstanding and righteous fellow. I've heard him making fiery speeches, fulminating against intellectuals; against the moral decay of the aristocracy; against incompetent bureaucrats; against both the greed of capitalists and the treachery of communists who dared challenge the Tsar."

"Didn't leave anyone out, did he?"

"I don't seem to remember him mentioning dwarves," Illya said with a laugh. "Iliodor reserved his most passionate denunciations for sexual misdeeds, personally visiting brothels to expose 'degenerates.' He was among the first in St. Petersburg to tout Rasputin's powers, which he claimed to have witnessed firsthand."

Houdini leaned forward. "Like what?"

"In Iliodor's hometown of Tsaritsyn, two women had purportedly become possessed by the devil," the writer said. "They writhed convulsively, screaming blasphemous obscenities while straining the chains to which they had been secured in their beds. Iliodor's own by-the-book ministrations—prayers, holy water, brandishing of the crucifix—failed to rout the demons. But with little more than a momentary laying on of hands and the muttering of a few words of comfort, Rasputin cured the ladies. Brother Iliodor instantly became a true believer."

"And yet ...?"

"Yet, I think he was jealous of Rasputin's powers," Illya said as he used a little shovel to feed the coal stove. "And he envied Rasputin's bedroom prowess as well. Iliodor took his vows of celibacy seriously. Was fanatical about it, one might say. Rasputin showed the prettiest of Iliodor's supporters attention that the monk refused to give them, kissing and fondling them right in front of Iliodor who, quite naturally, was infuriated.

"The final straw came when Rasputin allegedly attempted to rape a nun. Iliodor and the Archbishop Hermogen confronted him and threatened to inform the Tsar unless he repented. But the cunning rogue beat them to the punch by denouncing them to the Tsar as degenerates first. Tsarina Alexandra saw that both were banished to far-flung monasteries.

"After his downfall, Iliodor denounced Rasputin from afar and circulated rumors that the Tsarina was his former chum's mistress, as well as publishing letters he claimed proved this—which the Crown, of course, insists are forgeries. As a result, he was defrocked and banished from Russia. But it's said Iliodor snuck back into the country disguised as a woman and has set up his own religious settlement near Vyborg. Rumor has it he borrowed money to buy a flock of sheep and makes his living as a shepherd as he continues to preach to a meager group of followers."

"He sounds like a loony," Houdini said dubiously.

"That's indisputable, but I wager he'll be able to tell you quite a bit about his old comrade Rasputin, perhaps even where to find the chink in his armor."

"You've sold me," Houdini said, standing. "I'll make arrangements to find this colorful character."

"I'll come along for the ride. I met Iliodor once and somehow I think you'll fare better with an introduction."

Illya's flat was modest even by Russian standards and wretched compared to a typical New York tenement. On one wall hung a portrait of Karl Marx, Houdini noticed as he rose. He pointed out the bearded author of *The Communist Manifesto*.

"I thought you didn't go in for politics," he remarked.

Illya laughed. "Those belong to my roommate, Andropov. You met him at The Samarkand. Slight fellow with spectacles. He's a committed Bolshevik."

"A what?"

"They believe in workers owning the means of production. Economic justice. That the workers of the world must shake off their shackles and unite."

"That doesn't sound half bad," Houdini said. "But I bet the aristocrats and factory owners aren't crazy about them."

"That, my friend, is why their leader Lenin is now in hiding in Finland."

***

Houdini told Bess that his outing to the Coachman's Banya was a bust (leaving out his close encounter with the ballerina's bust). Bess related in detail what transpired in Rasputin's apartment.

"He seemed to genuinely care for the common folk who visit him," she noted. "You can see why so many are loyal to him."

Houdini looked at her piercingly and she caught the wariness in his eyes.

"Sweetheart, you don't think I'm going to fall for his act, do you?" she said, giggling. "The only guy I'm worshipping around here is you."

To the Imperial Couple, Houdini made the excuse that he'd been invited to perform by the mayor of Vyborg and would be leaving St. Petersburg for a few days. The Tsar assured him that this would be no problem, and that he'd entertain the children himself with their favorite games: Hide and Seek, Wizards, and Cossacks and Thieves.

Boris secured a troika, a sleigh pulled by three horses, and they made their way across the rugged terrain between St. Petersburg and the area outside Vyborg, near the Finnish border, where Iliodor's encampment was rumored to be— although its exact location was secret. With winter setting in, the journey was expected to take two days. Houdini had argued that they should take a car. Boris warned him that such a vehicle was unsuited to the snow-covered hills. It had seemed a dubious claim when they were in the vicinity of St Petersburg, which was barely above sea level and temperate by comparison. Now, as they passed conifer trees and over snow drifts, Houdini appreciated the policeman's foresight. He found the jingling of the bells comforting as the horses trotted undeterred over the pockets of ice that blanketed the road and crunched beneath its hooves.

While Boris drove the sleigh, Illya sat beside Houdini, jotting notes for his next volume of poetry in a journal.

"Is there an overall theme, if you don't mind me asking?" Houdini queried.

"Politics," Illya responded. "There's got to be more to say about Russia than simply that we love her."

"You ought to write love poems about women. The public eats that up. I know Bess gushes over them when they're printed in *The New York Times*."

"A writer needs to write what he knows and, alas, I haven't been lucky in romance."

Houdini shouted up to Boris, "How much further?"

"No more than ten miles, I would reckon, if that farmer knew what he was talking about." Hours earlier, they'd bribed

188 |*C. Michael Forsyth*

a grizzled peasant with a bottle of vodka to pinpoint Iliodor's hideout.

"I think we can rely on him," said Illya. "The Russian peasant is an honest drunk, unlike the Russian army officer who's given to exaggerating his past exploits with every glass. The Russian factory worker, on the other hand—"

"What in God's name?!!!" Boris cried out, pointing ahead.

Through the trees, Houdini saw a horse plowing through the snowbanks at the roadside, coming in their direction at a brisk trot. It was an odd place to see a wild horse, though Houdini had read that herds of that ancient breed, the Prezwalski horse, roamed Russia. As he squinted against the bright light reflected on the snow, he saw it had a saddle.

It must be a runaway, he thought, now noticing a rope tied to the saddle and stretched out taut behind the animal. *It's dragging something ...* Now it was Houdini's turn to yelp.

"God Almighty!"

He saw what the draft horse was dragging: a stumbling woman, her hands bound. She was stark naked, her skin as white as the snowbanks around her. She stumbled, screaming in terror as the animal launched into a full gallop, dragging her on her belly.

The men stared in astonishment as the horse dashed by with its burden.

"Turn around," Houdini hollered. Boris whipped their horses and yanked the reins. The troika nearly tipped over, then righted itself, as he struggled to bring the sleigh around.

It took several minutes for their troika to catch up with the horse galloping on the roadside. The woman's state had worsened. She was covered in scrapes from rocks that jutted from the snow. Though the cold must have been excruciating, at least the snow had protected her from most of the jagged stone. Without it, she would already have been ripped to shreds.

"Help me, in the name of God! Have pity!" she screeched.

"We can't catch it; it's fast for a farm horse," Boris shouted. "The pity is someone wasted it on this. And a usable saddle to boot."

Houdini shot the big policeman a dirty look. He didn't expect such black humor from the stalwart fellow, especially with the life of a helpless woman hanging in the balance.

"You can tell that to its owner after I beat the daylights out of him," the magician snapped. They were still several horse lengths away. He had hoped to leap on the runaway's back like a cowboy in a wild west show, but it was too far away. He settled for something just as daring.

"Houdini, no!" Boris roared as Houdini propelled himself through the air.

The American landed with a smack atop the woman and grabbed hold of her. Although the damsel in distress was well-endowed, there was nothing erotic about the embrace; her nude body was like ice. He wrapped his legs around her waist and reached for the rope. Normally, it would take him only seconds to defeat such a knot, but the horse's pull had made it taut. Snow churned into his nose as he, too, was hauled along at top speed.

He cried, "Whoa!" The horse didn't slow a bit. *I suppose she already tried that.*

CHAPTER FIFTEEN

Cult of the Khlysty

"Please!" the woman gasped in Houdini's ear as the horse cantered through the snow, dragging them both.

With his right hand, he hauled them forward on the rope, creating slack, while the nimble fingers of his left worked the knot that bound the victim's wrists. When the knot failed to surrender to the escape artist, he grabbed hold of a passing rock and began desperately slicing at the rope. It took several moments of frantic carving, but at last the rope snapped. The horse dashed on, glad to be rid of its load.

Houdini sat in the snow, panting beside the woman who lay face down, whimpering softly. Whatever monster had subjected her to this humiliating fate had lashed her first. The distinctive stripes of fresh whip marks crisscrossed her back and buttocks.

He rolled her over gently. "It's okay, kid, you're safe."

"Bless you, sir, bless you," she replied, shielding her breasts. She was in her twenties with light brown hair now a tangled mess full of leaves and snow. She might have been pretty once, but her face was disfigured by wart-like lesions.

Illya, panting as he stumbled through the snow, caught up with them.

"You seem to be a magnet for naked women these days, Houdini," he said. The writer hurriedly took off his coat and wrapped it around the woman's shoulders. "I wish I had something thicker, madam."

"Thank you, thank you, thank you," she murmured through chattering teeth. Houdini lifted her up and strode toward the troika.

"What's your name?"

"Chioniya Guseva," gasped the damsel in distress.

"I'm Harry Houdini."

She showed no sign of recognizing the name, and for once, such a slight didn't bother the magician. He approached the sleigh where Boris sat waiting. He expected the big man to rush forward to relieve him of the victim, but Boris made no effort to take her, looking on with a complete absence of sympathy, as though Houdini were presenting him with a drowned cat.

"Do you mind?" Houdini said with undisguised annoyance. "I'm a little winded. I don't get dragged by farm animals every day. Usually, it's just holidays."

The officer took the shivering woman with a grunt that might have either been from effort or disgust. He placed her in the back of the troika. Houdini climbed in beside her, bundling her in one of the blankets.

"What happened?" he asked once he'd tucked her in snugly.

"Brigands," she sobbed. "They took my money, my jewels, my clothing. And they, they ..." She couldn't bring herself to go on.

Rage coursed through the American. *What kind of monsters would do such a thing?* When he was traveling with the Welsh

Brothers Circus, the knife thrower's assistant was waylaid in an alley in St. Louis and violated by a pair of thugs. But even those sons of bitches didn't go this far.

"My friend Boris is a police officer," he told her. "He'll see that the bastards who did this to you pay. Boris, there must be a constabulary in the area?"

Boris snorted, lashing the horse, and the troika jerked forward.

"If you have something to say, feel free to jump in," Houdini spat.

"She's lying," Boris growled. "This is the traditional peasant punishment for prostitutes. Those scars on her face are from syphilis—a parting gift from one of her gentlemen callers."

"A tradition more honored in the breach than the observance," Illya said softly.

The pity that the disfigurement had instilled in Houdini transformed into revulsion. This apparently showed up his expression, because Chioniya brought up her forearm to cover her face in shame. Tears began to stream down her cheeks.

"Party girl or not, no one deserves to be treated that way," the magician told Boris sternly. "She needs looking after."

Illya passed her his handkerchief and she dabbed away her tears.

"In these times, people do terrible things to survive," he said gently.

Boris grunted noncommittedly and pointed to a ruined mill covered in vines, a landmark that was difficult to miss.

"Come on, if that farmer was right, Brother Iliodor's retreat is only a few miles away," he said. "They can patch her up there."

Houdini knew the still-trembling victim probably wasn't in the mood for a lecture, but he couldn't deny himself a moment of righteous indignation.

"A pretty girl like you oughtn't have had to stoop to that," he scolded her in a fatherly manner. "You could have found a husband, I bet."

She smiled wistfully. "I was married. To a fine gentleman. I did have furs once, jewelry. I had a life and I had my honor—until *he* came into my life."

Houdini felt a sudden wave of nausea coming on.

"Who?" he asked, but of course, he knew what she was going to say.

"Rasputin," she responded, uttering the name with venom. "It was my husband who introduced us. He hoped that the holy man could help me with my anxiety and sleeplessness. Father Grigori succeeded. And he also seduced me. I became his mistress. Oh, why dignify it? His whore. My husband kicked me out. My own family would not take me in. In the end, I was reduced to selling myself on the street."

Boris snorted again and spat to the side of the fast-moving troika.

"A woman who betrays her husband is worse than a whore," he admonished her gruffly.

Houdini shot him a fierce look of disapproval. Chioniya hung her head.

"You've never seen those eyes," she whispered. "No one can resist those eyes."

Houdini thought of Bess. *My wife has a lot more backbone than this pliant creature,* he told himself. *Doesn't she?*

Brother Iliodor's encampment, an assortment of ramshackle huts and tents, sat on a hill on the bank of the Vuoksa River. In the distance, they could see men working on a barge, erecting a tall banner at least twenty feet long. It bore writing in big, red Cyrillic letters, but it was difficult to read them as the banner rippled in the wind.

"What the heck is that?" Houdini asked.

"It appears that the good brother has a message he wishes to share with the world," Illya replied.

The settlement was surrounded by a crudely constructed fence. As their troika pulled up at the makeshift wooden gate, a pair of men in brown monk robes ran up, rifles at the ready.

"A proper Christian greeting," Illya remarked. Boris reached under his heavy fur coat for his revolver.

"Easy, big fellow," Houdini said.

Iliodor's followers were out of breath by the time they reached the gate. Before they could spit out a "who goes there," Houdini told them, "We are here to see Brother Iliodor."

"*Father* Iliodor, and he's seeing no one today," one of the guards retorted, directing the rifle at Houdini.

"He'll want to see us. We're here about Rasputin."

The monks looked at each other, conferred in mumbles, then elected the safest course: to let their leader handle this.

The monks tied the men's hands behind their backs and took them down to the makeshift village, pushing them roughly to speed them on. One of Iliodor's followers, a curly-haired young man, was gentler with the girl. When he saw the raw wounds on her wrists, he didn't tie her, but walked along beside her, refusing to look at her except in quick, chaste glances.

Supervising the hoisting of the banner stood Brother Iliodor, standing on the deck of the barge with arms akimbo, like the captain of a pirate ship. With a fleshy face and tiny ears, the monk resembled a prize hog on two legs. Defrocked or not, he wore a white cassock and a heavy cross about his neck. He railed against his men, calling them fools as they struggled to straighten the banner, which hung between two posts that had been erected on the barge.

"Mother Russia is not a place for Jews" the banner read. Houdini scowled.

"It seems he's found another enemy," Illya said.

"I don't know who I want to punch out more—him or Rasputin," the magician hissed.

They approached Iliodor, and one of the men escorting them called out softly at first, as if frightened to disturb him.

"Father ... Father ... FATHER!"

At last, Brother Iliodor turned, and when he saw the visitors, he charged down the ramp from the barge and toward them like an enraged bull.

"Who sent you?" he roared. "Are you more of his minions? I'll have you thrashed and sent back to him in irons!" His voice was a disconcertingly high-pitched screech, at odds with his bulk.

"Perhaps you don't recognize me," Illya said, stepping forward. "I am the poet and playwright Illya Volkov. We met at the dedication of the shrine to St. Sebastian."

"I can't be expected to remember every Tolstoy want-to-be who came to me with insipid drivel to curry favor with the Church," Brother Iliodor scoffed. "And these other jackals?"

"My name is Harry Houdini," the escape artist said calmly. "I'm a magician from America."

Iliodor raised his eyebrows. "I don't believe in magic. It's an accursed trick of the devil."

"Of course," Houdini said. "I don't mean real sorcery. I'm a stage performer. It's make-believe."

Iliodor pointed an accusatory finger. "So, a false magician then. A charlatan."

No winning with this nut, Houdini though.

One of the defrocked monk's aides whispered in Brother Iliodor's ear, "He's a celebrity. The world's most famous escape artist. I've read about him in newspapers."

The fat man crossed his arms and sneered skeptically.

"Well, I don't believe you are this Houdini," Brother Iliodor said. "Where is your proof?"

Houdini brought his hands in front of him, freed from the bonds, and presented them with a showman's flourish. Brother Iliodor scrutinized Houdini for a moment, then instructed his henchmen, "Untie the others."

Released from the ropes, Illya stepped forward, taking Chioniya by the arm. "Sir, we found a girl on the road. She's in dire need of medical attention."

Chioniya knelt before the robed clergyman.

"I was on my way to see you, to seek your protection," she said. "I stayed at a village where I was set upon by a mob."

"And why was that?" the defrocked monk demanded in a hostile tone.

She bowed her head. "I am a fallen woman and, to pay for a meal and lodging, I gave myself to the town blacksmith. He was not discreet about it. The villagers beat me and chased me from the town tied to his horse."

Brother Iliodor shook his head and waved dismissively, growling, "I have no pity for whores."

It was Boris who, to Houdini's surprise, came to the girl's defense.

"She says she fell victim to Rasputin," he said, approaching. "That he corrupted her."

"That Satan!" Iliodor shrieked. "So many he has ruined. But that very legion of victims, this will be his undoing." He turned to the curly-haired follower. "Take her to the Sisters of Justice and have them tend to her. When she mends, she may prove a worthy candidate for membership."

Chioniya looked tentatively at Houdini, who nodded. She allowed herself to be led off by the follower. Brother Iliodor now adopted a slightly less antagonistic attitude toward the men, as if the "gift" of the girl had put them in his good graces.

"You swear upon your lives you have nothing to do with Rasputin?" he said, a glimmer of paranoia still showing through his squinting eyes.

"That's not quite true," Houdini revealed. "We are here about Rasputin, actually. We want to find out the truth about him. We have heard that you know something about him that is … damaging."

"What I know about his evil would fill ten thousand books!" the cleric boasted. "Walk with me."

They trailed Brother Iliodor as he walked through the encampment, weaving through the rickety huts. Each follower he passed crossed himself reverently and in an unorthodox pattern, as if it were a secret salute. As they passed the barge, Iliodor pointed to it proudly.

"We will take it down the river, spreading the word to all the curious who flock to see it. I vow to preach from the deck until my lungs fail me."

I hope it sinks with you on it, you Jew-hating tub of lard, Houdini thought.

The men walked past a pen where about fifty sheep grazed, bleating.

"My followers raise them and sell the wool to maintain my ministry," the clergyman explained. "To the mighty, the life of a shepherd might seem a fall from grace, but it is a more honorable profession than priesthood in a corrupt church. It was the profession of David, of Abraham and many of the patriarchs."

"Your flock isn't very big, sir," Boris observed.

"Of course, we could not survive on that alone. We are grateful for the generosity of the peasantry whose donations give us sustenance."

Houdini couldn't wait to be out of earshot of this pompous ass, so he got right to the point.

"What is this you know about Rasputin?"

"I know everything about Rasputin," Brother Iliodor replied with a ring of self-importance. "He was my closest friend."

"And now your closest enemy," Illya put in.

Brother Iliodor nodded. This was a topic he clearly relished and Houdini braced himself for an extended sermon.

"The demon Rasputin controls the Holy Synod, which threw me out of the church," Brother Iliodor exclaimed. "Yes, he has those 'men of God' do his bidding. They have bowed down to the Devil. Oh, the cheats, serpents, murderers of God, traitors and hypocrites, godless servants of the Antichrist! Animals fed with the people's blood!"

He dripped with sweat, the exertion of railing at such a fever pitch while striding being a bit too much for him. He paused and dabbed his forehead with a handkerchief.

Then he continued, "They once offered me a pardon, you know, if I retracted my accusations against him. But I will not allow myself ever to be pardoned. I would rather be executed and go to hell than say one word about the king of demons, Rasputin, other than to denounce him. His blasphemous practices have contaminated the Imperial Family like a cancer, and Russia itself will perish from the disease."

Up until this point, the defrocked monk's grandiose blather had only succeeded in giving Houdini an earache. Now he took Iliodor's arm.

"Father, you said something about Rasputin's practices. Do you mean his womanizing?"

Brother Iliodor laughed, an unnerving cackle that would be at home in a sanitarium. "Rasputin's voracious whoring is the least of his abominations," he said. "Have you never heard of the Khlysty?"

Houdini shook his head.

"The Khlysty?" Boris said. "Some religious sect, banished centuries ago."

"Banished, but not destroyed, unfortunately," Brother Iliodor informed them. "Their heresies are manifold. Chief among their delusions is that Our Lord Jesus Christ did not return to heaven, but inhabited another body to continue His work on Earth. That He has been incarnated innumerable times with none of these many 'Christs' less holy than the original. Each Khlysty community, or 'ark,' has its own 'Christ.' A particularly powerful 'Christ' can supposedly combine pagan spells with Christian prayer to achieve miraculous acts of healing."

"And Rasputin leads such an ark?" Houdini asked excitedly.

Iliodor nodded. "He told me himself how he participated in their rituals. They believe each sin, followed by great suffering and profound repentance, brings one closer to God. So, they seek purification through bouts of boundless debauchery, a rite they call the Rejoicing. They contend that the Holy Spirit comes during the whirling and dancing and that resurrected in their sweat are the drops of Our Lord's sweat. But of course, it is the Devil and his horde of demons who possess the misguided fools."

Houdini frowned. "It sounds a little farfetched. This is the twentieth century."

Iliodor bellowed to an acolyte, "Go get Brother Mikhail."

They waited awkwardly for several minutes, Iliodor wearing a smug expression. Finally, the henchman returned with a young man with prematurely gray hair and eerily pale eyes. They looked as if the pigment had been scoured from them, and Houdini thought of Moses, transformed after seeing the burning bush.

"Tell them about the Rejoicing," Brother Iliodor commanded.

The man looked at his feet with embarrassment.

"Go on, my son," Brother Iliodor said, his voice softening with compassion that Houdini suspected might be counterfeit. "You have no cause for shame. You have renounced the heretics and left their godless world behind."

Young Brother Mikhail looked up at the visitors and reluctantly complied.

"I was a student at the university when my sister introduced me to the cult," he began. "We would meet in the cellar of a peasant lodge; beneath barns; the private tombs of rich members, but always underground. The rite commenced innocuously enough with our leader, whom we called The Christ, leading invocations and hymns, as you would see with many religious societies. Then he would announce it was time for the Rejoicing. The faithful formed a ring and began to sway in rhythm, then to whirl around and around, spinning faster and faster. We danced in a frenzy while The Christ slashed us with a whip until blood flowed, reserving an especially vicious flogging for any dancer whose energy flagged. We were no longer whirling people, but flying hair, billowing robes—no longer individual men and women, but a ring of ecstasy. When

The Christ commanded it, we flung off our robes. We danced until sweat poured from our pores in rivulets.

"In a state of intoxication beyond anything I can describe, we would collapse on the ground naked, and then ..." He faltered.

"Go on, my son," Brother Iliodor encouraged him.

"And then we would copulate indiscriminately and with no regard to familial ties. Fathers with daughters, brothers with sisters. I myself committed the sin of incest with my sister. You see, we were not men and women any longer, but something beneath beasts and yet greater than ordinary humans: spiritual entities, angels, demons co-mingling. Groaning, weeping, cries of passion echoed off the walls of the underground chamber. This obscene orgy would continue for hours, until candles flickered and died out. And everything was in darkness."

Brother Mikhail was by now sobbing. "Sometimes I think that because I participated in rites so blasphemous, I cannot escape hell and damnation."

Brother Iliodor stroked his back soothingly.

"No, because you have repented and the Lord has forgiven you, through me. Thank you, brother. You are free to go."

The man wiped away tears and snot with the sleeve of his robe and departed. Brother Iliodor turned to the visitors.

"So, you see it now, don't you? Evil in its purest form," the clergyman fumed, gesticulating wildly in the air. "No, beyond evil, the primordial chaos unleashed. Rasputin has unnatural power over others whom he uses to satisfy his carnal desires, and gains by drawing energy from his deceived followers. He grows still more powerful each day. First Russia, then, if he is not stopped, the world under his sway. For you see he is *not* a second Christ. Nay, just the opposite. He is Satan incarnate—the Antichrist foretold in the Book of Revelation."

Houdini looked at Boris, who was a ghastly shade somewhere between that of chalk and bone.

"Well, that's the bad news. What's the good news?" Illya said.

They heard a woman shriek and Boris swung around, reaching for his pistol.

Was someone interfering with poor Chioniya? Houdini thought. *After all she'd already been through? She's scarcely been at the encampment for thirty minutes!*

A creepy grin spread across Iliodor's piggish face. "Come, you are about see a miracle. Broken vessels made whole and strong."

They followed him around a ramshackle building that looked like a carpenter had constructed it while stumbling drunk. When they turned the corner, they saw fourteen women, each clad in a tunic and tights like those of a medieval page, over which they wore a kind of nun's headpiece and cape. On each tunic was emblazoned a red cross. The women were spaced out in a line like recruits undergoing basic training, led by a stocky female "drill sergeant" barking commands. Each woman stood before a dummy made of straw and kneed it in the groin, screaming with gusto as they did so.

"What the heck is going on?" Houdini exclaimed.

Brother Iliodor smiled proudly. "These are my sacred nuns. They are a holy order of women who have been ruined by Rasputin. I have dubbed them the Sisterhood of Justice."

The drill leader, distinguished by a blue robe, cried, "Strike!"

Each woman reached under her tunic and pulled out a butcher knife from a hidden sheathe presumably strapped to her thigh. With all their might, they thrust the blades into the dummies, first driving into the chest, then into the gut, then making a rapid upward tear that sent straw flying in all directions.

"That is right," Brother Iliodor squealed in delight. "From sack to sternum. Cut the devil's entrails from his body."

He turned to the visitors. "When the time is right, they will seek out Rasputin. One by one, until the job is done." From each dummy, there protruded at crotch level a foot-long dowel, the purpose of which was about to be made clear.

"Do not forget to emasculate the fiend!" Brother Iliodor shouted.

In unison, the women sliced at their targets and the wooden sticks dropped to the ground. Houdini, Illya and Boris clutched their groins reflexively.

Houdini shook his head, flummoxed. "I may be wrong, but doesn't the Bible say something about murder? That it's a violation of God's law?"

"Not when the victim is the Beast foretold in the Holy Bible," Brother Iliodor explained with absolute certainty.

Houdini gazed at the barge. The banner had finally been erected properly, rustling in the wind with its nauseating message.

"Mr. Houdini, surely you have seen Rasputin's powers over others," Brother Iliodor demanded, a trace of desperation in his voice. "Do you find it so hard to accept that he is the Antichrist?"

"You lost me at 'Christ,'" Houdini said with a cold smile. "You see, Brother Iliodor, I'm a Jew."

The defrocked monk recoiled in horror, as if Houdini had removed his hat to reveal horns.

CHAPTER SIXTEEN

The Hidden Temple

O n the road back to St. Petersburg, Houdini stared at the grey sky, trying to digest the bizarre tale. If half of what Brother Iliodor and Brother Mikhail had told them was true, Rasputin was an even more dangerous antagonist than it seemed before. He turned to Illya, who was busy scribbling in his journal.

"Another poem, Illya?"

"Not this time."

"A play?"

"An idea for a film," the writer replied with a faraway look in his eyes. "Nothing ambitious. Just two or three minutes. I know plenty of actors, and a fellow who owns a movie camera. Cinema will be the medium of the twentieth century. The moving image affects the heart more directly than a novel or poetry or opera."

Houdini was intrigued. He'd been filmed jumping into a river while handcuffed in Rochester, New York in 1909, and the footage fascinated him. He'd even been toying with the idea of appearing in an adventure short.

"What's it about?"

"About the very peculiar times we live in," Illya said with an enigmatic smile.

Houdini knew there was no hope of prying it out of him. "What do you make of what Iliodor said?"

"Well, he's mad as a hatter, of course. But even madmen can speak the truth. That's why we're so fond of holy fools. I've heard of cults like these. The Orthodox Church has always feared them. I think, Houdini, they represent the dark side of the Russian soul, an expression of something primitive and profane. An ungovernable force that must at all costs be repressed."

Houdini stroked his chin. "He said the Khlysty meet underneath barns. Is there such a place in St. Petersburg where that could be?"

Boris nodded. "Many on the outskirts of the city, south of the Fontanka River. The ground to the north and east is too swampy to think of building anything underground."

"We'll have to search them," Houdini said.

"There must be scores of barns!" the policeman objected.

"If there have been wild ceremonies, people would have seen some odd goings-on. Let's spread some dough around and find out where. That'll narrow it down some."

"Well ..."

"We'll split up, then. You take half, I'll take the other. And keep that camera ready. One picture of Rasputin 'rejoicing' with a bevy of those female fanatics will be worth a thousand words."

***

As Houdini and his companions made their journey back to St. Petersburg, Bess labored in the kitchen elbow-to-elbow with the Little Ladies, preparing borsht, one of Rasputin's favorite dishes. The red beet-and-cabbage soup was served with beef, potato, herbs, dill and a dollop of *smetana*, Russian sour cream.

"I can finish if you want to sit down," she told Anna Vyrubova, mindful of the woman's lame leg.

Rasputin's chief disciple shook her head.

"My leg used to ache when I stood for long stretches, but Father Grigori cured me of my pain," she said. "It only acts up on a cold night when I am in my cottage."

The image of this woman's existence as a spinster, alone in the little cottage, struck Bess as sad. She then pictured her own empty house, in particular the room that she and Harry set aside as a nursery when they first purchased the townhouse. It had long since been turned into a storage room for props.

"Do you think Father Grigori can cure any condition?" she asked diffidently.

Vyrubova looked at her solemnly and placed her hand on hers.

"Yes, he can. He has cured blindness and made the lame to walk. One need only have faith, total faith in him."

After lunch, Rasputin preached on the subject of sin, the importance of acknowledging one's weakness, surrendering "in abject shame," and accepting the Lord's forgiveness.

"We are, through sin, suffering and redemption, reborn," he proclaimed. "Say amen."

"Amen," his flock echoed.

Rasputin turned his radiant eyes on Bess.

"Your husband, he does not believe in the power of faith, does he?" he asked.

The sudden focus on Bess took her by surprise and she fell dumb. The other women fixed their eyes on her with an intensity that approached that of their master, like a pack of stray cats whose eyes shone in the moonlight.

"He ... he is a religious man," she said finally. "Harry practices the Hebrew faith. His father was a rabbi."

The women mumbled as if she had revealed that Houdini was an ax murderer, but Rasputin stilled them with his hand.

"I have no quarrel with the Jews," he said. "My business manager is a Jew. But you must realize that your prayers will not be answered until you abandon yourself completely to Christ."

She bowed her head. Their interfaith marriage had never posed any difficulty. They'd been married three times, first civilly, later by a Catholic priest and by a rabbi.

"Stand up," Rasputin commanded, and she found herself rising like a puppet on strings. He strode over and took her shoulders gravely. "Faith in powers beyond yourself will be your salvation. It will open a doorway to all that you desire."

He was so close she felt enveloped in his aura. Something akin to electricity surged through her.

***

When Houdini returned to the palace, and he and his wife were alone in their room, he told Bess about his discovery of Rasputin's involvement with the forbidden Khlysty sect. She poured a glass of water for each of them and he noticed her hand shaking.

"It all sounds screwy, doesn't it, sweetheart?" she said with false levity. "I suppose you'll be suspecting Father Grigori of human sacrifice next."

Houdini did not reply, instead quietly studying her face.

"You did say this man hates Rasputin," she pressed on. "He'd say anything to hurt him. Nasty rumors about sex. You certainly don't believe those awful things about Alexandra, do you?"

Houdini shook his head. "I'd hate to believe it. But Rasputin's powers of mind-manipulation, why they're uncanny. He tried to put the whammy on me and I almost fell for it. What he could do to a woman ..."

"Oh, because we're the weaker sex? Why I ought to ..." She raised a fist and shook it like a comedian in a burlesque routine.

Houdini laughed and took her in his arms.

"I just want you steering clear of him and his harem," he said.

"It's not a harem," she protested.

"Coven of witches, then. Any way you slice it, you're not going back to that place, and that's final."

She crossed her arms. "You're being a bully. I'm not at all sure I believe a word of this 'Khlysty' business, but if there's any truth to it, the Little Ladies know where and when it takes place. And how will we find out unless I keep mingling with them?"

"It's too risky," he said, shaking his head.

She nodded her head. He shook his head.

She nodded, and then stamped her foot and said, "You can't dangle in a straitjacket from a flagpole five stories up and tell me what's too risky."

"When I risk my neck, I've thought it through," he said emphatically.

"You trust your abilities."

"That's right!" he said, raising his voice. "You've nailed it right on the head."

"Well, I trust myself. Do you trust me?"

Houdini hesitated, taken aback. "What kind of silly question is that?" he growled. "Why of course I do."

"Then prove it."

Houdini bit his lip, weakening. "What I ought to do is put you over my knee."

"Promises, promises."

"Come here, you nut," Houdini said with a laugh. He brought her close and kissed her.

"Speaking of promises, you've got to swear on your mother you'll clear out as soon as one of those 'Little Ladies' lets the cat out of the bag," Houdini demanded, waving his finger at her.

"Scout's honor," she replied. "If there really is some kind of kooky devil's mass coming up, which for the record, I doubt."

The next morning, Houdini entertained the children. Much to their delight, he taught them how to perform his famous 21 Card Trick, in which each card represented a prisoner and one represented Houdini. Shuffled around from cell to cell, the performer's task was to find and "free" the magician. Anastasia was the first to master the trick, which she crowed about to no end.

That night, he set out to investigate the barns to the southeast of the city. He didn't want to risk using a car from the Imperial Garage again. The chauffeur might talk, and he didn't want word of his jaunt getting back to the Tsar.

He had the switchboard call a cab instead, arranging to be met outside the palace gates. As he made his way to the main door, he found his path suddenly blocked by Hercules, the largest of the Ethiopians, whose broad shoulders were built for wrestling a Cape buffalo to the ground. The magician was rattled to see him away from his post at the entrance to the Imperial Family's quarters.

"You are going out, Mr. Houdini?" Hercules asked in a deep voice.

"You speak English?" Houdini responded, evading the question, but genuinely surprised. The accent was distinctly American. *This guy is about as Ethiopian as Jack Johnson.*

"The truth is, suh, I'm from Alabama. My name is Jim Hercules."

"Well, it's a pleasure to meet you, Jim. Your name fits you," Houdini said with a smile, clasping his countryman's meaty hands. "How the hell did you find yourself in Russia?"

"I was a boxer back in the States," the giant revealed. "I was touring Europe, and the Tsar's mother saw me fighting in the ring. She offered me a job in the palace and I've been here ever since. I've seen newspaper stories about all the escapes you've done. Always meant something special to me. My great uncle, he was a slave in Alabama. He escaped by getting himself shipped to the north inside a crate."

"That took more guts than I have," the magician replied.

"I got me five children, and they are all fans of yours. I see them once a year when I visit home. They sure would be tickled if I got your autograph."

"Well, sure, I'd be delighted."

The Ethiopian-by-way-of-Alabama produced from his pocket a yellowed news clipping. To Houdini's surprise, he saw that it was an old one from his 1903 Russian tour, depicting his escape from the Siberian Transport Cell.

"Who should I make it out to?"

"You can make it out to me, suh. I'd be lying if I said I wasn't a bigger fan than any of them."

Houdini took his time to write in elegant longhand, "Don't let those lions in Ethiopia eat you. Your friend, Harry Houdini."

The behemoth chuckled at the joke, then said, "You didn't say where you were going at this time of night, Mr. Houdini."

"I'm performing at a nightclub for some extra dough, one of those with a lot of showgirls showing their bloomers. But I don't want it getting around. After all, the Tsar brought me here for his personal entertainment. I know it's a lot to ask for, but would you cover for me?"

Hercules covered his eyes with a broad hand.

"Mum's the word. You come and go as you please, Mr. Houdini. Come on, best you leave through the servants' entrance."

***

Houdini and Boris convened at the crossroads in a farming district southeast of the Fontanka River. They had agreed it wasn't fair to ask the young writer to join them in what might prove to be a dangerous mission. Plus, Illya was suddenly obsessed with putting together his little film, putting everything else aside.

"My informants tell me there've been rumors of loud singing here late at night," Boris told the magician. "It could just be some drunken peasants. Or ..."

Houdini held up his lantern and looked down the road. The cluster of barns and sheds, which probably looked picturesque during the day, was ominous by moonlight. A weathervane in the shape of a witch on her broom creaked as it turned in the wind. A dog howled in the distance, and it flashed through the escape artist's mind that dogs could supposedly detect the supernatural.

"You have your flashbulbs?" Houdini asked his bearish companion. Boris patted the pocket of his coat.

"There are a lot of barns," said the magician. "You take the ones to the left, I'll take the right. If need be, we'll inspect those on the north and south roads tomorrow."

"I don't know about splitting up, Mr. Houdini," Boris said, creases appearing in his brow. "I have a feeling in my stomach about this place. It smells of the devil's business."

"I know, you won't be around to rescue me again," Houdini said. "Don't worry, I've been working on my right cross."

Boris cracked a smile, though unease was still evident in his eyes. The men shook hands.

The first three barns the escape artist inspected were empty, and he began to think they were on a wild goose chase. However, when Houdini reached the fourth barn, his own sense that something was out of kilter kicked in. On its face, the structure appeared innocuous. It looked the way an American schoolboy might draw a barn, rectangular with a curved roof, a crossbar holding the double doors shut and even a rooster as a weathervane. But paint the color of blood had been recently applied, covering over rot. There was something artificial about the barn that reminded the magician of a miniature in Alexei's model train set.

It had rained the previous night. The mud beneath Houdini's feet sucked at his overshoes like quicksand, and he remembered how the city was built on a morass. What was below this slime? An endless sea of gook extending to the center of the earth, with eyeless worms slithering through it? Tunnels built in ancient times reaching out like tentacles for miles?

"Holy Toledo, is my imagination running away from me!" the escape artist muttered.

Houdini pulled aside the crossbar and cracked open one door just wide enough to slip inside. Despite his stealth, it creaked plaintively, like a sheep bleating to his herder that a wolf was afoot. At first glance, the interior looked so normal, it was as if it had been decorated by a theater's set designer for a cowboy musical. A pitchfork stuck out of a haystack; a horseshoe hung from a nail on a wall. A crippled cart leaned against a pillar, one wheel missing. The four stalls stood empty. One held a water bucket, as if left for a horse. But something stunk about the place, or rather *didn't* stink, he realized. There was no lingering hint of animal dung. No indication it had served as a barn for years.

In the dim light of his lantern, a white object the size of a rabbit's foot glittered and he bent to pick it up. It was a stone figurine of a winged being with horns and a mermaid tail. It was so worn, Houdini couldn't tell if the face was animal or human, or if the expression was benevolent or malevolent. It didn't look like any sculpture he'd seen in Russia, more like something out of Greek mythology.

No, more ancient, like those idols archaeologists had unearthed in Turkey a few years back, Houdini thought upon closer inspection. *Heck, the darned thing looks like it could have come from Atlantis.* At that point, he realized his imagination had taken flight again. *Okay, maybe just a good luck charm a Gypsy pawned off on a peasant?* He deposited the figurine in his breast pocket.

Suddenly, he did smell something, but not the scent of animals or their feces: smoke. The barn was on fire. He rushed to the door. Someone had slid the crossbar into place, trapping him in. Houdini smelled something even more alarming: gasoline.

Rasputin's henchmen mean to burn me alive!

CHAPTER SEVENTEEN

The Inferno

Houdini battered the barn doors with his shoulder, but they wouldn't budge. He felt the resistance of something massive propped against the doors from outside, so that even if he was able to manipulate the crossbar from inside, the doors couldn't open. With the speed of a seasoned sailor racing up a crow's nest, he scaled the ladder to the loft and pushed on the shutters. They'd been boarded shut from the outside. Houdini flung himself off the loft and landed on the haystack, not wasting the precious seconds it would have taken to climb down.

Those walls look pretty solid, but I bet you could smash through one with the right tool. He reached for the pitchfork.

A sledgehammer is what I need right about now, but this will have to do.

A burning timber from the roof crashed down, missing him by inches, and set the haystack ablaze. Houdini's sleeve caught fire. The magician dashed to the stall for the water bucket and doused it. He tossed the bucket aside and snatched the pitchfork out of the haystack, which had exploded into a bonfire. He plunged the farmer's tool into the wall. After a dozen rapid strikes, he succeeded in making a small hole.

218 |C. Michael Forsyth

Houdini reckoned that in five minutes, he'd produce an opening in the boards large enough to wriggle through. He was as flexible as any octopus.

The trouble is I'll be unconscious from smoke inhalation by then.

Already, smoke was filling his lungs. Flames licked from the walls like ravening wolves. In a less sturdily constructed barn, there might have been a chance of kicking down one of the weakening walls, but this one would survive just long enough to cook him alive.

Fine! I'll dig my way out!

The barn had an earthen floor. He'd tunneled through soil in his escape acts, but always with the help of a concealed tool. This pitchfork wasn't cut out for it, he found as he stabbed the earth and it stopped just a few inches deep. Below the surface, the ground was hard as stone. He dropped the pitchfork and stumbled back, coughing in the thickening smoke.

Houdini dropped to his hands and knees to draw in the remaining oxygen, and the reprieve gave him a chance to think.

Hold on. Below the surface isn't just hard as stone—it is stone!

Remembering the curious figurine in his pocket, it dawned on him that the place really had been used for forbidden ceremonies. That would mean there was a cellar. So, there must be a secret opening. But where? Desperate as a trapped rat, he looked all about the maelstrom of angry flames. It was even harder to see through the smoke than it was to breathe in it. A fiery beam tumbled end over end, like some monstrous thing hurled by Zeus, and he barely rolled out of the way as it smashed to pieces.

He had to find that trapdoor before the entire roof collapsed on him. *Where, where?*

That crippled cart conveniently kept a section of the floor out of sight, he recalled. Blinded by the smoke, he wormed over to where, in his mind's eye, it stood. He groped about and grabbed a wheel. With considerable effort, he rolled the broken wagon out of the way and used his forearm to rake away a superficial covering of earth. Sure enough, his hand found a metal handle. He flung open the trapdoor and slithered down headfirst, even as another burning beam smashed the cart into splinters. The hatch slammed shut overhead. The escape artist lurched down a ladder and landed on his face on a stone floor.

Houdini felt the sudden tomb-like coolness of his new surroundings and lit a match. The chamber was unexpectedly large, enough to comfortably accommodate forty people. And it was definitely a place of worship, although not necessarily of the most wholesome kind. In the center stood a stone altar on which there were engraved runes that seemed unimaginably ancient. They bespoke a time when men worshipped—and feared—gods *not* in their own image.

Tall candlesticks encircled the altar and it was not hard to picture some blasphemous ritual illuminated by their glow. Houdini lit one and in the faint light it offered, he spotted a doorway at the far end. Houdini hurried to it.

Beyond the doorway stretched a tunnel so narrow that worshippers must travel single file and so low that even the short-of-stature magician had to duck. The passageway stretched on and on, until he entertained the horrible notion that it was a circle that would take him back to where he'd begun. But after fifty yards, he ran into another ladder which led up to another trap door. When he emerged, he found himself in a thicket of bushes which hid the entrance. Hearing voices, he quickly blew out the candle and crept toward them on his hands and knees.

Two men stood around the barn watching patiently as the roof caved in and the whole building became a giant bonfire. They were still as prairie dogs. In the American south, you might have seen Ku Klux Klansmen guzzling moonshine and chortling as they torched a sharecropper's barn, but these guys were eerily still, watching their handiwork with a kind of reverence. He wondered what their eyes looked like. Was it the feverish gleam of religious fanatics?

Shots rang out in the distance.

Boris!

Houdini darted down the road his companion had taken, passing a handful of barns from which the lowing of cows and clucking of chickens could be heard. As he passed one, he heard groaning and turned.

The bodies of three men sprawled, partially on top of each other. In the moonlight, Houdini could make out a black, smoking hole in the center of one man's forehead. A short distance away, a large figure sat leaning against an outhouse. As Houdini approached, the man raised a pistol weakly.

"Take another step and I'll send you to hell," came Boris's voice, as low as a Kodiak bear awakened from hibernation.

"Boris, it's me," Houdini said. The policeman dropped his gun. Houdini knelt beside him and saw a bullet hole in his coat.

"I hit these three dogs; two others ran off with their tails between their legs," Boris boasted.

"That's some fine shooting, but we've got to get you to a hospital."

"I'm not going to last another five minutes, my friend. I've been hit three times."

"Three bullet wounds? Why, that's nothing to a big ox like you," Houdini said as he knelt beside his comrade. "Don't be a baby."

Boris opened his coat and gestured to his vest where blood was spreading like ink from a shattered fountain pen. He'd been shot in the heart.

"It's a careless mama who would let her baby get an injury like this." The wounded man unclenched his fist, revealing the camera watch. "I didn't get very much. Sorry I let you down."

Houdini took the watch and clasped the cop's hand. He could feel the life force ebbing from his friend.

"Is there anything I can do?"

"There is a flask of vodka in my other pocket. Just this once I will drink on duty."

CHAPTER EIGHTEEN

A Prophecy of Doom

At the palace, Houdini huddled in a tapestried alcove outside the banquet hall with Count Vladimir Fredericks, Prime Minister Stolypin, Archbishop Theophan and the Okhrana director Dzhunkovsky, all of whom had been invited to a state dinner. Servants scurried by, toting platters and crystal racks holding silverware. Four nights had passed since the magician's narrow escape from the inferno.

"I was able to get the film taken by Boris Stolypin developed," Dzhunkovsky said. He glanced around furtively and produced an envelope from his breast pocket. He shook out the contents into his hand. "We have circulated this photograph among my detectives and I have no doubt we will be able to identify the killer soon. Prime Minister, the men your cousin shot dead were all known criminals and I am certain this scum is of the same ilk."

Prime Minister Stolypin scrutinized the photo, then passed it to Houdini. The photograph showed a young man whose most identifiable feature was a rather unorthodox hairdo: a high, dark pompadour parted in the middle. His features, illuminated by the garish light of the flash and seen in high contrast, were hawkish and severe, as if hewn from oak with a hatchet. His expression was surprisingly neutral for a man who was about to fire a gun and was also at risk of being fired upon: neither angry, gleeful, nor scared.

"Hard to believe he was seconds away from putting a bullet in a man's chest," Houdini remarked.

"I've seen that look before on a man who was arrested for strangling his wife as she slept," Dzhunkovsky said quietly. "He claimed he had committed the crime while sleepwalking. The court did not believe him and he was sentenced to be hanged. The night before his execution, I visited him in his cell. As we spoke, it seemed that his mind was elsewhere entirely—and I realized that he was conversing with me in his sleep. I swear to you, the look in his eyes was exactly like this."

Houdini stared into the soulless eyes of the killer.

"Like a zombie," he mumbled.

"A what?" Count Vladimir asked.

"Something they believe in down in the Caribbean. People brought back from the dead to work the fields as slaves."

"Like a revenant, the undead," Bishop Theophan said, nodding with understanding. "In our country, we have legends about such creatures. Chief amongst them the *vurdalak*, which subsists on the blood of the living."

"Do any of you recognize him?" Dzhunkovsky asked, passing the photo around to the others.

The conspirators shook their heads in turn.

"I wouldn't expect it," the Okhrana chief said. "I'm sure Rasputin's enforcers are recruited from the gutter. Petty criminals, vagrants, those with weak minds."

"Even strong minds can be bent to his will," Prime Minister Stolypin pointed out. "He now counts many in the upper class among his minions, including those of the highest rank."

"Our aristocrats today are a far cry from those who fought beside Ivan the Terrible," said Count Vladimir. "Their blood is thin."

Stolypin returned the photo to Dzhunkovsky. The chief produced Boris's camera watch from his pocket.

"I've reloaded the film," he told Houdini. "Now you have a spare."

Houdini accepted the pocket watch, identical to his except it bore no HH engraved on the back, and he stared at it glumly.

"My cousin's funeral will be the day after tomorrow," Stolypin told Houdini. "Of course, I do not expect you to attend."

"He was a good man," Houdini replied, tightening his fingers around the watch. "I'll make sure he hasn't died in vain."

Said Archbishop Theophan, "It will be an honor to conduct the ceremony. I only wish that from the pulpit I could condemn the man we all know is behind the crime."

"We take a great risk being seen together like this," observed the Prime Minister. "Rasputin knows you must have allies in high places, Houdini. I've spoken against him, but so have others. He probably did not suspect me of involvement in your investigation until Boris's death, which has been reported in the newspaper. An article mentioned that he is my cousin."

"You must both be on the alert," Archbishop Theophan warned. "Those who oppose Rasputin are in grave danger. He is ruthless with his enemies."

"I'm not scared of that rat," Houdini said fiercely.

But of course he was. The fiendish mystic had at his disposal a private army of goons, fanatical cultists, femme fatales, Gypsies and mesmerized assassins. Plus, most daunting,

Rasputin's weird powers, the nature of which, and limits of which, remained unknown.

Count Vladimir Fredericks pointed to the face of a grandfather clock.

"The banquet is about to begin," he said. "It would be prudent if we each entered the dining hall separately." The brothers in arms quickly dispersed.

Houdini spotted Bess walking arm and arm down a corridor with Anastasia, and he caught up with them.

"Where have you been?" Bess whispered.

"Chasing around maids to pinch their behinds, what do you think?"

She swatted his own behind with mock dismay.

"Keep it up and I'll marry the next Russian bear-trainer I see," she warned him.

Tonight, Anastasia was clad in a frilly white gown with a high-necked collar, more like the formal attire of her older sisters.

"You look lovely," the magician said as he took her other arm. "Like a real little lady."

"I hate it," she said, wrinkling her nose. "There are so many bows. Can you teach me to escape from it?"

The dining table was long enough to host a Viking feast. Beside each gold-crested plate was a crystal rack holding knives, spoons and forks. Behind each chair, a footman hovered to serve his assigned guest.

In addition to the Imperial family, the Houdinis and the intrepid band of conspirators, a number of officials and dignitaries were in attendance. These included Sir George Buchanan, the British ambassador to Russia; Vladimir Dedyulin, Commandant of the palace and responsible for the Imperial Family's security, and Prince Vlad Orlov, chief of the

"You're a long way from home."

"As are you."

Something about the limey rubbed Houdini the wrong way. Despite his pleasant manner, he had a crafty look in his eyes that Houdini had seen in card cheats. It crossed Houdini's mind that Donatson might have fled England after bringing disgrace to his family, perhaps theft or a scandal involving a married woman.

Rasputin greeted Houdini with another warm embrace. His aroma wasn't as overwhelming as on their first meeting; he had at least bathed with soap, but beneath that scent lingered a hint of that goatish stench. Houdini cringed to see Bess accept his hug without recoiling. The Tsarina kissed her spiritual advisor's hand with her usual ardor. And while Houdini remained skeptical of the salacious rumors swirling around the two, the image flashed through his mind of the unholy holy man on top of her.

Rasputin uttered an extended grace asking God to punish hypocrites, conspirators and traitors.

"May hypocrites who praise our Lord while holding jealousy and anger in their hearts be met with swift and sure justice," he said, gazing at Archbishop Theophan, who was seated directly across from him.

The dinner conversation was loud and lively. Sir George, the ambassador, discussed his imminent departure on a diplomatic mission to the Far East. The delegation's chief goal was to ensure that in any future conflict, Japan would ally itself with Russia and England, not Germany.

"Surely, no one thinks that Germany is likely to go to war with us," Alexandra said with a nervous little laugh. "Wilhelm is Nicky's cousin."

"We have nothing to fear from Willy," Nicholas concurred. "Just as, in the end, there is little danger of war with England because your King George V is also my cousin."

"Blood is thicker than water," Fat Orlov opined.

"I must say I find the British habit of treating Germans as warlike quite incomprehensible," Alexandra said with a trace of irritation.

"Of course, you are also of German descent, so your affinity is natural," Sir George noted. "My point is that we would rather have Japan with us than against us."

"You can never have too many allies, I suppose," Bess said.

"I'm not so certain of that," Sir George observed. "Every ally is a nation you may be called upon to defend."

Tsar Nicholas said with certainty, "There is no stronger alliance than that forged by blood, Sir George. The friendship between our two nations will endure as long as I am alive."

"Here, here," said the English tutor Charles Gibbes, raising his glass. The dinner guests all followed suit.

Rasputin had been stuffing his face with his customary gusto. He paused from gorging himself for a moment and told Prime Minister Stolypin, "I am sorry to hear about the death of your own dear cousin."

Stolypin looked as if he were barely able to restrain himself from lunging across the table at Rasputin.

"I thank you for your kind words," he replied stiffly. "I take solace only in the fact that I am certain the fiendish perpetrator of the crime will be brought to justice."

Rasputin considered him as a child might look at a bug, contemplating whether or not to crush it between his fingers.

"I sense the Angel of Death lingering near you," he said loudly. Alexandra gasped and dropped her fork, which a footman hurried to replace. Stolypin blanched, but summoned the will to meet Rasputin's eyes.

"All of us are mortal, even the holiest," he said in a tone of defiance.

Rasputin nodded in agreement. Then he pointed in turn to Archbishop Theophan, Count Vladimir and Chief Dzhunkovsky. "And to this one, that one and that one, fortune will also be unkind." The men, singled out from so many at the table, could not disguise their shock.

"He's a regular Suzy Sunshine, isn't he?" Houdini whispered to Bess. But she looked as mortified as those Rasputin had marked for doom.

Alexandra began to grow faint. Her lady-in-waiting Anna Vyrubova, seated beside her, dipped a napkin in water and used it to dab her forehead.

"In America, we're not so hot on fate," Houdini declared in a strong, clear voice. "We believe that a man carves out his own destiny."

Rasputin's British flunky Donatson smiled. "That's what makes you and your countrymen so charming. That you cling to that illusion doggedly."

The French teacher Gilliard laughed, and the other guests quickly joined him in pretending this was all just pleasant dinner conversation. Eager to change the subject, the Tsar cleared his throat.

"Mr. Houdini has a great entertainment planned for tomorrow," he said, turning to the magician.

"It's a mystery I've been preparing for some time now," Houdini elaborated. "I'm to be buried alive in a coffin under six feet of snow, handcuffed, and escape from it."

"But how will you breathe?" asked Dr. Botkin in astonishment.

"Well, there will be air in the coffin of course, at first. But it won't last forever."

The children excitedly peppered him with questions about the act. Would there be an actual funeral? Would he be allowed to take a shovel into the coffin?

"What if you have to pee?" shouted Alexei, only to be shushed by his sister Tatiana.

Rasputin looked at the magician pensively.

"You will not survive," he intoned. It was stated so forcefully, it seemed more a command than prophecy. Bess clutched Houdini's knee under the table.

Alexandra, still reeling from the previous prophecy, cried, "You must call it off!"

Nicholas nodded in agreement. "It might be best to postpone the performance, Mr. Houdini. You have nothing to prove to the masses and we are sure of your abilities. Father Grigori's prophecies are unerring."

Rasputin's prophecy of doom struck Houdini like a punch in the gut, but he was darned if he was going to show it. Recovering, the escape artist forced his lips into a casual smile.

"Well, Father Grigori, thank you for your concern," he said. "But a medical expert from the University of Rochester said I was going to kill myself jumping manacled into the Erie Canal. And a Harvard man told the newspapers it was physically impossible to escape from a sealed milk can. They both had to eat their words."

"Nothing can defeat Harry Houdini," Alexei boasted.

"Shhh!" Alexandra scolded him, then turned to her husband. "You know, Nicky, all this daredevil tomfoolery, it's not having the best influence on the children."

Anastasia shot to her feet, throwing down her napkin.

"If you send Mr. Houdini away, I shall run away too," she exclaimed.

"Me too," Alexei echoed.

Olga, Tatiana and Maria all protested as well, though in less dramatic terms.

"No one is speaking of sending Mr. Houdini away," their father reassured them, while glancing at the Tsarina for support. "Are we, Sunny? But please, Houdini, do reconsider this endeavor in light of Our Friend's warning."

Alexandra took her husband's hand and squeezed it anxiously. "We must forbid it. Unless you have the blessing of Father Grigori."

All heads turned to the man of the cloth.

"I will bring all my humble powers of prayer to Mr. Houdini," he vowed solemnly.

"You see, Alix," the Tsar said, patting his wife's hand. "It's all taken care of."

This seemed to mollify Alexandra and the mood at the table lightened.

"We have less strenuous entertainment lined up for Thursday," Nicholas said. "Minister Stolypin, the Imperial Family will be attending a performance of the great opera *Tsar Saltan* at the Kiev Opera House. You are invited to attend."

"I would be honored," Stolypin said with a slight bow.

"And you too, of course, Mr. and Mrs. Houdini," the emperor continued.

"I'll be there," the magician replied. He couldn't resist directing a sly grin at Rasputin and adding, "Barring the unforeseen."

Most of the guests departed by car or carriage. Archbishop Theophan and Rasputin, however, were staying the night. While waiting for his car to be brought around, Rasputin's publicist Donatson stood beside Houdini, smoking a cigarette from a long holder.

"Are you quite sure you want to go through with this stunt tomorrow?" the Englishman asked. "Father Grigori's record for predictions is really quite impressive. Perfect, in fact."

"What do *you* predict?"

"I think that purchasing a coffin was a wise investment."

"Well, put your money where your mouth is," Houdini said. "Let's bet on it."

Donatson chuckled. "You would wager with your life?"

Houdini shrugged. "I'm already betting my life. At least this way, I can make a dime off it. What do you say? My skill against your boss's hoodoo."

The Englishman hesitated, then said with a smile, "Shall we say fifteen rubles?"

"Double it."

"Done."

The bettors shook hands.

Houdini, Bess, the Imperial Family and their black-robed spiritual advisor watched as, in turn, the dignitaries left. Prime Minister Stolypin got into his carriage and it took off behind a stream of others.

"Death is after him," Rasputin said sadly. Alexandra cried out in fear and, had she not leaned on her spiritual advisor for support, she would surely have collapsed.

***

Bess took hours to fall asleep and when she did, her slumber was plagued by vivid and unsettling dreams. In one, she saw her husband trapped in a glass coffin, beating frantically at the lid. His face turned blue and his cheeks inflated as he held his breath. She tried to open the coffin, but could find no handles. The oblong glass box then began to sink into an abyss, Houdini's face frozen in horror. Beside the grave towered Rasputin in a black robe and cape that fluttered behind him like bat wings. Bess dropped to her knees before him, imploring him to help. Father Grigori reached down and placed a hand on her head, stroking her hair paternally. Then he pushed her face gently into his groin. She pulled away, but some invisible force drew her back. Rasputin's gnarled, elongated fingers began to unbuttoned his fly as Bess knelt trembling, dreading what she was about to see, yet possessed by excruciating anticipation.

Bess sat up, drenched in sweat, trembling with fear and embarrassment. It was as if Rasputin had visited her in her sleep. She sensed his presence so strongly she was sure for a moment he was still in the room; she could smell that animal scent. Had he been there in spirit form, like those mediums she'd met in America who claimed they could use astral projection? His eyes in the nightmare were as magnetic as in real life, and behind those eyes was a terrible need. She thought of the tales her grandmother had told about nocturnal spirits that brought nightmares: the hag-like drudes, and the demonic alps that could take any form. When she married, Houdini had laughed at such superstitions and patiently chipped away at her beliefs over the years with appeals to science and reason.

But he doesn't know everything, Bess thought.

She lay back down beside Houdini, who slept with the tranquility of the guiltless. The magician's wife closed her eyes but was afraid to sleep, lest she find herself again in that dream and it continued just as it left off. The thought of Rasputin lurking in the palace tonight, free to seduce anyone he pleased, troubled her.

The girls! Foreboding overcame Bess and she tossed off the covers.

Bess was panting from exertion when she reached the nursery door, a lantern in hand. As she reached for the doorknob, the door flew open, nearly slamming her in the face. Out bolted the children's nanny Maria Vishnyakova in a frenzy, eyes wide.

"What is it?" Bess asked, trying to keep panic out of own voice. "Did something happen to one of the girls?"

"No, not to them."

Bess saw that the young woman's blouse was torn.

"Father Grigori, he took advantage of me," Maria Vishnyakova said, bowing her head in shame.

CHAPTER NINETEEN

Crime and Punishment

"**A**re you sure?" Bess asked, aghast at the nanny's accusation against Rasputin. "Are you sure you didn't mistake his intentions?"

"Ma'am, he was inside me. It was monstrous."

"Yes, monstrous for any man to behave that way."

"No, I mean *it* was monstrous. It hurt me badly. I was a virgin before now."

"Oh," Bess said, her cheeks reddening. "That." Like a photographic slide projected on a wall, the image appeared in her mind of a mammoth appendage boring into the girl.

"I must inform the empress," the flustered victim said, starting down the hall.

Bess restrained her. "No, no wait," she said. *To go off half-cocked and to make such a vile accusation against the Tsarina's most trusted advisor...*

"Perhaps we should tell Archbishop Theophan," Maria Vishnyakova suggested.

"Yes, yes," Bess said. "He'll know how to advise us."

Taking her by the elbow, Bess led the limping girl down the hall toward the archbishop's chambers.

After the nanny repeated the story to the old cleric, he brought her under the ceiling light and peered deeply into her eyes.

"Did you lead him on in any way?" he demanded with the severity of a Spanish inquisitor. Bess had the same thought. A young, pretty girl anxious for attention could put ideas in a man's head. Even a good man.

Maria Vishnyakova shook her head. "No, Father. Never. I make sure I don't even look in his eyes."

"Should we tell the Tsarina?" Bess asked.

"No. I will speak to her first," the Archbishop said. He turned to the nanny and placed his hands on her shoulders. "My child, would you be willing to tell your story to the Tsarina? In detail."

The nanny covered her mouth with both hands. "In detail? Again?"

"You must paint a picture in such vivid detail that the Tsarina will accept your word over that of 'Our Friend,'" the clergyman explained.

She nodded grimly. "Yes, Father."

"It is settled then," he said. "I will call upon you in the morning. You must steel yourself. Cowardice now will be the undoing of both of us."

He made the sign of the cross. "Bless you, child. You may have saved Russia."

***

As Bess returned to her room, a tall figure suddenly stood in her path. Silhouetted by the lamp behind him, he looked like the Minotaur guarding his Labyrinth. *Rasputin!*

Primordial terror seized her. Still, she marched forward and confronted him, holding up her lantern. Lit from underneath, Rasputin's fearsome features were more pronounced. He looked at that moment like Lucifer in a church play.

"Is it true what Maria Vishnyakova has said? That you forced yourself on her?" she demanded.

"I cannot speak of what happened," the holy man said with an anguished expression.

"Did you deflower her?" she pressed him, raising the light before his face.

Rasputin nodded, straggling hair falling over his eyes.

"Time and again she tempted me, but in the past, I always had the strength to resist," he said. "But my will was too weak. When she offered herself to me this time, I relented. I have disgraced myself! Oh, to have surrendered to such bestial behavior not a few feet from where the little ones sleep."

He bowed his head, sobbing in grief. Bess watched him, flummoxed. The girl had seemed so genuinely distraught. But she'd seen the way women threw themselves at the mystic. Certainly, Rasputin didn't need to rape anyone.

The Siberian looked up at her beseechingly, his eyes wet and shimmering, like a chastised dog. It was difficult to doubt his sincerity. At the very least, he truly believed that the girl had given her consent. Perhaps there had been a misunderstanding.

"Can you find it in your heart to forgive me, Malchik?" he pleaded. She was surprised that the spiritual guide to the Tsarina and the circle of noblewomen would make such a request. It both flattered her and awakened her maternal instinct. Like a mother comforting a child, she put her hand to his moist cheek.

"I am sure God will forgive you," she said gently. "Didn't you tell us that only through sin do we find redemption?"

He took her hand and kissed it.

"Bless you," he cried.

***

Bess straightened Houdini's bowtie as he dressed for the stunt. She hadn't told her mate about the melodrama that had unfolded in the dead of night. When all was said and done, she had heard only accusations; nothing had been proven. While initially she'd been sympathetic toward the nanny, having had a night to consider, she now leaned toward the suspicion that the silly girl had indeed pursued Father Grigori. When the inexperienced little minx found out she had bitten off more than she could chew, she panicked and lashed out.

Bess couldn't help feeling a certain resentment toward the nanny. It irked her that such a reckless simpleton was in a position to destroy Rasputin who, for all his faults, had done so many kindnesses to so many, uplifted so many people spiritually in her presence and kept the Tsarina mentally afloat. And, although she couldn't quite bring herself to admit it, Bess also felt a tinge of jealousy that the girl had been the object of the Siberian's carnal desires.

Seven raps came on the door in such a distinct pattern, it reminded Bess of a secret signal and reinforced her growing unease with the conspiracy against the starets. Houdini answered it and Archbishop Theophan scurried in as if he were being pursued, shutting the door behind him.

"You shouldn't be here," Houdini said. "You know how dangerous it is for us to be seen together."

"I fear he knows already that we're in league," the clergyman said. "Somehow through his mental powers, his spies, or some other manner that only God and the devil can tell. I am certain he means to destroy us all. But now, of course, we may have the means to destroy him first. I have an audience with Alexandra today."

"I don't follow," Houdini said.

"Mrs. Houdini has not explained the situation to you?"

Houdini turned to his wife and put an arm around her waist.

"Of course she has. Bess doesn't keep any secrets from me. Right Bess?"

Theophan looked at the clock over the fireplace.

"I must go to the Tsarina," he said nervously, reminding Houdini of the White Rabbit in *Alice in Wonderland*.

"Well, good luck," the magician said, extending his hand.

Archbishop Theophan shook it and then made the sign of the cross.

"If I fail, may the Lord protect you," he said.

As soon as the door closed, Houdini turned to Bess.

"Well, I'm all ears. What was that all about?"

Bess waved him away. "It was nothing."

"That's funny, because Theophan suggested it was everything."

"It's something that the children's nanny said. About Father Grigori. Something she claimed happened in the nursery."

Her husband stiffened. "The girls? Why, if that beast laid a finger on one of those innocent—"

"Of course not. He's not a monster, darling. A womanizer, yes, I'll give you that. No, she said that he interfered with her."

"Interfered with her?"

She gestured to her blouse. "He tore her blouse here."

Houdini's shoulders slumped. "So he's a masher," he said disappointedly. "That comes as no surprise."

Bess couldn't lie directly to her husband. "And she claims they had relations. The whole act."

Houdini narrowed his eyes.

She forced herself to continue. "Against her will."

"And you don't believe her?"

"I don't know what to believe. There are girls who make up stories, you know that. For attention. Or some other motive. And Father Grigori has many enemies. Someone could have put the idea in her silly head, paid her even."

Houdini studied his wife's face. He said slowly, "You don't have to call him Father, you know. He's not your priest."

"What are you getting sore for?"

"I'm not sore. It just sounds like you're taking his side."

Bess stepped forward and placed a hand on her husband's chest.

"You haven't seen the power he has over women," she said. "The Little Ladies have to bat off all the aristocratic women who flock to his apartment—who line up for their chance to spend a second in his presence. It's ridiculous to think he'd have to force himself on a girl."

Houdini sat on the bed and mulled that over.

"You're right. That is, everything you just said will *sound* right to Alexandra." He slipped on his wingtip shoes, and the master of knots tied them fast enough to set a world record. "Suddenly, I have the idea the Archbishop better not set foot in the Tsarina's boudoir. Come on!"

As they reached the Tsarina's private quarters, Houdini's heart sank to see Rasputin stride out energetically. If he'd been sent packing like his predecessor Monsieur Philippe, he showed no sign of it.

"I trust you slept well, Mr. Houdini," the mystic said, bowing in greeting.

"I slept like a baby," Houdini replied. "A clear conscience will do that for you. I hear you had a busy night."

Rasputin flashed his teeth in what was half smile, half the look of a predator about to lunge.

"I look forward to your performance this afternoon," he said. "I am sure this will be a day that the people of St. Petersburg will long remember."

A threat delivered as gently as a girls' softball pitch, Houdini thought. Rasputin took Bess's hand and kissed it. The sight of those thick, sensuous lips slobbering over his wife's fingers made the magician want to start throwing punches.

"A moment of your company is always a pleasure," the starets said. It was the sort of courtly gesture an English gentleman might make, Houdini thought, but this was no gentleman. Bess stared at the mystic for a beat, then pulled her hand away.

"Father," she said, bowing reverently.

"I will see you at the prayer circle tomorrow?"

"Of course."

"The Tsarina is just finishing with the Archbishop now," Rasputin said with a pleasant smile. "I think it will be quick."

When the towering figure disappeared around a corner, Houdini said, "I wouldn't mind shoving that joker's cross down his throat. His next stop ought to be prison where he can share a cell with other rapists and murderers."

"A fine thing to say on Sunday morning!" Bess admonished him. "You said you didn't believe her."

"Wrong, I said that Alexandra might not believe her. Me, I'd send my daughter on a date with Jack the Ripper before I'd trust her around that—"

"We happen not to have a daughter, if you haven't noticed," she snapped with equal vehemence and crossed her arms.

"Now who's sore?" he said, stepping closer. "What's that got to do with the price of tea in China?"

The door swung open and Archbishop Theophan emerged next. He was ghostly white and walked shakily, as if he'd aged ten years during the audience.

"She did not credit the girl's account," he informed them. "And she raked me over the coals for bringing such a 'foul accusation' against the Imperial Family's most trusted advisor."

"I could have told you that," Houdini said.

"Why didn't you?" the Archbishop cried bitterly. "I have ruined myself. I am to resign from my position and to report to a monastery in the hinterlands. A lifetime post."

Houdini glanced at his wife, then back at Theophan. "I figured you know the Tsarina better than I do."

"And what about the nanny?" Bess asked.

"Maria Vishnyakova's fate has not been decided, but the Tsarina hinted that she might be imprisoned for 'slandering' Rasputin," the deposed church leader replied.

The injustice struck Bess so hard her knees almost buckled. Although she'd done everything in her power to help the young woman, a gust of guilt swept through her.

"Let me speak with Alexandra," Bess said and rushed into the room.

"I am to be off the grounds in half an hour or be escorted by armed guards," Theophan told Houdini. "Like a traitor. A heretic who dared to insult her deity. And that poor girl ..."

"I'll walk you to the door," Houdini said. "If anyone can talk the empress out of it, it's Bess."

***

"Lies, lies, lies!" Alexandra screamed, pacing furiously about her mauve refuge. "An impudent tart like that daring to besmirch a man of God and that old fool spreading her calumny. An attack on Our Friend is an attack on the Throne."

"You are quite right, Your Imperial Majesty," Bess said, trying to keep up with the Tsarina. "I think, though, you should show mercy to the girl, even if she's a fool."

"She deserves to be whipped, publicly, like a village whore," Alexandra said. "Father Grigori is so right when he says the peasant ways are more righteous than our 'civilized' ways, with our anemic justice."

"Yes, but ... Christ says we should forgive sinners," Bess pointed out diplomatically. "And Father Grigori says the same thing. It is only by great sin and repentance that we can be purified. This girl fell from grace by seducing Father Grigori, but surely she can redeem herself."

The Tsarina's face softened. She took her American friend's hand.

"You are quite right. Oh, your simplicity, how you see through the fog of deceit and intrigue. I wish there was one of the courtiers here I could trust as I trust you, besides dear Anna of course." She sat on the divan and drew Bess down beside her. "If she recants and begs for forgiveness, she will be sent to a nunnery where she can spend the rest of her days doing penance," the Tsarina decided.

Bess breathed a sigh of relief. *A steep sentence for badmouthing a man of the cloth, but better than jail!*

Alexandra smiled and changed the subject. "Are you worried about your husband? His feat this morning sounds so hazardous."

"He is absolutely confident, and I am absolutely confident in him."

The Tsarina nodded. "And he will have Father Grigori beside him. That is what gives me faith."

"Yes, we know how powerful his prayers are."

The empress put her hands together and closed her eyes. "Praise be unto the Most High for bringing Our Friend into our lives. Amen!"

Not sure what to do, Bess clasped her hands and echoed her. "Amen!"

Alexandra turned to her, her anger abated like a storm passed. "Have you spoken with Father Grigori about your ... problem?"

"I beg your pardon, Your Majesty?"

"It's not too difficult to see that your soul is troubled. It is that you are childless, isn't it?"

Bess looked away. It was not a subject she broached with anyone other than her husband, mother, and the handful of doctors she'd consulted.

"I ... well ..." She halted, tongue-tied.

The Tsarina placed her hands on her friend's. "Father Grigori helped me. Now I have a son, and he protects that son as an eagle looks over its chicks. Go to him and allow him to bless you. His prayers are more powerful than those of any man, more than those of any priest in any church, even the Pope in Rome."

As Houdini and Theophan walked down the corridor to the main entrance of the palace, the toppled church leader shook his head in frustration.

"I fell into Rasputin's trap," he moaned. "His cunning is beyond measure. You are in grave danger as are Stolypin and the others. One way or another, he will bring down each of you. Forget about Russia, Houdini. You must think of yourself now, and of your precious wife. Flee Russia before it is too late. And in the name of all that is holy, don't tempt fate by burying yourself alive."

Houdini was about to reply when he looked up and saw Rasputin waiting for them beside a mirror that hung on the foyer wall.

"You dared to attempt to destroy me, and yet see who is destroyed," the mystic said in a voice as harsh as acid.

"You have won today, Rasputin," Archbishop Theophan said. "But one day the Tsarina will see you for the beast you truly are."

Rasputin guffawed. "It is you who are to be exposed. Now your twisted soul, which you have been able to hide from the world, will be visible for all to see." He pointed to the mirror. "Behold, villain!"

The cleric turned to the looking glass, then stumbled back, shielding his eyes as if from blinding light.

"Father, what's wrong?" Houdini said, grabbing Theophan's arm and turning the older man to face him.

Theophan removed his hand from his face for Houdini to see. One side looked normal, the other twisted into a grimace as if by palsy. The fallen clergyman recoiled in horror from his own image and stumbled out of the palace.

CHAPTER TWENTY

Buried Alive

That afternoon, a crowd numbering in the thousands gathered in a field near the Fontanka River, not far from where Boris had perished, to watch Houdini's feat. For weeks, he had been performing only privately for the Tsar, with a handful of additional shows for aristocratic guests. This was to be his first public exhibition—and his last, if some pessimists were correct. His assistant Franz and a second assistant, with the help of six muscular hirelings, had dug a hole six feet deep in a snow-filled ravine, the depth of which might have easily been another four. Prepping the spot had taken two days.

A coffin decorated with a large HH on the lid sat beside the hole, with ropes and pulleys in place to lower it on Franz's signal.

"Boss, suppose you tell me what's going on?" Franz whispered to Houdini.

"We're about to knock the socks off fifteen hundred Russians, that's what."

"All this cloak and dagger stuff, ducking out at all hours of the night?"

"I'll handle the cloaks and daggers," Houdini replied, clapping him on the back. "You keep coming up with tricks to keep the kids busy—and for Pete's sake, try to make sure nothing goes screwy today."

Franz sighed and returned to supervising the crew. Bess fussed over her husband, using a brush to put his bushy hair in place for the herd of photographers and reporters documenting the exploit.

"Quickly as you can, darling," she cautioned him. "No stalling for dramatic effect."

"Okay, okay, I won't stop for donuts on the way up."

"Ha!" she snorted. "You should be a comedian, not an escape artist."

"Sweetie, you know Franz and I have timed this exactly."

A familiar voice came from close by, declaring, "There's my star!"

The couple turned to see the writer Illya Volkov arriving with two companions in tow. One carried a motion picture camera, and a young assistant toted a tripod.

"I still have the camera for a week," he said. "I pawned my favorite books for the money to rent it, and I'm going to make sure I put it to good use."

"How is your movie project coming along?" asked Houdini. "I haven't seen hide or hair of you lately. You've missed some swell adventures."

"The scene's been filmed and developed," the writer—and budding film director—informed him proudly. "It's being edited now and I will soon screen it for the Tsar. Along with footage of your miraculous escape from the jaws of death, of course."

"At least one person has faith in me," Houdini said. "But you better set up quick. The fun begins in ten minutes."

Nearby, in chairs brought out for the occasion, sat the Imperial Family. Count Vladimir Fredericks, standing beside the Tsar, gave the escape artist an encouraging wave. Rasputin hovered over Alexandra's shoulder, while chatting with his English cohort Robert Donatson.

Prince Felix Yusupov, in a fine fox coat and hat, approached and pointed to Houdini's tuxedo.

"A very sharp burial suit," he remarked.

"I plan to get a lot of use out of it," Houdini retorted. "If this act goes over well, I have a lot of other places lined up to be buried. Under sand, wrapped up like a mummy maybe."

"How optimistic to plot out a sequel when the success of the original is still in doubt."

"That's me, an eternal optimist."

Houdini and Bess walked over to the royal party. Donatson tipped his hat to Bess, then extended his hand to her husband.

"Good luck, old boy."

"You're betting against me," Houdini reminded him.

"Well, on one side are my financial interests, and on the other side is my natural human sympathy for a man who's about to do something very brave and very stupid."

Houdini smiled and shook the Englishman's hand.

"Just remember to spell Houdini correctly on your check." The escape artist had made some quiet inquiries about Donatson, and he wasn't surprised to learn he was suspected of involvement in everything from diamond smuggling to blackmail. Yet, there was no denying the fellow had a certain roguish charm.

Rasputin stood beside Alexandra, holding her hand. She was trembling slightly, and Bess could tell it was more from jitters than the cold. The children sat behind them and hopped up excitedly as the American couple neared.

"Good luck, Mr. Houdini!" Tatiana, Olga and Maria shouted.

"He doesn't *need* luck," Alexei corrected them with a righteous air. "He is Houdini." Anastasia ran forward and hugged the magician's waist.

"He needs prayers then," she said. "If you die in that grave, I want to be buried in it too."

Alexandra restrained her youngest daughter, pulling her back to her seat.

"Mr. Houdini needs the prayers of only one person," the Tsarina reminded her. She signaled Rasputin.

The spiritual advisor of the Imperial Family raised his right hand to deliver a blessing, with the grandeur that the Archbishop of Canterbury would display in coronating a new King of England.

"Oh Lord, please overlook the vanity of this man," he began. "Let me be a conduit for your power and—"

Houdini snagged the mystic's wrist in midair.

"I'll take my chances without your blessing, if you don't mind," he said civilly, but with steel.

"Darling, no," Bess protested, her eyes widening in alarm. "What could be the harm?"

The emperor stood. "Mr. Houdini, the agreement was that you would only be allowed to attempt this perilous act with the spiritual help of Our Friend," he objected.

"I don't want this to be too easy," Houdini replied. "Why, with Rasputin helping out, the village idiot could get out of that coffin, isn't that right, Father Grigori?" He stepped closer to the starets and looked boldly in his eyes.

"In fact," Houdini said loudly enough for all close by to hear, "why don't you use all your power to try and *stop* me? And we'll see whose mojo packs more wallop."

"I forbid this," Alexandra declared shrilly.

"It is all right, Mama," Rasputin said, placing a hand on her shoulder. "This will be an opportunity for our visitor to learn humility and for the children to see what becomes of those who defy God."

Houdini stepped forward and said in a low voice only Rasputin could hear, "God? Last time I checked, you were angling for Antichrist." He dug into his pocket and drew out an object. "By the way, I believe this belongs to you."

The mystic looked at what the magician held in his open hand: the ancient figurine of the horned creature.

"I have no idea what such a thing is," Rasputin said, taking it hastily and thrusting it in a pocket. "But I thank you for the curious memento."

"You'll have more to remember me by soon."

Rasputin adopted a doleful expression and it seemed that tears might spring forth any moment. His searchlight eyes bored into Houdini.

"Your pride is your undoing, Ehrich Weiss. You think you are clever, but the truth is that you do not know up from down."

Rasputin's use of Houdini's birth name startled the stage performer. Yet he knew this was no proof of psychic ability. To have some stooge dig up that nugget of trivia wouldn't take much effort.

"So, your will against my body?" Houdini said. "I'll accept that challenge any day of the week." He turned to his assistant. "Franz, let's get this show on the road!"

As the hushed crowd looked on, Houdini called forth the most respected locksmith in the city, one Anatoly Gorokhov. Withdrawing a pair of shiny handcuffs from his coat pocket, Gorokhov stepped forward.

"Are those the handcuffs you showed me in your shop last week?" Houdini asked, projecting his voice as far as he could. The locksmith turned to the onlookers.

"These are the newest and finest handcuffs imported from America, recently invented by Mr. George Carney and employing the revolutionary new swing cuff design," Gorokhov announced. "No man has ever escaped from them. At Mr. Houdini's request, I will now throw the only key into the river."

The audience watched as the locksmith hurled the key into the water fifty feet away.

Houdini had suggested to Gorokhov that, for dramatic effect, the locksmith swallow the key in full view of the audience, but the Russian had politely declined. Gorokhov cuffed Houdini and then Franz attached leg irons to his ankles.

"Count Vladimir Fredericks, would you kindly inspect them and make sure they are quite secure?" Houdini asked. The old man's face looked as if half the blood had been drained from it and he seemed unsteady on his feet.

"Are you absolutely certain?" Count Vladimir asked in a low voice as he inspected the leg irons.

"I'm certain of one thing," Houdini replied. "If I fail, you must promise to get Bess out of Russia immediately."

"You have my word." The Count placed his hand on his shoulder. "Good luck, my boy."

Franz whistled through two fingers and a pair of the hired hands hoisted Houdini into the air. As gently as they could, they rested him in the coffin. Bess rushed over.

"I love you, you fool," she blurted out. "With all my soul and body."

"You'll prove the body part an hour from now," he replied with a wink. Franz closed the bottom portion of the lid.

"Father Grigori, care to do the honors?" Houdini called to the psychic.

The starets stepped forward and put a large hand with its perpetually grimy nails on the coffin lid. He reiterated in a raspy whisper, "Poor soul, you truly do not know up from down."

Rasputin slammed the coffin shut with such force that Bess jumped at the sound. Alexandra heaved a deep sigh. The Tsar took her hand comfortingly, as if she were a scared child. Franz yelled to the big lugs, who then used cables and pulleys to lower the coffin into the six-foot grave. With shovels, they began to fill the hole with snow and ice, then dumped in wheelbarrows full.

Inside the coffin, Houdini heard the thump of soil and ice on the coffin lid. He had, of course, already extricated himself from the cuffs and leg irons. Armed with an encyclopedic knowledge of handcuffs, he'd recognized the recently designed American-made handcuff the instant he saw it in Gorokhov's shop. The locksmith proudly expounded on the virtues of the new model, but Houdini already knew every feature. Over the following week, he'd had Franz make a key that could jimmy the lock. As soon as the lid closed, he'd clawed behind his back beneath the velvet lining and opened a small compartment where the key was hidden. He was out of the handcuffs before the first clump of snow landed on the lid.

As soon as enough snow had accumulated to cover the coffin and shield it from the view of spectators, he popped open a hatch built on the side of the seemingly solid box. He punched through a carefully painted white piece of cardboard that passed for snow in the eyes of a casual observer above. Then he slipped out, rolling into a small side room that Franz and his second assistant had built adjacent to the grave. The space was cramped, but held enough air for Houdini to take deep breaths to fill his lungs. The magician lay there for a moment and hyperventilated, saturating his blood with oxygen. They'd calculated that tunneling up would take another ten minutes—long enough for the audience above to grow worried. Houdini extracted a spade from its hiding place and began to dig.

With the calm efficiency of a mole for whom such work was a daily chore, he scraped the snow above his head and shoveled down past his frame to the crawlspace behind him. When the tunnel was large enough, he began to wriggle through.

Houdini wondered if he was digging too fast. Despite what he had promised Bess, he didn't want to pop up from the snow prematurely. Suspense was the key to his art. It was rarely the difficulty of an escape that made it shine, it was the onlookers' fear that the performer would fail—and possibly die. Still, a promise was a promise. He raced for the surface.

Up top, the children waited patiently for Houdini to surface. Men debated how much air a coffin contained and how long it could sustain a man, as if they were doctoral candidates in physics. Bess found herself wringing her hands. The clicking of Illya's motion picture camera as the film passed through it was maddening. She asked Franz how much time had passed. He looked at his stopwatch.

"Seven minutes, Bess."

She began to tremble, and that horrible premonition of her husband suffocating in the coffin resurfaced in her mind. She felt a small hand take hers and looked down to see Anastasia beaming up at her.

"Don't be anxious, Mrs. Houdini," the child said. "You know perfectly well he can handle something so pedestrian as this."

Beneath them, Houdini began to realize something was very wrong. He'd been digging at a good pace, and yet saw no hint of daylight above him, heard no chattering voices. His hands were growing numb and the ice gnawed at his skin.

For the first time in years, panic overcame him and he began to shovel faster and faster, scrambling forward. In his mind's eye, he saw Rasputin's leering face and in his mind's ear echoed the prophecy that he would not survive. He was finding it increasingly hard to breathe. He thought of people who'd been buried alive, remembering newspaper stories about authorities exhuming remains and, after opening coffins, finding the contorted bodies of those who'd been trapped inside.

But I'm out of my coffin and the open air is just a few feet away, he told himself, pushing on.

I should never have taunted Rasputin. What would have been the harm of him muttering some mumbo jumbo? For Houdini was seized by the horrifying conviction that by some evil paranormal power, the mystic was murdering him.

CHAPTER TWENTY-ONE

VAMPIR

Fear seized hold of Houdini. He could not shake the idea that his nemesis was demonic. *What was the word the Archbishop had used? Vurdalak.*

A creature of the night that could spread its evil like a contagion and had power over men, animals, storms. Could that be what Rasputin was? Houdini's mind, starved of oxygen, began to play tricks on him. He was in bed, his mother in a rocking chair beside him, relating a Hungarian folktale about such a powerful, indestructible being. But she used another word: *vampir.*

"The vampir feeds on the life force, the blood of the living. With each victim, he grows more powerful," Mama said. "In the old country, if villagers suspected that a man might rise from the grave as a vampir, they buried him upside down."

"Why?" he asked.

"So, if he escaped his coffin, he would claw his way down not up, and spend centuries burrowing toward the center of the earth."

Those words, spoken decades ago, snapped Houdini out of the hallucination. "You will not know up from down." That was the phrase Rasputin had drummed into his brain.

259

Somehow, I got disoriented. I've been digging down!

He twisted around in the tunnel and changed direction. His tremendous lung capacity was failing him. He couldn't think anymore, but his hands continued to work, furiously tearing snow out of the way.

Up above, Bess grew increasingly frantic. "How long has it been?" she demanded.

"Thirteen minutes," Franz said dismally. "He should have surfaced by now."

"We have to get him out," the escape artist's wife cried. "Tell the men to pick up their shovels."

"But you know the boss, he—"

Bess snatched up one of the shovels. "Do I have to do it myself?"

Franz relented, taking the shovel from her. He was about to give the order when Alexei cried out, "Look, his fingers!"

Bess turned and saw three fingers breaking the snow, the tips frighteningly blue. Houdini's wedding ring glinted in the sunlight.

"Franz!" she shrieked. She and the assistants rushed to the spot. Bystanders elbowed each other out of the way to aid them in hauling the magician out of the snow. His hair, encrusted in white crystals, looked like a mad professor's, and he shivered like a newborn taking its first bath.

A deafening roar of applause as if at a football match greeted him, and the world's greatest escape artist waved to the crowd obligingly. Bess wrapped a heavy fur blanket about him.

"You gave me one hell of a fright," she said. "I told you to go easy on the dramatics." She embraced him, lending him her warmth and life.

"Three cheers for Houdini!" chanted the crowd. The Tsarina stood and the crowd piped down.

"It is Rasputin who is the miracle worker," Alexandra asserted with great dignity. "He put his blessing upon Houdini before he entered the coffin." Those close enough to hear clapped dutifully, the response far more tepid than it had been for the heroic American.

"But Father Grigori only began to speak and Mr. Houdini shut him up, Mummy," Alexei protested beside her.

"Even half a prayer from him is potent," she retorted sharply. "Now, let us all give thanks to God and Father Grigori for the salvation of our dear visitor."

Houdini, his teeth chattering, tried to summon the will to correct her. As he endeavored to make his mouth work, Count Vladimir stepped forward.

"Wait," he said. "The people have a right to know what happened."

The Tsarina stamped her foot. "The people have no rights except what we choose to bestow upon them."

Daring to defy her, the count pointed a finger at Rasputin and spoke loudly enough for all those around to hear. "With all due respect, your Imperial Majesty, Houdini did not achieve this miraculous escape with Father Grigori's help; he achieved it despite ... despite ..."

The nobleman groaned and clutched his right arm in pain. "Despite his ..."

"Curse?" Rasputin suggested.

Count Vladimir crossed his arms over his chest and sank, groaning, to his knees, then keeled over onto the snow. Houdini flung himself to one knee beside the stricken nobleman and glared up at Rasputin with undiluted hatred.

CHAPTER TWENTY-TWO

A Night at the Opera

B y the time a horse-drawn ambulance took the unconscious nobleman away, the crowd had thinned to a few dozen people. Rasputin had left with the Imperial Family, consoling Alexandra in the car and quieting the concerns of the children. Houdini stood next to Chief Dzhunkovsky.

"First Archbishop Theophan, now Count Vladimir," Houdini said under his breath.

"You think that he caused the count's heart attack? But how?" the Okhrana director asked.

"Somehow, he planted the thought of death in his mind," Houdini said, staring at the icy grave from which he'd escaped. "He played the same game with me and it almost was the end of me."

"He really is more than just a charlatan, isn't he?" Dzhunkovsky said.

"Maybe. One thing's for sure. He's on to all of us. That makes it official: he's your enemy too, Dzhunkovsky."

"I am the enemy of every criminal in Russia," the head of the secret police said through gritted teeth.

"I mean it, Dzhunkovsky. Your life is in as much danger as mine."

The Okhrana chief sighed. "It is Prime Minister Stolypin I'm worried about. He's already been the target of assassins. Scarcely a month after taking office, as he was writing at his desk, a bomb planted by revolutionaries exploded. A wall of the house collapsed and thirty-two people including visitors and servants lost their lives. The minister's daughter was badly maimed. Since then, he has had guards around him day and night."

"Double them—and put extra men on your own guard detail too," Houdini advised, picturing the gruesome scene.

"Very well, but how can I protect myself or anyone from Rasputin's mental powers?"

"He tries to get into your head, but you can stop him if you keep your guard up. He got in my mind just now, but I booted him out."

"My will is as strong as any man's," Dzhunkovsky declared. But his eyes betrayed his doubt. "Rasputin will surely make another attempt to destroy you. No one would blame you if you withdrew from this now. You are not a Russian. This is not your fight."

"It is now," Houdini replied, turning from the Fontanka River and striding toward the car where Bess sat waiting.

***

When they reached the palace, Houdini ushered Bess into their room and slammed the door behind them.

"Bess, you've made your last visit to that maniac's home," he declared. "He's after me and that means he might harm you to get to me."

She shook her head. "Father Grigori wouldn't hurt me."

"Because you're one of his Little Ladies now?"

"That's what he thinks."

"And you've outsmarted him?"

"Now you're catching on. You're not the only one in this family with a mind and a will, you know."

Houdini punched his palm so violently that she stepped back.

"You're calling it quits on this little spy mission and that's final," the escape artist declared.

He marched into the bathroom and she hurried in after him. He took from his coat the two pocket watches, his own and Boris's, and wrapped them in a handkerchief. Then he secured them under the sink for safekeeping, using tape from the medical kit. Perhaps he was becoming paranoid, but the last thing he could afford now was some light-fingered minion of Rasputin's lifting the miniature cameras.

"I'm going to bed," he announced. "That act wiped me out."

"Wait, darling," his wife said, blocking his way. "The women say that he's preparing to take them on a trip away from the capital."

"To a gathering of the Khlysty?"

"Well, what do you think?"

He stroked his jaw. "Where?"

"That's just it, he didn't say. But Anna Vyrubova told me that he will make the announcement next week."

Uncertain now, Houdini ran both hands through his hair, as if to stimulate his grey matter.

Bess hugged him and said, "Please, darling, let me just continue until then."

He nodded reluctantly. The only way to defeat Rasputin was to complete his mission: to catch the fiend with his pants down in the middle of that ungodly ceremony.

***

Two days later, Houdini and Bess sat beside the Imperial Couple and their two eldest daughters in their box at Kiev Opera House, watching the composer Rimsky-Korsakov's most famous work, *Tsar Saltan.*

The party had traveled to Kiev on the Imperial Train, a mini-palace on wheels. Among its extraordinary features: a dining table that could seat twenty; a mahogany-paneled, lushly carpeted lounge car; and luxurious tubs designed so that water would not slosh out even when the train rounded a bend. Maria, Anastasia and Alexei had been left behind, for their parents knew they would squirm far too much during the performance.

Prime Minister Stolypin, sitting beside other dignitaries, occupied an orchestra seat below them. A small army of policemen surrounded the building and guarded the doors. No assassins could reach the Imperial Family or the Prime Minister unless they, too, came as an army. Yet Houdini kept looking about nervously with his opera glasses at the exits; the boxes on the other side of the theater; the aisles whenever a patron rose to visit the restroom. His eyes scanned everywhere but the stage.

"Do they need to put a girl in a tutu on stage to get your attention?" Bess whispered to him.

"Knock it off," he whispered back.

The production was spectacular, featuring the greatest voices the Houdinis had ever heard, augmented by sound effects such as thunderclaps, hoofbeats and cannon fire. Unseen machines moved castle walls and mountain peaks, simulated storm clouds and ocean waves. Under normal circumstances, Houdini would have puzzled out how the ingenious mechanisms worked, but his mind was elsewhere. Where would Rasputin take his disciples? Russia was the biggest country in the world and the mystic's secret Khlysty temple could be anywhere in it.

During the second intermission, Tsar Nicholas leaned over to Houdini.

"I see that with no pretty ballerinas, it is hard to hold your interest," he said with a chuckle. "When we return to St. Petersburg, the entertainment may be more to your liking. Our friend Illya Volkov has produced a short film. He will present it at the palace."

Houdini was not paying attention. His eyes were on a young man in evening attire making his way up the center aisle. He was not drifting about trading quips and gossip like the others, but striding with determination, a soldier on a mission. Peering through the opera glasses, Houdini spotted the distinctive part in the middle of his hair.

Boris's killer!

Prime Minister Stolypin had risen and turned his back to the stage to chat with a portly dignitary and his wife.

"Stolypin, watch out!" Houdini shouted. But despite his having the lung capacity of a whale and practice projecting his voice in a large auditorium, he could not be heard over the hubbub. Without hesitation, the daredevil launched himself over the railing of the emperor's box.

CHAPTER TWENTY-THREE

The Automaton

As the would-be assassin marched down the aisle of the Kiev Opera House toward the Prime Minister, Houdini sailed through the air from the Imperial Family's box. He caught a side curtain and skidded down with the agility of an aerial acrobat. Treading nimbly over the backs of chairs and past startled patrons, he raced toward the intended victim.

"Stolypin! Someone stop that man!"

The Prime Minister turned in time to see the young stranger, and instantly recognized his cousin's murderer from the photo.

"You!" he snarled.

In response, the man drew a Browning revolver from his waistband and fired two shots at the official's chest. Only the closest audience members turned their heads. To the rest of the murmuring crowd, the sound was barely audible, no louder than if a pair of opera glasses had fallen.

Houdini leaped over several rows and tackled the assailant, grabbing his wrist and twisting it. Two more shots fired into the air before the magician wrested the revolver away. Glaring into the shooter's face, he saw the man's expression was blank. No triumph, no remorse.

Houdini turned to the Prime Minister, praying that despite the close range, the assassin had missed his target. But Stolypin's uniform was bloodstained, as was his hand where he clutched his chest. Stolypin slowly sank into his chair and began to unbutton his tunic.

As officers finally appeared and wrestled the assassin to the floor, Houdini hunched over his mortally wounded ally. Stolypin placed two bloody fingers on Houdini's cheek.

"You alone can stop him," he murmured. Then he gave a final gasp, and his eyes became as glazed as those of his assassin.

***

Days after the assassination, Houdini met with Dzhunkovsky at the Okhrana chief's villa on the outskirts of the city. It was a modest country estate with a now-frozen fountain on the front lawn. Light streamed into the secret police chief's study through the bay windows. *A pretty peaceful spot to discuss murder and revenge*, Houdini thought.

"Stolypin gave me this as a token of friendship," Dzhunkovsky said gloomily, toying with a sapphire ring on his right hand. "He was one of the few noble politicians I ever met."

"They're a rare breed in America too."

"Death was after him, just as Rasputin warned."

"His predictions certainly have a way of coming true, don't they?" Houdini replied with a smirk. "Have your boys dug up any proof linking Rasputin to the assassin?"

"The murderer claims to have no memory of the incident, nor of who sent him," Dzhunkovsky replied, swiveling back and forth in his rolling desk chair.

"That's convenient."

"I wouldn't believe him, save for the soulless gaze in his eyes throughout my entire interrogation."

Houdini shuddered. He'd read that a man couldn't be forced by hypnosis to commit an act that he would find repugnant in his normal state. *But what if the hypnotist convinced you that your friend's head was a nail, then put a hammer in your hand?*

"A new Prime Minister has already been chosen," Dzhunkovsky informed him. "Vladimir Kokovtsov."

"Kokovstov?" Houdini frowned. The name sounded familiar.

"You might have met him socially. A big fellow with a barrel chest and a booming voice to match."

Now Houdini recalled: the man who had made a spectacle of himself singing with the Gypsy band on Rasputin's command at The Samarkand!

"He'll be a puppet," the magician fumed, slamming his fist on Dzhunkovsky's desk.

The official nodded. "Yet another in the growing cast of marionettes whose strings that fiend controls."

Dzhunkovsky's housekeeper, a heavyset woman in her sixties with graying hair in a bun, rolled in a tray filled with pastries, a teapot and cups.

"Tea in your sugar, sir?" she asked Houdini, after filling her employer's cup.

"Four lumps please," the guest replied. She poured tea into his cup, moving with the fluidity of a machine.

"Rasputin has an array of weapons at his disposal," Dzhunkovsky said, leaning back in his chair. "Hired thugs, the blessing and support of the Tsarina, and now, there can be no doubt, hypnotized assassins. I'm beginning to fear there is no way to stop him."

"He's planning a big Khlysty ceremony," Houdini told him. "Bess is trying to find out when and where."

"Are you sure that's wise?"

"Not sure at all."

The housekeeper passed each man his cup. Houdini scrutinized her face to see if she was eavesdropping, but her face was a complete blank. Apparently, she remained oblivious to events outside the confines of the household, even if the fate of her nation hung in the balance.

"I could order the arrest of every member of his band of fanatics," Dzhunkovsky pointed out, stirring his cup furiously. "That would throw a wrench into his wicked scheme."

"Not if you want to keep your job," Houdini replied. "I'll get you proof, all right. Even the Tsarina won't be able to shield Rasputin if we present a photograph of him knee deep in some kind of Satanic orgy."

"You're right, of course," Dzhunkovsky admitted and brought the teacup to his mouth. His pinkie was extended, an incongruously effete gesture for the stalwart Russian, Houdini thought. Suddenly, with the speed of a mongoose seizing the throat of a cobra, Houdini slapped the cup out of the other man's hand.

"What the devil?" the secret police chief cried.

"Poison!" Houdini explained. "Just look at her."

Dzhunkovsky stared at his housekeeper and saw that she bore the same stupefied look as Stolypin's assassin.

"Ulyana, what's wrong with you?" he uttered in disbelief.

She said nothing, but calmly plucked the bread knife from the table and lunged at him. Like lightning, Houdini blazed to intercept her. He kicked Dzhunkovsky's chair, rolling him out of harm's way, while reaching out to snare the housekeeper's wrist. He twisted it behind her back and the knife clattered to the floor.

The housekeeper put up no further resistance.

"This woman has been in my employ for ten years," Dzhunkovsky gasped, shaking visibly. "Ulyana, why did you attack me?"

She stared blankly at him with a docile smile, as if she'd only been using the knife to butter bread.

"Don't you know who I am, Ulyana?" the Okhrana chief asked, taking her face in his hands.

"Of course I know who you are," the woman replied. "You are Ivan Federoff, who murdered my father fifty years ago."

Houdini and Dzhunkovsky looked at each other in alarm.

CHAPTER TWENTY-FOUR

The Silver Screen

The Little Ladies, gathered in Rasputin's living room, sat in a semicircle around their idol as he raged against high society.

"You are too worldly," he condemned his audience. "St. Petersburg stinks of corruption and the stench is on you. To purify yourselves, you will have to journey far from here. To the real Russia. The peasant girl who bathes nude in the river has more morality than the shameless adulteresses and vain housewives of this city."

The women looked about excitedly, like schoolchildren whose teacher had announced a class trip.

"Begin packing," their master ordered them. "And no finery. We are not putting your extravagance and vanity on display. Only humility is to be rewarded."

Bess raised her hand timidly.

"But where are we going?" she asked. The mystic's eyes sparkled with merriment.

"By week's end, I will tell you, Malchik," he said.

One piece of unhappy news put a damper on the gathering. The husband of one member, Olga Lokhtina, Rasputin's first patron in the city, had followed through on his threat to kick her out without a single ruble if she continued to worship the mystic. She expected family members to take her in, but they turned their backs on the disgraced woman. At recent meetings, she had seemed increasingly agitated and Bess had not seen her in days.

While Rasputin rested in his room, his chief disciple Anna Vyrubova filled the Little Ladies in on how to prepare for the trip, and Munya raised her hand.

"Shouldn't we find Olga Lokhtina and inform her about the retreat?" she asked.

"Under no circumstances. She is not coming with us," Anna Vyrubova told the others. "Father Grigori says that her spiritual sickness would bring disharmony to the pilgrimage. Furthermore, no one is to admit her to the premises."

The disciples mumbled anxiously, shaken by the sudden prospect that they themselves might become persona non grata at a moment's notice.

Vyrubova shushed them. Sternly, she said, "It is up to each of us to be sure that we have the spiritual purity to be worthy of being in the Father's presence."

***

Following the assassination of the Prime Minister, the Imperial Family was confined to the palace, the most opulent prison in the world. The children's usual gaiety evaporated as ennui set in. Houdini invented a battery of new tricks and games to amuse them, but even those failed to lift the glum mood.

The Tsar called everyone to the sitting room and with great jubilation—that to Houdini's ears sounded forced—announced that tonight would be a rare movie night. And not only would they see the usual films of the family at play, they would view Illya Volkov's newly-completed film.

"No one in Russia has seen it yet," Nicholas announced. "The premiere will be right here." The girls squealed in delight and Alexei bounced up and down.

That night they gathered in the palace's Mountain Hall. About thirty other aristocrats were in attendance, including the Tsar's mother Maria Fedorovna, his sister the Grand Duchess Xenia, and Prince Felix Yusupov.

Yusupov greeted the Houdinis, telling them, "I have just come from the hospital. I was visiting dear Count Vladimir, whose Maker is, it would seem, not ready to receive him."

"He's recovering then," Houdini said with a sigh of relief. Perhaps his allies weren't dropping off like the ten little Indians after all.

"In body, yes, but his mind not so, I'm afraid. He's addled, as if he'd become senile overnight."

"How awful," Bess exclaimed.

Houdini shuddered inwardly, unnerved by the notion that a person's wits could suddenly evaporate.

"He'll return to his post soon, I imagine," Yusupov rattled on. "He's a fixture here and the Tsar wouldn't think of replacing him. However, I'm certain that one secretary or another will take over many of his duties."

"Perhaps it would have been better if he'd died," Houdini muttered.

"Now, there's a cheery thought," Yusupov said. A footman signaled that the lights were about to dim.

Houdini and Bess took their seats beside Illya. Houdini had seen plenty of movies. Nickelodeons were all the rage in Manhattan. For a nickel, audiences sat on hard wooden chairs in the cramped theaters, gawking at a collection of ten to fifteen short films that ran continuously. The subjects ranged widely, from the view from moving trains to boxing championships, to comic vignettes.

Houdini was especially fascinated by the film pioneer Georges Méliès, who used trick photography in *The Conjuring of a Woman at the House of Robert Houdin*. The short was about Jean-Eugène Robert-Houdin, a nineteenth-century French magician whom Houdini idolized—so much so that the American paid homage when concocting his stage name. Lately, producers had undertaken more ambitious projects, such as the costume drama *Les Misérables* and a sixty-nine-minute epic, *Dante's Inferno*.

Despite his familiarity with the medium, Houdini could not escape being mesmerized by the flickering images that appeared on the twelve-foot screen. The vignettes featured the Imperial Family enjoying moments of domestic tranquility: roller-skating on the deck of the royal yacht, picnicking, riding bicycles, playing tennis. At one point, the younger children rode the Tsar's back as he romped around on all fours.

That could be any father in the world, Houdini thought.

Beside him, Illya whispered, "There is someone who might be able to help you." He placed in Houdini's hand a small piece of paper. "Here is the address."

With Houdini's co-conspirators dropping like flies, he was certainly ready for reinforcements.

"I'll see you there at noon," he said. "I promised Anastasia I'd teach her how to pick a lock."

"I don't expect to be there," Illya replied with a wry smile.

"Why not?"

"You'll see in a few moments."

Following the home movies, the projectionist screened footage of the magician's escape from the icy grave. Unlike previous occasions, when Houdini's ego ballooned at the sight of his escapes on the silver screen, a chill ran up the magician's spine as he watched the coffin descend.

After the workmen filled the grave with snow, the camera remained fixed in place, pointed expectantly at the grave. The image on the scene remained immobile for what seemed to Houdini a vast amount of time. The irrational thought struck the magician that his cinematic self might fail to arise. The screen flashed black for a second—presumably when the camera assistant changed film reels. Then the movie continued with the camera panning over the rapt audience. The Tsar's younger children's eyes shone with excitement. Olga, Tatiana and the Imperial Couple looked on with what looked like grim certainty that the escape artist was doomed.

Houdini watched Bess wring her hands on screen. It might look melodramatic to others, but he could tell her fear was genuine. The camera swiveled to Rasputin, who stared at the ground as if willing Houdini to remain beneath it. Unexpectedly, the mystic turned and looked directly at the camera.

Beside Houdini, Bess gasped. Rasputin's gaze was so intense, you'd swear he was looking straight at her from the screen. She gripped her husband's forearm. On screen, the magician finally emerged from the snow. The audience in the screening room clapped along with the crowd in the film.

The lights came on again. As the projectionist changed reels, the Tsar stood to introduce the next segment.

"Our dear friend Illya Volkov, the poet and playwright, has created a film. He has told us nothing of the story, but from what we have seen of his plays, we can be sure it will be entertaining."

The children chattered as excitedly as chipmunks. Illya stood up.

"Film is the new medium through which the truth is told," he announced. "I believe that movies will be to the twentieth century what novels were to the nineteenth. Copies of this film have been distributed and it will be seen in every movie house in Russia. You will be the first to view it."

"We are honored," Alexandra said.

"The honor is mine, Your Imperial Majesty." Illya took his seat beside Houdini. The lights dimmed again, then the screen flickered back to life.

The opening shot was an exterior of a building. Houdini recognized it as a miniature replica of the palace, crudely made from a shoebox like something a child might do as a school project. The next shot took the viewer into a gaudily decorated room, crammed with papier-mâché busts and treasure chests brimming with fake gold. At the center of the room were two thrones. In keeping with the exterior, the set had all the sophistication of a third-grade play. On one throne, a woman wearing a tin crown perched, busily knitting a scarf that had already reached a preposterous seven feet in length.

The door flew open and a man strutted in, sporting a blatantly pasted-on mustache. He wore a crown that looked a bit too large for his head.

"The king," Alexei and Anastasia declared in unison. The Queen popped up and the couple embraced. From behind his back, the King presented her with a bouquet. His mate pecked him on the cheek, whirled and placed the flowers in a vase.

The door burst open again, and in rushed a tall man in a monk's robe with a false beard that reached to his knees. An enormous cross hung around his neck, and he made the sign of the cross.

"It's Father Grigori," the children cheered happily. Houdini's hands tightened on his chair. Illya had cast the part well. The elongated beard and exaggerated movements gave him a buffoonish quality, yet even this mere shadow of Rasputin radiated menace.

The royal couple rushed to greet the visitor. The Queen reverently kissed the holy man's right hand, while the King dropped to his knees and smothered the left with kisses. Bess heard mumbling of dismay nearby, but in the darkened room couldn't see any expressions.

The Queen turned and picked up the flowers her husband had just given her. While her back was turned, the Monk leered at her bottom, then gave it a spank. The children laughed. But Bess heard a sharp intake of breath behind her, followed by discontented murmuring.

The Queen turned, giggled coquettishly, then passed the bouquet to the Monk. He sniffed them, smiled, then drop-kicked the flowers out the window of the crude set.

Top of the line burlesque, Houdini thought. *But Illya must be off his rocker!*

The King was still slobbering over the Monk's hand, an adoring hound. The Monk yanked the hand away, then sat and pointed to his right boot. The King pulled the boot off and kissed his foot. The Monk shook his head and took from his pocket a box labeled "shoe polish" in big, black Cyrillic letters.

He sat on the throne and pointed imperiously to his boots, kicking the left one off too.

The King polished the boots with the fervor of a schoolboy desperate to please his headmaster. The mumbling of the small audience gave way to graveyard silence. The Monk hopped off the throne, looped an arm around the Queen's waist and began to lead her off. The King appeared oblivious at first, then started to rise in protest. The Monk stopped him with a broad hand covering his face. For a moment, the monarch swung his arms in the air comically as the Monk chatted with the blushing, giggling Queen.

The Monk finally released the King, allowing him to flop to the floor, then he led his prize behind a black curtain at the back of the set.

In the real world, the lights burst on and the Tsar was on his feet, face purple with rage. The Tsarina had fainted.

"Olga, take the children to their room!" he roared. For the first time since the Houdinis met him, he sounded like a man with the power to sentence other men to death.

"But Father, it's so funny," Alexei complained.

"It's not over," Anastasia said, pointing to the screen.

"It most certainly is."

The projector had been switched off. As the film sputtered out, an image, rendered ghostly grey by the brightness of the room, was faintly visible: stockings, a crown and a wig flying from behind the curtain. Olga grabbed Alexei's hand and dragged off the protesting child as the rest of the brood hurried after her. The Tsar pointed at Illya, who sat with his hands on his knees, bracing for the inevitable.

"Commandant Dedyulin, put that man in irons," Nicholas commanded, his voice trembling with fury. "Have anyone who was involved in the making of that abomination arrested."

The head of palace security obeyed, and within seconds, officers seized the poet, playwright, film auteur and now enemy of the realm.

"You cannot silence the people," Illya shouted, thrashing about in the guards' grasp. "The film is being shown all across Russia, in coffee houses and taverns and cellars."

"See that every copy is hunted down and destroyed," Nicholas thundered. He fell into his seat, exhausted by the rare expression of rage. Alexandra leaned back in her chair, moaning, as her lady-in-waiting Anna Vyrubova frantically fanned her.

"Alix, I swear to you that traitor will never see the sun again," the Tsar said emphatically.

"How dreadful," Bess whispered to Houdini. "To put on such an obscene spectacle in front of the children. I hope they jail him for twenty years."

"The obscenity is that this sewer rat Rasputin has got his teeth in the Imperial Family and no one can shake him loose," her husband replied, watching his friend being dragged from the room.

"You don't honestly believe that Rasputin has slept with the Tsarina, do you?" Bess demanded. "She's the most pious woman I've ever met."

"If he hasn't taken her body, he's taken her mind. Which is worse?"

CHAPTER TWENTY-FIVE

The Inner Sanctum

The next morning found the palace mired in a malaise even deeper than it had sunk after the Prime Minister's assassination. Alexandra became suspicious of everyone save "Our Friend," and possessed by a general fearfulness. She found every excuse to keep little Alexei by her side. Among the girls, only Anastasia maintained an avid interest in magic, and she lingered to learn more handcuff escapes after her older siblings drifted off one by one. When the time came for her mathematics lesson, Houdini stopped her before she left.

"I have a present for you," he told the Tsar's youngest daughter.

"Is it ...?"

He withdrew from his pocket a small, flat leather case and passed it to her. Anastasia beamed when she saw the tiny sharp pieces of metal within.

"My very own lock picks?"

He tousled her hair and grinned.

"Every princess should have one," Houdini said.

Shortly afterward, Houdini and Bess parted company following a long goodbye kiss. She was off to what she pinkie-swore would be her last trip to a gathering of the Little Ladies, he off to seek the mysterious source of help offered by Illya. When she arrived at Rasputin's home, the mystic was already holding court in the parlor, in the midst of his adoring disciples. Rasputin was in high spirits. Instead of the usual drab attire he wore at the prayer circle, he was decked out in a lilac silk shirt with a crimson waistband and striped English trousers.

"You are cheerful this morning, Father," Bess remarked.

"I am always cheerful before a pilgrimage. Tomorrow we embark on our spiritual journey."

"Tomorrow?" Bess squeaked.

Rasputin looked at her like a doctor about to announce a diagnosis of incurable cancer.

"You are not ready," he informed Bess.

"It's just I need to make some arrangements with my husband," she explained, flustered.

"No, I do not think you are ready to be initiated," he said in a sterner tone. "You are too uncertain. Not sure whether to stride toward the light or to stay in the bleak marsh with the masses of the spiritually ignorant."

He showed his back to her. Bess slipped around in front of him, barely staving off an urge to drop to her knees.

"No, I am ready," the escape artist's wife pleaded frantically. The thought of being left behind filled her with a sudden dread. The master stepped close to her, feral power emanating from his eyes. Rasputin took her hands and drew them to his lips.

"Yes, I believe you are," he said. "Come with me to my room. We will pray on this."

She looked at the other women, who buried their faces in their prayer books. Only the former nun Akilina looked up.

She smiled knowingly at the novice and gave a nod of encouragement. Rasputin led Bess by the hand to his bedroom. She felt her throat becoming dry as they crossed the threshold and entered the inner sanctum.

Rasputin's bedroom looked nothing like a monastic cell, nor was it an opulent bachelor's den. For such a larger-than-life character, it was surprisingly prosaic, looking like any one of a thousand suites across St. Petersburg. In the corner close to the wall lay in wait a narrow bed with a red fox bedspread, a present from Anna Vyrubova. In the opposite corner, lamps burned before a small statue of a boy, an icon of Artemius of Verkola, the sixteenth-century child saint whose corpse allegedly showed no sign of decay.

Portraits of Nicholas and Alexandra hung on the walls along with crude engravings of biblical scenes, handmade by peasants who'd made the pilgrimage to the holy man. Other items donated by the Little Ladies littered the room, holding places of honor to varying degrees, from the doorway to the night table inches from where the master slept. Displayed at the center of Rasputin's desk was a large, gold-plated pocket watch with the state coat of arms. It was, Bess surmised, a gift from Tsar Nicholas II himself.

Rasputin sat down. Still gripping her hand, he pulled the magician's wife close to him, her legs between his knees. He addressed her in the soothing voice of a father confessor.

"Are you truly happy in your marriage?"

"Yes, of course I am."

"And yet, he has not given you a child. He makes love to you regularly?"

She blushed. "Yes. It's not for lack of trying."

Rasputin nodded sympathetically. "Then it is something else. Have you not prayed to our Lord to make you fertile?"

"Yes, Father Grigori."

He stroked his beard like Solomon weighing the fair division of an infant.

"The problem is that you have not shown enough faith," he decided. "Your husband is not a believer in Our Lord Jesus Christ. He does not believe in miracles."

"You know that he is Jewish," Bess protested. She pulled away from him gently, but he held her in place.

"Mr. Houdini is more than that," Rasputin said. "He is a skeptic and will go so to his grave. So, the burden rests upon you. It will take all your faith, and complete purity of soul."

Bess bowed her head. *Whose soul is completely pure?* she wondered glumly.

"You have a daughter already in your heart," Rasputin said.

How could he know that? Only she and Houdini had ever spoken of their imaginary daughter.

"She is real in your heart, and she can be real in your womb," Rasputin assured her kindly. He placed his hand on her belly and she jumped a little at his touch. "Is that what you want?"

"Yes," she whispered, tears beginning to roll.

"What are you prepared to do?" he asked in a low octave, scarcely above the rumble of a tiger.

"I would do anything."

"That is not true," Rasputin disagreed, withdrawing his hand. "You will go only so far, and then fear stops you at the very brink. Perhaps you do not truly want to be healed?"

"I do, I do!" Bess insisted with the desperation of a death row inmate begging for a reprieve. He smiled beneficently and took her small hand again.

"You must sin, sin greatly, and then seek the Lord's forgiveness. Only a vessel that has been cleansed can receive His miracles."

"I understand."

"Do you?" asked the master of minds, drawing her into his lap.

***

A stocky man leaned up against a lamppost across from the flat to which Illya had dispatched Houdini, casually reading a newspaper and enjoying a smoke. Thanks to the number of cigarette butts around the man's feet, Houdini pegged him as a lookout immediately. The American almost turned around there and then, but curiosity got the better of him. He mounted the stairs of the grungy tenement, excusing himself as he passed an elderly couple for whom the ascent was like scaling the Alps.

He rapped on the apartment door. After a moment, it cracked open a few inches, and through the gap, Houdini could make out the pinched nose and spectacles of the poet's roommate Andropov.

"Illya said you might come, but I had my doubts," Andropov said in his reedy tenor.

"There are cats less curious than me."

Andropov stepped back and admitted the magician. The pasty-faced young man was far from alone. Eight fellows sat around the room in a semicircle, on chairs, stools and boxes, around a bald man with a goatee seated at a writing desk. A youth of about fourteen perched on the windowsill, keeping a watchful eye on the lookout below. Houdini had obviously interrupted a meeting, and it didn't take a Harvard graduate to figure out the subject. On the wall hung a large banner bearing the hammer and sickle—the symbol of the Bolsheviks.

"This is the American?" said the bald man, raising an eyebrow.

"Illya Volkov says we can trust him," Andropov told him.

"Too much is at stake," said a scrawny man in a corner. It took a moment for Houdini to place the face, then it came to him. It was Igor, the craftsman from Faberge's shop. Upon reflection, it wasn't surprising that the disgruntled worker bee had trained his stinger on the ruling class.

The leader—for that was what the bald man surely was—beckoned Houdini forward.

"Mr. Houdini, it is an honor to meet you," he said.

"And you are ...?"

"My name is Vladimir Ilyich Ulyanov, but I am known in our circle as Lenin. Volkov has told us of your campaign against Rasputin." He invited Houdini to take a seat on an unoccupied box beside his desk. "We, too, believe that is the key to changing Russia."

"So, you want to create a democracy?"

"How naïve you Americans are," Lenin replied with a dismissive laugh. "Your simplistic notion that there can be true liberty while workers remain in chains. No, we shall create a dictatorship of the proletariat."

"The proletariat?"

Lenin gestured to the rough men around him. "The common laborers. We will give them ownership of the means of production. The shirt factory shall become the property of those who sweat over sewing machines; the vast estates of the aristocrats will become the farms of those who till the soil."

"Sounds like paradise," Houdini said, although he really thought it sounded like a pipe dream. "And what does Rasputin have to do with it?"

"Whoever controls Rasputin controls the empire, as surely you must now realize. He has the power to bring it tumbling down."

"Whatever you know about Rasputin, you must tell us," Andropov interjected.

"The truth is, I don't know anything," Houdini confessed. "I've been at this for weeks and I'm not any closer to getting the goods on him. Don't you have your own spies?"

Lenin gave a smile of the superior intellect at work.

"Indeed, we have a comrade who has infiltrated Rasputin's entourage of pampered aristocrats, but our agent has thus far been unable to obtain the critical information we need. If the two of you work in concert ..."

"Who is it?" Houdini interrupted.

One of Lenin's followers, a big bruiser with a handlebar mustache and biceps the size of footballs, chortled.

"Do you hear that? He wants us to tell him who The Hummingbird is!"

His comrades laughed along. Lenin paused, opened a jar on his desk and began to leisurely apply an ointment that Houdini assumed must be some kind of baldness cure.

The Bolshevik leader said to Houdini, "Before I tell you more, I must extract from you a promise that when you find proof of Rasputin's depravity, you do not take it to the Tsar, but bring it here to me."

"Why not the Tsar?"

"Our goal is not to destroy Rasputin, but to control him," Lenin explained.

"You mean to blackmail him, then. "

Lenin's condescending smile returned. "Let us say that we might enter into an arrangement with Rasputin that guarantees him security in the current regime for as long as it lasts, and also guarantees that it will not last long."

The American rose and said, "I'm not crazy about dictatorships, whether it's the proletariat or some fellow in a tin helmet with horns. If I get my hands on a smoking gun, the last thing I'd do is turn it over to you."

What meager warmth the communist patriarch had thus far projected now evaporated. He screwed the lid of the ointment back on and wiped off the residue that was on his hands onto a scrap of paper on the desk.

"Then I am afraid I must see to it that you do not leave this room," he told Houdini and snapped his fingers.

CHAPTER TWENTY-SIX

Temptation

Two of Lenin's lackeys grabbed the magician by either arm. He struggled manfully, to no avail. The big bruiser with the handlebar mustache and bulging biceps stalked toward Houdini, his huge mallet of a fist raised. Houdini swung up both feet and booted him in the chest. The enforcer stumbled back, then charged again like an enraged silverback. Houdini braced himself for a combination of blows sure to include a jaw-shattering uppercut, but a sharp cry put brakes on the beating.

"Police!" shouted the youth sitting by the window. "I see a signal from Yermilov!"

Two of the men helped Lenin to his feet and hustled him toward the door, while others scrambled about picking up maps and papers.

"The back stairs!" the father of Russian communism cried, and he and his colleagues shot out of the apartment. They had abandoned their guest without so much as a backward glance. Houdini went to the window and saw a dozen plainclothes detectives swarming into the building.

Last thing you need now is to be mistaken for a revolutionary, he thought. As soon as the flapping coat of the last cop vanished through the front door below, Houdini slid the window open and climbed out. On cat feet, he walked along the narrow ledge, shooing pigeons out of the way as he turned a corner.

Reaching another apartment, the escape artist jimmied the window and climbed into a small room with a sewing machine and baskets of clothes. Perhaps the resident did seamstress work, Houdini thought. He eased the door open and tiptoed down a hallway. He passed another small room where a metal tub was half full of water.

A shriek startled him, and he spun to see a blonde woman in her forties emerge from a kitchen, clad in a loosely tied bathrobe and carrying a bucket. Letting the robe fly open, revealing a generous bosom and flash of yellow, she raised the bucket as if to toss the contents at him.

"It's scalding, I warn you!" she snarled. "It's just come from the stove."

"I say hot but not scalding," retorted Houdini.

Taking a new tack, the occupant of the apartment put down the bucket and hastily knotted the robe.

"Get out before my husband arrives," she said with the severity of a Temperance Society matron. "He'll bash your head in, I promise you!"

Houdini backed up, raising his hands.

"Whoa, whoa, sister. I didn't mean to scare you. I'm not some kind of—" Houdini stopped, hearing the patter of policemen's brogans on the steps. "How would you like to make ten rubles?"

"You insult me!" the lady of the house replied, crossing her arms in fury. Then she added, "To do what?"

Moments later, fists pounded the door of the apartment. Two stalwart Russian policemen, Sergeants Petrov and Koslov, stood outside, demanding entrance.

"Go away," a woman's voice came back indistinctly. "I'm indisposed."

"We are the police. Come open the door at once," Petrov shouted.

"I am in the bath, you fools!" the woman yelled louder.

Petrov nodded and broad-shouldered Koslov bashed the cheap door. It gave way easily and the officers entered, looking about the modest dwelling.

"You'd better steer clear," the housewife called out to them. The officers followed the sound of her voice to a door and pushed it open. There, sure enough, a woman sat in a metal tub full to the rim with suds.

The lady let loose an eardrum-piercing shriek, covered her chest and slid deeper into the tub, so that only her knees and head poked out of the bubbles.

"A thousand pardons, ma'am," Sgt. Koslov said, backing out.

"I regret to say we must search your apartment," Sgt. Petrov informed her.

"Be quick about it," she snapped. "Don't stand there gawking like a twelve-year-old boy; there are only two rooms besides the front room and this one."

Blushing and averting his eyes, Sgt. Petrov pushed his fellow officer out of the room, leaving the bathroom door open. They scrupulously checked behind the curtains, under the bed, in each closet and cupboard, then returned to the bathroom.

"Sorry to have troubled you," Sgt. Petrov said. He turned to go, and then, as if a light bulb had switched on over his head, he slowly faced her again.

"Wait a moment," the officer said. "Madam, I must ask you to step out of the tub."

"Do you think I've been sitting on a man?" she asked incredulously. "On which part exactly do you imagine?"

"We are just doing our duty to the emperor," the sergeant responded, red as a tomato. "We are looking for Bolsheviks."

"I know what you hope to see, lecher, and it's not my party card," she replied. She sighed, then added, "Hand me a towel."

Shielding his eyes, the officer took a towel from a rack on the wall and handed it to her with an outstretched hand. The buxom blonde clambered out, draping the towel around her.

The officer stuck a hairy arm into the water, causing bubbles to slosh over the top. He fished around for a few moments, then satisfied there were no revolutionaries holding their breath below, he lurched to his feet.

"Ten thousand pardons, ma'am," he said, tipping his hat.

"Ten thousand pardons, a million pardons. When my husband comes home, you can be sure he'll report you both," she fumed. "A pair of dirty Peeping Toms."

The shame-faced cops scrammed, closing the bathroom door—behind which Houdini stood. He waited with a finger to his lips until he heard the outer door slam.

"How did you know they wouldn't look behind the door?" the housewife marveled.

"One thing I've learned in show business is that the easiest way to distract a rube is a nice pair of melons," he replied cheerfully.

"You know, my husband really won't be back for several hours," she said, biting her lower lip.

Houdini shook his head, drew out his wallet and counted out ten rubles.

"Buy yourself something nice to greet him in."

****

"Turn around," Rasputin gently instructed his newest disciple, who sat in his lap like a trusting child. Bess rotated away from him to face the bedroom mirror. Her own reflection looked like a stranger's. Father Grigori's face seemed more familiar than her own, his expression kind and reassuring.

"I am loyal to my husband. What you are suggesting, it's not possible," she said, barely above a whisper.

"You think that the marriage is about him. Your husband is the planet and to him, you are merely a lifeless moon," the spiritual leader told her softly. "You can hardly breathe in the coldness of space." He stroked her arms sympathetically. "Yet, do you not see what you truly are? A star, burning bright. With more energy than a hundred thousand Houdinis, untapped and awaiting release?"

The fine hairs of her forearms stood on end. All of her senses were heightened, keen to his fetid breath heating the back of her neck, the goatish stench of his unwashed armpits, his unadulterated masculine energy. Her head swam as his words carried her up to dizzying spiritual heights, while at the very same time, she felt herself being overtaken by something primal and animalistic. They were suddenly spirit to spirit, ape to ape.

Through her skirts, she felt that legendary organ beneath her buttocks, and the gossip mongers had not exaggerated. It was a weapon that would obliterate you and complete you at once.

"How else are we to find forgiveness if we do not first sin and then repent?" Rasputin asked. He took hold of her right breast, with no more forewarning than a farmer would give a cow when grasping its udder. Her heart pounded and her breathing quickened.

"If God did not want us to fornicate, he would not have put lust in our hearts," the miracle worker preached. "Just as he does not begrudge a thirsty man lapping water from a river, so he does not fault a woman and man for satiating their physical desires."

"But the Holy Bible, Father ... adultery? Thou shall not ...?" she said in a voice as weak as the mew of a newborn kitten.

"Do not believe the priests," the mystic said, his eyes meeting hers in the mirror. "They prattle endlessly about sin. But think of the wild animals. Do they fear sin? There is wisdom in their simplicity. Those fools in their pulpits preach that sin is evil, but they do not understand the great paradox, that sin is God's greatest gift. He gives us sin so that we may repent. And repentance brings joy to the soul and strength to the body. Without sin, there is no life, no joy. It is only through it that your body will be restored to health. I will teach you to sin."

"We are not animals," Bess gasped, hardly able to speak or think.

Rasputin smiled. "Of course we are."

His manhood was now at full attention, a workman's tool ready to do labor.

"Unbutton your top," he commanded her. "You desire this, as you always have deep in your heart. You want to know what it is like to be degraded, to fall utterly from grace and surrender to your most base desires."

Bess did as she was instructed. She watched herself in the mirror as her breasts became exposed. She appraised them as if they were another woman's. They were small, but well-shaped and delicately beautiful, she thought. Rasputin's reflection loomed above hers now, a satyr's face. The savage leer frightened her for a moment.

"Please," she moaned. Then their eyes locked again and she was lost. She was powerless to resist him, physically unable to move. He placed his hands, with their dirty nails, on her waist.

"Hike up your skirts," the mystic commanded her. As she obeyed, she saw the stockinged legs of the ghostly woman in the mirror appear.

Rasputin whispered in her ear, "You fear that I am polluting you, but I am not. I am purifying you."

***

When the cab dropped off Houdini at the palace, he mounted the steps, musing about the tangled web into which he'd blundered. Now, in addition to Rasputin's legion of automatons, etcetera, he had these ruthless communist revolutionaries to contend with. Plus, he had to factor into the equation the revelation that a Bolshevik spy lurked amidst Rasputin's ranks. He was glad that this was his wife's last day in the cult leader's den.

As he mounted the palace steps, a horn beeped behind him. He whirled to see an automobile roll to a stop: an ostentatious, canary-yellow Rolls Royce Silver Shadow. The chauffeur was a young fellow with a head of thick, luxuriant hair the color of midnight and a natty mustache. His passenger was the ballerina Natasha Stepanova, the magician's one-time steam room companion. She wore a Parisian dress that matched the color of her car and a broad hat festooned with peacock feathers, tilted rakishly to one side. Wearing a sunny smile, the dancer waved him toward her with a handkerchief. Sighing, Houdini trotted down the stairs.

"I almost didn't recognize you with clothes on," he said. "You have a hell of a nerve showing up here at the palace. If it were up to me, you'd be tied to a horse like one of those backwoods harlots and hauled off. Better yet, four of them, in different directions."

"If you continue to insult me, I won't give you some valuable information," she said, adjusting her hat nonchalantly.

Houdini folded his arms across his chest. "As if I'd believe a single syllable coming out of those scarlet lips of yours."

"It concerns your wife."

He grabbed the car door and leaned in the window. "Bess? Is she in trouble? That's nothing to joke about."

Natasha smirked. "She might be 'in trouble' soon. Rasputin has taken her into his bedroom."

He raised his hand to slap her. She didn't cower; he realized a girl like that had probably taken her share of smacks.

"Why are you telling me?" he demanded.

The vixen smiled. "Now you are in my debt."

He turned and started up the steps two at a time.

"Where are you going?" Natasha called to him.

"To call for my driver."

"Don't be a silly goose; there isn't time for that." She patted the seat next to her. He had to admit she was right. By the time he got to a phone and called the chauffeur, and the guy brought the car around, precious minutes would have flown by. Houdini scowled and hopped into the back seat beside her.

"Step on it, pal," he shouted to the driver.

Tires screeched as the car did a 360-degree turn and made for the palace gates. He eyed Natasha warily, maintaining a safe distance from her on the seat.

"You don't have to sit all the way over there," she said. "I'm not going to bite you."

"That's what Dracula's daughter said."

The car, with its six-cylinder, fifty-horsepower engine, made the fourteen-mile trek to St. Petersburg with astonishing speed. It roared through the streets, weaving between cars, horse-drawn carriages and peddlers' wagons. The chauffeur pounded the horn repeatedly, scattering pedestrians.

"I hope you appreciate that Joseph here is putting my new car at serious risk of dents," Natasha remarked lightly, holding her hat in place. Her eyes shone with excitement; she clearly relished the thrilling race against time.

"If we ding it, tell whichever big shot gave it to you it was for a good cause," Houdini snapped.

Before the car had even fully stopped outside Rasputin's apartment building, Houdini sprang out. He gave Natasha no backward glance, and left the door hanging open.

"You're quite welcome," she called to the magician as he dashed past the procession of pilgrims and into the courtyard.

Houdini bolted to the front door where a pair of toughs, each over six-foot-two, stepped forward to block his way. One, with a short neck, broad shoulders and overhanging brow that made him look like a full-blooded Neanderthal, stopped Houdini in his tracks with a hand to the chest.

"Where do you think you're going, pipsqueak?"

"I'm going up to see Rasputin. It's an emergency!"

"You have to wait your turn," the modern-day caveman grunted, gesturing at the stream of petitioners stretching down the block and disappearing around the corner.

"Don't you know who I am? I'm Harry Houdini," the magician insisted.

Unimpressed, the doorman shrugged and told him, "The actress just beyond the lamppost performed before the King of Spain last year."

"I'm a guest of the Tsar!" Houdini protested.

The Neanderthal's colleague, leaner and sporting a villainous eyepatch, whispered in his ear. Whatever the news, it piqued the henchman's interest, because the Neanderthal grinned maliciously at the magician.

"Well, it seems there's been a misunderstanding. There are strict orders *not* to let you in," the under-evolved doorman said, taking obvious pleasure in the revelation.

"You don't understand. My wife's up there!" Houdini cried, grabbing the Neanderthal's lapels. The doorman slapped his hands away.

The eyepatch wearer—whom Houdini now recognized as one of Rasputin's companions at The Samarkand tavern— elbowed the Neanderthal.

"Oh, I think we do understand," he snickered. "Don't worry. After an afternoon with Rasputin, your wife will be willing do tricks a street girl wouldn't dream of. You'll owe him a box of cigars for his trouble."

"Yes," added the Neanderthal, trying to match him in wit. "He'll loosen up her morals, and other things too."

Houdini socked the doorman in the jaw, laying out the jokester flat on his back. The escape artist bashed the eyepatch wearer aside like a quarterback breaking through a defensive line. But the Neanderthal, spitting out blood, grabbed Houdini's ankle, bringing him down.

Together, the roughnecks tussled with Houdini like alligator wrestlers until they finally got him by his arms and legs. They carried him through the courtyard and tossed him unceremoniously into the street.

"Don't come back, if you know what's good for you," the Neanderthal bellowed, using his sleeve to wipe blood from his prognathous jaw.

Houdini crawled to his feet, aching all over from the manhandling. He knew he wouldn't fare any better in Round Two. Bess said there was a back entrance, he remembered.

The escape artist raced around the corner and located a narrow alley jam-packed with smashed crates, shattered vodka bottles and heaps of garbage where scuttering rodents picked at the meat clinging to chicken bones. It stank of urine and so many other unpleasant aromas, it would drive a bloodhound mad. He found the side door locked, then looked up to the third-floor window.

Houdini hopped onto the ledge of a first-story window. Then, hand over hand, he began to crawl up the side of the building, a house fly braving the web of a tarantula.

***

Rasputin stood behind Bess, whose blouse was unbuttoned to the waist, massaging her breasts with practiced fingers. Though he was much taller than her, that magnificent member pressed against her, from the small of her back to the undercurve of her backside. It throbbed with life; she imagined it coiling it around her and crushing her like a constrictor. Yet what an end that would be, breath and life slowly ceasing, the soul ascending to a higher realm.

He fiddled with her undergarments, unbuttoning and
unbowing until finally her knickers fell to her ankles. The
mystic dropped his trousers and positioned himself; his phallus
waved back and forth in the air impatiently, a devil's trident
made of flesh. He grabbed Bess's waist.

"Put your hands on the chair, Malchik," he commanded her.
"The little boy will finally become a woman."

Bess obediently bent forward at the waist and reached for
the back of the chair. Then abruptly she pulled back and
grabbed the large, callused hands at her waist.

"Wait," Houdini's wife wheezed. "Wait ... just ... one ...
moment."

"You have made me wait long enough," Rasputin growled.

Staring into the mirror, Bess now saw Rasputin's true face.
Absent was any speck of human warmth or affection, only
animal hunger. Yet she could not tear her eyes away from his.
All she could do now was wish, with what tiny spark of will
still flickered within her, that the mirror would shatter.

Break! Break! Break! Holy Mother of Mary, break!

CHAPTER TWENTY-SEVEN

Goodbye, Cruel World

G lass cascaded in all directions as Houdini leaped through the window and landed in a crouching position on Rasputin's bedroom floor.

"You filthy rat. Get your hands off her!" he screamed.

Rasputin stepped away from Bess, who hurriedly began to tug her undergarments and skirts back into place. Wild-eyed with fury, Houdini rushed the mystic. Bess, covering her bosom, interposed her body between them.

"It's my fault. Don't hurt him!"

"Get out, Bess," her husband barked.

"But—"

"I'll deal with you later. I said beat it!"

Holding her blouse in place, Bess fled the room. Rasputin had pulled up his trousers and buttoned them. While another man might have panicked when confronted by an aggrieved husband, the mystic maintained a beneficent smile and raised his hands, Christ-like.

"My brother, do not be enraged at your wife," he advised Houdini. "Woman's nature is weak. They are creatures of the flesh."

"Don't worry about her. I'm going to clobber you to death."

"Strike me, if that is what your heart tells you to do. The Lord says that when a neighbor smites us, we are to turn the other cheek."

"I've heard enough scripture from you for the day, you pig," Houdini shot back. With a right hook given bone-splintering force by rage, he punched the cross-wearing Casanova in the nose. The blow would have spun the head of an ordinary man halfway around. However, this was no ordinary man. Rasputin stood his ground, and another few jabs from the American were all it took to inflame his peasant blood. Roaring in anger, he swung one of his sledgehammer fists.

So much for that hokum about turning the other cheek, Houdini thought.

Houdini ducked the wild haymaker and slugged his opponent in the belly. Rasputin howled in pain, then grabbed Houdini under the armpits, lifted him off the ground and tossed him like a toy across the room. The American landed on a small table, knocking it over. Houdini rolled to his feet holding the table and smashed it over Rasputin's head.

The hulking Russian stumbled back, blood running down his forehead. Then he burst forward with a flurry of punches that drove Houdini to the wall. The manipulative court psychic had left the building; this was one hundred percent pure Siberian brawler. With one mighty hand, he took Houdini by the throat and lifted him clear off the floor. Houdini pounded his enemy's chest with his fists, but the blows landed as harmlessly as fairy breath. Dangling in the air, he found it difficult to breathe as Rasputin's iron fingers began to crush his windpipe.

Rasputin's ferocious grin looked like it belonged on a man-eating tiger, not a human. As Houdini tried to shove Rasputin away, his hand brushed aside the hair that concealed the mystic's forehead, revealing a lesion that resembled a budding horn.

Maybe Brother Iliodor was right; this guy is the Devil!

In desperation, Houdini reached with both hands and grasped the jeweled cross hanging from the larger man's neck. He twisted the chain so that it tightened on Rasputin's throat. Summoning all his strength, Houdini began to garotte his opponent. At first, Rasputin did not even seem to notice and continued to throttle the magician.

For the love of Mike, doesn't this bastard need to breathe? Houdini wondered, growing faint.

But gradually, the mystic's grip on Houdini's throat weakened. Rasputin dropped his opponent and sank to his knees. Houdini kneed him in the chest, bowling him over onto his back, then sat astride Rasputin, continuing to choke him.

"Mess with my wife, will you?" he shouted. "Why I oughta choke the life right out of you, you son of a bitch." Yet, he hesitated. If ever a louse deserved to be squashed it was this louse, but he couldn't quite bring himself to finish off his opponent.

Light still burned in Rasputin's eyes. As impossible as it seemed, he spoke.

"You cannot destroy me," he rasped. It was a calm statement of fact.

"You want to bet?"

The door burst open and the Neanderthal, Eyepatch and a third gorilla tumbled into the room.

"Assassin!" Eyepatch spat and reached into his pocket.

As he drew out a revolver and pointed it at the magician, Houdini yanked off the cross, breaking the chain, and hurled it. It struck the gun, knocking it out of the henchman's hand. The weapon struck the floor and discharged, putting a bullet through the eye of the Tsar's portrait, then skittered under the bed.

Rasputin's henchmen pounced on him like hyenas, but Houdini ducked around them. There followed a frenetic melee straight out of a theatrical farce, then Houdini jumped through the shattered window. Eyepatch dropped to his belly to retrieve the gun.

The Neanderthal rushed to the window and stuck his head out, but saw no sign of the magician in the trash-strewn alley below. He heard shoes scraping the bricks above him, looked up and saw Houdini scaling the wall. The Neanderthal reached, but his hand fell a hair short of Houdini's ankle.

"He's headed for the roof," the Russian cried. Eyepatch elbowed him out of the way and took a shot at Houdini as he scrambled over the top. The bullet missed and took a chunk of mortar out of the wall.

Houdini stood on the roof, panting, as he assessed the daunting distance between Rasputin's apartment building and the next. The gap was at least fifteen feet. He glanced around, looking for some other avenue of escape. Just as he concluded there were no other options, the roof door burst open and Eyepatch and the Neanderthal charged out. The gunman fired twice at Houdini, who danced out of the path of the bullets. With no other alternative, he ran full speed toward the edge of the roof and launched himself through the air. A bullet whizzed by.

Houdini's arms swung like windmills as he sailed over the span. Far below in an alley, a pack of stray dogs waged a turf war with feral cats. The magician smacked the slanting, snow-covered roof. A bullet kicked up snow just inches from his head. Houdini then lost his footing and slid off the roof. One hand caught the ledge and he dangled by it, four stories up. Eyepatch grinned triumphantly and took careful aim.

"Let me have the gun," the Neanderthal said. "How can you gauge distance with that stupid thing over your eye?" Reluctantly, the one-eyed minion passed the revolver to the Neanderthal. The brute turned sideways and pointed the firearm as if he'd been permitted first shot in a duel, taking infinite care with his aim. He pulled the trigger and the revolver clicked, empty. He watched in frustration as the American clawed his way onto the other roof.

***

Bess sat on a bench at a small park in the shadow of a statue of Peter the Great, her tear-stained face buried in her hands, wishing he could come to life and cleave her in two with his broadsword. Whatever otherworldly trance Rasputin had placed her in was broken now; she could think clearly. But that was little consolation.

What have I done? How could I have been so weak?

It was more than just his will being stronger than hers. Part of her had wanted to surrender to Rasputin. Purified? No, she felt unclean from her fingertips—that had raked his brutish hands at the last moment—to her toes, which had curled in anticipation. She clasped her hands and held them to her forehead, eyes closed.

"God forgive me. God forgive me!" Bess prayed.

Hands pulled hers apart and yanked her to her feet. She opened her eyes to see Houdini glaring at her. She'd never seen such fury in his eyes.

"You better have more to say than prayers!" he cried. "How could you, Bess? After all we've been through? The life I've given you."

"You can't understand."

"You're right about that. And here I thought you loved me!" He threw her hands away from him.

"I do, husband, believe me," Bess said, reaching for him.

He stepped out of range. "You have an odd way of showing it."

"We agreed that I should infiltrate his group."

"Yes, not to sleep with him. For God's sake, Bess!" He turned away, not bearing to look at her. She grabbed his arm despairingly.

"You don't know what it was like. Those eyes."

"Yeah, yeah, yeah. Those big, dreamy peepers of his. You can't hypnotize someone into doing something they wouldn't do anyway."

"But I didn't, sweetheart. I didn't go through with it."

"You didn't because I got there in time to stop the pair of you," he cried, shaking his arm loose. "Otherwise you'd be one of his harem girls right now, fawning over that goat. I've had enough of you, Bess. You're either a tramp or such a moral weakling it doesn't matter. Do you have any idea how many floozies come by my dressing room after a show, batting their eyelashes? I could have my pick of the litter. But do I try any funny business? No!"

Bess lowered her head like a schoolgirl caught stealing from a teacher's purse. Houdini waved her away in disgust.

"I might as well have tied the knot with a streetwalker."

The floodgates opened and Bess bawled, not like an adult but as unrestrained as an infant. Houdini felt a rush of sympathy and instinct told him to reach out to her, but he resisted manfully. *I have willpower, unlike her.*

"I never want to lay eyes on you again!" he yelled, attracting the attention of a passing pushcart vendor.

Bess stared at him in horror, then turned and rushed off down the street, brushing past a pair of workmen carrying a large mirror.

Houdini slumped onto the bench his wife had occupied a moment before, worn emotionally—and physically too, from the exertion of climbing the building, battling Rasputin and darting across the rooftops of St. Petersburg. Could his wife of seventeen years, his sweet Bess, have really fallen for that monster? Or was she right? Did the mystic exercise some kind of abnormal power no woman could resist? He recalled being trapped under the snow, digging the wrong way. Nearly killing himself all because of that suggestion Rasputin had planted in his brain, like the egg of some hideous parasite.

Who am I kidding? If I'd been in Rasputin's bedroom and he ordered me to put a gun to my head, odds are two to one I'd have done it. He sprang to his feet and hurried off in the direction his wife had fled.

Fifteen minutes later, the escape artist stood at an intersection, befuddled, unsure of which direction to take. Looking down each street in turn, he saw nothing but bustling strangers. A seagull squawked and he turned. In the distance, Houdini saw the Fontanka Canal. Barges stacked with crates drifted along it, tugged by boats. An awful thought struck him.

She couldn't. She wouldn't. Please, God, no!

He bolted in the direction of the canal, elbowing his way past factory workers, street vendors, fishmongers and other citizens of St. Petersburg who now seemed to be deliberately blocking his way, like chess pieces placed by an unseen hand.

After nearly bowling over a child, being cursed at by two old ladies, and bumping into a brawny sailor who threatened to thrash him, Houdini reached the canal. He looked over the two-foot stone wall, expecting to see his wife's flailing hand or her red and green scarf floating by, but there was no sign of Bess.

She must be submerged!

He tore off his jacket, kicked off his shoes and hopped onto the barrier, preparing to swan dive in.

CHAPTER TWENTY-EIGHT

Kidnapped

J ust as Houdini swung his hands overhead for a headfirst dive, he heard a voice he recognized as his wife's carried on the wind, faint, distant, but unmistakable.

Bess! Thank God!

He turned to his left, and about one hundred feet away, he saw Bess speaking to a woman beside an elegant, black-and-gold carriage. The woman put her arm about Bess comfortingly and gestured to the vehicle. Bess started to climb in, then thought better and retreated. To Houdini's surprise, the tall woman grasped Bess's wrist. The magician began sprinting in stockinged feet toward them.

"Hey, hey!" he cried. The woman looked up and when she saw Houdini, she smiled. He recognized her now, even without the geisha makeup—and that iron grip clinched it. Effortlessly, she hauled Bess into the carriage behind her. Before Bess's head disappeared into the vehicle, she saw her husband charging to the rescue.

"Darling!" she screamed.

As the carriage took off, Houdini bounded from the street like a kangaroo and just barely caught the rear with both hands. The magician was dragged through the streets, cobblestones shredding his pants legs. With Herculean effort, he climbed up the back of the carriage. Gripping the roof, the escape artist worked his way around to the window and looked in.

The face of the Geisha greeted him, in thick pancake makeup and blood-red lipstick, so close he could smell her jasmine perfume. She grinned, cocking an eyebrow, then out shot a fist that would have rocked Jack Johnson back on his heels.

Houdini lost his grip on the roof of the carriage. He tumbled head over heels for several yards, hearing brakes squeal and horns blare as drivers tried to stop before squashing him. The magician rolled to his knees, his hands and forearms scraped and bleeding, clothes torn and dirty as a hobo's. He watched in dismay as the carriage vanished into the distance. Through the cloud of dust, he could make out an emblem that looked like a Y on the rear.

A brawny older man in a bloodstained butcher's apron helped Houdini to his feet.

"Are you all right?" the butcher asked.

"I'm fine. Get me to a telephone."

A tailor's shop down the street had a phone, and the proprietor was kind enough to let Houdini use it. After a switchboard operator connected him to the headquarters of the Okhrana, Houdini got Chief Dzhunkovsky on the line.

"Bess has been kidnapped," Houdini shouted into the mouthpiece, holding the horn-shaped receiver to one ear. "Right off the street near the Fontanka Canal. You've got to—"

"Slow down, Houdini," Dzhunkovsky interrupted him. "We'll send men at once. However, you must come to headquarters immediately. You're wanted for questioning."

"Me, wanted?"

"Yes, you're accused of violently assaulting Rasputin. It's not true, is it?"

"I might have known that rat would squeal, and he didn't waste a minute, did he?" Houdini said with a bitter laugh. "We mixed it up, sure, and believe me, he gave as good as he got. But that doesn't matter now. What matters is finding Bess. The carriage had some kind of symbol on the back, looked like the English letter Y. Any idea what it means?"

"Nothing that I can think of immediately. I can have an expert comb through our records of radical groups. But Houdini, you must surrender yourself."

"Not while my wife is missing," Houdini said. He slammed down the phone, then told the tailor, "I need to place one more call."

***

Shoving a footman out of the way, Houdini stormed into the mansion of the Grand Duchess Militsa, in which he'd last set foot the night of the masquerade ball. He found the older of the two Black Sisters curled up in an armchair in her sitting room, dressed in a black silk robe of oriental design. Her devotion to the occult evidently had not waned. Tarot cards were spread out on a round mahogany table before her, on which a crystal ball also rested. Kindling crackled in the fireplace beside her. A chessboard sat on a little round table nearby, a game still in progress.

Militsa smiled at the magician as though he were a party guest who'd arrived promptly.

316 |C. Michael Forsyth

"This is an unexpected pleasure, Mr. Houdini," she said, placing down a card. "You left rather abruptly your last visit."

"Where is she?"

"I'm sorry, I'm at a loss."

"That Amazon of yours. The one who was at the ball that night?"

She laughed. "Oh, her. You regret abandoning her?"

"She has my wife."

"I don't think she has much use for women."

"She's kidnapped her. I'm sure she's in cahoots with your pal Rasputin."

"And what has that to do with me?" she replied with a bored expression. "Rasputin no longer does my bidding. He's outgrown me, so he believes."

Two footmen rushed into the room, and the Grand Duchess waved them away.

"Well, surely you know who that female viper is and where I can find her," Houdini demanded.

"Perhaps, but it would be indiscreet for me to reveal this person's identity."

"Look, I've never hit a woman and I won't start now," he said in a low voice seething with menace. He picked up a poker from the fireplace. "But I sure wouldn't feel bad about smashing every Ming vase, mirror and window in this place."

The threat didn't faze Militsa, who made a steeple of her fingers and looked at him sympathetically.

"It would give me great pleasure to oblige, but you see this is more than a matter of discretion on my part," she explained. "I've given my word of honor. And this person has pledged to keep my secrets in return. To break my oath ... well, surely you're familiar with the concept of karma?"

"Yes, and you're about to see it in action." He raised the poker over the crystal ball, polished beryl set in a bronze base. "So help me God, I'll crack your toy to smithereens."

Militsa leaped up reaching for him, displaying fear for the first time.

"Don't!" she cried. "That's a Druid artifact from before the birth of Christ, the last remaining one of its kind. If you knew what I had to do to acquire it—"

"I don't care if you had to make whoopee with Nostradamus," he snarled. "Going once, going twice ..."

"You already know who it is!" she blurted out.

"What?"

She pointed to the ancient sphere. "The answer is buried in your mind," she said. "With the crystal, I can help you see it."

Houdini rolled his eyes. "I don't have time for your tomfoolery."

"If I fail, you may smash the crystal if you wish."

The magician frowned. He saw something in her eyes he'd never seen there before: an ounce of sincerity. He nodded and sat beside her. She rose and went to a cabinet, then returned with a decanter and two crystal goblets. Into each, she poured a syrupy green liquid.

"You're not expecting me to drink that, are you?" Houdini said, pushing away her hand as she offered him a glass. "What kind of dope do you think I am?"

She laughed. "So untrusting! It is only *La Fée Verte*, The Green Fairy."

"Absinthe?"

She nodded. "See, I'll sip it first." She drank from the glass. Then her tongue flickered over the rim, capturing an errant drop.

Houdini had never sampled absinthe, but he knew it was an alcoholic drink derived from grand wormwood, green anise, sweet fennel, and other herbs. Creative geniuses such as Vincent van Gogh, Edgar Allan Poe and Lord Byron indulged in the spirit and it was a favorite of Bohemians and devotees of the occult who claimed to have had extraordinary visions under its influence. However, friends of the magician who'd imbibed The Green Fairy reported, with disappointment, that such claims were exaggerated. He assumed it was a combination of intoxication and an over-active imagination that produced any hallucinations.

"You have a closed mind, Mr. Houdini," Militsa said, pushing the goblet on him again. "You must open it." He accepted the goblet and sipped stingily.

"More," she encouraged him.

"Down the hatch," he said with forced bravado, turning the goblet up and draining its contents. His hostess rose and dimmed the lights.

"Clear your mind, banish all troubling thoughts," she instructed the magician. "Gaze at the ball. You see nothing else in the room, hear nothing but my voice."

Houdini obeyed, concentrating on the dull globe. He'd seen enough charlatans who claimed expertise in crystallomancy to be highly skeptical of the process. His hope was that the want-to-be sorceress would slip up and reveal the identity of his wife's kidnapper.

"O, powers that lie beyond, we beg thee, enter this crystal," she implored with the flamboyance of a Broadway stage actress. "Let this vessel be a window through which we can see truths unknown."

The ball began to shimmer, as if lit not only by the fire but some inner source that sent sparkles reflecting off the facets within. As Houdini continued to stare, the absinthe kicked in and he felt woozy. The magician grabbed the arms of the chair for support and to keep him anchored in reality. Now a mist began to fill the ball. It swirled before his eyes and he sensed that at any moment, the mist would peel back, revealing some phantasmagoric image.

Instead, it was his sense of smell that the crystal ball ignited. He could detect the Geisha's jasmine perfume, as if she were standing right beside him. So strong was the effect that he had to fight the urge to turn and look for her. Looking away from the ancient crystal would break the delicate trance, instinct warned him. He allowed the olfactory hallucination to fully overtake him. His sense of smell heightened; he became like a dog, experiencing scents ten thousand times more acutely, suddenly aware of their subtleties and overlapping layers. Beneath the jasmine, Houdini caught a whisper of another aroma, partially washed away with soap and water perhaps, yet lingering.

That scent. He had smelled it before. But where? He shut his eyes, blotting out the world before him, so that for a moment, he existed only in a universe of smells. And then he had it.

Yusupov. Yes, that obnoxious cologne of his! The exaggerated feminine voice, the remarkable strength in the hands. Of course, the Geisha was a man! With the realization, Houdini's trance broke

"You mean that was Yusupov?" he ejaculated excitedly. "Disguised as a woman?"

Militsa smiled coyly. "If that is what the crystal revealed."

***

Jim Hercules sat behind the wheel of a puttering Russo-Balt automobile. Dressed in street clothes instead of the genie costume, he'd have fit in pretty well back in America. But here, with his black skin and tremendous bulk, he remained exotic; the John Henry of Russia. He sat up as his passenger came stumbling down the stairs of Militsa's palace and rushed to the car.

"Thanks for the lift, Hercules," Houdini said, shaking off the remnants of the stupor. "But I don't think I can ask you to go on the next leg of the journey. There'll be rough stuff."

"Like I told you on the telephone, Mr. Houdini, I'm not afraid of trouble." He produced a large pistol from his pocket. "That's why I brought this hog leg."

Houdini climbed in beside him. "All right, then. Let's get moving."

Less than a half hour later, the car pulled up in the courtyard of Yusupov's palace, a sprawling three-story building on the banks of the Moika River. At least twenty enormous columns graced the entrance.

"Lend me that pistol, Hercules," Houdini asked. The big man handed over the weapon.

"Do you want me to go in with you?" Hercules asked.

"No, wait here. If Yusupov tries to leave, grab him with those big mitts of yours. I'm going to sneak around back and find another way in."

"Are you sure, suh?"

Houdini clapped Hercules on a shoulder that lived up to the man's name.

"Just be careful. Don't mind how prissy he acts, the guy throws a mean left jab."

"Not as mean as mine, I reckon."

The estate had to be crawling with servants, Houdini realized. He made his way around the building looking for a side entrance. Within minutes, he found steps leading to a cellar. It was bolted from the inside, but it was a small task for the escape artist to defeat the lock and enter.

Houdini made his way through a dark, narrow brick corridor, pushing past spiderwebs and kicking aside an occasional rat. He recalled Yusupov's story about the forgotten torture chamber beneath his other palace in Moscow, and imagined he might run into skeletons hanging from chains like in some hokey haunted house in an amusement park. However, he saw nothing more remarkable than patches of black mold.

The magician pushed through a door leading to a cozy basement room, surprisingly well-appointed with a fireplace, couches and oriental rugs. Yet, innocuous as it appeared, something felt wrong about the room. A sense of foreboding came over him. Houdini was not one to give much credence to premonitions, but the thought struck him that something dreadful would take place here—or perhaps had already.

He climbed a stairway and tiptoed through the palace, which was every ounce as lavish as the Tsar's. Had he not been on so urgent a mission, he would have lingered to gawk as he worked his way through a maze of rooms, each more spectacular than the last. He passed through halls full of Greek and Roman statues; a magnificent private theater modeled after the Mariinsky Theater; under intricately carved arched doorways high enough to accommodate the Cyclops; and beneath painted ceilings that rivaled the Sistine Chapel, adorned with angelic beings. Everywhere gold glimmered:

fireplaces, mirrors, clocks, even wallpaper embossed with gold. It was a temple to opulence.

He dodged servants, whose voices and footsteps echoed on marble floors. Ahead he saw a staircase, and assuming it led to Yusupov's bedroom, started up the stairs. But as his foot met the first step, he felt the unmistakable pressure of a gun poking his back.

"Mr. Houdini?"

"You got me," he sighed.

"Prince Felix has been expecting you," his captor said in a calm voice. "Kindly come this way." The uniformed footman gingerly took Houdini's pistol and placed it in his pocket.

The footman marched Houdini through several hallways, then into an elegant dining room lit by a crystal chandelier. A shield hung on the wall, emblazoned with the Yusupov coat of arms, a pair of lions rampant bearing an oval enclosing a stag, a crossbow and a heroic knight. Beneath the shield, crossed swords were mounted.

Fresh flowers adorned the table and at its head sat Yusupov, applying caviar to a slice of bread. Close beside him dined a man in aristocratic attire. He was darkly handsome with full lips, meticulously coiffed hair and broad shoulders. A second footman was serving them. The table was set for three.

"Mr. Houdini! How kind of you to join us," the prince greeted him. "May I introduce my dearest friend, Dmitri Pavlovich, cousin of the Tsar."

The pretty boy raised a glass to the magician.

"Please have a seat. We were just sitting down to lunch," Yusupov said, waving his hand at an elaborate spread of delicacies. "Help yourself to anything that catches your eye. Be careful of the mushroom soup. It's just come from the kitchen and it's extraordinarily hot. Do you prefer Gray Sevruga caviar or Imperial Golden Osetra?"

"I prefer to see my wife, and if you prefer to keep your head on your neck, you better tell me where she is!" Houdini snarled, starting toward the table.

The armed footman grabbed his sleeve and restrained him. Yusupov smiled.

"Dmitri, would you excuse us?" he said. "I do want to make sure that package is delivered on schedule."

The handsome man stood, but hesitated. "Are you quite certain?"

Yusupov nodded. "I'm sure I'll be able to handle Mr. Houdini myself."

"Very well. You know where I'll be."

The second footman handed Dmitri a cape. He bowed to Houdini.

"Sir," he said, and marched out. Yusupov turned to the footman bearing the pistol.

"Anatoly, keep the household staff in the west wing. My guest and I are in need of privacy."

"Yes, your Illustrious Highness." Pocketing his pistol, the footman left, followed by the servant who'd been overseeing the meal.

"Mr. Houdini, please have a seat," Yusupov said genially.

Grimacing as if he'd been asked to sit beside a rattlesnake, Houdini drew back a chair close to the prince and sat.

"Look, I know you're the one who snatched Bess," he shot. "In spite of that silly getup of yours."

"I should hope you would," the nobleman said with a little chuckle. "I expected you hours ago. Didn't you notice the Y on my coach? For Yusupov? It's a private joke to have it on the vehicle when I use it in disguise."

Houdini saw the emblem in his mind's eye and cursed himself for missing so glaring a clue.

"You *wanted* me to find you?" he asked.

"Of course. As you failed to show up in a reasonable time, I was just about to write a note for you with my address." The aristocrat gestured to a notepad, ink and pen on the table.

"Sorry to inconvenience you. What's all this about? You're in cahoots with Rasputin, aren't you?"

"Oh, just a little game."

"Okay, you've had your fun. Where is my wife?" Houdini said, driving his fist into the table with such force, the silverware rattled.

"You'll never guess."

"I'm not about to guess. You're about to tell me, or I swear I'll rip your tongue out." Houdini stood, shaking his fist inches from Yusupov's face.

"Well, you're in a disagreeable mood and that is understandable. I assure you, your wife is safe," the nobleman said. Then he giggled. "Or more accurately, *in* a safe. My personal safe."

"What? Are you insane?" Houdini barked. He reached for the nobleman and clutched his ruffled shirt. "If one hair on her head is hurt, I'll see you're locked up for kidnapping."

"Evidently you do not know how the law operates in Russia," replied Yusupov without an iota of fear. "Aristocrats don't go to prison."

"We'll see about that. Take me to the safe. Now, or so help me God—"

"Oh, the safe's not here," Yusupov said, popping a last piece of caviar and toast in his mouth. "It's on the road. My companion Dmitri just set off for Lake Ladoga, where it will be deposited."

CHAPTER TWENTY-NINE

An Impossible Rescue

Hercules had, of course, been suspicious when he saw the safe being loaded onto a motor truck. It didn't look like a robbery, he thought. No thieves would be brazen enough to pull a heist in broad daylight. And Mr. Houdini had told him to watch out for Yusupov, not his lackeys. But it sure was odd to see a safe being carted out of a house instead of into one. He stepped in front of the truck waving a tire iron.

When Dmitri saw the giant black man appear in the driveway, his jaw dropped.

"Should we mow him down, sir?" offered the driver, Rasputin's one-eyed henchman.

"No, stop," Dmitri replied.

The truck rolled to a stop. The back door slid open and out poured four roughnecks who rushed Hercules, fists raised. The "Ethiopian" swung the tire iron into the cranium of the first man with such power that it nearly took his head off. The second received a poke to the gut that sent him to his knees, clutching his abdomen and screaming bloody murder. The remaining pair tackled the giant, but he flung them away like toy soldiers.

"Get us out of here," Dmitri cried. The driver hit the gas and the truck tore off past the brawlers, tires squealing.

Meanwhile, inside the palace, Houdini released Yusupov's lapels and headed for the doorway. Then he whirled about.

"What's the combination?" he demanded.

"Mr. Houdini, surely you can crack an ordinary house safe," the perfumed aristocrat said, dabbing his lips with a lace napkin. "I assure you, the number is very simple. An important date every patriotic Russian should know."

"Tell me the combination or I swear to God I'll bash your head in," Houdini growled, charging back into the room.

Yusupov stood, casting the napkin aside. "I can do better than that." He removed his ascot, reached into his shirt and pulled out a chain from which a key dangled.

"Hand it over," Houdini exclaimed.

"Oh, let's make it interesting," Yusupov said. He went to the wall where the two sabers were displayed and tossed one toward Houdini. It clattered to the floor in front of the magician.

"Forgive the cliché," the nobleman said, taking the other saber from the wall. "I go to the theater quite a bit and I have a weakness for melodramas. Also, it's a bit of a hike to the sword cabinet." Houdini picked up the saber and started forward warily. He had monkeyed around with swords before. The sword swallower in Welsh Brothers Circus had taught him the basics: the proper stance, how to lunge, parry and retreat. However, he was no match for the nobleman, trained since boyhood in the art. Utterly at ease, Yusupov danced about and effortlessly turned aside Houdini's artless thrusts.

"Rasputin put you up to this, didn't he?" Houdini shouted.

"That would be telling," his opponent replied with a jackal's grin.

Yusupov sat in a dining chair and crossed his legs, as Houdini slashed at him from every angle to no effect. He yawned, then stood and took the aggressive role. The prince pressed forward, chasing the helpless American around the room. The sword flew out of Houdini's hand.

"That was smashing. Such agility," Yusupov remarked. "Give me a month to train you!" He picked up Houdini's sword with his own and tossed it back to him.

The guy really does go to the theater too much, the magician thought.

Houdini snatched the blade out of the air and glared at his opponent hatefully. Yusupov marched steadily toward him, as dispassionate as his blade was deadly. Houdini backed up against a door and it fell open behind him. He tumbled into a spacious kitchen. Copper pots and pans of every shape hung from a rack near the ceiling, and on the eight-burner stove, steam still poured from a pot of mushroom soup.

Yusupov entered and let the door close behind him, eager for the unequal contest to continue. Houdini, on the other hand, decided it was time to put an end to it.

He hurled the saber at Yusupov's head. The nobleman pranced out of the way of the projectile with the grace of a bullfighter. In the instant he was distracted, Houdini rushed forward, grabbed the soup pot and tossed the contents into Yusupov's face.

The prince shrieked in agony and dropped his sword, clutching his face.

As he stumbled back against the door, Houdini seized a pair of carving knives from the counter. He'd achieved greater mastery of knife-throwing than swordsmanship in the circus, and he had briefly incorporated a William Tell act in his performance. (He'd jettisoned it after he nicked Bess's ear).

328 |C. Michael Forsyth

Houdini tossed the first knife at Yusupov, pinning his right
shirt sleeve to the door. He barreled forward into the prince
with his shoulder and drove the second knife through the left
sleeve into the door. As Yusupov hung helpless, like a
scarecrow, Houdini yanked the key from his neck.

"Thank you," Yusupov gasped.

"What?" Houdini said, bent over and trying to catch his
breath.

"The spell ... you've broken it."

"Are you Sleeping Beauty now?"

"The trance Rasputin put me in."

Houdini recalled his encounter with Rasputin, how the
flame had snapped him out of it. The magician was skeptical,
yet something was different in Yusupov's eyes. For the first
time, there was genuine human emotion: anguish mixed with
shame.

"Are you on the level?"

Yusupov nodded. "I've been in his grip for years, acting on
his orders blindly. Today he had me waiting in the carriage
nearby his apartment in case your wife fled from him. My
purpose here at my home was only to delay you until the safe
arrives at the lake. Rasputin plans for you to drown while
attempting to rescue her. In some places, Lake Ladoga is more
than seven hundred feet deep."

"Where is this lake?"

"I'll show you."

The escape artist frowned for a second, then pried the
knives from the door, freeing the master of the house.

Racing out of the wooden doors of the palace—three times
taller than a man—Houdini and Yusupov almost crashed into
the colossal figure of Hercules. The car was behind him, engine

running. Some distance away lay a stack of the defeated minions, all unconscious.

"Mr. Houdini, suh, a truck left," Hercules cried. "I think maybe Miss Bess—"

"I know," Houdini interrupted him. "Hop in."

"Wait," said Yusupov. "My car, a Prince Henry Vauxhall, is far faster. She's been clocked at seventy miles per hour."

Houdini hesitated, then nodded and yelled at his fellow American, "Hercules, head for the police station and tell the cops to meet us at the lake."

***

Prince Yusupov's cherry red two-seater sped down the road north along the Neva River, its three-liter engine delivering sixty horsepower.

"How did you get mixed up with Rasputin?" Houdini shouted to the nobleman over the roar of the sports car's engine.

"I went to him for a cure for my affliction."

"What's wrong with you?" From what Houdini had seen of the aristocrat on the tennis court—not to mention his swordplay—he seemed as fit as a circus acrobat.

"You recall how we met at the Grand Duchess Militsa's ball?"

"Yeah, you were dressed like a girl. It was a costume party."

Yusupov bit his lip, then launched into a confession.

"It wasn't the first time. Since I was a youth, I was fond of disguising myself as a girl. My older brother catered to this peccadillo and took me to parties in that guise. He found it amusing to introduce me to various gentlemen. By and large they were tantalized, not disappointed, to discover my true sex."

Houdini was hardly shocked by the revelation. In show business, he'd met enough homosexuals to fill an orchestra pit.

"Get to the point," he said sharply, as the car screeched around a bend. Surprised that the showman evinced no revulsion, the nobleman forged ahead.

"I went to Rasputin and he promised that he could cure me through prayer and by his extraordinary gifts. In the course of our many sessions, I found my desire for other men begin to weaken, giving me hope. Only my feelings for Dmitri remained and these became increasingly platonic. Indeed, all my interests subsided, except the desire to be in Rasputin's presence, which became like an addiction. He began to have a power over me. I had to do his bidding."

Houdini shook his head. "Did it ever occur to you that there's nothing to cure? You were made that way and that's all there is to it?"

"Tell that to the church and the nobility," Yusupov said, smiling bitterly. "I would be shunned, perhaps banished."

"I get it," Houdini said. "Just swear you'll never let yourself be controlled by Rasputin again."

Yusupov clenched his jaw with determination in his eyes as he sped up.

"He is now my mortal enemy, and I swear to do everything in my power to bring about his destruction," he declared.

Miles ahead, the truck rattled down the road, and Bess, scrunched in the thirty-six-inch-high safe, felt every bump. She pounded on the door.

"Let me out, you rats!" she hollered. "When my husband catches you, he'll rip you limb from limb."

Up front in the cab, beside the driver, all Dmitri could hear were muffled cries. This disquieted him, but his loyalty to Yusupov, his friend since childhood and lover of several years, was absolute. They each had wives, of course, both considered rare beauties, but the noblemen's hearts belonged to each other. And so, when Felix had made the extraordinary request that he take on this unsavory assignment, he obliged without hesitation.

Yusupov's custom-built Prince Henry Vauxhall went up on two tires as it made a sharp turn, and Houdini held his breath, certain it would turn over. But it came back down and roared ahead, the passing trees becoming a blur.

Looking ahead, Houdini and his newfound comrade saw an enormous lake surrounded by fir trees. The area nearest to shore was frozen over, and a wooden pier jutted out into this portion. Houdini saw a truck slowly backing up to the pier. Two men stood on the pier, directing the driver by waving their arms.

"There they are," Yusupov cried. He gunned the engine and tore off toward the lake. To Houdini's horror, he saw men unloading a large safe from the truck and using a dolly to wheel it down the pier.

"We'll never make it," he yelled to Yusupov. "We've got to take a shortcut across the ice."

"I'm not sure the ice can hold her."

"Jump out and I'll drive."

Yusupov scoffed. "No gentleman would honor such a request. No, this is the least I owe you. Besides, I can't have some Yank denting my most cherished automobile."

He drove off the road, down a steep embankment and onto the ice. Momentum propelled the car forward, and as it skidded left and right, the Russian wrestled with the steering wheel.

"Houdini, there's something I ought to tell you," he said, anxiously.

"Sorry, I'm spoken for," Houdini interrupted him, hanging onto the side of the car for dear life.

"No, the combination, in case—"

Before Yusupov could complete his sentence, the car skidded across the ice and flipped over three times, then smashed into the bank near the pier. Houdini was thrown clear of the vehicle and landed on his back on the ice, sliding to the shore like a hockey puck. The escape artist scrambled to his feet, slipped on the ice and fell down, then crawled on his elbows to the bank. The car, banged up like a tin can, rested on its side, with one of the tires rolling away. Yusupov sprawled over the steering wheel, head bleeding. It was hard to tell if he was dead or only unconscious, and Houdini didn't have time to check. He scrambled up the embankment and dashed onto the pier, drawing the key to the safe from his pocket.

He saw four men at the end of the pier: Dmitri, the driver Eyepatch, and two henchmen who'd met them there, standing beside the safe. Watching Houdini race toward them, Dmitri signaled with his hand and the men shoved the safe off the pier.

"No!" Houdini screamed.

As the safe hit the ice, it smashed through with an awful crack that sounded as if the earth itself had split asunder.

"Bess!" Houdini shouted in despair as he ran to the end of the pier. The two henchmen, one of whom the escape artist recognized as Rasputin's enforcer the Neanderthal, grabbed hold of him. While the Neanderthal held Houdini back, Dmitri pried open the magician's hand and grabbed the key.

"Wait, your friend Yusupov has switched sides," Houdini protested.

"Unlikely," Dmitri replied. As the magician looked on helplessly, the prince's lover pitched the key into the hole the safe had made.

"We can't make it too easy," Dmitri said. "That would be cheating your fans." He pointed to the hillside overlooking the lake, where dozens of people stood, mostly in peasant dress. Others sat in chairs or on picnic blankets, and they had apparently been waiting for quite some time.

"They've come to watch you perform," the handsome aristocrat explained. He plucked from his breast pocket a paper and waved it before the escape artist. Houdini stared in astonishment at a crude flyer that showed a woman trapped in a safe and Houdini swimming down after it. Over the picture in big, bold type was, "Watch Death-defying Houdini Free Woman from Sunken Safe!"

"Why, you filthy son of a bitch," Houdini snarled, lunging for him with such force, Eyepatch and the Neanderthal could barely restrain him.

"I suggest you conserve your energy," Dmitri said. He nodded and his men released Houdini. The instant that happened, the escape artist took in an enormous breath and swan-dived off the pier. In midair, he heard the crowd applaud.

The 550-pound safe plunged straight to the bottom of the lake, twenty feet down this close to shore, in a matter of seconds. Houdini's descent, powered by the momentum of his headfirst dive and then the strength of his arms, took longer. The water was scarcely above freezing, but he was used to cold water. He regularly took baths in ice water to brace himself for water escapes. Within thirty seconds, he reached the bottom and grasped the handle of the safe.

Inside, Bess fought hysteria. The safe was nearly airtight, "nearly" being the operative word. Water jetted in from all sides of the door and was already up to her knees. Houdini pounded on the door. Two longs, a short, two longs: their secret signal.

"Darling!" Bess cried.

The magician had identified the Swiss-made safe from a distance and knew that this model typically had four numbers. He couldn't see worth a damn in the dim illumination provided by the hole in the ice, but his free hand quickly found the dial. With his ear pressed against the door, he began to manipulate the lock.

First, he had to determine the contact points on the lock. Its drive cam had a notch in it like the wheels in the wheel pack, sloped to allow the lever to pass through when it came around. When the nose of the lever made contact with this slope, there would be a small click. By listening for the click, he could determine which numbers on the dial face corresponded to the left and right side of the notch.

Every cloud has a silver lining. In this dire dilemma, it was that the water amplified the sound. Within forty-five seconds, Houdini found the first number of the combination: 5.

The water was up to Bess's waist now, but she struggled to keep panic at bay. She knew Houdini wouldn't be able to pull the door open anyway until the pressure was about equal on both sides.

My husband will save me! she forced herself to believe.

Another click and Houdini had the second number: 8.

His fingers were numb now, barely able to feel the dial. The cold attacked his body like a thousand pins. His lungs, though they had a greater capacity than an ordinary man's, ached. He'd been underwater three minutes now. Time was running out. He knew the only hope was to guess the last two numbers of the combination. And that, he knew, was an impossible task.

CHAPTER THIRTY

Enemy of the State

The water in the safe was above Bess's neck now. She pressed her lips against the top, sucking in the dwindling air.

If only Yusupov had a chance to spit out the combination! Houdini thought. But he'd given a clue, hadn't he? "A date every patriotic Russian should know." What date?

His lungs were about to explode; any second he would have to give in, open his mouth, and that would be the end of him— and Bess. *I've failed her. And she'll die thinking I hate her.* The lack of oxygen slowed his thought processes, but he desperately fought to keep the wheels of his brain turning.

A patriotic American would say July 4, 1776, or 7-4-17-76, Houdini reasoned. Russians have no Independence Day. They never ditched their monarch; they have a Tsar.

The Tsar's birthday!

The last four numbers had to be a year. Nicholas said he was 26 when his father died in 1894. Which would make the date of his birthday May 18, 1868. 5-8-18-68! The escape artist dialed 18, then 68. Houdini heard a click as the safe unlocked.

The magician wrenched open the safe as his mouth opened, and the carbon dioxide bubbled out.

Bess lurched out of the safe, wrapped her arms around her husband's waist like an octopus and planted her mouth on his. She blew into his lungs, restoring enough oxygen to revive him. He opened his eyes and looked into hers, the most welcome sight in his life.

Good old Bess!

Together they kicked to the surface.

Houdini and his wife broke the surface, gasping for air, to the wild applause of the crowd—who believed they were merely witnessing the climax of a stunt by the fabled magician. With his last ounce of strength, Houdini pushed Bess out of the water. He began to sink back down, but she caught his hand.

Bess felt her husband's hand slipping out of hers. Then, suddenly, a man knelt beside her, grasping Houdini's forearm: Yusupov.

Still bleeding from a nasty head wound, the nobleman called to Dmitri, "Help me, you fool."

"But I thought ...?" his companion said, still bewildered. While Houdini was beneath the ice, the two had argued, and even engaged in a brief shoving match, as Yusupov heatedly tried to explain that he was no longer Rasputin's puppet.

"In the name of God, Dmitri!" the prince cried, clinging to the magician with the tenacity of a starving polar bear with its paws on a seal. Bess, unable to assist any further, suddenly passed out and tumbled over. Dmitri dropped to his knees and took her place. Together, the aristocrats hauled Houdini onto the ice.

Houdini's face and hands were an awful, inhuman blue, as if he'd joined the ranks of the living dead. He looked up at the pier, where the Neanderthal and Eyepatch looked on with anger and frustration. Behind them, a dozen policemen charged toward the pier.

Houdini clutched Yusupov's forearm and gasped, "Get Bess back to the palace."

"But—" the prince protested.

"Please!"

The nobleman nodded, and he and Dmitri carried Bess up the embankment. Houdini sprawled on the ice, shaking convulsively, barely conscious himself. Though his vision was growing blurry, he saw the policemen scramble down the embankment, one of them tumbling on the way. Slipping and sliding comically, like bumbling coppers in a movie short, they made their way to Houdini.

The magician clung to wakefulness as his rescuers approached, hoping he had the energy to blurt out the essential details of Rasputin's fiendish murder plot before fainting, and also praying that he'd awaken with all his fingers and toes attached.

Two plainclothes officers hoisted the escape artist to his feet. Coincidentally, these were Sergeants Petrov and Koslov, the same cops who had fruitlessly searched for him in the apartment of the bathing housewife.

"Mr. Houdini, I have orders to place you under arrest," Sgt. Petrov informed him.

Houdini collapsed in their arms, darkness overtaking him.

***

Houdini woke up on a narrow bunk, cocooned in a pea-green woolen blanket. Moaning, he peeled it back and saw, to his dismay, that he was decked out in prison stripes. The magician sat up, glancing around, and found that he was in a concrete cell. Light streamed in from a tiny window, casting the unmistakable shadow of bars on the floor. In a corner, a figure sat with his back to him at a small and primitive wooden table.

"Where am I?" Houdini croaked.

"You and I are guests of Peter and Paul Fortress," replied his cellmate in a voice Houdini instantly recognized. "Specifically, the Trubetskoy Bastion."

"Illya?"

The poet turned to face him. "I wasn't sure that you would wake up. Hypothermia has killed many a Russian."

"How long have I been out?"

"At least two days. Nine hours here, and I must say, you've been dreadful company. On the brief occasions that you spoke, it was to mumble your wife's name."

Houdini tried to climb out of the bed, but his legs gave way and he sank back down.

"But what am I doing in prison?"

"You were arrested on suspicion of having made an attempt on the life of Rasputin," Illya said. "It's a bold move even for him, trumping up such a ridiculous charge."

"It's not ridiculous," Houdini admitted. "I came within an inch of choking the life out of that son of a bitch and I wish I had."

Illya stared dumbfounded as that confession sank in. Then he laughed and said, "I imagine you had a perfectly good reason."

"You bet I did."

Houdini quickly took stock of their dismal surroundings: walls thick enough to withstand a battering ram; an iron door with a miniscule opening for a guard to peep through; a barred window high above the floor.

"Do they honestly think they can hold Houdini?" the escape artist snorted. Their cell measured about twenty by ten feet. The table at which Illya had been writing was bracketed to the wall, and on it sat an electric lamp covered with a convex glass. A porcelain basin was affixed to the wall under a water tap in one of the corners, and next to it sat a bucket for stool. The window was about eighteen by twenty-four inches, with glass framed in iron, and bars on the outside cemented in place. Through the window, about ten or fifteen feet away, loomed an external wall as tall as the bastion itself.

As Houdini's mind went into high gear working out a possible means of escape, Illya banged on the door. A few minutes later, the slot on the door slid open, revealing a pair of beady eyes and bushy eyebrows, a wart between them.

"What do you want, Volkov? Another book? The Bible isn't good enough for you?" the jailor grumbled. "If you had read it more often, you wouldn't be in this predicament."

"Mr. Houdini is awake," Illya said. "Be a good fellow and bring him some food."

The jailor grunted in the affirmative and the window slid shut.

"Thanks," Houdini said. "And by the way, thanks for introducing me to the Bolsheviks. A more interesting bunch of cutthroats I've never met."

Illya looked puzzled. "Lenin said only that he wanted to talk, to see if you could help each other with the Rasputin problem."

"Well, we did have a nice little chat before his boys started playing Punch and Judy with me."

The poet winced. "Sorry about that," he said.

An explosion in the distance made Houdini jump.

"What in God's name?" he demanded.

"You'll get used to that," Illya said with a chuckle. "Every day at noon, a cannon is fired from the Naryshkin Bastion. It's an old tradition, so I've been told."

Illya went on to tell Houdini the history of Peter and Paul Fortress. It was built by Peter the Great in 1703 on a small island near the north bank of the Neva River, designed to defend against a Swedish invasion that never materialized.

Twenty years later, it found new life as a prison for aristocrats and political prisoners, first among them the disgraced son of Peter the Great. The fortress soon housed the torture chambers of The Third Section of His Imperial Majesty's Own Chancellery, a secret police force that was a forerunner of the Okhrana. In the early 1870s, the main prison block, the Trubetskoy Bastion, was constructed within the fortifications. It came to accommodate revolutionaries of various stripes, from anarchists to socialists.

A half hour after Illya's request, the guard brought Houdini's meal. It was far less scrumptious than the fare that the performer was accustomed to at the palace: just two slices of black rye bread and a mug of warm water.

"This is all we get to eat?"

"Heavens no," his cellmate replied. "We'll be treated to meat stew for supper, possibly even a fruit."

"I won't have to worry about gaining weight," Houdini said gloomily.

As the escape artist gnawed the dry bread, a fist banged on the iron door and the guard's voice announced, "You have a visitor."

Houdini stood, brightening in relief as Dzhunkovsky walked in.

"Back in the land of the living," the Okhrana chief said, and gripped his hand. "You were half-dead when they carried you to the hospital on a stretcher."

"Thank goodness. I thought I'd rot in here," Houdini said, sitting on the bed to put on the rough leather slippers that served as shoes. "I hope you brought some clothes."

"Not so fast." Dzhunkovsky turned to the guard and said, "I need to interrogate this prisoner. Take Volkov away."

"You can speak freely in front of Illya," the magician said. "I trust him completely."

"I find it difficult to trust traitors," Dzhunkovsky replied coldly, turning toward the poet. "That excrement you dared to call a film ..."

"... tells you that you can be sure he hates Rasputin as much as we do," Houdini finished.

Dzhunkovsky sighed. "Very well." He told the guard, "Come back in ten minutes." As soon as the guard was out of earshot, the Okhrana chief pointed at Houdini accusingly.

"Why on Earth would you attack Rasputin? I had no choice but to order your arrest."

"I was defending my wife's honor."

"I know that. Mrs. Houdini made a statement to that effect, and I am working on securing your release, but you can rest assured, the Tsarina is furious. I myself am facing the ax. Rasputin has told her that I am 'not a righteous man,' the death knell for any official in Russia. I will be lucky if I land a position as the chief dog catcher in the northernmost Siberian village. His Supreme Majesty is in Moscow, and when he returns, your fate will be decided."

Houdini paced back and forth furiously. "Rasputin tried to have me killed. Hasn't Yusupov reported that to you?"

"Yusupov? What has he got to do with it?"

Of course he hadn't come forward, Houdini thought. *Yusupov couldn't go to the police without implicating himself. After all, he'd been the one who orchestrated the kidnapping, and he has no proof that he'd acted on Rasputin's orders.*

"What about Bess?" he asked. "Is she all right?"

"Rasputin has taken all the Little Ladies on his jaunt out of the city, your wife included."

Houdini stopped pacing and grabbed the Okhrana chief's shoulders.

"What? Already? Where to?" he cried.

"Our spies have been unable to discover that. They left in the dead of night."

"If she went, it wasn't willingly."

"I can't say," Dzhunkovsky said. "She's been surrounded by Anna Vyrubova and her flock of harpies since her return to the palace."

Houdini slammed his fist on the table, rattling the lamp so it flickered on and off.

"You've got to let me out of here, or damn it, I'll break out."

"Do not attempt it," Dzhunkovsky warned him. "That will only make matters worse. I assure you, it is impossible. I swear that I am doing everything I can to secure your release. If I fail, I'm certain the American embassy can help you."

The magician shook his head violently. "Don't you see, there's no time? Rasputin has some kind of ritual planned. I'm not going to sit here while that nut sacrifices my wife in a volcano or whatever madness he's cooked up."

"I'm sorry," replied the director of the secret police. "I must go now. I'm already putting myself at risk of being fired immediately by visiting you and if that happens I will be of no use to you at all."

Houdini growled under his breath in frustration, then said, "I understand your position. Let's not part enemies." He extended his hand and the men shook, Houdini grasping the other man's forearm.

After Dzhunkovsky departed, Houdini began pacing even more frantically.

Illya said, "Well, it sounds like I'll be enjoying the pleasure of your company for a few weeks at the minimum."

"Like hell. I'm busting out of this dump tonight."

"That won't be easy. The only man ever to escape was the anarchist Prince Peter Kropotkin in 1876."

Houdini stopped walking and looked at the poet. "How did he do it?"

"Bribery. I don't mean to discourage you, Houdini, but this prison is tighter than the Bastille."

"Mark that slammer down as next on my list," Houdini said fiercely. "I'm getting out tonight, I tell you."

Replied the poet, "Mind if I tag along?"

CHAPTER THIRTY-ONE

Prison Break

Houdini was, of course, famous for jailbreaks. He had scores of letters from police chiefs worldwide attesting that the escapes were genuine, including one from the superintendent of Scotland Yard. In Washington, D.C., he escaped from the infamous Murderers' Row, managing to open the doors of eight other cells and shuffle the prisoners around, so that befuddled guards discovered each convict in the wrong cell. After slipping out of a cell in Boston City Prison, Houdini scaled the wall and phoned the flabbergasted warden from half a mile away.

Houdini relied on subterfuge in addition to skill and agility. When possible, the escape artist visited the jail cell beforehand and asked the jailer for the key for a moment to test the lock. Surreptitiously, he made a wax impression of the key using a small box filled with wax that he kept in his palm. He used that impression to make a duplicate key. Often, he was handed a master key, which fit all the cells in the block—making possible that seemingly explicable rearrangement of prisoners in Boston.

Hiding the key presented a challenge. One trick Houdini used was to hide it in his wooly hair, another was to tape it under his instep. Searchers generally inspected between the toes without checking beneath the foot. If he was barred from seeing the cell in advance, Houdini did indeed use the trick that Dzhunkovsky's predecessor Lebedoeff had gotten wind of. Bess would rush into the cell and give him a long farewell kiss—exchanging the key from her mouth to his.

Unfortunately, none of these ploys were now available to Houdini. The magician sat in his bed, posed like The Thinker, schemes of varying degrees of daring flitting through his mind, only to be shot down one after another as unfeasible. By late afternoon, he'd hatched a plan.

When the sun set, they had their final meal of the day: a slab of under-seasoned beef, a potato and tea. After wolfing down the food, Houdini sprang to his feet.

"Illya, get the sheets off the beds."

"Now that's a bit hackneyed isn't it?" the writer replied. "I was expecting something slightly more original. And there's the little matter of the bars, isn't there? A three-year-old child couldn't slip between them."

"Let me worry about the bars, you worry about unmaking the bed."

From his pocket, Houdini withdrew an object he'd purloined during the handshake with Dzhunkovsky: the Okhrana chief's sapphire ring.

"Ideally, you'd want a diamond for this," he told Illya. "But any stone that's harder than glass will do."

"The hand truly is quicker than the eye," Illya marveled. Standing on the chair to reach the window, Houdini used the sharp edge of a facet to begin cutting the glass.

"Twist the sheets into a pair of ropes and knot each end," he told his cellmate over his shoulder, as he delicately moved his makeshift cutting tool.

"I still don't see how ... well, you're the professional," Illya said.

While Houdini gingerly scored the glass, his comrade twisted and knotted the bedsheets, turning them into a pair of serviceable ropes. Houdini had swiped some grease from their plates before they were taken away and left it in on the windowsill to congeal. Now he dipped his fingertips into the gluey substance, then placed his hands on the glass, spreading out his fingers like a frog.

"A suction cup is what we really need here," he explained to Illya, "But this will have to do. Use your mug and gently tap around the edges of the glass."

His apprentice did as he was told, using the bottom of the mug to tap the glass where Houdini had deeply scored it. When Illya had worked his way around the perimeter, Houdini instructed him, "Back up, and be ready to take the glass from me."

Houdini stepped back from the window, the glass adhering to his sticky fingers.

"I'm going to pass it to you now," he said. "Be careful. If you drop it, the guard will hear."

"I do get the general idea of what we're up to," Illya replied, taking the glass from him as it slid from Houdini's fingers. He laid it on the table.

Houdini took one of the sheet ropes and tied it to the now-exposed bars.

"Pass me the other one," he ordered Illya.

"I take it back. I have no idea what we're up to," the bewildered poet said as he handed the sheet rope to the escape artist.

As Houdini secured the makeshift rope to a second bar, he told Illya, "Take your mattress off the bed." The Russian hauled off the mattress. Houdini pushed the bed frame onto its side.

"Help me get the bed frame into position."

The two men positioned the bed frame so that it stood on one side facing the wall at a 45-degree angle. Illya held it in place as Houdini tied the makeshift ropes, which hung from the bars to the metal frame.

"Ah, now I'm beginning to see what you're up to," Illya said, smiling.

"Do as I do," Houdini commanded him. He sat with his back braced against the wall and his feet planted on the upturned bed frame. The writer joined him.

"Now, on the count of three we kick," Houdini explained.

"And that's supposed to ...?" Illya asked. "I can't see how this could possibly—"

"One ... two ..."

On the count of three, both men kicked the bed frame. They tried again and again, and on that third kick, Illya heard the bars begin to loosen.

"It's really working," he said excitedly.

"One more time!" ordered Houdini.

There was an awful grinding sound as the bars tore loose from the concrete. It took only a little extra twisting by Houdini's powerful hands to dislodge those two center bars. They repeated the procedure with the remaining bars.

Illya looked in amazement through the window at the full moon hanging in the night sky. Houdini smiled triumphantly.

"Now, hackneyed or not, we use the sheets the old-fashioned way," the escape artist said.

***

Crouching in the shadows beside Knverkskiy Moat, which surrounded the island, the two escapees watched six guards patrolling the long stone bridge to the mainland, rifles slung over their shoulders. The leap from the roof of the bastion onto the outer wall had been harrowing, as was climbing down with the sheet ropes, but this presented an even greater challenge.

"And there's no other way off the island?" Houdini whispered.

"There's a dock on the other side, but I'd bet the only poetry trophy I haven't hocked that it's as well-guarded as this, if not more so," Illya replied.

"We need a diversion," Houdini said.

"Or invisibility cloaks," the poet suggested.

"Something that would set them all off running. A fire?"

Illya's smile was faintly visible in the moonlight as he said, "I have just the thing. Come on!"

A few minutes later, the guards lounged on the bridge exchanging views on the merits of communism. They were forbidden from drinking on duty, but one had brought a flask that they surreptitiously passed around.

"Wealth distributed equally. Who could disagree with that?" argued Guard Number One.

"And what about the fellow who's too lazy to work?" said Guard Number Two.

"Why, he'd be compelled to work, of course," Guard Number One explained.

"And jailed if he didn't," Guard Number Three put in.

"Ah, compelled," said Guard Number Four. "At least we'd all still have jobs."

Their discussion was interrupted by an explosion on the other side of the fortress.

"The cannon!" cried Guard Number Five.

"Could it be Kasparov, drunk again?" suggested Guard Number Six

"Are we under attack?" Guard Number One said, unshouldering his rifle along with the others.

"From whom, the Swiss?" Guard Number Three said sarcastically. "Come on!"

The guards ran off.

"Good thinking," Houdini whispered to Illya. Naryshkin Bastion was more than a hundred yards away, far enough that it would take at least fifteen minutes for the guards to reach the cannon, argue about how it could have fired by itself and return. By that time, he and Illya could sprint across the bridge. However, there was one hitch. There remained a single guard, Number Four, on the bridge.

"We could overpower him," Illya suggested. "Strangle him and throw him off the bridge."

"Are you ready to commit murder, Illya?"

"Well, no. I was rather hoping you would do the honors."

Houdini pointed to the river. "We cross the ice."

"It's not completely frozen over," his friend protested. "You see, over there, patches of open water." Large sheets of ice slowly drifted down river, separated by black expanses of several feet.

"We jump from ice floe to ice floe," Houdini said. "You played hopscotch when you were a kid, didn't you?"

"I was more fond of jacks. And if we fall in?"

"We swim. I'm not looking forward to another dip in the drink so soon, but if need be ..."

"I can't!" Illya insisted.

"Shh! Of course you can. You're young and—"

"Can't swim. You'll have to go without me."

"In a pig's eye," Houdini declared. As urgent as the need was to escape and find Bess, he wasn't about to leave his friend behind. He patted the Russian's cheek. "Trust me, Illya. Just do as I do, exactly, and you'll be fine."

The ice closest to the island was thick and immobile, so it was relatively easy to traverse the first six yards. But as they ventured beyond that point, Houdini could feel the ice moving under his feet and had to hold out his arms like a tightrope walker to keep his balance. He looked back to see Illya, a few feet behind him, doing the same.

As gaps between the floes began to appear, Houdini jumped them. Soon he was hopping from one sheet of ice to the next, Illya following suit. The ice drifted more quickly the further out they got, the floes bumping up against each other like logs. Although the obstacle course became more challenging as they neared the middle of the moat, Houdini also became more adept with each leap, gaining a better sense of timing.

"This might catch on as a sport," he remarked, looking back over his shoulder.

Illya shook his fist. "You know, I'm beginning to think I *could* kill a man."

Suddenly, a large spot of light appeared on the ice a few yards away, and looking up, the magician saw that its source was the bridge. The beam moved slowly toward them as Guard Number Four swiveled a carbon arc searchlight about. The spot crept along the ice toward them.

"Do you think he heard us?" Illya whispered.

"Maybe it's just dawned on him the cannon could be a diversion. Come on!"

354 |C. Michael Forsyth

As the two figures hurried across the river, Houdini was forced to throw caution to the wind and jump from one momentary perch to the next like a mountain goat, relying on instinct. The final gap was formidable, at least twelve feet.

"We'll have to get a running start," he told his companion over his shoulder.

He backed up and ran. As he did, he could feel the ice shifting under his feet. He launched himself into the air and came down on the thick ice near the mainland. It cracked on the impact, and the magician was relieved that he didn't fall through.

Houdini looked back to see Illya, wild-eyed with panic as the ice floe he stood on began to spin around in the current. The young man lost his balance and almost tumbled into the water. Houdini wanted to cry out words of encouragement to the writer, but now he could see the other guards returning to the bridge. He ran along the river as the sheet of ice bearing his friend drifted.

"I haven't got all night," he called softly to Illya.

Illya turned to the sound of his friend's voice. He gritted his teeth, charged and leaped with his eyes closed. The Russian landed sprawling face-forward on the ice and skidded on his belly the rest of the way to shore. Houdini knelt and scooped him up.

"Now that wasn't so hard, was it?

***

Ten minutes later, the two escapees huddled in an alley between a barber's shop and a shoemaker's.

"I've got to get back to Tsarskoe Selo," Houdini said. "Bess would leave a note for me or word with someone."

"You may not be so welcome in the palace these days," Illya pointed out.

"I probably won't use the front door."

The poet laughed. "Yesterday, I would have said that to sneak into the Tsar's home was unimaginable even for you. Can you use my help?"

"The stakes are a lot higher for you, Illya. You face life in prison. Skedaddle. I'd leave the country if I were you."

The Russian shook his head. "No, I think I'll find Lenin and do my part for making change in this country. You know, I'm still a patriot at heart."

"Just watch yourself. If those jokers take power, I'm not sure there'll be much room for poets."

CHAPTER THIRTY-TWO

Anastasia's Gift

Although Houdini had escaped from scores of prisons around the world, he knew that breaking into Alexander Palace would be a far more difficult task. He'd seen the walls, the guard towers, the legion of fierce mounted Cossacks. Given several days, of course, he could concoct a method of entry unaided, but he didn't have that luxury.

The escape artist huddled in an alley, wearing a coat he'd pinched during the night from a clothing store, courtesy of an easily jimmied window latch. He'd stolen a few hours of sleep as well, but it was an uneasy rest, permeated by nightmares of blasphemous rituals in a black forest. He raced through the woods calling after Bess and heard only mad cackles in reply. Now, his waking mind was just as troubled. What if Bess didn't leave a note revealing where Rasputin and his acolytes were bound—or worse, left a farewell letter telling him she'd joined the cult forever?

Suddenly, a giant shadow fell upon Houdini. He jumped up in a boxing stance, half expecting to see Rasputin's face. But it was Hercules, whom he had again contacted through the palace switchboard.

"Jesus, you almost scared me to death," the magician blurted.

Hercules chuckled. "First time anybody ever accused me of sneaking up on 'em, me being as big as I am."

"Thanks for coming."

"Well, you're an American like me. Do you need help getting out of the country?"

"No, I need help getting into the palace."

Hercules ran his giant hand over his jaw. "Mr. Houdini, I would like to help, but ..."

"I know, you've got your job to think about."

"It ain't just that, suh. I made a promise to those folks in the palace. I know it don't seem like much to a man like you. I know I'm just a doorman, like one of those you see outside a fancy hotel or nightclub. But those are their children in there."

Houdini leaned against a wall, digesting what he'd just heard. Hercules was his only hope. The switchboard operator had told him that "Mr. Houdini's assistants" had been deported.

"I know you're a whole heck of a lot more than just a doorman," he replied. "Listen to me, though. If Rasputin isn't stopped, he's going to cause the death of those children and their parents. The people won't stand for his nonsense forever."

Hercules pondered the magician's words for a moment, then said, "Okay, what do you want me to do?"

***

The guard at the service entrance to Alexander Palace was half asleep, but the sight of Hercules rolling in a wooden crate on a dolly piqued his curiosity.

"What in St. Peter's name is in there?" he asked.

"A set of toy cowboys and Indians for Alexei," the American explained.

The guard whistled. "It must contain every tribe."

"Plus teepees and canoes, horses, wagons and buffalo," Hercules said with a horse laugh. "The finest set in the world, naturally. The Tsar ordered it all the way from St. Louis."

"As if that boy needed more toys!"

"That ain't for us to judge, now is it?" Hercules admonished him.

"I was just making an observation," the guard said sheepishly.

"Well, keep your opinions to yourself and, gosh darn it, give me a hand with this."

Once inside the bedroom that Houdini and his wife had occupied, Hercules helped Houdini out of the crate in which the small man had been folded up like a bat. There was no sign of recent habitation.

"It's like I told you, suh, they packed up all your things," the doorman said.

Houdini opened a dresser drawer, found it empty and slammed it shut.

"She would have left a note," the magician mumbled.

"I don't know. They didn't leave much time for that. Those ladies, Miss Vyrubova and the others, they stuck to her like white on rice."

Houdini went into the bathroom and reached under the sink. There was no note. However, he did find the small pouch in which he'd put the two cameras. When he examined the pouch, he found that his pocket watch with the HH engraving was missing, along with a pair of flashbulbs. Only Boris's remained.

Bess, you little fool!

She'd taken the camera to snare Rasputin—to catch him with his pants down, literally—at the Khlysty rite. Part of him was thrilled to know that she wasn't in Rasputin's thrall. The other part was terrified at the thought that his wife was heading into the belly of the beast with that madman and his band of fanatics.

"They did let her say goodbye to the children," Hercules remembered suddenly. "Anastasia hugged her forever."

"What? You've got to take me to the nursery!"

Hercules groaned and pinched the bridge of his broad nose. "The personal quarters of the Imperial family?"

Minutes later, Hercules rolled the crate into Alexei's playroom while the second Ethiopian—who also did not hail from Ethiopia, but rather from Nigeria—held the door for him.

"Let me help you open it," the African said.

"You go on about your business," Hercules said gruffly. "This ain't a two-man job."

"I like to see the new toys," insisted his coworker.

Hercules rolled his eyes. "Buy yourself a doll at Christmas," he grumbled in a miles-deep voice that warned he would brook no foolishness today.

The African shrugged and left. As soon as the coast was clear, Hercules reopened the crate, took Houdini's hand—like a child's compared to his own—and pulled him to his feet.

"What now?" he asked the magician.

"You go round up Anastasia and bring her here," Houdini replied. "I'm just praying Bess told her something."

Hercules looked around at the indoor playground. "You sure you'll be all right?"

Houdini smiled and stuck out his hand. "Thanks for everything, Hercules. If you ever decide to come back to America, you have a job waiting for you."

Gripping his hand, the giant smiled. "Depending on how things go, I may end up having to take you up on that."

After Jim Hercules departed, Houdini sat on the crate and waited. His eyes roamed around the room at the jumble of toy circuses, train sets and cavalries, and wondered what the average Russian child played with. *A rusty tin soldier? Dirty rag doll? Maybe the socialists are onto something.*

Suddenly, he heard a creaking sound behind him.

"Boo!"

He jumped to his feet, to see Alexei pushing open the door to a toy cabinet and emerge, unfolding his limbs.

"Alexei, what the devil are you doing?" Houdini exclaimed.

"We're playing hide and seek. Anastasia is the searcher," the boy replied. Houdini came forward to hug the child, but the Tsarevich skittered back warily.

"They said you were in prison," Alexei said, pointing his finger at the magician.

"Well, I busted out, of course. To see you."

Alexei screwed up his face skeptically. "Mama said that you hurt Father Grigori. Is that true?"

Houdini knelt beside the boy and put his hand on his shoulder.

"Yes, it's true," he admitted. "You see, Father Grigori isn't a very nice man. Oh, he pretends to be. But he's like that old witch in Hansel and Gretel who lives in a gingerbread house and lures in children by pretending to be kind and offering them sweets."

Alexei scowled. "That isn't true. You're the pretender!"

"Alexei, you've got to believe me," he said, shaking the six-year-old's shoulders a little harder than he intended. Did Bess say goodbye to you?"

The boy nodded.

Houdini asked him, "Did she say anything to you or your sisters about where she was going?"

"When she kissed Anastasia, I think she whispered in her ear," the Tsar's son recalled.

"Alexei, please, run and find Anastasia," the magician said. "Please? As a favor for your pal Houdini? When you get back, I'll explain everything. I promise."

The Tsar's son looked at him uncertainly for a moment, then, his mind settled, he nodded and ran off.

Houdini scanned the playroom in search of a place to hide until either Hercules or Alexei returned with Anastasia. Climbing back into the crate would be pushing his luck. The toy cabinet from which the boy emerged moments ago? Too small. The suit of medieval armor in the corner, given to Alexei during his Knights-of-the-Round-Table phase? Without the help of a squire, donning it would take forever and make one hell of a racket. He finally elected the simplest choice: standing behind a curtain.

He was barely in place when he heard the door open. Feet crossed the room almost soundlessly. The man must have taken off his shoes, for he tread the wooden floor with the stealth of a Navajo warrior. Houdini braced himself, suddenly fearing the guard might take no chances and thrust through the curtain with a sword.

Should I surrender?

"I see your feet," came a cheery voice as the curtain ripped open. There stood Anastasia.

"When Hercules told me you were here, I scarcely believed him," she said.

Houdini embraced her. "You know I wouldn't let a few prison walls and some old moat keep me from my little escape artist in training."

"Is it true you fought with Father Grigori?" she asked, crossing her arms.

"Yes, and I had a good reason."

"I believe you. But what?"

"We don't have time for that now. Did my wife say anything to you before they left?"

"Yes. She said—"

The playroom door burst open and five Imperial Guardsmen stood pointing rifles, led by Commandant Dedyulin, chief of palace security.

"Move away from the Grand Duchess, sir," barked the commandant.

Houdini retreated and one of the men pulled the girl aside.

"He wasn't going to hurt me," she protested.

Alexei pushed his way between two guards' hips into the room and pointed at Houdini with a cold glare.

"You see, I wasn't fibbing," he told Commandant Dedyulin.

"You traitor!" Anastasia cried.

"You're the traitor," Alexei yelled back. "He is an enemy of Our Friend, Father Grigori, and any enemy of the starets is an enemy of Russia."

Parroting his mother, Houdini thought, grimacing.

"Come with us quietly, sir," Commandant Dedyulin said. "There's no reason for the children to see any rough business."

Anastasia squirmed in the arms of the guard, stomping her feet, putting her hand to her forehead as if she was going to faint and making a variety of other melodramatic gestures.

Finally, she broke away from the guard, ran forward and squeezed the magician's hand.

"You are our real friend," she declared.

"Goodbye, kid," he said as the men gently pulled her away.

***

Houdini sat in a jail cell of the palace guardhouse. His hands were cuffed tightly behind his back, and a young Cossack officer sat across from him, a pistol in his hand.

"I wish you wouldn't point that thing at me," Houdini said.

The Cossack, whose brawl-battered face and cynical expression suggested experience beyond his years, took a drag on the cigarette he held in his other hand.

"You expect me to trust those handcuffs, I suppose," the guard said with a mirthless smile. "I didn't just fall off the turnip truck, you know."

Houdini's captor had every right not to trust the handcuffs. The truth was, the magician was free of them almost the instant his rump touched the chair. Moreover, he didn't even have to rely on his extraordinary flexibility. Anastasia had snuck one of her lockpicks to him when she grasped his hand.

And that was not the only gift the Tsar's youngest daughter had given him. She'd also told him where Rasputin had taken Bess and his troop of followers. *What a clever little imp, with all those theatrics!* Every one of the girl's gestures had represented a letter in the "mind-reading" code he had taught her.

P... O ... K ... R ... She only got that far, but Houdini knew what the rest must be: Pokrovskoe, the name of Rasputin's hometown in Siberia. Houdini knew where he had to go, and thanks to his little accomplice, his Russian captors would have no idea where he was bound. Now he just had to get out of the cell without being shot.

"I sure could use a smoke," Houdini said. "Do you have another one of those things?"

"They're not cheap, you know."

"I need something to settle my nerves. Doesn't even a man condemned to death get a cigarette? I only beat up a guy."

The soldier grunted. With his Mauser still trained at Houdini, he deftly removed a cigarette carton from his breast pocket and tapped one out. He placed the smoke in the magician's mouth and lit it. All with one hand, as if he'd practiced the steps in front of a mirror.

Where is a clumsy doofus when you need one? Houdini thought.

The guard retreated to his seat. "They ought to pin a medal on you for attacking Rasputin," he said with grudging admiration.

"You don't think much of him?"

"The biggest whoremonger in St. Petersburg," the Cossack sneered. "He keeps the princesses of the pavement gainfully employed—picks them off the street in the dead of night and takes them home. Usually, he doesn't make love to them, though. He has them strip for him while he does nothing but look at them with those devil eyes."

"One of them told you this in bed?"

The guard waved the pistol in disgust.

"I don't have money to waste on such creatures," he informed Houdini. "I have a fiancée, a girl with a good head on her shoulders. She's an apprentice at a seamstress shop and she's saving money to open her own business."

"What's her name?"

"What is it to you?" the young man said, squinting suspiciously.

Houdini yawned. "Just making conversation. You're on duty for an hour at least, right?"

The man considered Houdini through narrow eyes, then his face relaxed.

"Darya," he said.

"Do you have a picture?"

The Cossack rested the pistol in his lap and pulled a wallet out of his breast pocket. He extracted the photo of his sweetheart, the cherubic blonde Darya. As he raised his head to present the photograph to his prisoner, a blow struck him in the face with such force the chair rocked back and he rolled backward out of it, knocked out cold.

Fifteen minutes later, when the commandant shook Darya's loving fiancé awake, he severely reprimanded the soldier for having let the prisoner escape. Still, in later years the Cossack would point to his bent nose with pride and brag that it was the great Houdini himself who broke it.

CHAPTER THIRTY-THREE

A Deadly Present

The train leaving for Siberia sat in the station as the last few stragglers climbed aboard. A ragged man with a ridiculously long beard and thick glasses climbed the steps and was intercepted by the conductor and a porter.

"I'll take that," the porter said, reaching for the man's battered wicker suitcase.

"Zat eez not necessary," the old man said, clutching the bag to his chest as if it were a beloved pet. The porter wrestled it from him. The passenger tried to shove his way past the two railroad employees, but the conductor, a portly fellow with a drooping mustache, stopped him.

"Not so fast. Let's see your papers and your ticket," the conductor rumbled. Dismay flashed across the traveler's face.

"I thought I vould take my seat first," the ragged man, whose clothing reeked of tobacco, protested weakly. "Vat eez this all about?"

"We have orders to keep a lookout for someone," the conductor said.

"Who?"

"Never mind who. Do as you've been told," the train worker replied.

The passenger dug into his pocket, pulling out an array of lint-covered items: a can opener, a tin of sardines, a ball of twine. It seemed he might be stalling for time. At last, he produced a crumpled ticket and a folded-up identity document, which the conductor then scrutinized over his glasses.

"Very well, sir, welcome aboard," the conductor said, stepping aside and allowing the passenger aboard.

"My suitcase please," the ragged man said huffily.

"I am afraid it must be searched first. There is evidence of a plot to blow up trains on the Trans-Siberian and we must take every precaution. The porter will bring the suitcase to your seat."

Seeing that the porter showed no sign of surrendering the bag, the scruffy passenger squeezed past him.

"I promise you vill see no tip from me," he growled.

The conductor turned to the porter. "Well, greenhorn, don't just stand there twiddling your thumbs, unless you want to be fired your first day on the job," he chided him. "Do you need a kick in the behind to get you started?"

The porter nodded meekly and scurried off with the suitcase. The conductor shook his head in weary contempt as the new fellow swayed on unsteady legs down the corridor.

Moments later, after ducking into a water closet at the end of the car, the "new porter" adjusted his collar. The stolen uniform didn't fit badly except for the neck. Houdini pulled a map from his pocket and consulted it. Rasputin's village Pokrovskoe lay sixteen hundred miles from St. Petersburg in Western Siberia, two hundred miles east of the Ural Mountains. The train was due to arrive in the city of Verkhoturye in six days, then he'd travel by road to the provincial capital of Tobolsk, and down the Tura River by boat to Rasputin's hometown.

With the Tsar's Cossacks at his heels, the escape artist had stowed away on an Imperial train that made the fourteen-mile run from Tsarskoe Selo to the St. Petersburg train station. Finding the Trans-Siberian line was easy; sneaking aboard the baggage car less so. As a diversion, the master of misdirection had been forced to stoop to the childish trick of throwing a stone at the station bell.

Houdini made his way to the kitchen. He hadn't eaten since his stint as a guest of the Tsar at Peter and Paul Fortress and he hoped to steal a bite. Visions of steak topped with onions floated cloud-like through his mind. There was no restaurant car for the common folk, so most passengers brought their own food with them. The enticing, intermingling aromas of stews, cabbage, sausages and other vittles filled Houdini's nostrils as he passed through the aisle, and the scents fueled his appetite.

Stepping from the cars occupied by the peasantry and bourgeoisie into those of the rich felt like crossing through a looking glass from one universe into another. The train boasted two elegant dining cars, with ornate ceiling lamps and high-backed chairs upholstered in red and gold. Drapes framed windows that gave a panoramic view of the passing countryside.

After gorging himself on every scrap of food he could get his hands on, Houdini changed along with other porters into their white stewards' jackets. There'd be no need for further baggage handling for a couple of days.

"Watch your step," a fellow steward warned Houdini. "Passengers of the highest rank are aboard. They are accustomed to service from the cream of the crop."

As he passed the open door of a private compartment, Houdini heard a booming voice that sounded familiar. He glanced in and was alarmed to see the enormous Grand Duke Nikola Nikolaevich, Militsa's brother-in-law, whom he'd met at the palace on his first visit to Russia.

"My mission to the East is vital, my friends," the nobleman was telling two-well-heeled companions. "Despite our avoidable defeat by Japan, we must not cede the Orient to the Orientals. While the Tsar has his attention in the West, some of us must attend to Russia's interests there."

"It sounds as if we hardly need a Tsar, with you on the case," jested a plump, ruddy-faced companion.

"His Supreme Majesty has no more loyal subject than I," replied the grand duke sternly, clearly unamused by the jibe. "All the more reason that I must intercede when necessary on his behalf."

Houdini turned down his cap and tried to slink by. But at that moment, the nobleman turned and looked directly at him.

"We're out of wine. Bring another bottle of Chateau Lafitte," Grand Duke Nikolai said, and immediately returned to the conversation.

He doesn't recognize me, Houdini realized. *Servants are invisible to some swells, whether you're in the States, England or Russia.*

"Yes sir," he said, and hurried off.

For most of the journey, Houdini managed to duck assignments to the grand duke's compartment. He also kept conversations with his peers to a bare minimum. Although his Russian was pretty good, railroad slang was a language unto itself. In his years traveling by rail with the circus and shooting the breeze with rail workers, he'd picked up some colorful terms. To "pull the cow's tail" meant to yank the whistle cord;

"throwing away the diamonds" was when the fireman missed the fire door with a shovelful of coal, and a "boxcar tourist" was a hobo. However, it was hard to keep the corresponding Russian idioms straight.

As the train roared eastward billowing black smoke, the landscape became increasingly bleak. Grassy plains through which broad rivers wound gave way to a frozen wasteland of snow that sparkled like a sea of diamonds. The land seemed uninhabitable, but on his occasional glimpses through the window, Houdini saw passing villages, most little more than clusters of unpainted log huts amongst which geese and pigs roamed freely. When traveling past larger towns, he often spotted the onion-shaped dome of a church, painted yellow or blue.

The terrain grew steadily more mountainous as the train approached the Urals. Firemen fed the furnaces at a furious rate, and it took every morsel of power for the locomotive to make the steep climb. Amidst snow-enshrouded pines and silver-leaved birch trees, animals could be seen from the train: sable, foxes, even bears. These mountains, three hundred million years old, were among the most ancient in the world, yet despite the eons still towered, miraculously uneroded. Across that barrier, the travelers passed from Europe into Asia, from a continent where modern science held sway, to a land of mystery and mysticism, where civilizations of unimaginable antiquity had been born and had withered away.

Soon after they descended from the Eastern slope of the Urals, Houdini's luck ran out. As was inevitable, he was ordered to bring a tray of drinks to the grand duke's table in the dining car. Entering, he saw that Nikolaevich and his three previous companions were the sole occupants. Presumably, the huge cigars they puffed had routed the other passengers.

Who would dare ask this intimidatingly tall aristocrat with a chest studded with medals to put out his stogie?

Once again, the grand duke was holding court.

"It was made for me as a gift at an expense of more than three thousand rubles," he bragged, "and when I return to St. Petersburg, I will make a gift of it to the Tsar."

"It is not only beautiful, it is unique," the nobleman's tubby companion said, blending jealousy and awe.

Houdini placed the tray on the table and was about to make a hasty retreat when he got his first look at the object that Nikolaevich was so proudly displaying. It was a jeweled snuff box. Unmistakably the one he'd seen in Faberge's shop on the workbench of the Bolshevik conspirator Igor.

"You press the jewels of various colors in the right order and, voila, the box opens," the grand duke explained.

"Ingenious," his plump companion marveled.

"I've always had a good head for puzzles," Nikolaevich boasted. "The devilish thing has gotten the best of me up until now. Between now and when I return from Siam to present the gift to the Tsar, you can be sure I'll solve it."

"Let me have a go at it," the friend begged.

"No, I," the second companion pleaded in a squeaky voice.

Houdini could barely prevent a gasp from escaping his lips. The box must be a device to assassinate the Tsar, rigged to activate when opened. The grand duke looked up to see the steward still hovering over their table. Wearing a look of irritation, the nobleman was about to ask why he was just standing there when Houdini rested the drink tray on the table.

"Sirs, excuse me, your window is slightly open," the fake steward said.

"I don't hear any wind," observed the squeaky-voiced gentleman who sat closest to the window.

"Here, allow me to adjust it," Houdini insisted. He leaned over the table and struggled with the window. As he did so, the train rocked a bit and he lost his balance, knocking two of the drinks over, sending brandy splashing into the grand duke's lap.

"You clumsy oaf," the nobleman roared in dismay, struggling to his feet. "Have you never stood on a train before?"

"A thousand pardons, sir," Houdini replied, frantically wiping the liquid with napkins. "I'll be back with towels in an instant." He hurried off before the tongue-lashing became any more severe. Nikolaevich resumed his seat, examining his trousers.

"It will take a miracle to get that stain out," he grumbled.

"Please, let me try the box," his chubby companion said.

"If you insist. I'll grant you five minutes."

"That's a bit stingy." He held out his hand expectantly.

"I already gave it to you," Nikolaevich replied with some annoyance.

"You're mistaken. Look in your pocket."

The grand duke checked his jacket pocket. He blanched, then looked about, befuddled.

"Perhaps it's under the table," the squeaky-voiced man said, and ducked to look. As Houdini reached the car door, grinning at his own ingenuity, it opened with a frosty gust and he was greeted by another familiar face: Robert Donatson, Rasputin's publicist.

He must have boarded in Moscow. Are they holding a convention of everyone I know in Russia? the magician thought. *Headed to Siberia to meet his master, no doubt. And unlike the* self-absorbed Nikolaevich, the Englishman instantly recognized Houdini.

"You!"

Before Houdini could reply, the grand duke's bass voice trumpeted. "Stop, thief!"

Houdini tried to push past Donatson, but Rasputin's British flunky blocked his way. They struggled for a moment, as Nikolaevich and his compatriots caught up. Together, they tackled him to the floor. In the melee, Houdini's cap fell off.

"Why, look, it's Houdini," the grand duke declared in astonishment. His expression quickly changed to rage. "Assaulting the Tsar's spiritual advisor and now theft?" he growled. "Give me back the snuff box this instant!"

"Get these numbskulls off me, then," the American responded. The wealthy passengers released him.

"I'll get the soldiers," the squeaky friend said. "This is no fit work for a gentleman." As he exited the car, Houdini withdrew the jeweled box from his pocket.

"The man who opens this box will die," he informed his captors dramatically. "It was designed to assassinate the Tsar."

"Preposterous," Nikolaevich scoffed. "Next to myself, Faberge is the most loyal subject in Russia."

"I tell you, this box is deadly," Houdini said, waving the jewel-encrusted gift. "A Bolshevik in his shop made it."

Donatson frowned. "You must admit it would be deucedly clever, Your Serene Highness. I certainly wouldn't open the box if I were you before it's carefully examined."

"If he's right, then it must be a bomb," the fat fellow said, a trace of panic in his voice. "We should throw it off the train." He went to the window and began to pry it open.

"That box cost me three thousand rubles," the grand duke rumbled. "I'd throw you off the train first."

"It's too small to contain a bomb," Donatson observed.

"I think I've got it," Houdini announced. "Anyone have gloves?"

"You can use mine," Donatson said, pulling a sturdy leather pair out of his jacket pocket.

"Now see here ..." Nikolaevich protested. Before the nobleman could utter another word, Houdini slipped on the gloves. His fingers began to dance over the surface of the Faberge box.

"This is mad; he's going to blow us to kingdom come," the panicked, plump companion said. "You fools can stay here if you want." He hightailed it to the door, squeezing past Donatson.

Even through the leather, Houdini's sensitive fingers could detect minute movements within the box. He touched a ruby, then an emerald, a sapphire and then an amethyst.

"If you're thinking what I think you are, I'm not entirely sure those gloves will save you," Donatson said.

CHAPTER THIRTY-FOUR

Here's Where I Get Off

The Faberge snuff box popped open and as it did, Houdini quickly removed his hand. Only the magician's superhuman reflexes spared his life, because just where the tip of his index finger had rested, a small needle sprang out.

"What the devil?" the grand duke exclaimed. Donatson gingerly took the box from Houdini and sniffed the point.

"Tetrodotoxin, I'd wager," the Englishman said. "From the blue-ringed octopus. So potent, the poison from one animal can kill twenty-six men in minutes."

Odd that he'd be an authority on poisons, Houdini thought. *Or is he just trying to show off?*

As if Donatson had read his mind, Rasputin's publicist added apologetically, "Don't mean to bore you. Books about marine biology are a guilty pleasure of mine."

And I'm Abraham Lincoln, Houdini thought. *Unless they put out books with scented pages now.*

Nikolaevich sat down, visibly shaken. Such a display of weakness was rare for the nobleman, the magician suspected.

"Unbelievable! Houdini, I owe you my life," he said. "And possibly the Tsar's himself. When I tell him what happened, you can be sure these silly charges regarding that charlatan Rasputin will be dropped."

"I'll hold onto this as proof," the Englishman said. He closed the box, causing the needle to retract. Houdini snatched the deadly instrument from him and pocketed it.

"If you don't mind, I'll present it to Tsar Nicholas myself," the escape artist said.

Donatson opened his mouth to challenge him, but the grand duke said, "Agreed. I grant your request."

At that moment, Nikolaevich's plump companion returned, accompanied by five soldiers with long Mosin–Nagant rifles slung over their shoulders.

"I am afraid that for now, until the charges are formally dropped, you must remain in custody," the grand duke said. "We must return you to St. Petersburg."

This time, Houdini's guards did a better job of shackling him. His feet were placed in irons, his hands cuffed at the front, in full sight. While frisking the escape artist, the soldiers found Anastasia's lockpick and took it away. For good measure, he was bound to the chair with heavy rope. In a cramped compartment, three soldiers sat staring at him sternly, with rifles in their laps, two across from him and one beside.

Houdini seethed with frustration. The train could reach Verkhoturye in less than two hours. There, he'd be placed on a train headed west. And these guards would mind him all the way. He didn't attempt small talk, for there was no hope of distracting these determined fellows nor a ghost of a chance they would underestimate his ability to free himself.

The soldiers, however, didn't share his preference for silence. They bombarded him with questions about his escapes. Was it true that he had escaped from a milk can, and from a diving suit and from a boiler tank and from the belly of a giant sea creature? Yes, yes and yes, he told them.

"You should do an act in which you escape from inside a cannon before it fires," the soldier beside him suggested. "While in a straitjacket, of course."

"Ivan's father was a trapeze artist in the circus, so he thinks he knows all about showmanship," a fellow soldier explained with a sigh.

"It's not a bad idea, really," Houdini replied, picturing an audience perched on the edge of their seats as the fuse burned on an enormous cannon.

Kapow! Ka-Pow! Ka-pow! Ka-pow! Shots rang out in the distance with the rapidity of firecrackers. The soldiers leaped to their feet, rifles at the ready.

"Anarchists!" one cried, throwing open the door.

"What about him?" asked Ivan, the soldier who'd suggested the Human Cannonball Deathtrap, as Houdini was already calling it in his mind.

"He can guard himself for a minute. Let's go!" cried the third soldier.

"I'll keep an eye on him; you go on," Ivan said. His compatriots stormed out of the car in the direction of the gunfire. Ivan went to the door, cast a glance anxiously in both directions, then shut it. He remained on his feet, ready for action.

Smarter than he looks, Houdini thought.

"Is this some kind of trick of yours?" Ivan demanded of the magician. Houdini smiled innocently and shrugged.

The light in the car dimmed as the train entered a tunnel.

"Odd coincidence that the distraction takes place just as we enter a tunnel," Ivan said in an accusatory tone.

"Don't behave like a paranoiac," Houdini replied, his face in the shadows. "A Russian soldier must be brave." The next moment, they were plunged into complete darkness.

Ivan grabbed Houdini's shoulder, while keeping his rifle at the ready.

"Don't you dare move," he ordered with a scowl. Standing over the captive, trying to maintain his balance, the soldier trembled like a child in the dark. Houdini could hear his rapid breathing over the rumble of the train.

"I've got you and I won't let you escape," Ivan shouted at Houdini defiantly.

That was just before a hard object struck the soldier on the back of the head and he collapsed.

Poor Ivan recovered a few moments later as the train emerged from the tunnel and light filled the car.

"No, no, no!" he cried. The great Houdini had vanished.

***

In the well-appointed private compartment of Robert Donatson, a bewildered Houdini waved away the Englishman's offer of a brandy.

"What gives?" Houdini demanded. "Why did you spring me?"

"I thought Americans were acquainted with the phrase 'thank you,'" Donatson said with an easy smile. "Unless freeing you before you had a chance to extricate yourself has wounded your pride."

"I suppose you were the one who fired the shots," Houdini said, rubbing his wrists where the handcuffs had been.

"Guilty."

"I don't understand. You're one of Rasputin's cronies."

"That's one of the hats I wear," the Englishman replied, taking a sip of the rejected liquor himself.

"What's your game?" the magician asked, stabbing at him in the air with his index finger. "You know about bombs, poison, and you walk around with guns."

"I am in the service of His Majesty's government," Donatson revealed.

"A spy?"

"Our government is concerned that there may be a war in Europe," Donatson explained as he lit a pipe. "We need to know what the Russians will do, what they're capable of, and what role this fellow Rasputin may play in the Tsar's decisions. My department chief thought you might be doing the same sort of thing for the Yanks."

"The only thing I'm doing is tracking down Rasputin and saving my wife," Houdini replied fiercely. "He's here in Siberia."

"Yes, I know. I'm to meet him there after his 'special gathering.'"

"Then you know about the Khlysty?"

"Yes, I've been trying like the devil to find out where precisely the proceedings will take place. He's close-lipped when he chooses to be."

"I think it's Pokrovskoe, Rasputin's old stomping grounds. I'll find them."

"I sincerely hope so," the agent said. "I am under orders from our Prime Minister only to observe Rasputin, not to interfere with his machinations. But I shouldn't be disappointed at all if you manage to undo him." He added with a shudder, "The things I've seen that man do ..." Donatson shook off his revulsion. He opened a black attaché case and withdrew a map.

"I'm afraid you can't hide in here much longer," he said. "We've got to get you off this train."

"How, jump?" Houdini said. "From a locomotive going seventy miles per hour?"

"No, that would be suicide. You'll jump from a locomotive going twelve miles per hour."

He spread the map out on the desk and pointed to a train route demarked in red. "The train will slow in approximately six minutes when it makes the turn around this mountain. You'll jump from the platform between the cars at just the right moment and the snow bank will break your fall ... I should think."

"And assuming I don't break my neck, how far will I be from Verkhoturye?"

"No more than a hundred and fifty miles, I estimate," the Englishman said.

"Oh, just around the corner."

"You can make it on foot to this village here," Donatson said, pointing to the map. "Find a farmer who can take you by wagon to the Monastery of St. Nicholas in Verkhoturye. They can help you arrange transportation from there."

"A monastery?"

"It's where Rasputin received his early religious training," Donatson confirmed.

"He ought to ask for his money back," Houdini said. "They missed the part about murder and rape."

"Speaking of money, you'll need this," continued the British agent. He produced an envelope from the attaché case. "Thirty rubles. Quite sufficient to pay your way."

"Now, I can't—"

"I still owe you from our wager, remember," Donatson reminded him. "Your escape from the icy grave."

"I figured you'd welshed on that bet," Houdini replied.

"Oh, ye of little faith."

The spy also supplied Houdini with a set of fresh clothes and a heavy brown coat. They were about to slip out of the compartment when they heard voices in the corridor and a sharp knock on the door to the adjacent stateroom.

"Blast it," Donatson said. "Change of plans." He pointed to the window. Houdini slid it open and a tsunami of frigid air blasted into the room, nearly bowling them over.

"Do you see the bend up ahead?" Donatson asked. Squinting in the wind, Houdini saw the train tracks winding around a mountain. The magician nodded, beginning to feel the locomotive slow.

"You'll land in hot water over this, won't you?" Houdini said.

The Englishman laughed. "I imagine they'll chalk it all up to your talent for self-extrication."

Houdini climbed out of the window and clung, waiting. The locomotive had slowed considerably, chugging along now at no more than 30 mph. As Houdini held onto the window frame, waiting for the right moment, a knock came at the Englishman's door.

"One moment," Donatson said, "Just getting my trousers on."

"I must ask you to unlock your door at this instant," came a gruff voice from the other side. The spy looked at Houdini apologetically.

"I fear you must make the jump prematurely," he said.

The magician looked out at the pines rushing by. The train was still going better than 20 mph. He gave his newfound friend a grim salute, then took the death plunge.

CHAPTER THIRTY-FIVE

The Madwoman

The village of Pokrovskoe stood on the Western Siberian steppes, a landscape of vast plains and forbidding forests. Marshy in the brief summer, the terrain was blanketed by snow and ice during a winter that lasted six months. Its people were hardened by the inhospitable climate; the evidence could be seen in their wind-weathered faces and callused hands. They relieved their life of hardship with extended drinking bouts, characterized by frenetic dancing, raucous laughter and epic fist-fights that sometimes lasted until dawn and left all participants unconscious on a tavern floor. Unlike peasants in the west, they'd never known the yoke of serfdom. Their spirits were as untamed as wild horses.

During the warm seasons, men, women and children labored in the fields. Others loaded goods on ships that stopped on their journey down the Tura River. The village was also a staging post where travelers exchanged horses and stocked up on supplies for the grueling eastward journey across the wasteland. Rasputin's father had made his living raising horses for this purpose. As the three wagons bearing the mystic and his entourage of female followers and bodyguards arrived in the village, Bess could see men loading carts and sleighs for the outbound trek on the icy, potholed road.

Rasputin was greeted as a conquering hero by residents who waved and cheered enthusiastically and competed to be the first to help unload the wagons.

"What is the news from St. Petersburg?" one asked.

"Did you put in a good word for me with the Tsar?" another joked.

"Will you preach to us tonight, starets?"

"Of course, my friends, but first I must rest," Rasputin told his neighbors.

Bess did notice one elderly denizen look fearfully at Rasputin, make the sign of the cross and take refuge in her cottage. But the starets paid this no mind. His spirits rose from buoyant to ecstatic at his homecoming.

"The cities of the west are putrid with over-civilization and the arrogance of men," he told the Little Ladies. "Now, breathe in the pure air of Siberia. Some of you still reek of decadence, but here you will be cleansed."

Bess was surprised at just how ordinary Rasputin's home appeared, a good-sized peasant house with a certain rustic charm. In the front room was a fireplace with an icon of St. Simeon on the mantle, a plain wooden dining table and a few chairs, one of these a rocker for the man of the house. She was surprised to discover that Rasputin had a wife, Praskovia, and three children, Maria, Dmitri and Varya.

"Welcome, sisters," said Praskovia, embracing them. She was a reasonably attractive woman with fair hair and vacant blue eyes.

Rasputin's wife supervised the Little Ladies as they carried in their overnight bags. The oldest child, thirteen-year-old Maria, assisted her father's disciples while observing their every movement with saucer eyes almost as intense as her father's.

Rather than helping, Rasputin announced that he was retiring to his room for a nap. On the way, he grabbed a fistful of Akilina's prodigious rear end.

"A Siberian would find a woman with such strong, plow-pulling hips a true prize," he said with a robust guffaw.

It startled Bess that Rasputin had groped his acolyte in full view of his wife. A short time later, she and Praskovia made a bed together while engaging in small talk. The peasant woman spoke only Russian, but that was fine with Bess. Her Russian had steadily improved in the company of the Little Ladies, and by now they conversed entirely in that language.

Unable to contain her curiosity any longer, Bess asked Mrs. Rasputin an indelicate, but obvious question. "Doesn't it bother you that your husband ... enjoys the company of so many women?" she asked in a low voice.

"That he makes love to them, you mean?"

Her frankness made Bess blush, and she nodded.

"I am happy that God has blessed me with a mate so virile and full of vitality, he has that much to spare," Praskovia replied.

Well, that's one way of looking at it, Bess thought. The other women were in a tizzy, chattering like squirrels, eyes sparkling. Anna Vyrubova's face in particular was aglow with a passion that Bess found unnerving.

"The day after tomorrow, we travel to the place where we will have our spiritual retreat," the chief disciple told Bess. "Others are already gathering as we speak."

"You've been before?" Bess asked nonchalantly.

Vyrubova nodded with a blissful smile. "The Grand Gathering is like nothing you've experienced. It will transform you utterly, body and soul."

"It's a sort of mass, then?"

"Sort of a mass," Vyrubova echoed her with an amused expression. "One might put it that way, yes."

Bess shivered. The woman's hungry eyes bespoke an experience quite unlike Sunday service.

At suppertime, the guests sat at the table with Rasputin and his family, then afterward, peasants crammed into the cottage to hear the holy man's sermon.

The Little Ladies were to sleep three to a bed. It came as no surprise to Bess that Vyrubova selected her as one of her bedmates. Houdini's wife felt relief when the ballerina Natasha Stepanova snuggled in between them. By now accustomed to the luxurious king-size bed at the palace, it was a shock to the system for Bess to find her flesh pressed against the dancer's toned, fragrant body.

"Well hello, sister," Natasha told her with an insouciant smile. "This is how we Russians sleep, those of us who grew up without riches. I had a brother on either side." She placed a hand on the American woman's hip, leaned in and whispered in her ear. "Don't worry, I will protect you from that one."

"I'm not worried, sis," Bess yawned, turning away. "There were ten of us in my house, so believe me, this is no big deal."

***

Houdini trudged through the two-foot drifts, glad for the sturdy boots Donatson had given him, but yearning for snow shoes. The fur hat and gloves kept the biting cold at bay—or more accurately, staved off pure agony. He rubbed his left shoulder, which still ached from the injury he incurred in the leap from the train.

Hours before, he had made the jump and crash-landed in a heap of snow. He tumbled downhill for twenty feet, gathering icy crystals as he rolled, a human snowball, before finally colliding with a tree. He dislocated his shoulder, but it wasn't the first time for that; indeed, he could do it at will to escape from straitjackets. With a grimace, he shoved it back into place and knelt watching the locomotive vanish into the distance, the mournful whistle tooting.

He had been marching steadily for miles now, with no town in sight, but at last he came across a road. Tracks in the snow told him that at least it was trafficked. Horses had passed since the last snowfall and there were wheel tracks as well. The sun was close to setting to his left, so he headed right, eastward.

After another two miles, unable to walk any further, Houdini sank to one knee on the road. *Just need to gather my strength*, he told himself. But the wind was picking up and the temperature steadily dropping. He wasn't sure if he could survive the night.

Houdini will not be defeated by snow!

He forged ahead, wrapping his scarf around his neck yet another time and bowing his head to keep the wind from his face. His hands were buried in his pockets, but even with the gloves and heavy coat, he was sure he'd lose a finger or two to frostbite before the adventure was over.

Two hours later, the magician collapsed to both knees. The sun had almost disappeared, and with it, all but the faintest glimmer of hope.

"Whoa, whoa, get out of the road, you idiot!"

Houdini looked up to see a covered, horse-drawn sleigh driven by a peasant, who was pulling on the reins with all his might. The two horses came within a yard of trampling the magician. The driver sat bundled up in a heavy coat and blankets. Beside him, a woman held up a lantern.

"Are you trying to get run over?" the driver yelled down at Houdini.

"I ... I need to get to the Monastery of St. Nicholas in Verkhoturye," he managed to utter through chattering teeth.

"Why, we're headed to Verkhoturye now," the wife offered.

"The monastery, he said," the driver of the troika corrected her. "That's out of our way. Chesmensky is expecting those pickles."

His limbs stiffened by the cold, Houdini slowly reached into his pocket and pulled out the money pouch.

"I can pay five rubles."

"Well, I suppose the monks might be in need of pickles," the husband grunted. "Fine, fine then. Climb in the back."

***

Bess was awakened by the sound of a commotion outside: men's voices berating a squawking woman. She tied her robe and hurried to the window. Through it, Houdini's wife saw a crone in ragged clothing struggling to enter the doorway, with Rasputin's men shoving her back.

"All I want is to kiss his blessed hand," the woman said. Her eyes bugged out like a frog's and her hair was in disarray.

"Keep that wretched creature away from me," Rasputin told his chief acolyte Anna Vyrubova. His whole body trembled and he covered his ears. "I can't stand her howling." It was the first time that Bess had ever seen fright in his face. Vyrubova nodded and ran to the kitchen.

"Who is she?" Bess whispered to one of the Little Ladies, Elena Dzhanumova.

"Don't you recognize her? That is Olga Lokhtina," Elena replied. "After her husband threw her out, her relatives disowned her. She became penniless and has since wandered the streets."

Now Bess could recognize the face, although it was difficult to reconcile it with her memory of that high-spirited, regally attired society woman she'd met in Rasputin's apartment and who had boasted of being the mystic's first adherent in St. Petersburg.

"Be on your way, hag," the eyepatch-wearing bodyguard snarled at Lokhtina. "And find somewhere to take a bath. You smell like an outhouse!"

Bess felt a rush of sympathy. "Why are they being so cruel to her?"

"Surely you can see that she has gone mad," Elena replied. "And her madness disturbs Father Grigori."

Vyrubova returned from the kitchen wearing an expression so venomous, Bess half expected to see a butcher knife in her hand. Instead, the leader of the Little Ladies was armed with a bucket of water. Standing at the front door beside the guards, she tossed the water over the madwoman, drenching her from head to toe.

"Yes, baptize me!" Lokhtina shrieked. "Crucify me if you wish, but let me see the Master's eyes."

"That's enough out of you, nutso," said the Neanderthal, nodding to his companion. The men charged the wretched woman with raised sticks and chased her off down the road, shoving, beating and cursing.

Bess looked around in disbelief at Rasputin's disciples. The women had returned to their tasks as if nothing untoward had happened.

"Well, if you won't do something, I will," she said angrily. "At least we can make sure she has something to eat." Disgusted at the behavior of her companions, Bess snatched up a loaf of bread, wrapped it in a napkin and headed out the door.

When Bess caught up with the madwoman, she was crouched behind a barn. Her appearance was even wilder after getting roughed up. When Bess offered her the bread, Lokhtina took it and clutched it to her bosom protectively.

"How long have you been out here?" Bess asked.

"He would not see me in the capital, so I came here and have waited because I knew he would return. I must see him, you understand? He can spit on me if he wishes; I only want to kneel at his feet one more time."

"Surely you must have relatives who can take you in? You'll die out here."

"Then let me die. Who else can make me whole again?"

"You mustn't talk like that," Bess said, kneeling beside her. Lokhtina grabbed her hand with desperate ferocity.

"Please, you must say a word for me, just a word. Tell him that I'm better. I won't scream or beg."

"Yes of course," Bess said. "You must let me go now, Olga." She pried her hand loose and stood up.

Olga Lokhtina shook a finger at her. "You think you're so high and mighty because you are his newest conquest," she croaked. "But one day you'll be just like me. All of you will." She began to laugh to herself, and Bess took the opportunity to back slowly away, leaving the wastrel cackling.

As she walked back to Rasputin's house, Bess thought about the prostitute Chioniya whom her husband had rescued from being dragged naked by a horse. How many other women had Rasputin ruined? Abandoned to lunacy and degradation? She entered the house with a renewed determination to fulfill her mission to expose him.

Bess found the mystic sitting by the fireplace, his devotees bringing coffee and fruit to his chair. He seemed less agitated now, with the unbalanced woman out of his sight.

"Father Grigori, I can't stand the anticipation," Bess said, nestling at his feet. "Where is the ceremony to be held, Father?"

Rasputin took her hand. "You are eager to play your role in the Grand Gathering?"

"Oh, yes, Father!" she declared with every bit of enthusiasm she could muster.

"All in good time," the mystic said.

Rasputin had made no further sexual advances toward Bess since the incident in the apartment, instead treating her to cryptic remarks and seemingly sarcastic comments about her "high-mindedness."

The return of Pokrovskoe's favorite son was, of course, an occasion for celebration. A steady stream of peasants flowed through the door bearing gifts and pleading to be healed. More so than in St. Petersburg, these gifts were in the form of livestock and edibles: live pigs, goats and mules, sausages and smoked hams, as well as finely crocheted blankets. The Little Ladies facilitated the process, greeting the petitioners, taking their gifts and keeping the visitors in an orderly line. Bess watched in amazement as the starets placed a hand on the knee of a swineherd who'd hobbled in on arthritic knees. A few gentle words said over him, and the man strode out with the pep of a fifteen-year-old boy stepping out on his first date.

The faithful always thanked Rasputin profusely, with an abject humility befitting those in the company of Jesus himself. A select few promised in hushed tones to see their master at the Grand Gathering. Bess got the sense that these individuals had performed some special service for the mystic that earned them the right to attend. It irked Bess that these humble peasants with patches on their coats were privy to the location of the ceremony when she was not.

"Is it mainly Father Grigori's neighbors who will join us at the Grand Gathering?" Bess asked Anna Vyrubova.

"Oh, you'd be surprised at the rank of some of those who will come from afar for spiritual awakening," the Tsarina's lady-in-waiting said. "Princesses, dukes, captains of industry."

Toward the end of the afternoon, Bess and the former nun Akilina greeted at the doorstep a freckle-faced girl of about sixteen. One arm was in a sling, Bess could see, although it was partially concealed by her heavy coat.

"My name is Yaroslava Kozelsky," the visitor said. "I have heard the great Father Grigori is here. As you can see, I am in urgent need of his services."

"Come in, please," Bess said, taking her hat.

"May I take your coat?" Akilina said, reaching for her. The newcomer pulled away.

"It is all right. I'm still cold," Yaroslava explained.

"Come by the fire then, and warm yourself, before Father Grigori comes from his room," Bess urged her. As Akilina went to get Rasputin, Bess led the visitor to the fire.

"Have you come from far?" Bess asked.

"From Tyumen, ma'am. It is about sixty miles to the west. You are English, yes?"

"American."

"I should like to go to America someday," the girl said wistfully.

"Our weather is nicer, that's for certain."

"It is not the weather. It is the country. Russia is sick." A pall came over her face that suddenly made her look older. Rasputin returned from his room, accompanied by Vyrubova, Akilina, and several of the other Little Ladies.

"Father Grigori, this is Yaroslava," Akilina said. "She is in need of succor." The comely teen curtseyed clumsily.

"Show me, my child," he said with a benign smile. The girl turned away and threw off her coat. As she turned back, she brandished a glittering object that had been hidden by the sling, which was rigged to fall away.

"I'll show you hell," she shrieked.

"Grigori, a knife!" Bess cried.

Yaroslava lunged savagely at the big Siberian, screaming, "Die, devil!"

Either Bess's warning or animal instinct spared Rasputin's life. He caught the girl's wrist as it arced down and twisted it until the knife dropped to the ground. The holy man's disciples flew to his side and pounced on the would-be assassin. They struck and clawed at her with such ferocity Bess feared they would rip her limb from limb.

Elena and Rasputin's housekeeper Dunya hauled Yaroslava to her feet, each taking an arm and holding them apart so far, it looked as if she might rip like a paper doll.

"Who let this she-devil into my home where my children sleep?" Rasputin bellowed in fury. Bess was about to apologize when Akilina took the blame.

"Forgive me, Father, she seemed so sincere," the former nun said, bowing her head in shame.

Rasputin cut her off. "See to that one, Anna."

Vyrubova grabbed Akilina's forearm and pulled her aside. She picked up Rasputin's belt, which he'd carelessly tossed over a chair.

"Flagellate yourself," she commanded. "Twenty strokes." Without objection, Akilina took the belt and disappeared into a back room. Rasputin approached the girl, who struggled in her captors' arms.

"Are you one of those she-wolves sent by Brother Iliodor?" he demanded.

Yaroslava bared her teeth. "I am one, and more will come until we finish you."

"What have I ever done to you, child, that you should harbor such un-Christian feelings toward me?"

"Nothing to me, because I was only six when you came to our village ten years ago spreading your gospel," she said. "But my sister was thirteen—younger than I am today. You corrupted her. She was a child and you corrupted her."

Rasputin sat in his chair and ran his hands through his long, straggly hair. He began to shake his head repeatedly.

"Her name was Katrina," the avenging angel said, her voice growing stronger. "After you dishonored her, she threw herself in the river and drowned." The word "drowned" appeared to exacerbate Rasputin's state of agitation. He mumbled some incoherent phrases about Christ and forgiveness. Then finally he muttered, "I remember no such person."

"Such insolence, to besmirch the name of our teacher," Anna Vyrubova screeched. "She deserves to be beaten in the village square!"

"Strip her and turn her over to the bodyguards," Elena proposed angrily. "They'll know what to do with a lying blasphemer!"

Their vigorous support somehow helped the spiritual leader to regain his composure. Rasputin's eyes took on a fierce and frightening new look, glittering in the firelight.

"Put her before me," he ordered.

His followers forced the girl to her knees. With a single finger, Rasputin gently tilted up her chin and peered into her eyes.

"She will do me no harm," he said calmly.

"Best you have your witches kill me now," Yaroslava cried. "Let me live and I promise I will slay you. I took an oath before Brother Iliodor as a Sister of Justice."

"Oh, your heart is so full of hatred for me?" he said softly and soothingly.

"Yes!" she cried, and spat in his face.

Rasputin wiped the spittle from his beard, then said, "Long before you took an oath to that fool Brother Iliodor, you swore obedience to me. Have you forgotten, child?"

The teenager looked up at him in confusion. For the first time, Bess saw uncertainty in her eyes. Rasputin gripped the peasant girl's shoulders and looked down at her, summoning all his concentration.

"Look deeply into my eyes, Yaroslava," he ordered her. "You are a child again and a child must obey."

She tried to look away, but he took her head in his hands and forced her to meet his gaze.

"I say that you do not hate me, you love me," he stated in a deep monotone. The defiance in the girl's face began to dissipate.

"You love me and will obey me in all things," Rasputin intoned.

In an equally monotonic voice, Yaroslava echoed him, "I will obey you."

Her eyes were so vacant, they looked like those of a sightless person. Bess shuddered at how quickly the would-be assassin had acquiesced. Rasputin nodded to his followers who, with some reluctance, released Yaroslava.

"Stand up," he said. As the girl obeyed, there was something ghastly about her movements, like a marionette operated by unseen strings.

"Give her the knife," Rasputin told Elena.

"But Father," his followers protested. He clapped his hands, commanding instant obedience. Elena picked up the knife from the floor and handed the weapon to the girl who only moments before had tried to plunge it into Rasputin's chest.

"Slit your throat," he said in a voice still just as gentle. Without hesitation, the girl raised the knife to her throat.

Bess shrieked, "For the love of God, Grigori, no!"

The mystic winked at her and quickly said, "My little boy objects. All right then, Yaroslava, just cut your nose. But be careful. Only a nick, here, to spoil your looks a little." He tapped the wing of his right nostril. "We cannot have a noseless girl roaming my village frightening the hogs." Seeing a look of disapproval on his wife's face, he added, "You will feel no pain, Yaroslava."

The peasant girl put the knife point to one nostril and carved a superficial incision a half inch long. Bess covered her own face with horror. However, if Yaroslava experienced even a scintilla of pain, she showed no sign.

"That is enough," Rasputin said, and gently removed the weapon from her hand. He stabbed it into the dinner table with a loud thunk. Then he laughed and fell into his chair by the fireplace.

"Now we will see how much this one loves her old Father Grigori," he announced to his followers. "On your knees," he commanded.

The girl dropped to her knees before him, as if those puppet strings had broken.

Rasputin stuck out his feet and called to his daughter. "Maria, bring Papa some polish. My boots could use a good cleaning. He roared with laughter and his followers echoed him like a Greek chorus.

He pointed to Bess. "If it were not for the delicate sensibilities of the wife of the great Harry Houdini, my assassin might be performing a very different service."

Bess folded her arms, scowling, and even a few of the other Little Ladies seemed put out by his off-color remark. Now the starets turned solemn.

"Have I sinned?" he asked his disciples. "Monstrously. Enough for ten men. My shame at my own degradation pains me more than any knife aimed at my heart. And that is why the Grand Gathering is so important to my salvation, and the salvation of all our souls. It is only through ultimate sin that can we find ultimate redemption."

Rasputin's daughter brought pieces of cloth, polish, and a small bowl of water, and placed them beside the kneeling peasant girl. With a trickle of blood running down her face like a tear, Yaroslava began to methodically wipe the muck and pig feces off the bottom of her new master's boots. From the next room, Bess could hear the crack of the belt as Akilina punished herself for her folly. Natasha Stepanova stood beside Houdini's wife, watching the assassin-turned-serving-wench silently go about her work.

"That poor creature," Bess whispered.

"Nothing gives our Master greater pleasure than to turn one of Iliodor's assassins into a household slave," the dancer replied, taking a bite out of an apple. "He even dispatched one to go back and kick the good brother in the groin."

"Surely he doesn't mean to keep her in that stupor indefinitely."

"When he tires of her, he'll give her away to some bumpkin who has done him a favor," Natasha said, shrugging indifferently. "At least that's what he's done in the past."

"But she's so young!"

Vyrubova, who had come up behind them, interjected, "If Father Grigori had turned her over to the police, she would spend the rest of her youth in prison. He has been exceedingly generous."

Right, thought Bess, incensed. *He deserves a gold medal for decency!*

CHAPTER THIRTY-SIX

The Teacher

Nikolayevsky Monastery of Verkhoturye loomed large before Houdini, its gleaming white walls and multiple domes adorned with crosses, a far cry from the grim medieval fortress he'd envisioned. But it could have looked like a giant outhouse for all the magician cared. He was just glad to be indoors again, at long last.

Founded in 1598, Verkhoturye was one of the oldest Russian settlements east of the Urals. For centuries, the town had thrived as manufactured goods were shipped through it to new settlements in eastern Siberia, while traders brought furs bound for cities in the west. Since remote times, for reasons that remained a mystery, Verkhoturye had been considered holy ground. Forty places of worship sprang up in the area, most prominently the monastery, famous for the miracles of its patron saint, St. Simeon.

In 1692, an earthquake caused the coffin of a long-deceased local holy man named Simeon to rise from the ground. Peering through the shattered remnants of the coffin, peasants were stunned to see that Simeon's corpse was virtually undecayed— a sign of sainthood. Soon after, cases of miraculous healing began to crop up in the vicinity. These were attributed to Simeon, and the pope canonized him. The remains were removed to the monastery, where the relics drew tens of

402 |C. Michael Forsyth

thousands of pilgrims each year. So, naturally, when Houdini arrived at its doors, the monks who admitted him assumed he was one of these pilgrims.

"You have come to see St. Simeon?" said a tall, giraffe-necked monk with a jutting Adam's apple who greeted Houdini.

"Is he in charge?"

The monk laughed. "No, you're quite right. I mean his remains. The line in the chapel is quite long, but you should be able to pray before the reliquary within three quarters of an hour. You can touch his fingers, which remain uncorrupted."

"Gee, that sure sounds like something," Houdini replied. "But I need to see the abbot."

"Father Anatoly is quite busy," the monk began, then saw the fire in Houdini's eyes. "However, if the matter is truly urgent ..."

"Nothing could possibly be more urgent."

"Very well, then."

Houdini followed the monk through immense halls with glorious ornaments ranging in style from the Italian Renaissance to the Ukrainian baroque, all of which, the magician reckoned, had been paid for with donations from the legion of pilgrims. Gold-painted icons of Russian saints lined the hallways. The gawky, long-necked monk provided Houdini with a running commentary as they passed.

"This is Xenia, patron saint of St. Petersburg, who gave all her possessions to the poor and wandered the streets for forty-five years, a fool for Christ ... Here is St. Gabriel of Bialystok, only six when he was martyred, drained of his blessed blood by Jews ..."

Sure, always blame the Jews, Houdini thought, but knew this was no time to argue.

"... St. Demetrius of Uglich, the son of Ivan the Terrible, who rejected his father's cruel ways and later was murdered during the Time of Troubles ... and that is St. Nicetas Sylittes, a twelfth-century hermit and healer who bound himself in chains and enclosed himself within a pillar."

"Man after my own heart," Houdini remarked.

As they reached the abbot's office, the chatty monk pointed out a statue of a bearded man bearing a scroll.

"Our patron saint, Simeon," he said reverently. "It is the soil of his grave through which the power of Our Lord acts. Those who've rubbed it on their bodies have seen diseases of the skin vanish overnight."

Yuck! Houdini thought. *I don't think the boys at Wilson's Acme Cream have anything to worry about.*

The abbot, Father Anatoly, reluctantly took a break from bookkeeping to grant Houdini an audience. He listened to the magician's story with a grave expression, interrupting at rare intervals to ask for clarification. When he was fully up to speed, he sighed deeply.

"You know, to be in accordance with the law, I should send a telegram to the capital informing the authorities that you are here. And I should place you in one of our cells until they arrive," said the wizened, seventy-five-year-old abbot from behind his desk. Houdini stood up.

"If that's your plan, you might as well let me out the front door and get it over with," the escape artist said testily.

"Wait," Father Anatoly said, gesturing for him to sit. When Houdini retook his seat, the abbot went on.

"I know Rasputin must be stopped. We bear some responsibility for him, for what he has become, this I know only too well," the head monk said, toying sadly with a paperweight in the image of St. Simeon.

"When he first came to us, we were impressed by his sincerity. After all, he had come hundreds of miles from his village on foot. Although he was barely literate, he was insatiable in his quest for enlightenment and would spend hours asking theological questions of our most learned brothers and joining us in prayer. Too, we were impressed by his spiritual power. Word of his healing gifts had already reached us and it was obvious that this was no ordinary man. He had the potential to be a saint himself. It was I who suggested that he spend time in the company of the hermit Makary."

"Makary?"

"A wise man who lives outside the monastery and serves as our swineherd. Over the years, he had groomed others with special gifts, though none so special as Rasputin. I think after that apprenticeship began, Rasputin's powers truly blossomed. Makary told him that to achieve his full potential, he must make a pilgrimage to Mount Athos in Greece and pray for further guidance. Again, by foot, a journey of more than a thousand miles. When I saw him after his return more than a year later, he was not the same."

"How so?" Houdini asked, leaning forward.

The abbot gave a shrug of resignation. "I cannot say. He seemed even more imbued with spiritual energy, like an engine charged. But a wildness, too, seemed to have been unleashed. His vices became an embarrassment to the monastery and we were forced to banish him. That was the last I saw of Rasputin."

"But not the last the world saw of him," Houdini said.

"Sadly, no. Your allies in St. Petersburg, Stolypin and the others, were right. He will bring the empire down."

"Then you know that you must help me. Can someone take me by wagon to Pokrovskoe?"

Father Anatoly shook his head. "We've just had a heavy snow; that road is impassable."

"Just get me to the Tura River. I can take a boat from there."

"The Tura is frozen solid this time of year. No, at this time, the only means is by sled."

"Dogsled?"

The abbot gave an apologetic smile. "Not exactly."

***

Houdini stood outside the corral, skeptically regarding a reindeer as it rooted around in the snow for food. Its lumbering companion idly chomped on hay that hung from either side of its muzzle.

"They don't look very fast," the magician said. The owner, a beefy, strong-jawed fellow of about eighteen, looked hurt.

"She can run fifty miles an hour, faster than most horses," he said defensively. He patted the creature's face. "It's all right, Ludmila, he didn't mean it."

Father Anatoly smiled. "Forgive Hans, Mr. Houdini. The reindeer are like his girlfriends. I have told him it is really time he settles down with a wife. Unless we can convince him to join us as a brother, of course."

Hans blushed. "Plenty of girls like me," he insisted. "They are not keen to marry because I have no money. I am still in debt to my uncle, from whom I borrowed to buy Ludmila and Galina. But once my business takes off—"

The abbot interrupted him, telling Houdini, "Hans transports furs from eastern parts. He stopped here to make a delivery and pick up icons painted by the brothers for the return trip."

Houdini touched Ludmila's antlers thoughtfully. "How fast can they go pulling a sled?"

"I usually figure twenty-five miles in a day," Hans answered.

The magician thought of Bess in the clutches of Rasputin, and told him, "We need to go faster, much faster."

The youthful driver pointed to the sled, which was already loaded with goods.

"If I unload it and we take only the minimal supplies, food and water, we can race across the snow much faster."

Houdini clasped Hans's hand. "Do it. You get me to Pokrovskoe in two days and you'll have enough money to pay off your uncle and then some."

Father Anatoly told Hans, "I will send Brother Konstantin to help you."

"Give me two hours to be ready," the sled driver said, eyes bright with dreams of a wife and big cottage.

"Mr. Houdini, you may rest up for the arduous journey in my quarters if you wish," the abbot said.

Houdini shook his head. "Where can I find this Brother Makary?"

***

Bess and Natasha Stepanova, side by side, packed their overnight bags for the trip to the site of the Grand Gathering.

"What do you know about this ceremony?" Bess asked the ballerina.

"I haven't been. I'm a 'virgin' like you," the redhead said. "But from I've heard, no one returns from it with any semblance of virginity."

"It's nothing more than one big, happy orgy then?" suggested Bess, trying to disguise her disgust. She had heard of wealthy degenerates who gathered in mansions for drunken sex parties in the States.

"I know only that you needn't pack a great deal of undergarments," Natasha said, then tittered at her own wit.

"Hush your mouth, you know-nothing," Anna Vyrubova snapped, coming up behind them. She glared at Natasha, then adopted a more patient tone with Bess. "It is a communing of spirits. We all bond together, regardless of age or gender. But mere words are insufficient. You must experience it for yourself." She moved on to assist the others.

"No concern for gender," the ballerina mimicked Vyubova with her trademark smirk. "Not your cup of tea, Bess, but I gather that will be far from the biggest taboo broken."

Bess gulped. She squeezed Houdini's watch in the pocket of her skirt, as if it were a rabbit's foot. A moment later, Rasputin stomped into the room on heavy boots and tossed Natasha's bigger suitcase on the floor in front of her.

"Pack it all," he commanded.

"Beg pardon?" the dancer responded, eyes widening.

"You're going home."

"What? I've been dreaming of my initiation for a year!"

Rasputin grabbed her roughly and looked into her eyes.

"Do you take me for a great fool?" he roared. "Do you think I can't see that you are insincere? Taking you to this holy rite would be casting pearls before a swine."

"How dare you talk to me that way!" she shot back.

"I will talk to you as I please because you are a whore."

Reflexively, Natasha raised her hand to slap him. He caught her wrist and twisted her arm behind her back.

"Seducing the great men of society, members of the government," he growled.

"To whom you sent me," she cried, "to gain sway over them—the ones with wills too strong for you to master."

"You did not bring me Houdini, though, did you? Are you in league with that heathen?"

"You're mad!"

He wrenched her wrist higher, between her shoulder blades, and she yelped in pain, her knees buckling.

"You're hurting me," she protested.

"Not half the pain you deserve."

Hearing the ruckus, the other disciples gathered round to gawk.

"Do you not think you were seen speaking to a man at the train station in St. Petersburg, and the same man again when we stopped in Tobolsk?" he demanded. His eyes were wild with what Bess took to be paranoia.

"Am I forbidden from speaking to any man but you?" Natasha replied.

Vyrubova spat angrily, "Listen to her insolent tongue!"

Rasputin shoved the ballerina away and she fell on the floor.

"Please, Master," Natasha begged, rising to her knees and elbows. "Let me prove my loyalty to you."

Bess did not consider the redhead her friend, but found it painful to watch her grovel. Vyrubova showed no such squeamishness. Her eyes glowed in triumph at the sight of the haughty performer debased. Rasputin's rage must indeed have been in full flower, because the lecher didn't pause to entertain the implicit offer. With his booted foot to the dancer's upraised rump, he sent her sprawling onto her face.

"Get that trollop from my sight," he bellowed, quivering with fury.

Natasha lay weeping, unable to meet the eyes of the other Little Ladies, who witnessed her fall from grace with embarrassed silence. The Neanderthal entered and Vyrubova pointed to the disgraced disciple with a contemptuous sneer.

"Take that thing to the village post office," she said. "She can send a telegram for her 'gentleman friend' to come and haul her away."

Bess knelt beside Natasha to help her to her feet, but the dancer waved her away and rose with the poise she'd demonstrated on stage. She straightened her shoulders, straining to regain her dignity.

"You are the biggest pack of fools I've ever seen," she told them, and laughed.

***

An overpowering stench told Houdini he was nearing the pigsty, a stone's throw from the monastery walls. Close by stood a wooden shack as modest as the monks' dwelling was ostentatious.

He saw a stooped, old man with waist-length white hair emptying a bucket of slop into a pig pen. Honking joyfully, the animals collided with each other, rushing to leftovers from the monastery: vegetables, bread, bones to which bits of meat clung.

"Hello," Houdini called to him.

The man looked up. His face was as deeply creased as an old leather glove. He wasn't clad in a monk's robes, just the rough, patched garments of a peasant.

"Are you the holy man?" Houdini asked.

"As you can see, I am the swineherd," the other replied in a cracked voice that matched his face.

"I think one of your swine is on the loose," the American said, stepping forward.

That got the man's attention. The bent Methuselah came from the pen and closed and latched the gate behind him.

"Are you Father Makary?" Houdini asked.

"Makary is enough."

"My name is Houdini," the magician said. "I've come from St. Petersburg in search of Rasputin."

Every Russian reacted to the mystic's name—some with fear, some with awe, some with disgust. Makary's expression was merely pained.

"You seek healing?" Makary asked. "Be careful what you wish for. To be healed by Rasputin comes with a price. You need no intermediary between you and the Almighty, my son."

"I'm not looking for him to heal me," Houdini said.

Makary fixed him with a soul-searing gaze that reminded Houdini disconcertingly of Rasputin's, yet seemed benign, devoid of menace.

"You have come to destroy him," the hermit said. Houdini nodded.

The ancient shook his head. "That will not be so easy."

"I'm starting to get that idea. That's why I need your help."

"What is it you want, my son?"

"Rasputin must have an Achilles heel. I need to understand his power. It's not really supernatural, is it?"

The hermit considered the question. "His mind is more powerful than that of most men," Makary replied. "Some call it this one thing, some another."

Houdini rubbed the back of his neck. "This isn't what I call helping."

The hermit began hobbling toward his shack and extended his elbow for Houdini to assist him.

"Mother Russia is not truly a European nation," he said as they walked. "It is Asian and this land is home to Eastern traditions far more ancient than Christianity. Some of us have, in our travels, learned practices known to the mystics and Zen masters. Mind over flesh. The power to exert one's mind over another's."

"Hypnotism, then?"

"If you will, but nothing like the party tricks dilettantes perform to amuse the idle rich in parlors of London and Paris. As it is practiced by true masters, it is a powerful tool that transforms the subjects and their reality."

Houdini opened the door to the shack for Makary and followed the hermit in.

"And Rasputin learned this from you?" he said.

The old man sighed wearily and took a seat at a wooden table in the center of the humble abode, which was warmed by a fireplace.

"Rasputin was a gifted student," Makary said, lighting a single candle to illuminate the room. "When he came to me, he already had strong natural abilities. He was highly sensitive to the emotions of others, could 'read' them. Something beyond ordinary intuition, perhaps something dwelling in that twilight between the normal and the unknowable. I helped him to hone his abilities."

"You put dynamite in the hands of a madman," Houdini remarked, though he hadn't meant to hurl the accusation out loud.

Makary winced. "I thought he would use his powers for good," the hermit explained. "And at first, he did. His abilities as a healer of souls, minds and bodies were far beyond anything I had ever witnessed. But the carnal side of his nature was just as strong as the spiritual side.

"I sent him to the monastery at Mount Athos in Greece, a center of spirituality, in the hope that he might conquer his demons. But there, unfortunately, he saw monks engage in degenerate behavior, including the sin of homosexuality, and he began to view the life of celibacy as a farce. He realized that his destiny was not to be a monk, but to be something else. Something ... more. The spiritual and bestial in him ceased to wage war, but instead fused and fueled each other."

"I've seen his bestial side, all right," Houdini said. "The pervert makes a career of corrupting women, especially married ones."

"The opportunity to bed women is not what drives him," Makary replied, shaking his head. "Nor does he seek wealth. No, it is a lust for domination, power for power's sake. Since he left my tutelage, his strength has increased a hundred-fold, and at the same time, he has sunk deeper into darkness. You have heard of those obscene rituals?"

"Yes, the Khlysty business."

"That is what his followers believe, but beneath the surface is something even more sinister and blasphemous."

"Devil worship?" Houdini suggested, raising his eyebrows.

The old man rose to get some sticks from a stack in the corner and fed them to the fire.

"More ancient than the fallen angel Lucifer of the Christian faith, more ancient than the gods of Rome or Babylon," Makary said. "As his power over men and women grows, so does his quest for spiritual forces darker and deeper, deeper and darker, the unknowable, the unthinkable. And his followers sink with him into this moral cesspool, an abyss from which there is no escape."

Houdini fought down the dread that was rising in him like bile.

"Inescapable isn't in my vocabulary," he said. "How can he be stopped?"

"I've wondered that myself," Makary replied. "I've sometimes thought that if his own power could somehow be turned against him ... But of course, I am too old and weak to oppose Rasputin now."

Houdini got up and went to the hermit's side.

"This ability to hypnotize others as Rasputin does, can you teach it to me?"

"I've just told you how dangerous these mental powers are," the hermit protested.

"And that it's the only way I can battle him," retorted Houdini.

Makary hesitated, then asked, "How long are you prepared to stay and study with me?"

The magician scratched his jaw and calculated the time, then said, "Well, Hans said that we ought to be able to leave at 3:00."

The hermit groaned and ran both hands through his white mane.

"You expect me to teach you in one hour what took Rasputin years to master?"

"I'm a quick learner," Houdini replied with a confident smile.

The Grand Gathering

W hen Rasputin and the Little Ladies reached the site of the Grand Gathering, they were not the first to have arrived. Already assembled were at least two dozen men and women. Most wore white robes with cowls, similar in design to those a monk might wear. Six of the men wore red robes, emblazoned with peculiar symbols that resembled hieroglyphics, and Vyrubova told Bess these were Khlysty deacons. The attendees greeted Rasputin joyfully and embraced the women as if they were long-lost relatives. Indeed, Rasputin didn't behave at all like a cult leader, but like a beloved family patriarch hosting a reunion.

The Little Ladies now numbered thirteen. Rasputin's wife Praskovia and his children had not accompanied them; they'd been dispatched to the home of Praskovia's mother. Vyrubova clapped her hands to gain the attention of the women.

"We must don our holy attire for the Rejoicing," she announced.

She led the contingent through stone halls from whose walls ancient tapestries clung, riddled with holes and mold. One depicted a unicorn battling a bear, another St. George defeating the dragon. There was no electricity; torches lit the way. The Little Ladies entered a chamber that served as a changing room. On hooks, scores of white robes lined one wall—suggesting to Bess that many more followers were expected. The other walls were taken up by cubbyholes, filled with the neatly folded clothes and shoes of the worshippers who had preceded them.

"Remove all of your clothing, even your undergarments, and put on the worship robes," Vyrubova instructed in the manner of a hospital nurse. She supervised the proceedings with the keen interest that Bess had by now come to expect. The women assisted each other in unlacing their corsets and unfastening elaborate brassieres that reached all the way to the waist. Around Houdini's wife, white hobble skirts, garters and stockings cascaded to the floor.

Bess stood behind the Little Lady named Barbara Uexkuell, unlacing her corset, while Elena undid the American woman's.

"Have you been to the Grand Gathering before?" Bess asked Elena over her shoulder.

"We three and Vera Zhukovskaya are the novices," Elena answered. "The others won't tell us anything about it."

Rasputin's disciples Munya, Akilina and Princess Shakhovskaya stripped beside them. The princess pulled off her chemise, trimmed in lace and ribbons, while Akilina wiggled her hips out of her slip and dropped her drawers, exposing her big, rosy behind.

"It seemed this day would never come," the former nun exulted. "Now the Rejoicing is just hours away."

In her performing days with the Floral Sisters, Bess had become used to changing with other women backstage and changing rapidly. No one saw her exchange the pocket-watch camera from its hiding place in her knickers to the pocket of the robe. When the women were outfitted in their robes, Vyrubova looked at them approvingly.

"I see apprehension in the eyes of some of you," she said. "You have nothing to fear. You shall journey to a place beyond shame, or fear or judgment."

"The Radenie," Munya said in hushed reverence.

Bess prided herself on how well she spoke Russian now. This was the first time in many conversations that a word was spoken that she didn't understand.

"Radenie?" she repeated.

"The sacred circle dance," Akilina explained.

Each hour, more followers arrived, from all social castes and all corners of the empire and, Bess suspected, far beyond it. Some of the pilgrims' accents and garb were so unfamiliar to Bess, the fanciful notion struck her that they could be time travelers. The Khlysty cult included male and female as well as young and old, from fresh-faced boys and girls barely in their teens to wrinkled crones and men with wisps of white hair clinging to their skulls. But all such distinctions dissolved as the new arrivals donned their robes. No titles or formal terms of address were used, nor even last names.

People chatted about small matters or sat reading books of devotion. A nervous energy permeated the air. Yet everyone seemed on high alert, despite their casual chit-chat, like baboons aware that a leopard is on the prowl. Soon, at least ninety people packed the building, filling every hall and alcove. Bess found herself squeezed against a little bald man with reading glasses, who was mumbling passages from the Bible he held to his nose. He tucked in his groin to avoid contact with her.

"Strange to be embarrassed, since soon we will all be one," he said. "Force of habit, I suppose."

***

The pair of reindeer blazed across the snow, hauling the sled behind. Known as caribou in North America, they were a species exquisitely adapted to the unforgiving wasteland, wanderers that roamed up to three thousand miles a year. But Houdini wasn't satisfied with their performance.

"Can't Donner and Blitzen go any faster?" he shouted to the driver.

"Not without collapsing from exhaustion or tipping us over," Hans replied. "And don't you recall? Their names are Galina and Ludmila."

"Sure. Wait, aren't those girls' names?"

"They are girls."

"But the antlers?" Houdini said, pointing at the horns.

"Males shed their antlers in December, after mating season," Hans explained. "Cows keep theirs through the winter until after their calves are born."

Houdini leaned back in the seat. "Tell me more."

"Well, they're very fast swimmers—" Hans began enthusiastically.

"I was just kidding," the magician said. The young man pouted and Houdini regretted his teasing. "How do you take these long runs without going crazy?" he asked.

"Well, we sometimes pass the time by singing," Hans said, brightening. "Do you want to begin, or shall I?"

"Knock yourself out," the magician replied.

In a robust voice, the young man belted out a peasant song:

"Nadya girl, what do you need?
You don't need anything but chocolate,

Chocolate's cheap, it's just a few rubles.
There's no chocolate, but you can have candy.

Why am I bald, without a hair left?
Because I've had too much fun with young women!
She danced a karapet, ripped up her boots,
And all that was left on her legs were stockings and gum.

A luscious young lady danced the karapet,
And a young Cossack squeezed her.
She danced a karapet and fell into the bushes—yes!
We'll all soon be walking to the christening."

Houdini listened politely, trying to decipher the bewildering lyrics. Then, at the boy's beckoning, he returned the favor and shared some American songs. By the time they passed Tyumen, the nearest town to Pokrovskoe, Houdini had learned the Russian folk song by heart, and taught his eager pupil the words to "Yankee Doodle Dandy," plus four Al Jolson tunes.

The monotony of the landscape was occasionally broken by structures such as windmills and the crumbling walls of abandoned fortresses. In the distance, soon after passing Tyumen, Houdini saw what looked like a medieval castle looming above a gloomy forest.

"What is that place?" he asked, elbowing Hans and pointing to the structure.

"That was an outpost of Ivan the Terrible," Hans revealed. "His enemies were sent here, those whose lives he was generous enough to spare. He exiled them to Siberia instead of putting them to death."

'That was mighty white of him."

Hans grimaced as he tugged his red cap down over his ears. "I'm sure there were some who suffered his tortures who would have preferred the executioner's ax."

"Thanks for the history lesson. How far are we from Pokrovskoe?"

"No more than thirty miles. And it's a good thing." Hans pointed to the dark skies. "There hasn't been snow this way in a while, as you can see from the ground, but a blizzard is on the way."

***

The sled arrived in Pokrovskoe just over an hour later. Houdini's first stop was the post office, a little outpost without any of the pretensions of the majestic government buildings of St. Petersburg. Despite Houdini's efforts to seem nonchalant in his queries, he drew suspicious glances, as any stranger in this remote village might. The postmaster told Houdini the location of the faith healer's home.

"Is there anywhere in town that he might hold a gathering?" Houdini asked.

The postmaster thought for a minute. "He used to hold prayer meetings on his own property years ago."

With his finger, the postmaster beckoned Houdini to lean in, then he whispered, "There were rumors of odd goings-on there and some years ago, the authorities raided the place, but they found nothing."

"Maybe they didn't look hard enough," Houdini said.

They found Rasputin's home empty, although the abundance of suitcases confirmed the earlier presence of the

Little Ladies. Searching among the luggage, Houdini found a blue suitcase he recognized as his wife's. He opened it and found most of her clothing inside. On top lay the red and green scarf he'd given her last Christmas. He drew it to his face, breathed in her familiar scent, and sighed. Nearby, Hans poked the fireplace, stirring up orange embers that still clung to life.

"We can't be more than a day behind them," Hans told Houdini reassuringly.

As they exited the home, Houdini saw in the distance a large barn with a makeshift cross in the place of the weathervane. Outside it, they could make out two figures sitting on a bench.

"We have one more stop here," Houdini told the reindeer driver.

***

"It is time," shouted one of the Khlysty deacons over the clamor as he raised a lantern above his head. The participants covered their heads with hoods and followed him in single file, like medieval penitents. Bess looked around for Rasputin, but he was nowhere to be seen. At the end of a hall, they came to a great iron door that looked like it was meant to restrain the whole host of hell. The red-clad deacon unlatched two bolts and swung the door open. Then he led the party down a spiral staircase. There was no clattering of shoes on stone, only the patter of bare feet and the rustling of robes. As they descended into darkness, Bess clenched the watch in her fist, deep in the pocket of the robe, as if it were a talisman against evil.

The stairway entered into a large chamber lit by seven torches, each on a stone column. In the middle stood an altar hewn from rock. It reminded Bess of an illustration in her old children's Bible of Abraham preparing to sacrifice Isaac on a stone altar. Nearby, five cauldrons bubbled, emitting fumes that filled the chamber with an intoxicating incense. The pilgrims knelt as they filled the chamber, the Little Ladies clustered together. It took nearly half an hour for the entire horde to take their places. They knelt tightly pressed together, looking up expectantly at the altar where the deacons stood.

"Let the Rejoicing begin," the deacons exclaimed.

***

The reindeer brought the sled to a halt in the back of Rasputin's house.

"All right, wait here," Houdini told Hans.

"What if you need help?" the big lad asked, frowning.

"Do just as I told you, and you'll be helping, believe me." The men shook hands, then Houdini strode toward the chapel.

A pair of motorcycles leaned against the building, and beside it their owners sat on the bench, smoking cigarettes. Houdini recognized them as his old pals the Neanderthal and Eyepatch. As Houdini neared, he listened intently for chants or, at the very least, hymns. He heard nothing, but reminded himself that the ceremony was likely held underground. When the duo saw him coming, they rose to their feet.

"It took you a long time to get over here," the Neanderthal said.

"You boys aren't religious, I take it?" the magician said.

"Come back on Sunday morning," the Neanderthal growled.

"I recognize you," Houdini said. "You're the ape who threw my wife in the lake. Not nice."

"Run along, little man," Eyepatch said, throwing away his cigarette. "We don't want to have to give you another beating."

"Does Rasputin have you goons hypnotized?" Houdini asked. "No, I doubt it. You don't have the brains for it. Just pays you bums to do his dirty work."

The thugs looked at each other, nodded, then lunged for the escape artist, who—much to their surprise—spun about and bolted. Houdini, who won medals for track in his youth, sprinted ahead of them. The Neanderthal and Eyepatch watched him disappear around the corner of Rasputin's cottages. A second later, from behind it, the sled took off, the man in Houdini's hat and brown coat whipping the reindeer to full gallop. Roaring in frustration, the Neanderthal cried, "Come on!" to his cohort. The two rushed back to the chapel, retrieved their motorcycles and took off after the sled.

As Houdini heard the sound of motorcycle engines die down, he snuck from behind the house and made for the church—now dressed in the reindeer driver's fur coat and red cap. He slipped into Rasputin's chapel. It was a paragon of simplicity, with only a dozen pews, a single rough-hewn cross and a pair of candlesticks sitting on the altar. *Quiet as a tomb,* Houdini thought, beginning to doubt that Rasputin and his flock of fanatics could really be anywhere about. If they were, it could only be in an underground chamber. He scrutinized the altar, looking for any type of mechanism.

That cross looks fishy, he thought.

He grasped the top of the cross and pulled down. Sure enough, it was a lever. The dais on which the altar stood rotated on a track two feet to the left, revealing an opening and a narrow brick stairway. An unidentifiable stench wafted up from below. As uninviting as the hidden cellar was, Houdini stealthily descended into it. As he did, the temperature dropped with what felt like unnatural rapidity.

The opening above provided just enough light for Houdini to see that the underground chamber was unoccupied. There were signs, though, that something unsavory had taken place there in the past. Odd, pagan runes adorned the walls, and a well-worn, blood-stained whip lay abandoned on the floor. There was an altar here too, but made of stone, and carved into it were more of the ancient symbols.

Well, it was worth a try.

Houdini trotted up the stairs into the chapel, where he was met by two ugly and familiar faces. The henchmen had returned and stood side by side in the aisle, which was barely wide enough to accommodate the shoulders of both.

"I told you he was here," Eyepatch told his associate, as proudly as if he'd just invented the wheel.

"We gave your little boyfriend a good thrashing before we let loose his reindeer and overturned his toy," the Neanderthal said with a nasty chortle. "Wept like a baby."

Houdini started forward, clenching his fists.

"You don't want to do that, Yankee dog," the Neanderthal warned him. "You'd best take a seat in the pew. The ceremony will be over soon, and when we take you to the Master, he'll decide what to do with you."

Houdini turned, grabbed a candlestick from the altar and charged them. He banged the Neanderthal in the chest and rammed the bottom of the candlestick into his belly, causing him to double over, moaning in pain. A wallop from the base of the candlestick sent Eyepatch crashing into the pews, shattering them. Houdini hopped over the fallen men and made for the door. But the Neanderthal dove for his legs like a Notre Dame linebacker and brought him down.

After wrestling Houdini to the floor, the men hoisted him up by his arms and legs and tossed him down the opening beside the altar. He tumbled all the way down and landed with a smack on the brick floor.

Groaning and holding his aching head, Houdini looked up to see the light disappearing as the men pushed the upstairs altar back into place. The gears of the wheel on which the dais turned made an awful, grinding sound.

"You stay here to guard him," he heard the Neanderthal say.

"I don't think he's going anywhere."

"You do know what this Houdini's profession is, right? I'll go to the forest and tell the Master."

"He won't like being interrupted. Not during the Rejoicing."

"They'd have just started," the Neanderthal assured Eyepatch. "The climax is always at noon."

Crouched on the floor in utter darkness, Houdini heard the sound of a motorcycle as it zoomed away.

CHAPTER THIRTY-EIGHT

The Beast Cometh Forth

Bess knelt shoulder to shoulder and hip to hip with her fellow worshippers. The proceedings had dragged on for at least three hours. Hymns, prayers, more hymns. She was beginning to wonder whether all the talk about mad cavorting and orgies was baloney. The gossip of ignorant fools. All she saw around her were the earnest faces of believers seeking spiritual enlightenment. The deacons led prayers and gave simple homilies that would not have been out of place in any Orthodox church, or even the pulpit of the Catholic church she'd attended as a child. Yet there was a comfort in nestling with the rest of this flock, singing and rocking in unison.

Now Rasputin himself took his turn on the dais, standing in front of the altar.

"The Christ!" many of the attendees whispered excitedly.

Rasputin, who wore a purple cassock, raised his hands and gestured for them to settle down.

"Am I The Christ?"

"Yes!" a chorus replied. Rasputin shook his head.

"Tonight, in this place, there is no I, there is only we. We all become one with Christ, one with each other. Here we die in the fires of ecstasy, our sinfulness is burned away, and are reborn as a new being."

His eyes glittered, and it seemed to Bess that they did not merely reflect the torchlight, they emitted light.

"We join with forces that were old when Jesus was born, before Abraham. We bathe in those primordial waters, a baptism more transformative than any priest ever dreamed. As Our Lord sayeth, I come to baptize you not in water but in fire. Willingly we let those flames incinerate us. And when we are reincarnated, it is as pure beings, children of light."

Bess listened, suddenly overtaken by doubt about the righteousness of her mission. At first, the sermon sounded like highfalutin blather. But as this strange man of the cloth continued, the truthfulness of his words became more apparent, his logic inescapable. She became aware of the energy in the room, like ions rearranging before an electrical storm. She sensed that something terrible and marvelous was about to take place. And now she felt an irresistible urge to be part of it.

"Yes!" voices around her muttered, roared and sang around her, caught up in the rapture.

"Yes!" whispered Bess.

***

Houdini threaded the whip through the gears of the wheel beneath the trap door and tied it securely with a square knot. The hard part had been locating the lash in the dark, crawling and groping in the underground chamber beneath Rasputin's chapel.

Now comes the easy part, the escape artist thought as he stepped back and pulled.

Upstairs, stretched out on a pew, Eyepatch unwrapped the lunch that one of the Little Ladies had prepared for him. He didn't mind being excluded from the Grand Gathering. Father Grigori had solemnly informed him that his role—watching out for any blasphemer who came by his old chapel in search of the faithful—was a far more critical role. And of course, the fistful of rubles he'd stuffed in his pocket was an ample consolation. He sank his teeth into the black bread and cured beef sandwich and chewed noisily. So noisily that he failed to hear the stockinged feet that tiptoed toward him from the altar. By the time he looked up, it was too late.

Houdini stood over Eyepatch, brandishing the candlestick with the base aimed squarely at his forehead.

"Don't make a move or I'll bash your pea brain in," the American snarled.

"How did you ...?" Eyepatch sputtered, spitting out a mouthful of bread.

"Shaddup!" snapped Houdini. "Where is Rasputin?"

"I ... I don't know," the henchman stammered. Houdini raised the candlestick as if to strike.

"Try again."

"I won't tell you!"

"You'll tell me, or I'll take your fool head off."

"The Master will do far worse if I tell. He can put visions of hell in your head."

Houdini saw that the fear in the minion's single eye was genuine and sensed that all the rough stuff in the world wouldn't make him cough up the truth.

"Have it your way." He clobbered Eyepatch—although not with all his might—and the hoodlum keeled over, unconscious.

Now the words of the other tough guy came back to him. The Neanderthal had said that he was going to the forest to speak to Rasputin. He pictured the castle he and Hans had passed on the way to Pokrovskoe. *A castle built by Ivan the Terrible!* He recalled Yusupov's story that beneath another of the tyrant's fortresses, underground chambers used for torture had been found. Houdini hurled away the candlestick and bolted out the door toward the second motorcycle.

***

On their knees, Rasputin's followers rocked, swayed and shook feverishly as he thundered at them. His fervent speech energized them, yet by the same token, he seemed to draw energy from them as if they were living batteries. In Bess's eyes, he loomed larger, the torchlight casting weird shadows that extended his figure in all directions, so that he was in all corners of the chamber, on everything, in everyone. The fever infected Bess too. Her entire body shivered; she was burning up, yet freezing too, unable to remain still, her thighs opening and closing. Rasputin flung up his arms, robes fluttering as if he was some colossal bird of prey.

"Let the Radenie begin!" he cried. All around Bess, the faithful scrambled to their feet.

"Radenie! Radenie! Radenie!" the mob chanted. Unable to control her own body, Bess found herself rising with them, pulled aloft by some unseen force.

"Radenie!" she screamed with the others.

Fortunately for Houdini, the snowstorm that Hans had warned him about still held off. The road back toward Tyumen was relatively clear and, going full throttle, Houdini made the trip to the castle in less than an hour. With its crumbling outer walls and broken parapets, the structure at first seemed unoccupied. But, driving the bike into a courtyard, Houdini found sleighs and carriages parked. Neighing led him to a large stable housing the horses of visitors. It was just beginning to snow when Houdini wheeled the motorbike in and leaned it against a wall. The motorcycle that the Neanderthal had driven was propped up nearby, so Houdini knew he had to watch out for Rasputin's hulking enforcer.

Hurrying through the castle, the escape artist followed a trail of candelabras to the changing room, where he found the cultists' robes. Now he could hear in the distance the chanting, like an eerie siren call. He rid himself of his coat and clothes, tucked them in a corner and dressed himself as one of the Khlysty.

Clad in a hooded white robe, Houdini found the door to the underground chamber and descended the spiral staircase. He followed the voices, which sounded far more like the howls of lunatics in the bowels of Bedlam than Gregorian chants.

What he beheld as he entered the underground chamber shocked him as it would any rational man. The description of the Khlysty ceremony he'd heard from the former cultist at Brother Iliodor's camp hardly did it justice. Scores of worshipers danced in a circle around a high altar, bumping each other like stampeding bulls. That is, if one chose to call this chaotic twisting, leaping and throwing up of the hands dancing. It was more like madness in motion. There was no music; the only accompaniment was bestial chanting intermingled with hysterical laughter, whoops of joy and inhuman screeches. On the dais around which the wild-eyed fanatics swept towered a giant figure who lashed them on with a cat-o'-nine-tails: Rasputin.

"Faster, faster, my children!" Rasputin roared above the cacophony.

It wasn't difficult for Houdini to infiltrate the frenzied worshippers. He moved along with them, trying to avoid flailing arms and legs. He had the awful sense that if you stumbled and fell, you'd be trampled. Dancing along with the cultists, he looked around for Bess, but it was impossible to pick her out from among the hooded figures. Rasputin egged them on, puppeteer and slave master, and the worshippers picked up their pace. Some of the hoods flew back and faces appeared: grinning crones with faces so craggy they looked like reanimated mummies, alongside fresh-faced adolescents, their innocence ripe for the taking.

All around Houdini, men and women swirled about, hair of all colors, blond, red, black, flying in all directions as if blown by the gusts of an invisible cyclone. Some worshippers sprang like rheboks, others spun in place, mad tops. Yet despite the lack of uniformity there was a oneness to them. Each moment they seemed less like individuals and more like a whirling cloud of insects. Growing dizzy, he thought of that children's book *Little Black Sambo*, in which a tiger raced around a tree so furiously it became nothing but a yellow blur.

Rasputin abruptly tossed the lash aside and thrust his right hand skyward. At this signal, the red-clad deacons took all but one of the torches and extinguished them in the cauldrons. The remaining torch gave faint illumination to the increasingly bizarre scene.

Robes began to sail off as the participants continued to dance. Men hopped up and down, their genitals flapping. Women thrashed about, arching their backs and bucking. In the darkened chamber, it was impossible to distinguish whole bodies. Houdini saw only flashes: bouncing breasts; leathery reptilian skin, grey pubic hair. Houdini slipped off his own robe and moved with them, the pocket watch in one hand, a flashbulb tucked in his armpit. Fortunately, he'd mastered the art of concealing tools of escape, even when nude. A pixyish female figure brushed by him.

Bess?!!!

He struggled through the fleshly merry-go-round after her, elbowing his way past hairy shoulders, sidling between wide hips. He caught her hand and spun her around. It was a girl of no more than fourteen, her eyes rolled back so that only the whites could be seen.

Suddenly, Rasputin threw his head back and raised both arms, fingers outstretched as if beckoning a deity. But surely not the God of the Christians or the Jews. He bellowed out a word in no tongue Houdini had ever heard and that he suspected was more ancient than Latin, or Greek or Egyptian, perhaps hadn't been spoken in the light of day for thousands of years.

Responding to a command—whether they understood its meaning or not—the worshippers collapsed to the floor, some on hands and knees as if transformed into hogs, others fully prostrate. Houdini dropped with them. Then, just as Brother Iliodor's follower had described, the worshippers crawled toward each other and launched into an orgy that would have put the Romans to shame. All around him, Houdini beheld a rollicking sea of flesh, with serpentine limbs slithering, buttocks rising and falling. The sounds of flesh smacking against flesh, grunts and moans filled the chamber.

Beside him, the teenaged girl he'd mistaken for Bess moments earlier now straddled a potbellied man with bristly warts, rocking and rolling her hips furiously. In front of the magician, a plump brunette knelt on all fours, rump raised in obscene invitation. Hers was not the only offer. On his right, a hag with withered dugs sank her claws into his forearm and tried to pull him on top of her. Houdini shoved the lust-crazed creature away and clambered over hairy backs and jiggling thighs to an oasis free of flesh.

Kneeling in the midst of the writhing mass, he shut his eyes and gasped in despair, "Bess!"

A small feminine hand touched his.

"What, dear?"

In the dim light, he saw Bess kneeling beside him, naked as a jaybird. He was speechless as she dragged him from the pile of bodies and behind one of the stone columns.

"What are you doing here?" Bess whispered.

"I heard there was a swell party going on. But where's the gin?"

"I thought you were in prison."

"You know how I hate being cooped up."

She unclenched her fist and showed Houdini the watch in her hands.

"You needn't have put yourself out," she said. "I'm about to take his picture. Sorry I took yours. I didn't see the engraving."

"Where have you been keeping that thing?"

"You don't want to know."

"You must really want to nail this guy."

"Do I ever."

Her husband pointed to the dais, where Rasputin rose up from the darkness.

"Speak of the devil," Houdini said.

The mystic stood before the altar in all his glory, utterly nude, his chest matted with dark hair more befitting a wolf or a goat than a human. At his feet, two women knelt caressing his engorged manhood like craven devotees of Priapus.

Houdini readied himself, Boris's watch in one hand and the flashbulb in the other. He'd been fantasizing about this moment for so long and now his prey was finally in his sights.

Caught you red-handed, you weasel.

He twisted open the lens cover and prepared to toss the flashbulb. But what he saw when he brought up the camera could not be possibly be real. For Rasputin had been transformed from a man into a monster. In place of his bearded face was a goat-like head crowned by horns, a grotesque mockery of humanity. The Beast Incarnate.

CHAPTER THIRTY-NINE

The Blizzard

After a few seconds, the master illusionist made sense of the scene before him. Houdini saw that there had been no supernatural metamorphosis. A pair of the red-robed deacons had placed a beast mask over Rasputin's head. The acolytes stepped back reverently. Makary was right, Houdini realized. This ceremony was rooted in something older than any heretical Christian cult, older than the worship of golden calves or Apollo.

"It's no good, we can't see his face," Bess whispered, shaking his arm.

Three women were now stacked in front of Rasputin. It wasn't clear which one he was plowing into from behind at that moment or which orifice; all wore expressions of ecstasy and agony, absolute bliss and absolute horror. Houdini stared for a moment and while on one level he was aware that he was witnessing something otherworldly, on another it couldn't be earthlier: a lecher satisfying himself with infatuated dupes. Houdini knew of a medium who had convinced a gullible widow he was channeling her husband's spirit to get her into bed, and another who hoodwinked a patron of the paranormal arts into believing he was the reincarnation of Casanova, the world's greatest lover. This lowlife belonged to that brotherhood of bamboozlers.

"I'll pull off the mask. You take the picture with your camera," Houdini whispered to his wife. "The timing's got to be just right."

"Be careful, sweetheart," Bess replied, and pecked him on the cheek.

Houdini wound his way through the heaps of bodies, some piled four high, past raised feet with curling toes, pumping rumps, and plunging organs. Insinuating himself between Rasputin's deacons, he stepped behind the mystic. Rasputin's broad back seemed unnaturally hairy, just this side of human, and it struck Houdini that if he hesitated one more second, Rasputin really would transmogrify into some monstrous demon-god. With one hand, he grabbed the horns of the mask and pulled up. With the other, he hurled the flashbulb to the floor.

Light exploded as if God—the one true God, the one his rabbi father praised—had cast down a bolt of lightning. At the same instant, Bess snapped the photo of the mystic at the climax of his four-way romp. For one brief second, in that garish light, the true Rasputin appeared to her: nothing more than a frightened animal. Houdini pushed past his enemy and took his place at the side of his wife, who still pointed the sub-miniature camera. When Rasputin spotted his adversary, his look of deer-like panic turned to an equally animalistic rage.

"Sacrilege!" he roared. "Seize the blasphemers!"

The cult leader's male followers must have been too spent from the rigors of intercourse to leap into action, for it was the women who rushed toward Houdini, claws outstretched. More screeching she-beasts—the Little Ladies in the forefront—converged on Bess, raking at her skin with merciless talons.

Houdini grabbed the single remaining torch from a column and swung it left, then right, like St. Michael with a flaming sword, clearing the attackers off Bess. He held the snarling, yipping wolfpack at bay. The magician saw the enraged false prophet barreling through the crowd toward them, fists clenching and unclenching in a titanic rage, his deacons at his heels. Houdini glanced at the arched entranceway a few yards away and committed the path to memory. Then he tossed the last torch into the cauldron, casting the chamber into utter darkness.

That didn't put an end to the mayhem. Houdini heard the rending of flesh as the she-devils blindly clawed and bit each other like starving rats in a barrel. He grabbed Bess's wrist.

"Come on!"

Counting on his memory, and accustomed from his stage act to operating in total darkness, he led his wife to the stairs. They scrambled up the winding stone steps and emerged on the ground floor. The escape artist whirled and shut the door, then slid the bolts into place.

"That ought to hold them for a while," he said. They hurried to the dressing area and threw on their clothes.

"Give me your watch," Houdini said. He stuffed it in his coat pocket along with his own. In the distance, they could hear a great thumping against the basement door as if the Minotaur were trying to bust out of his prison.

"The door won't hold long, will it?" Bess said, trying to keep the terror out of her voice. Houdini turned and took her shoulders.

"Look into my eyes," he said.

"This is no time to get romantic."

"Cut it out. Look into my eyes."

***

They hurried to the stable where Houdini had propped the motorbike against a beam. Bess looked at it skeptically.

"I suppose I'm expected to ride on that contraption," she said.

"We could run, but I didn't bring the right shoes for it," he said, donning the goggles and helmet that hung from one of the handlebars.

"Have you ever driven a motorcycle before?" she asked.

"Of course. How do you think I got here?"

Houdini got the engine started and they climbed on, Bess holding her husband's waist.

"Where do you think you're going, Yank?" came the Neanderthal's voice from behind them. The big thug approached, toting a double-barreled shotgun. Better prepared for a confrontation now, he also bore a holstered pistol on one hip and a sheathed knife on the other. The magician sighed.

This guy is really starting to get on my nerves.

"I knew you would get out of the basement of that chapel," the henchman said. "How did you do it?"

"I'll tell you in a postcard," the escape artist replied. He twisted the grip, applying the throttle, and the bike shot out of the barn. The Neanderthal screamed bloody murder and fired at them. Houdini leaned to the left and the bike tilted so far over Bess was sure it would tip over. That maneuver saved their lives; the shot cluster blew right by them.

The Neanderthal turned to his own motorbike and saw that the tires had been slashed.

"Damn you!" he cried, and kicked it over.

***

The Houdinis zoomed down the road toward Tyumen. From there, perhaps a troika or dogsled to the train station. The snow was compacted and the road pocked with treacherous patches of ice. The bike kept skidding and it took tremendous effort to keep it upright. Houdini drove as fast as the conditions allowed. Push the vehicle any harder and they were sure to tip over and careen into a tree.

Just as Hans had warned, the snow began to come down now, fast and furious. The wind picked up and the freezing air sought every means of entry to their skin, creeping in through the crevices between their scarves and coats, through button holes and the openings of boots. Fighting to keep control of the bike, Houdini's fingers gripped the handlebars tightly. Despite his thick gloves, the sweat on his hands began to freeze and his fingers started to swell up like sausages.

Snowflakes clouded Houdini's goggles, and he soon could no longer see the road ahead. But it was relatively straight and, trusting instinct, he forged ahead into what was becoming a full-fledged blizzard. Bess clung to her husband. She was suddenly possessed by the horrible thought that Rasputin had sent the storm, that in his rage he could control the weather as he could control minds. She looked back over her shoulder toward the castle from which they'd fled and, in the distance, could see at least ten horses.

"They're after us!" she cried. Houdini looked back and saw their mounted pursuers gaining on them. He leaned forward and accelerated, nearly blind, into the white maelstrom.

Too late, Houdini saw an enormous tree that had fallen onto the road, blocking their path. He yanked the brake lever as hard as he could—too hard, because the front brakes seized, causing the bike to skid, fall on its side and crash. The magician and his wife were flung clear and landed in a snowbank on the side of the road.

Houdini helped Bess to her feet.

"Are you all right, sweetie?"

She nodded. "But when we get home, we stick to the streetcar."

The riders surrounded them. The Neanderthal dismounted and strutted forward.

"You know, I'm getting a little tired of your mug," Houdini said. "You've got a face even a mother couldn't love."

Rasputin's ugly enforcer slugged Houdini in the jaw with such force that the American fell to the ground.

"That's for slashing my tires," he growled.

CHAPTER FORTY

The Torture Chamber

The Little Ladies Dunya and Akilina held Bess still while Anna Vyrubova sat on a stool searching her for the watch. The members of Rasputin's prayer circle showed not a glimmer of their former comradery. Their eyes burned with hatred.

Houdini's wife gasped as Vyrubova's hand thrust roughly into her private parts. It was the first sound she'd made since entering the room. Bess had ignored their commands, so the women had no choice but to strip her by force. Whatever longings the fat, crippled Russian might have expressed in the past, there was no mistaking her touch for a caress. She made sure her captive squirmed in discomfort. Finding nothing, Vyrubova stood.

"You treacherous little fool," she screeched. "You denied yourself the world when you betrayed our savior. You were offered unimaginable spiritual rewards. Now, whatever punishment you receive, you richly deserve."

Bess's only response was a look of raw disgust. Vyrubova slapped her.

"Get her dressed," Vyrubova ordered the Little Ladies.

Moments later, Rasputin, three deacons and the Neanderthal surrounded the American couple in a dark room that had evidently once served as a torture chamber, if the

443

grizzly medieval devices on hand were any guide. Houdini recognized the Iron Maiden, the Iron Chair and the Rack. He'd once incorporated a replica of the latter into his act. The decor reminded the escape artist of a tableau in a wax museum—particularly the man-sized cage that hung from the ceiling housing a skeleton turned half to dust. But these were no props; blood on the rusted implements gave witness to the fact that they'd been used in the past to torment unlucky souls.

"You have searched him thoroughly?" Rasputin demanded.

"From head to toe, Master," the Neanderthal replied.

"And the woman too?"

"Vyrubova herself did that," the henchman said with a crooked smile. "You can be sure she took her time."

Rasputin glowered at Houdini. "You will tell me where it is," he commanded.

Houdini met his eyes fearlessly. "Sure, right after hell freezes over."

The mystic seemed rattled for a moment, then shrugged his shoulders.

"It does not surprise me that the power of the Holy Spirit fails to move you."

"Oh, that's what it is now, is it?" Houdini said with a defiant laugh. "I thought it was good old-fashioned hypnotism."

Ignoring him, Rasputin moved on to Bess. She tried to avoid his gaze, but he took her face in his hands and jerked it toward him with such force it looked as if he might twist her head off.

"You will tell me where your little camera is," he ordered.

She looked at him blankly.

Rasputin stepped back, aghast. His powers had never failed him with any woman. He repeated the command in a lower octave, his voice reverberating around the room. Bess merely stared at him with a perplexed expression, as if he were talking in gibberish.

"It's okay, it happens to the best of us," Houdini cracked.

The frustrated mystic stomped around the room like a caged predator.

"You cannot stand between me and my destiny," he cried to Houdini. "You will regret the day you came to Russia."

"I'm already starting to wish we'd picked Paris," the escape artist replied.

Demonstrating initiative, the Neanderthal put his knife to Houdini's throat and snarled at Bess, "Talk up, you silly American cow, or so help me God, I'll slice your husband's throat so deep his tongue will fall out."

Her eyes widened in fear, but she did not speak.

"She's as stubborn as he is," he said with grudging admiration. "But give me an hour and she'll talk, or he will."

Rasputin nodded. "Your wife will suffer grievously," he told Houdini with such deep sadness it looked as if tears might appear. "And it is your fault, magician."

***

Rasputin's minions strapped Houdini to the rack, his ankles tied to one roller and his wrists to the other. The fiendish device worked simply. A handle and ratchet mechanism attached to the top roller allowed the torturer to gradually increase the tension in the ropes, inducing excruciating pain. The ropes would pull until the muscle fibers stretched to their limits, the victim's joints were dislocated and, if the interrogation failed to yield results, the limbs actually separated from the torso.

What his captors didn't know was that having freed himself from a replica of such a contraption multiple times, Houdini was confident that he could escape the rack within a matter of minutes. That was the good news. The bad news was that Neanderthal and one of the Khlysty deacons were just a few feet away, securing Bess in the Iron Chair.

The metal seat, which bore an ominous resemblance to an electric chair, was studded with scores of small pikes, on the seat, the back, the sides and the arms. Bess screamed as the spikes poked her flesh, not quite breaking the skin.

"I'm going to murder you for this!" Houdini cried, straining against the ropes.

The Neanderthal patted the deacon on the back. "I can handle it from here," he said. "I spent seven years as an interrogator for the Okhrana, till the filthy hypocrites sacked me. And we only had whips and thumbscrews, nothing so fancy as this. You see now, how I was right to restore this old 'junk' to working order? You never know what will come in handy."

The Khlysty deacon left through a heavy wooden door, and the Neanderthal turned his attention to the captives.

"You have made a lot of trouble for the Master. He is very unhappy with you," he scolded the magician.

"I'm not a fan of him either right now," Houdini replied.

"You will tell me where the camera is," the henchman said, leaning casually on the rack. "Either right now or after a lot of pain. I have extracted plans, secrets, and the names of accomplices from spies and revolutionaries. Men far more devoted than you. You think you're tough, but a pampered

American will not endure this kind of suffering long. You are no Russian; you are soft."

"You'd be surprised how much pain I've been through, how many times I've dislocated my shoulders, how many bruises I've racked up and how many bones I've broken," the escape artist replied, raising his head.

"We'll see." The Neanderthal gave the handle a turn and Houdini felt his arms being pulled almost from their sockets. Houdini groaned—but not loudly.

"I thought this was going to be a lot worse," he said. "I'd like to get one of these for my house. I figure a little bit a day, and I can gain two inches."

The Neanderthal looked at the American admiringly.

"You are quite a fellow," he said. Then he walked to the Iron Chair where Bess was squirming with discomfort. Every time she shifted her weight or position, the spikes bit her back and buttocks. They had not yet drawn blood, but the sharp points had already penetrated her skirts and were beginning to dig into her skin.

"I have never liked hurting women, ma'am," the Neanderthal said. "Some men do, of course; they get a perverse pleasure from it. But not me." He tightened the straps holding her arms to the chair, and she screeched as the spikes cut slightly into her flesh.

The Neanderthal patted her cheek. "You haven't even gotten to the awful part yet."

"I swear to God you won't get out of this room alive," Houdini yelled, lifting his head and craning to see what was going on. Now he understood the fiendish cunning of this torture. The chair sat on a slanted sheet of polished metal with the downward edge placed in the fireplace. Every time Bess moved, the chair slid an inch or two closer to the fire.

"If you can keep still, the chair will take a long time to reach the fire," the Neanderthal advised. He tightened the strap holding her to the back of the chair.

Bess screamed and thrashed, and the chair slid down several inches.

"But as you can see, it is very difficult not to squirm," the torturer said. "And believe me, that chair will get very hot as you get closer. Won't you tell me where the watch is? I really don't enjoy this."

Instead of answering, she screamed in English, "Stop! Please stop!"

The henchman covered his ears. "Quit babbling! I didn't go to school, woman. No French tutor either, believe it or not. Russian, please."

Houdini could take it no more. "All right, you win, you animal. I'll tell you where it's hidden."

"Yes?"

"Let my wife out of that thing first."

The Neanderthal burst out laughing and pointed to his overhanging brow. "I know I look like an ape-man, but I don't have the brains of one." He gave the chair a nudge and it slid closer to the fire. Houdini could see the reflection of the flames in Bess's terrified eyes.

"The camera is in the jeweled snuff box," he blurted out finally.

"What jeweled box?"

"Knock it off. The jeweled box that was in my pocket. You found it and kept it for yourself."

Rasputin's enforcer scowled. He shook a finger at Houdini. "If this is a trick ..."

"I'm in no position to pull tricks and I don't have time for yapping while my wife is in that infernal contraption."

The Neanderthal pulled the Faberge snuff box from his trouser pocket and tried to pry open the lid.

"What the devil is this? The box won't open. No tricks, eh?"

"It's a puzzle box," Houdini explained. "You press the jewels in a certain order to open it. It was a gift for the Tsar."

"I might have guessed. Silly aristocrats with too much time on their hands."

"Let me out of this thing and I'll open it for you."

The henchman let out another guttural laugh. "You must think I'm the stupidest man in Russia."

"You'd be pretty stupid to think Rasputin won't come to check on us soon."

The Neanderthal glanced at the door nervously.

"Tell me how to open it."

"It's complicated," Houdini said. "I don't exactly remember; it would be better if I had it my hands."

The torturer turned the crank, stretching Houdini further on the rack. The magician moaned.

"All right, all right," the words shot out of his mouth. "First, touch the ruby on the top. It's the red one."

"I know what color a ruby is," the Neanderthal said irritably as his thick index finger pressed the stone.

"Sorry to insult your intelligence. Now the emerald on the right side. Then the sapphire beside it."

The Russian grinned as he followed Houdini's instructions.

"You see, I knew we could be friends," he said. "Everyone wins. I get this precious box, the Master gets his film and, who knows, he might even let you live."

"Now the amethyst on the left side," Houdini told him.

The Neanderthal hesitated.

"Purple," Houdini said patiently.

The Neanderthal pressed the gem and there came an audible click as the box opened.

"Eureka!" the henchman exclaimed joyfully, then "Ouch!" as the needle pricked him. He dropped the box, spilling the two watches onto the floor. The Neanderthal looked at the wound and licked it.

"I warned you, no tricks," the Neanderthal yelled angrily. He drew the pistol from his holster.

"No!" Bess screamed as he marched to Houdini and put the pistol to the magician's head.

CHAPTER FORTY-ONE

The Hummingbird

The Neanderthal suddenly stumbled back, dropping the pistol and clutching his throat. Rasputin's chief enforcer dropped the weapon and keeled over backward, gasping, to the floor.

Bess called out to Houdini, "What's going on? Everything that man said sounded like gibberish, and Rasputin too, all of them."

"I hypnotized you," Houdini explained. "I gave you a suggestion that you couldn't understand Russian. It was the only way—"

"To stop me from spilling the beans. You have a lot of nerve," she scolded him. "What a rotten trick!" As she railed against him, the chair jiggled and continued its trek toward the fire.

"I'm sorry, sweetie," her chastened husband replied.

"Well, don't just sit there. Get me out of this horrible thing."

"Yes, ma'am." Houdini compressed his right hand and worked it out of its bindings, then used it to untie the left.

Bess was now less than a foot from the fire and drenched in sweat. As she writhed from the heat, the chair accelerated downward, and the small spikes ripped through the back of her dress.

"Darling, please!" she screamed.

The next thing she knew, she was in her husband's arms, freed from the devilish implement of torture. The Neanderthal lay dead, eyes staring into the void.

"I love you," Bess cried, embracing her mate.

"And I love you, sweetie. I'm so sorry about those awful things I said in St. Petersburg," Houdini said. He rapped the Iron Chair. "You know, this would make a swell addition to the act."

She punched him in the shoulder. "I guess we know who'll be sleeping on the couch for a week."

Houdini picked up the snuff box and watches, and he deposited them in his pockets. As they stepped over their fallen tormentor's corpse, Bess pointed out the color of the Neanderthal's shirt.

"See, what did I tell you? Yellow!"

***

Houdini was not fond of horses. He gave them a wide berth on the streets of New York whenever one pulling an apple cart trotted by. But he'd ridden them in the past and knew beggars couldn't be choosers. On a mare he had stolen from Rasputin's stable, he and Bess now headed toward Tyumen. The snow had stopped, but the drifts were high and it was slow going. Bess clung to the magician's back, her face buried in the fur coat he'd swiped from the castle.

"He'll be after us, you know," Bess said.

"I know."

"We may not be so lucky again. And—"

"You think that was luck?" Houdini interjected. "Brains, I think."

"Yes, genius," Bess said, stroking his back. "The question is, is beating Rasputin worth our lives?"

Houdini mulled this over, picturing his wife screaming as she slid toward the fire.

"Fine then," he said. "If there's no other choice, if worst comes to worse, I'll turn over the film. But only if there's absolutely no other choice."

"Promise?"

"Scout's honor."

By the time they reached the town, the horse was exhausted.

"She couldn't go another foot," Bess said.

Houdini patted the mare. "Thanks, Betsy, but this is as far as you go."

They turned the horse in at a stable, trading it for ten rubles. Houdini suspected it was worth more, but there was no time to bargain, and another of Rasputin's henchman had lifted his money pouch. He asked the proprietor where they could procure a dogsled driver, and the man directed him toward a building a few streets away where the driver was probably loading up supplies.

"His name is Gurkin and he's a very disagreeable fellow," the stable owner said. "He may take you if he's in a good mood, which is unlikely."

But all Bess heard was, "Yego zovut Gurkin, i on ochen' nepriyatnyy chelovek. On mozhet prinyat' vas, yesli u nego khorosheye nastroyeniye, chto maloveroyatno."

What did he say?" Bess asked.

"Sorry about that." Houdini clapped his hands in front of her face.

As they made their way through the small town, Houdini kept a sharp lookout for Rasputin and his minions, who couldn't be far behind. As they neared the building where various people were loading sleds with goods, he spotted the most unusual vehicle he'd ever seen: an automobile with skids under the front wheels, and in the back, caterpillar tracks.

"What in heaven's name is that?" Bess asked.

"Our ticket home," her husband replied.

"Do you really think he'll give us a ride?"

"If he doesn't, the Russian police will have to add car theft to my list of crimes."

A small crowd gathered around the driver, a tall man with a mustache and thick black hair, peppering him with questions.

"It is a prototype of the one the inventor Kegrasse has designed for the Tsar," the driver was telling them. He looked familiar to Houdini, but he couldn't place the face.

"It's like Sikorky's Aerosani, then," one gentleman suggested.

"That one uses a propeller," another know-it-all pointed out. "A conventional engine is more practical."

"It must have cost a fortune. Who does it belong to?" a third man asked.

"Some rich ballerina from the capital," a female onlooker replied. "She's in the supply store."

Houdini looked over in surprise as the owner of the vehicle emerged from the building. It was Natasha Stepanova, his onetime bathhouse companion.

"Duck!" Houdini said to his wife, and the two took cover behind a sleigh parked right beside the sled car.

"All right, begone," the mustachioed driver barked in a manner that suggested he relished opportunities to boss others around. Houdini finally pegged him as Natasha's chauffeur. The crowd dispersed, some grumbling about what pushy snobs the wealthy were. When they were gone, Natasha stepped close to the driver.

"Are you certain you placed the charges properly?" she asked in a low voice that Houdini had to strain to hear.

"Exactly according to the diagram our top explosives man drew," her companion replied.

"And there is enough to bring down the Kuznetsov?"

"Well, enough to destroy anything trying to cross it. Dynamite does not come cheap."

"I suppose that is adequate," Natasha said, apparently unimpressed.

"Yes, at least I completed *my* mission," the driver said gruffly.

"Don't be so smug, comrade," Natasha replied. "The Americans have done our work for us, and they can't have gotten very far."

"We must find them before Rasputin does. Our orders from Lenin are clear."

"I am well aware of our comrade's orders."

"This Houdini is a slippery devil," her cohort cautioned her. "He really can escape from anything."

"Slippery or not, The Hummingbird always gets her man," Natasha responded.

"On her back, usually," the driver said with a laugh. The woman stood close to him and wagged a finger an inch from his nose.

"Watch your tongue," she said. "Don't you dare mock the sacrifices I have made."

Natasha's co-conspirator gently pushed her finger away.

"Don't start getting it in your pretty head that I really am your servant," he said, moving in on her with a hint of menace.

She shoved him away. "We can't stay here bickering. I know where we can intercept them. Come on."

"As you wish, Comrade Stepanova," he replied, opening the door for her.

"Thank you, Comrade Stalin."

So, Natasha is The Hummingbird, the Bolshevik spy, Houdini thought in amazement as the car drove off, the caterpillar tracks helping it to traverse snow that would have stopped an ordinary automobile dead. Of course! She'd never seemed fanatically loyal, and now it was clear she wasn't—at least, not to Rasputin. From her no-nonsense tone, he suspected she was just as devoted to Lenin and his philosophy as the mystic's disciples were to him.

"I never really liked that hussy," Bess remarked to Houdini. "And now she's going around blowing people up."

"You've got to give the kid credit for being more than just a pretty face," he replied, earning him a kick in the shins.

They didn't arrive at the dogsled a moment too soon. The musher Gurkin, in his eighties, craggy-faced, with spectacularly bushy grey eyebrows, was in the final stages of harnessing his eight dogs. He pet the lead dog affectionately.

"We have a long ride ahead of us, Nika," he said. "But when we get to Tobolsk, I promise to buy you a pound of beef liver."

Suddenly, the biggest of his Siberian Huskies began to snarl. Gurkin whipped about, pulling an ice ax from the sled, displaying reflexes that belied his advanced age.

"Hold on, old timer," Houdini said with his hands raised. "We don't mean you any harm. We want to rent your dogsled."

Gurkin chortled. "Have you ever driven one before, boy?"

"Well, you whip the dogs and say mush, right?"

"Wherever my dogs go, I go."

"Naturally. That's what I meant. You've got to get us to the railway station in Verkhoturye."

"That's three-day's journey in the wrong direction. The owner of the Red Boar is waiting for his shipment of vodka and cigars," he said, pointing to his cargo. "Can you imagine the fights that will take place if they run out of drink again?"

"I'll pay you handsomely," Houdini promised.

"How handsomely?"

"Five rubles."

"Ha!" old Gurkin said, and spat on the ground. "Enough to take you a quarter of the way, perhaps."

The escape artist reluctantly reached into his coat pocket and took out the snuff box. He pointed to a blue gem.

"This sapphire is worth fifty rubles, at least," Houdini said. "Get us to Verkhoturye in one piece and it's yours."

The old man narrowed his eyes. "Where did you get that from?" he inquired suspiciously.

"Maybe I won it in a card game, maybe it fell off a watermelon cart."

The old man shook his head and returned to adjusting the harnesses.

"These are poor weather conditions for travel. You foreigners can't tolerate Russian winters, I assure you. Stay at the inn and when I return, I can take you wherever you wish."

Bess advanced. "Please, you've got to help us. We're in a terrible jam. Rasputin is after us."

The old musher turned back to them, his cross expression turning friendly.

458 |C. Michael Forsyth

He laughed and said, "Why didn't you say that in the beginning? If I'd known that devil was involved, I'd have agreed to do it for free!"

***

Across the white plain, the dogs raced as if chasing an invisible prey. Each was outfitted with a harness and they were hooked in pairs, with the harnesses attached by tug lines. These were in turn tied to a central gang line that pulled the sled. The old man, puffing a pipe, controlled the dogs utilizing verbal commands, from his position standing up at the back of the sled.

The journey was tranquil, the only sounds the panting of the dogs and the slushing noise of the runners passing over the snow. It was monotonous, but Bess had certainly had her fill of adventure in Siberia, and even her daredevil husband felt due for a little monotony.

"How much longer to Verkhoturye?" Houdini asked the musher.

"That depends on two things," said Gurkin. "The first is whether it snows again."

"And the other ...?"

"And the other is whether those wolves catch up."

The magician turned to see a pack of at least nine wolves running along a hillside, parallel to them, like shadows of the sled dogs. The beasts were gigantic, nearly the size of the dire wolves that preyed on hapless cavemen in prehistoric times.

Bess screamed.

"Don't worry, they're just protecting their territory," Houdini assured her. "Isn't that right, old fellow?"

"Actually, I believe they are hunting us," the musher said.

CHAPTER FORTY-TWO

Wolves of Two Kinds

As the enormous Siberian wolves chased the dogsled, Houdini couldn't help thinking once again of the vampirs of Hungarian folklore. *Couldn't Dracula in that book command wolves and rats?* The old sled driver cried to the dogs and they bolted faster, but unhindered by any burden, the wolfpack was gaining on them. Houdini cut short his flirtation with superstition. Putting fear aside, he racked his brain for a way they could escape being eaten alive.

"I'm going to have to borrow one of your vodka bottles," he told Gurkin.

"I could use a stiff drink myself right now, but you'd better find another way to calm your nerves," the old man replied. "They'll be upon us in a minute. Here's a knife; I'll use the ice ax."

Taking the knife, Houdini climbed forward on the sled and untied the rope holding down the canvas that covered the supplies. He busted open a box, which was chock full of bottles. Plucking one out, he yelled to the musher, "I need an old rag."

"Here's my handkerchief, if you don't mind a little snot," Gurkin yelled ahead. He passed the cloth to Bess, who handed it to her husband. The largest wolf, seemingly the leader, was now only a few feet behind the sled, its lips pulled back to

461

reveal a row of saw-like teeth. Several others were at its tail, while more were closing in from the left and right.

Houdini stuffed the handkerchief into the mouth of the vodka bottle and secured it with the stopper.

"Now I need a light," he yelled to Gurkin.

"Ah, now I see," the old man said. "Ma'am, in a compartment under the seat, there is a box of matches."

Bess found the matches and passed them to her husband. "I don't get it," she said.

"You will in a second," Houdini assured her, lighting the cloth. He tossed the bottle at the enormous alpha wolf just as it leaped for the sled. The bottle struck its target dead on and burst into flames. The beast crashed down in the snow, its fur afire. It scampered off yelping into the snowdrifts.

The second bottle missed its target, as did the third. But the fire rattled the pack and when his next throw set another unlucky member on fire, the rest scattered, whimpering.

"Darling, you may not get invited to the next ASPCA benefit dinner," Bess said in relief.

"At least we're off the menu."

Houdini secured the goods.

"A nice invention," the old man complimented him. "I've always known it was dangerous to store alcohol near fire, but I've never seen it used as a bomb before."

The magician smiled proudly. "Mark my words, one day they'll be known as Houdini cocktails."

Six miles away, a trio of dogsleds raced across the snow. The musher on the lead sled pointed to an orange flame in the distance.

"Did you see that?" he said to the man beside him.

That man, one Grigori Rasputin, stood up in the sled and extended his finger like a long, misshapen carrot.

"That way," he declared.

"Are you sure, Master?"

"God Himself is guiding us, my son," the mystic said.

***

Gurkin's dogsled was making good time. By nightfall they would reach Verkhoturye, he told the American couple.

"When we get back to New York, the first thing I'm going to do is take a hot bath," Bess said, snuggling against her husband under the fur blanket.

"Is there room for two in our tub?" he replied. "If not, I'm going to buy us a new one." They nestled together, forgetting the crusty old man behind them.

"Darling, everything's going to be different when we get home," she said. "We don't need children, real or make-believe, to be a family. All you need to be a family is love. Isn't that true, darling? ... Darling?"

Some sixth sense had alerted the magician and he sat up. He twisted around and looked behind them. Far away, he saw an object streaking across the snow.

"More wolves?" asked Bess.

"The human variety."

Gurkin withdrew a spyglass from his coat and looked back.

"Three sleds, no more than four miles behind us," said the musher.

"They won't catch us, will they?" Bess asked anxiously.

"Bah, of course not. I won the Tyumen to Tobolsk race five years in a row." The old man cried to the dogs and they picked up speed.

They maintained their lead over their pursuers for several hours. Sometimes Rasputin's sleds narrowed the gap, but the old musher was always able to put distance between them. He pointed to a bridge up ahead.

"We'll take a shortcut under the Kuznetsov Bridge and up the Tura River," Gurkin told them.

Houdini gulped. "What did you say the name of that bridge is?"

"Kuznetsov."

The Kuznetsov, the one that Natasha and her Bolshevik comrade had talked about blowing up!

As they neared the bridge, Houdini borrowed the spyglass and looked ahead at the wrought iron structure, which spanned about three hundred feet and rose forty-five feet above the waterline. It was an open-spandrel arch bridge with abutments on either bank and a broad upside-down U in-between. From that arch rose six columns that held up the road deck where the train tracks lay. Through the spyglass, Houdini could see that a bundle of dynamite sticks had been strategically placed high on one of the support columns, just below the tracks.

"Slow down," he ordered Gurkin.

"You need more lessons in Russian, my friend," the old man said. "You said 'slow down' not 'speed up.'"

"I know what I said. There's a bomb on that bridge, rigged by the Bolsheviks."

The driver shrugged. "Well, that's nothing new. They're always up to tricks like that. It has nothing to do with you, does it?"

"Stop right here," Houdini said when they were about twenty feet from the bridge. Bess looked back frantically at their pursuers, no longer dots on the snow but discernible as sleds, dogs and men.

"He's right, isn't he, darling?" she said.

"Hundreds of people will be on the next train," he reminded her. "If we let fanatics blow people up willy-nilly, we've been kidding ourselves about helping Russia." He patted her shoulder. "Don't worry, I'll be up and down in a jiffy." He planted a kiss on Bess's lips and jumped from the sled.

***

The train bearing the double-eagle insignia of the Russian military tore down the tracks toward the Kuznetsov Bridge, transporting 427 soldiers westward. In a forward car, officers amused themselves with songs and card-playing.

Lieutenant-General Sozryko Khoranov, highly decorated for his heroism in both the Russo-Turkish and Russo-Japanese wars, was engaged in a poker game with a young Cossack officer named Konstantin Agoev, along with two foreign diplomats returning from a peace conference in the Far East.

"I will be happy when we are back in Moscow," Agoev said. "Humans were never meant to live in Siberia."

"You'd best become accustomed to true cold," Khoranov replied soberly. "Russia's greatest weapon is her winters. Ask Napoleon if you don't believe me."

Sir George Buchanan, the British ambassador to Russia, looked at him over his cards.

"Hopefully, Europe will never see another leader so bent on conquest," he said. "In those years, England, France, Prussia, Austria, Spain, all caught up in the bloody conflagration."

"All that stands between peace and calamity is men of reason such as ourselves," said the United States ambassador Curtis Guild. "The great nations may all be standing in gasoline right now, but as long as we talk instead of tossing matches, the world is safe."

Khoranov shook his head. "With all due respect, Ambassador, peace is best achieved through strength. As long as each side has an army massive enough to defend itself, no one will be foolhardy enough to light the first match."

***

Like a West Indian lad climbing a coconut tree, Houdini shimmied up the support column toward the girder to which the bomb was secured. His experience performing "human fly" stunts put him in good stead. Once, to celebrate their fourteenth wedding anniversary, he'd climbed three stories to a hotel window to present Bess with a rose clenched in his teeth.

Within five minutes, Houdini reached the girder at the top of the column, just below the rails. He'd never defused a bomb, of course, but he had a rudimentary understanding of how dynamite worked. A spark was needed to set off a blasting cap, triggering a small explosion that detonated the dynamite itself. Ten sticks of dynamite were taped together and tied to the girder. A wire ran from the bomb, snaking around the metal beams and running to a hillside. There, he assumed, hid a Bolshevik saboteur ready to push down the detonator when the train approached.

Using Gurkin's knife, Houdini started to cut the ignition wire. Just then a shot rang out and a bullet ricocheted off the beam beside him.

The Bolshevik has a rifle, Houdini realized, ducking a second shot.

Bess borrowed the spyglass from Gurkin and watched with trepidation as her husband dodged gunfire and cut through the wire. She then looked back to check on their pursuers. Her heart almost leaped out of her chest at the sight of Rasputin standing up at the lead sled, whipping the animals with the same crazed expression as when he'd scourged his whirling bacchants. She looked back up at Houdini—then hearing a distant sound, turned and saw a funnel of smoke approaching.

"Darling, come down, there isn't time," she called up to him.

Houdini had sliced the wire running to the detonator, but the sniper didn't give up. Bullets continued to strike the metal around the escape artist with an awful clang. *So that's what he's up to. If a bullet hits that bomb, it'll blow up the train and me with it!*

The magician began to cut through the rope that secured the bomb to the beam. Looking down, Houdini could see Rasputin's sleds bearing down on Gurkin and Bess, now no more than half a mile away. He could also feel the vibration of the approaching train through the metal.

He yelled down to Gurkin, "Get moving!"

"Do nothing of the kind," Bess ordered the musher.

"Which one of you is in charge?" the old coot grunted.

"If you're married, you know the answer to that one," she said.

"Ah, we wait then," Gurkin said and rested on the handlebars.

Finally, Houdini cut through the rope and clutched the dynamite to his chest. Dodging the gunfire from below, he tried to slither around to the far side of the beam, out of the line of fire. By now, the locomotive was rumbling onto the bridge and the intense vibration rippled through the train trestle, causing Houdini to lose his balance.

Bess screamed in horror as she saw her husband fall from the beam, tumbling toward the ground forty-five feet below.

CHAPTER FORTY-THREE

On Thin Ice

Houdini lay flat on his back in the snow like a stunned squirrel, the bomb still tucked in his folded arms, as Bess knelt shaking him back to consciousness.

"That was the most foolish stunt I've ever seen," she scolded him. "You're determined to make a widow of me yet, aren't you?"

He looked up and saw the train puttering safely away. Bess helped him to his feet and planted a kiss on his lips.

"If I went for the hero type, I could fall for you," she said. Old Gurkin pointed to the pursuers, and Houdini was alarmed to see that the distance between them had been reduced to the length of a football field.

"Stop your yakking," the driver said grumpily. "I'll drive off, I swear. I won't be skinned alive by those barbarians." He shook his head as the couple piled into the sled in front of him.

"You Americans would be better off if you learn to keep your nose out of foreign affairs," Gurkin grumbled. He cried a command to the dogs and the sled pulled away.

Rasputin's teams were catching up. On each sled in front of the driver sat two men bearing rifles. Gurkin looked over his shoulder and growled.

"We've got to lighten the load," the musher cried. "Cut the cargo loose."

"But your client?" said Houdini.

"The two of you can jump if you prefer."

"Looks like I'll owe you another gemstone," the magician said.

He cut the rope binding the cargo, and boxes flew off the dogsled. A crate sailed through the air and struck one of Rasputin's henchmen, knocking him clear off the sled and scattering cigars onto the snow. Houdini tried to hold onto the two crates containing the vodka—hoping to repeat the trick he'd used to rout the wolves—but they slipped from his hands and joined the rest of the jettisoned goods. Unencumbered by the weights, Gurkin's dogs picked up speed and their pursuers fell behind.

Then a loud report of a gunshot came from behind them.

"Wonderful, they're shooting at us now," Bess cried. Two more gunshots followed. Behind them, they heard Gurkin grunt in pain. Bess turned around and saw their driver slumped over the handlebars.

"Darling, he's been hit!"

The magician climbed out of the bed of the speeding sled and nimbly worked his way onto the footboards behind the wounded musher.

"Hang on, old fellow," he said, keeping Gurkin from tumbling off. He looked behind them and saw one of the riflemen take aim. His shot missed Houdini's head by half an inch.

"How do I control the dogs?" he said in the wounded man's ear.

"Try saying mush," Gurkin groaned.

Fortunately, Houdini remembered most of the commands the driver had cried out to the Huskies. "Gee" for right, "Haw" for left and most salient now, a loud kissing sound Gurkin had used to make the dogs run faster. Imitating him, Houdini urged the dogs on.

"Watch a couple of New Yorkers lick Ruskies in a dogsled race!" he cried ahead to Bess. "It's like beating the English in a fox hunt."

"Don't pick out a spot for the trophy yet, dear," Bess called back. "Just talk to the dogs for now."

Just when Houdini thought they might outrun their pursuers, Gurkin's dogs slowed down and began barking. They were at a spot where the frozen river emerged from between two mountains into bright sunlight.

"What's eating them?" Houdini asked frantically.

"The ice is too thin here, Gurkin whispered. "They can tell."

Responding to slight changes in moisture on the surface through their paws, the dogs barked plaintively and whimpered. No amount of coaxing could propel them forward. Perhaps their master might have had better luck than Houdini, but he was barely conscious. The magician climbed off the stationary sled and helped Gurkin to its bed.

"Is there anything I can do for you, old timer?" Houdini asked.

"I could use my pipe."

Houdini took the matches and lit the pipe, then gently placed it between the old Russian's lips.

"Too bad we've lost the vodka," Gurkin said. Houdini covered him with the blanket.

"Hang in there," he told the musher.

Houdini rose to meet Rasputin as the mystic's dogsled skidded to a stop about twenty feet away. The big Siberian hopped off and walked purposefully toward them. Bess climbed up from the seat and stood beside her husband, clasping his hand.

The mystic, clad in an ankle-length fur coat, stopped about ten feet away. He wore a triumphant expression.

"Did you really think you could defeat a Siberian on the snow?" he said, letting loose the full-throated laugh of a buccaneer. His men echoed his laughter like a pack of hyenas.

Houdini smiled. "Well, I've always had a fair amount of luck."

"I am afraid that has run out." Rasputin gestured behind him to the rifle-bearing henchmen who'd stepped from the sleds. Houdini recognized a couple of the deacons and his old nemesis Eyepatch.

"You have been a naughty boy," Rasputin said, wagging a finger at him. "I should be in front of a fireplace now, enjoying a bowl of beef soup. You will give me the camera. Now."

Bess glared at him defiantly. "You ought to learn to say please," she said. "It's rude to boss people around."

The mystic thrust out his right hand, palm up. "Harry Houdini, if you give me the film right now, I promise that I will allow you to live and you may return to your home country," he said. "If you are so foolish as to disobey me, you will be beheaded by my followers with the ax that Mrs. Houdini is holding behind her back. But first, you will witness them buggering your wife half to death. I will finish and your last sight in this world will be Rasputin splitting her in half and the look of bliss upon her face as she meets the sublime. I give you one minute to decide."

Bess clenched the ice ax. She would use it to cut her own throat before she let that happen. Houdini reached into his pocket and slowly withdrew the watch.

"You make a good case," he said.

Rasputin smiled like a fox with a chick on a platter before it.

"No, darling," Bess cried.

CHAPTER FORTY-FOUR

An Old Acquaintance

Houdini flicked open the pocket watch and consulted it.

"What are you doing?" Rasputin growled, folding his arms impatiently.

"I just want to check the time," Houdini said, calmly. "I'm supposed to be giving you one minute."

"I said that *I* am giving *you* one minute," the mystic corrected him.

"Yes, we'll see about that."

Rasputin's henchmen glanced at each other uneasily.

"Well, you make a good case for turning over the film," the magician continued. "On the other hand, fellows like you aren't very good for the world. You're extraordinary all right, but you're a louse. And it's up to people like me who maybe aren't quite so extraordinary stop to you."

He looked down at the watch. "Well, isn't this a kick in the head. I just noticed this darned thing doesn't keep time."

Houdini flipped the watch closed and returned it to his pocket. He slowly turned his back on Rasputin and his men.

Ahead was ice no Siberian dog would dare tread upon, but perhaps a fleet-footed American could.

"He's going to run!" shouted Eyepatch.

"Do you think I am too honorable to order you shot in the back?" the mystic called to him.

"I don't think too much honor is one of your faults," Houdini responded. He turned to face his adversary, dramatically brandishing a stick of dynamite that he had removed from the bomb. The lit fuse sparkled. Rasputin's men backed up fearfully.

"He has dynamite!" one of them hollered, falling in the snow and scrabbling backward like a crab.

"Shoot him, you dogs!" Rasputin cried.

Loyal Eyepatch alone raised his rifle, but before he could fire, Houdini tossed the stick of dynamite at Rasputin. The Siberian instinctively bounded to the right, out of the way. The explosive landed on the snow-covered ice, while Rasputin's men ran for their lives.

The dynamite exploded with thunderous noise fifteen feet from the Siberian, knocking him off his feet. The ice cracked, split, and the floe tipped over. The Tsar's spiritual advisor bellowed in terror as he tumbled into the freezing water below.

Rasputin's sled dogs, spooked by the deafening noise, turned and stampeded, while his men scrambled back from the widening breach in the ice. Gurkin's dogs were startled as well, and—their fear trumping their caution about the thinness of the ice—they took off in the direction in which they'd been traveling. Houdini had flung Bess and himself face forward on the snow in the seconds after he tossed the stick of dynamite and before it exploded. He helped his wife to her feet, and together they ran after the departing dogsled, just barely managing to hop onto the foot boards.

Houdini looked back to see Rasputin floundering in the frigid water. Eyepatch knelt a short distance away, hands clapped over his still-ringing ears.

"Come!!!" Rasputin commanded the disoriented man.

The one-eyed follower crawled like a faithful dog to his master and reached for him. Rasputin clutched Eyepatch's arm, but in trying to haul himself out, succeeded only in pulling his henchmen headlong into the river. Eyepatch's boots vanished below the surface as the mystic struggled, his heavy and now water-logged coat dragging him down.

As the dogsled carried the Houdinis to safety, Bess looked back to see Rasputin's eyes, then whole head disappear beneath the water. His hand continued to reach up, the fingers positioned oddly as if he were giving a benediction.

He said he would drown and join his brother at last, she thought.

"That's the end of him, darling ... isn't it?" Bess asked.

***

Houdini had picked up just enough mushing know-how to get them to a small village twenty miles away. Miraculously, the rugged old geezer survived the journey; the bullet had narrowly missed his left lung. Bess had been able to staunch the bleeding with a pressure bandage she fashioned from a spare shirt in the sled. The village doctor/barber told them there was no way Gurkin would have made it without her care.

Houdini asked around in the village for an experienced driver to take them the rest of the way to Verkhoturye—and ideally, a fresh team of dogs as well. No such luck. However, he did hear word of a young man who was making a rest stop there who might be able to help him.

"Hans!" Houdini cried in astonishment when he found the husky fellow brushing his reindeer in a stable. "Aren't you a sight for sore eyes!"

Hans embraced him like a beloved uncle. "When I recovered Ludmilla and Galina, I looked everywhere for you," the Russian said. "I was afraid those ruffians had killed you. I was on my way home, only because I asked everywhere and couldn't find you. Don't think I abandoned you lightly."

"Don't worry about it," Houdini replied with a broad smile. "You came along at just the right place, and just the right time."

Houdini had to pry off another gem from the Faberge snuff box to buy their tickets, but the next morning they were seated in a private compartment on a westbound train in the Verkhoturye station. The "all aboard" cry had been called and the locomotive sat rumbling. Houdini drummed his fingers on his knee waiting for the train to start moving. He'd seen Rasputin's shaggy head and outstretched fingers descend into the Tura River, but doubt nagged at him like a splinter in flesh.

"Aren't you worried about being arrested by the Tsar as soon as we arrive in St. Petersburg?" Bess asked.

"The Grand Duke Nikolai will put in a good word for me," Houdini replied. "Hopefully, he informed the emperor by telegram. But I think we've worn out our welcome in Russia."

"I won't miss it," his wife replied.

Houdini took her hand. "Sweetie, I'm sorry I put you through all this. When Prime Minister Stolypin and the others asked me to get mixed up with Rasputin, I should have told them thanks for the offer, but no thanks."

"Well, you can make it up to me," she said.

"You name it. The biggest diamond in the world."

Bess smiled, mischievously. "You don't have to buy me anything. We have almost a week on this train."

Houdini grinned. "I better latch the door."

As he got up, Bess leaned over to draw the curtains. Through the glass she saw something that took her breath away. Near the railroad tracks a most unusual vehicle was parked: a car with caterpillar treads in the back and skis in the front.

"Darling!" she gasped as the magician reached for the latch.

The door popped open, nearly hitting him in the nose and Natasha entered, holding a dainty little .40 caliber Remington Derringer. Behind her loomed her mustachioed accomplice Stalin.

"Excuse me, do you have the time?" the lady spy said, waltzing into the compartment. "I would very much like to see your pocket watch."

CHAPTER FORTY-FIVE

The Fate of the Film

"That camera's not worth a shootout over. Rasputin is dead as a doornail," Houdini informed the gun-slinging redhead.

"It is not a shootout if only we are armed," Stalin corrected him, drawing his own, much bigger pistol.

"Rasputin is very much alive," Natasha said. "A dip in cold water isn't enough to kill a Siberian."

Houdini frowned at the news. Every time it looked like the mystic was down for the count, he bounced back.

"And I suppose you're going to give him the film that proves what a swine he is," Houdini growled in frustration.

"Of course not, silly boy. I am going to turn over the photograph to Comrade Lenin," she said, amusement in her eyes. "We will have control over Rasputin, and whoever controls Rasputin controls Russia."

"So, you're a Bolshevik, eh? A true believer? I never figured you for a sucker."

"We will build a great nation," Natasha contended in a new tone of sincerity. "Not a society where some who are wealthy by accident of birth exist as parasites on the backs of those who work, but a society where all are equal."

"You plan to give up your fancy cars and gowns from Paris?" Houdini asked.

"Gladly."

"Enough speeches," Stalin said gruffly. "We're not here to recruit them." He pointed his pistol at Bess. "Turn over the camera or we will shoot your wife."

"Easy, easy, big fellow," Houdini said, stepping in front of Bess.

"Forgive Comrade Stalin," Natasha said. "He can be a bit of a bully when he's impatient. And the train will be leaving the station in five minutes." Then she purred, "You're not going to make this difficult will you, my dear Harry?"

He reached into his jacket pocket and withdrew the watch.

"You're making a mistake, you know," Houdini told her, forking it over. "You'd be better off with the Tsar than with that bald icepick Lenin running Russia."

"In a few years, we'll see, shan't we?" the ballerina said. She inspected the sub-miniature camera closely. "I knew what you were up to when I saw this in Bess's luggage. We've been using them for over a year now—although personally, I prefer our makeup-compact cameras." She tucked the watch in her cleavage and buttoned her coat.

"And now the other one, if you don't mind," Natasha said.

"What makes you think we have two?" Houdini asked innocently.

"I telegraphed St. Petersburg and our source in the Okhrana was able to confirm that you were supplied with a second one. We have eyes everywhere."

"You owe them no explanation," her comrade groused, then warned Houdini, "We could just as easily shoot you and search your bodies."

Reluctantly, Houdini produced the second watch and gave it to Natasha. The communist agent passed the watch to Stalin, who buried it in the pocket of his bearskin coat.

Natasha gave Bess a cheeky smile and said, "I hope you don't mind." She moved closer and puckered up to kiss Houdini on the lips.

"I do mind, you tramp!" Bess said, rising. She kicked Natasha in the shin and as the Russian woman stumbled, Houdini's irate spouse jumped on her, swinging. The derringer skittered on the floor, but before Houdini could reach it, Stalin picked it up.

A tornado of hair pulling, scratching and clothes ripping erupted on the floor of the cramped compartment before Stalin pulled Bess off. Houdini pushed Bess behind him.

"Are you trying to get us both killed?" he admonished her.

Natasha stood up, straightening her clothing. "Quite the little spitfire when you're ready, aren't you?"

The train whistle blew.

"Let's get out of here!" her companion said. They both began to back up out of the compartment. Then Natasha stopped and looked at Bess.

"You think we have no pickpockets in Russia? Hand it over," she demanded.

Bess sighed and unclenched her left hand, revealing the watch. Glaring, she turned it over to the ballerina. Natasha took a small purse from her coat pocket, deposited the watch and snapped shut the purse, which she then shoved deep into the recesses of her mink coat.

"Check your pocket," she ordered Stalin.

"I would know if—" he protested.

"Check it," she insisted.

Grumbling, the tyrant-in-making plucked the camera from his pocket and waved it sourly. "Satisfied?"

Natasha smiled. "Where was I? Oh, yes." She stepped forward and pressed her scarlet lips against Houdini's. He held back for a second, then couldn't resist returning the kiss, taking her in his arms. As if it had a mind of its own, his hand slid over that marvelously firm backside and lingered there until she pulled away.

The red-haired vixen licked her lips. "*Now* I am satisfied."

"Can we go now, comrade?" demanded Stalin, looking as if smoke might pour from his ears. "Or, if you need more time for your goodbyes, I can pull down the bed."

"Adieu," Natasha said as the two Bolsheviks backed out of the compartment. "Perhaps I will be sent to spy on America one day."

As the train rolled out of the station, Bess and Houdini sat at the window and watched the pair return to their car.

"Please tell me all that wasn't for nothing," Bess moaned. Houdini smiled and held up Natasha's purse.

"Good thing we have better pickpockets in New York than in Russia." He opened the purse and showed her the watch. The sleight-of-hand artist used his fist to wipe off the Russian spy's lipstick.

"I hope you weren't worried?" he asked.

"Of course I was worried," Bess replied, flipping the watch over. "I was afraid you'd get mixed up and give her the wrong one."

But he hadn't. Houdini pointed to the HH engraved on the back of the watch.

***

Back in St. Petersburg, Houdini and Chief Dzhunkovsky sat outside the Tsar's study awaiting an audience. The director of the Okhrana grasped a brown eight-by-ten-inch envelope with both hands, as if he feared that at any moment a bird of prey might swoop down to snatch it.

"With the photograph enlarged, the evidence is even more damning," the official said. "That scene of debauchery ... beyond blasphemous."

"It sure wasn't Easter mass at Father O'Reilly's church," Houdini agreed. He saw that Dzhunkovsky was tapping his foot restlessly.

"Relax, chief," he assured his companion. "We've got that skunk nailed but good."

A buzzer sounded, and the two men rose and entered the study, where the Tsar sat at his desk. It was a small room with simple leather chairs, a sofa covered with a Persian throw and a table spread with maps. A bookcase housed busts, photographs and souvenirs of the emperor's travels to England and Germany. Nicholas II received them graciously and indicated that they should sit.

"I understand that you gentlemen have something to show me," the monarch said. His manner was pleasant, but his furrowed brow told Houdini he had been forewarned.

"Indeed, Your Supreme Majesty," Dzhunkovsky said eagerly. He pulled the photograph from the envelope and passed it to the Tsar. As the ruler looked at the photo, it began to shake in his hand. Nicholas turned pale and sprang to his feet, recoiling. He swayed as if his blood pressure had suddenly dropped and placed his hand on the desk to steady himself. Houdini and the boss of the secret police exchanged hopeful glances. After a moment, the Tsar recovered and stood erect.

"Rasputin has already confessed to us completely regarding this incident," he informed them, placing the photo on the desk. "The starets was with the cast of the local theater company as they were changing clothing for their roles as demonic females. They drank too much and the cavorting got out of hand."

"Cavorting?" Dzhunkovsky repeated in bewilderment.

Houdini groaned. "Let me guess, *The Bacchae.*"

Looking a bit puzzled, the Tsar replied, "No, *Faust.*"

Houdini burst out in laughter, unable to contain himself.

"I'll give Rasputin this much: the guy has cast-iron testicles," he said. "A lesser man would've packed his bags and hightailed it out of Russia in shame."

"Your Supreme Majesty, that is not what the photograph shows," objected the flustered Okhrana chief. "It depicts Rasputin's participation in an illegal Khlysty ceremony."

"I must disagree, Chief Dzhunkovsky," Nicholas replied. He pointed to details of the photo. "The magic symbols on the wall tell us this is clearly a theatrical set. The horned mask held by the man behind Father Grigori is most likely part of the devil costume for Mephistopheles. It all fits Our Friend's explanation to a T. His relations with these women is, of course, unacceptable, but in his defense, I think we all know that actresses in general do not have the highest morals and can cause any of us to abandon our scruples."

What is the penalty for socking a tsar? Houdini thought. *Because I've got to smack some sense into you!* He leaned forward and placed a hand on the desk.

"With all due respect, Your Majesty, you must deep down realize that's all malarkey," he said emphatically. "You can't be ... you can't be such a sap."

"Houdini!" Dzhunkovsky cautioned the American, grabbing his arm to restrain him. Houdini threw off the chief's hand.

"Tsar Nicholas, I saw that twisted black mass with my own eyes," he declared. "I don't expect you to take my word for it, but accept the evidence of your own eyes!"

The emperor closed his eyes and sighed.

"You do not understand," he said wearily. "My wife Alix, she adores Father Grigori. Her trust in him is absolute. Unfathomable to you, perhaps, but boundless. Her sanity is dependent upon that faith. My dear Houdini, I know that your intentions were good and your quick actions spared the life of Grand Duke Nikolai—or just as likely my own—for which the Empire owes you an eternal debt of gratitude. However, I must ask you to leave Russia. And Chief Dzhunkovsky, I must ask for your resignation."

Dzhunkovsky bowed. "You will have my letter of resignation this afternoon."

Houdini stared at the monarch, dumbfounded. *I've had it all wrong. The problem isn't Rasputin. His only trouble is that he's a wolf. It isn't Alexandra. She's just a fool. It's you, wrapped around her little finger. The people deserve better than this.*

"And what of Rasputin?" the magician asked bitterly. "Will he get a promotion for this or just a medal?"

"Our Friend has repented and vowed to us that he will never engage in such disgraceful behavior again."

Houdini shrugged. "Well then, all's well that ends well," he said with a bitter smile.

Like hell it's over.

CHAPTER FORTY-SIX

The Bell Ringer

"**B**ess, Bess, Bess. How could you have betrayed me?" Alexandra wept, throwing herself down on the divan in her boudoir. "To violate Our Friend's trust, to insinuate yourself into his circle and conspire to destroy him!"

"It's not me who's betrayed you," replied Bess firmly.

"To make an accusation of heresy and abomination against the holiest man in Russia!"

"I am sorry, Alexandra, but right this minute your husband the Tsar is looking at indisputable proof."

With no knock or forewarning, the door opened and Rasputin swept into the room in long, priestly robes. He now wore a plain wooden cross about his neck. Rasputin rushed forward and fell to his knees before the divan, bawling just as hard as the Tsarina.

"I come for the third and final time to express my shame, though I know I am not worthy to be in your sight," he cried, head bowed. "Banishment is too good for me. There is no land harsh enough to expiate my sins. Have me whipped through the streets of St. Petersburg."

"You have apologized enough," Alexandra said, placing a hand on his shaggy head.

"A thousand apologies would not be enough," Rasputin insisted, choking on his tears. "That I could have surrendered so completely to lust and drink!"

She ruffled his thick, greasy mane and said, "I know that despite your sweet and gentle soul, and the bright light of your spiritual power, you are a man and vulnerable to temptation. And the same light within you that makes you a beacon for we who seek a path to God also lures wanton seductresses. You are forgiven."

He buried his face in her lap and she stroked his head, comforting a chastened child. The Tsarina turned to Bess, who stood watching the scene with disgust.

"Now, Bess. It is your turn," she said sternly. "I want you to apologize for the awful things you have said about Father Grigori practicing the rites of the Khlysty. To admit that you were mistaken."

Bess stared at the Siberian, who knelt on the floor, tears rolling down his cheeks—crocodile tears, she thought with contempt. He no longer held power over her now. It was like staring at a zoo animal. But, swallowing her pride, she said finally, "I mistook what I saw, starets. I beg your forgiveness."

"Thank you, Bess, thank you," Alexandra said, standing. She took Rasputin's hand in her own and with the other, she clasped Bess's. "Let us pray."

Together, the trio recited:

"Our Father, who art in heaven, hallowed be Thy name.

Thy kingdom come. Thy will be done, on earth as it is in heaven.

Give us this day our daily bread, and forgive us our trespasses, as we forgive those who trespass against us,

and lead us not into temptation, but deliver us from evil.

For Thine is the kingdom, the power and the glory

of the Father and the Son and the Holy Spirit, now and forever. Amen."

Alexandra stood, warmth spreading across her face, renewed. She embraced Bess.

"I want you to know that you are still my friend," the Tsarina assured her. "Although you are across the sea, you have a place in my heart and will always be in my prayers."

"And I will be praying for you too, Your Imperial Majesty," replied the magician's wife.

Bess left quietly, leaving the mystic with his patron. When the door closed, Alexandra bade Father Grigori sit beside her. Wiping his tears away, he joined her on the divan. The Tsarina picked up a Bible.

"Come, Father Grigori, let us both seek comfort in the words of Our Lord."

Rasputin took her hand and smiled sweetly. They were interrupted by a gentle tinkling sound. Puzzled, Alexandra turned and saw that it emanated from a bell that sat on her shelf—the one that Monsieur Philippe had given her long ago to warn her of the presence of evil.

She stared at Rasputin, bringing her fingers to her lips.

***

Jim Hercules escorted the Houdinis through the palace, holding a suitcase in either hand. Four footmen and another of the Ethiopians followed, carting the rest of their luggage. They had said their goodbyes to Olga, Tatiana and Maria. Alexei had adamantly announced he was boycotting the parting and Anastasia was nowhere to be seen. As Bess walked beside

Houdini, she handed him the makeshift tuning fork she'd used just outside Alexandra's boudoir.

"Do you think it worked?" she whispered to her husband.

"You heard it ring, didn't you?"

"Yes. But I don't know if it convinced her."

Houdini put his arm around his wife's shoulder. "She knows now, in her heart. No telling what she'll do about it. It's time for us to go home."

When they reached the grand entrance. Houdini stopped to shake the former boxer's hand.

"It was an honor meeting you, Mr. Houdini," Hercules said, beaming.

"Don't forget, when you get back to the States, look me up," Houdini said. "It's a waste of brains and muscles to stay stuck at that door like a cigar store Indian."

As footmen opened the outer doors for them, they heard the clatter of shoes on the marble floor. Anastasia ran to them. She hugged Bess and threw herself into Houdini's arms. He picked her up, squeezed her tight, then put her down.

"Can't you stay a little longer?" she said. "You still haven't taught me the trunk escape."

"I wish I could. But there's a whole world out there that has never seen Houdini." He wrapped an arm around Bess's waist. "Plus, we have a houseful of pets at home to take care of."

"Perhaps we will return someday," Bess told Anastasia.

The child pouted. "It will be so awfully boring here."

"That I don't believe. I've seen how you kids make your own fun," Houdini said. "Also, you have all those magic tricks to practice."

"And my escapes?" she said, her smile returning.

"Well, naturally. You never know when you might find yourself in a jam."

***

Houdini and Bess sat in the waiting area of Nicholaevsky Railway Station in St. Petersburg, named after Nicholas I. While Bess perused an American newspaper, Houdini took in the magnificent architecture in the style of the Italian Renaissance, most notably the Venetian windows and two floors of Corinthian columns. Passengers from an arriving train poured past him. Out of the sea of faces, he recognized a woman carrying one small bag. He stood up in surprise, taking off his hat.

"Chioniya? Is that you?"

The prostitute he'd saved from a humiliating death dragged naked by a horse was dressed in a black coat and hat, like a widow, with a woolen scarf hiding her scarred face.

"Mr. Houdini! Where are you going?" she replied.

"Home to America. What about you?" He hoped she'd found work in St. Petersburg, perhaps in a shop or at least a factory.

The woman looked around to see if they were being observed, then came close to him.

"I am here for Rasputin," she whispered.

"I think we may have stopped him," he told her. "Turned the Tsarina against him."

"Nothing can stop Rasputin except death," Brother Iliodor's convert said with a bitter smile. "While he lives, he is a danger to Mother Russia."

He knew in his heart she was right. But he doubted that she had the capacity to assassinate the Siberian mystic, so superior in physical strength and will.

He called to Bess, "Sweetie, I'll be right back. Chioniya, come with me. I need to talk to you privately for a moment."

A train whistle blew.

"Don't you have a train to catch?" the Sister of Justice asked.

"This will take only a few minutes."

Fifteen minutes later, Houdini returned and casually took his seat beside Bess.

"Now what was that all about?" she asked, standing and folding her arms crossly. "The train is boarding. Who was that girl?"

"You ought to know by now I only have eyes for you," Houdini said, taking her arm and leading her toward the train. "You know what's the first thing I'm going to do when we get to New York?"

"I can't guess."

"Take you dancing."

CHAPTER FORTY-SEVEN

The Assassin

Grigori Yefimovich Rasputin swept his plate off the breakfast table, sending freshly made lamb dumplings rolling across the floor.

"You can't cook. You make love like a dead chicken. What good are you?" he roared. His wife Praskovia gave a sigh of the long-suffering and bent to pick up the shattered dish.

The mystic had been in this foul mood for months, ever since the emperor banished him to Siberia. Oh, officially it was no banishment. Tsar Nicholas had sheepishly explained that it was a temporary move, to protect him from the dangerous gossip of courtiers who'd learned of his disgrace.

"It will be like an extended vacation," the simpering fool had assured him. So far, that "vacation" had eaten up all of 1912!

Even the Tsarina had failed him, acceding to his ejection from the palace. Although he had used prayer and spiritual power to drive the memory of that blasted bell from her conscious mind, he still sensed deep within her a particle of distrust.

One day soon the Imperial Couple would see the error of their ways—this he foresaw, and his gift of prophecy never failed him. When the royal brat Alexei became sick again, Alexandra would call for him, begging him to return and save her son's life. But he would exact a price. No decision would be made in the capital without his say so, and those who had thwarted him would be cut down like wheat before a scythe. And he would make true all the lies that had been spread against him. The Tsarina would be on her knees, kissing more than just his hand this time. The daughters, too, he would plow through them, like a lumberjack clearing a virgin forest. He would break them all to pieces and from those shattered bits mold them again to his liking. But that triumph was thousands of miles and who knew how many months away.

It was the deceiver Houdini who was to blame for his current exile, that false magician with his bag of tricks: watches that were cameras, boxes full of poison, sticks of dynamite.

Houdini!

When Rasputin saw Praskovia stooping to clean up the mess, he shouted at her again.

"Stop that! What are you doing? I won't have my wife on her knees like a scullery maid when I have servants in the house. Call the wench!"

Praskovia turned and called to the back, "Chioniya!"

He toyed irritably with the horn-like bump on his forehead he'd been left with in his youth after stealing a horse and getting struck with an ax by the owner. A moment later, Chioniya drifted into the front room, ghostlike.

"Don't just stand there," her master said, pointing to the pieces of broken china and chunks of food. Listlessly, she got a broom and dustpan and went to work cleaning up.

When his former worshipper had arrived at the cottage in Pokrovskoe two months earlier, he recognized her as soon as he opened the door. Knowing at once she was yet another member of that imbecile Iliodor's corps of girl assassins, he knocked her out with a single blow before she had a chance to utter a word and he disarmed her. And, as he had with each of the previous would-be killers, he had just as easily broken her will and enslaved her.

Now she knelt on her hands and knees scrubbing the remnants of the sauce from the floor. The impulse to take her briefly seized him. But then Chioniya scooted around, and the syphilis scars on her face reminded him of why he hadn't despoiled her.

Disease-ridden whore! With that face, he couldn't even palm her off on a local bumpkin as a reward for carrying out some underhanded deed as he had the peasant girl Yaroslava. This one's only use was the most menial chores: emptying the chamber pots; cleaning the cinders from the fireplace; shining his boots.

The housekeeper Dunya returned from town with an armful of supplies, including salt and, more critically, vodka. She had a newspaper tucked in her armpit. Praskovia helped her carry in the bags.

"Let me see that paper," Rasputin said, rising. "I want to know what those fools are up to in St. Petersburg."

Dunya shooed him away. "Just the usual nonsense. It's really only good for kindling." She walked toward the fireplace.

The mystic snatched the newspaper from her. "Do you really think you can hide anything from me?"

"No, Father Grigori," she said, lowering her head. "Forgive me."

He laid the three-week-old copy of *The Vedomosti* on the table, and carefully perused it. Barely literate, it took him a few moments to find the article his housekeeper knew would rise his ire. When he spotted the headline, his face darkened with rage.

Houdini to Return to Russia. Famous Escape Artist Announces Third Engagement.

"Read it!" he demanded.

Dunya, herself no literary scholar, read haltingly from the article: "Mr. Houdini states that his third tour to Russia will take him to the outermost regions of Siberia, including the village of Pokrovskoe. 'I hope to drop in on my old pal Rasputin,' Mr. Houdini told reporters."

"When is he coming?" Praskovia inquired.

"It doesn't say."

"Surely the Tsar would not allow him to return?" Rasputin's wife asked her husband.

Rasputin circled the room, raging. "The arrogance of that imp. To think he can defeat the lion in his own lair. I will end him." Finally, he saw a use for Chioniya.

"Stand!" he ordered her.

"Yes, Master," she mumbled as if talking in her sleep. When she was on her feet, Rasputin held her shoulders and bored into her eyes with his own.

"You will leave this house and you will forget you were ever in it," the mystic commanded her. "You will go to the town square. And you will wait until you see the face of Harry Houdini." He pointed to the magician's photograph in the paper.

She looked at the photo and then back at Rasputin with confusion in her eyes. "Wait for Houdini? I do not understand."

"Wait in the square for however long it takes. And when Houdini arrives in the square, you will kill him."

She shook her head, "Kill Houdini? But Houdini is my friend. Houdini is good."

Rasputin's voice became more strident. "And I tell you Houdini is your enemy. Houdini is a great sinner. He is evil."

The woman squirmed and screwed up her ruined face in the familiar manner of someone resisting a suggestion. Rasputin momentarily feared that his powers were failing him. He had been so stricken by dread of this lately, that to brush up, he'd secretly visited a doctor who claimed to be an expert in hypnotism.

"You hate Houdini. Houdini is evil. Houdini must die," the mystic repeated, putting bass into his voice and retracting his pupils to pinpricks.

"I hate Houdini. Houdini is evil. Houdini must die," Chioniya finally mimicked Rasputin, much to his relief. The mystic went to a drawer and retrieved the knife that the former prostitute had brought to assassinate him. He placed the weapon in her hand.

"I am sure that Brother Iliodor taught you how to use this properly." He thrust into an imaginary victim and ripped upward. "Make sure that Houdini is disemboweled, so that death comes slowly. Kill the deceiver Harry Houdini."

Chioniya raised the knife. "Now?"

"No, not now, half-wit!" he snapped. *I have really scrambled this one's brain*, Rasputin thought, sighing, and gently pushed her hand down. "At the town square."

"The town square," she echoed.

"Do you understand your instructions?"

"I am to wait in the town square, and when I see Houdini, I am to kill him with this knife." Behind her eyes there was nothing, and Rasputin was satisfied that her obedience would be blind and total.

"Do you have any questions, my child?" he asked her, more patient now.

"How long am I to wait, Master?"

"Until Houdini comes. I do not care if it is a week or a month or a year or ten years. You will wait in the square."

The mental slave frowned a little. "How am I to feed myself, master?"

"How you feed yourself is not my concern," Rasputin grumbled, annoyed again. "If you must return to the life of a prostitute, whore yourself. If with that face, no man will have you, then beg." He flung the newspaper into the fire.

***

Chioniya waited in the square for weeks that turned into months, months that became more than a year. It was not until June of 1914 that the time came for the assassin to execute her Master's command. As Rasputin had foreseen, he had wormed his way back into the Imperial Couple's good graces, and when he visited Pokrovskoe, as he did that summer, it was of his own accord.

That day, Houdini, Bess and the magician's assistant Franz Kukol walked down a foreign street, dodging a gaggle of children who brushed by in pursuit of a dog.

"This show will really knock their socks off, boss," Franz said.

"Once we work out all the kinks," Houdini agreed.

Bess looked around. "It feels odd to be back here."

Houdini felt a tug on his coattails. He looked down and saw a soot-faced urchin.

"Shoeshine, sir?"

"No thanks, kid."

Franz stopped and smiled at the youngster. "Come on, Boss. We have plenty of time."

Houdini nodded. "Fine. You first. I'm going to find a newspaper stand." His assistant settled down on the boy's rickety stool, as Houdini turned to Bess.

"I'll be back in a minute, sweetie," he said, giving her a peck on the cheek.

Bess watched her husband disappear into the distance, and then an unease suddenly came over her, a premonition that something terrible was going to happen. She hastened after him.

"Darling, wait!"

At that moment, Rasputin was walking hurriedly down the street toward the Pokrovskoe post office. In his shaking hand, he held the telegram he had received from the Tsarina.

"Archduke Franz Ferdinand of Austria-Hungary and wife assassinated in Sarajevo. What does this portend? Urgently need your wisdom," the message said.

Just as when the mystic first read the telegram a half hour earlier, apocalyptic images flooded his mind: billowing, life-stealing gas; trenches filled with dying men; war machines dueling in the sky; blood, blood, blood.

Horror is coming, like none the world has ever seen, he thought. But perhaps the chain of events he foresaw could be averted if he sent a telegram forewarning His Supreme Majesty in time.

"Perhaps I have done more harm than good in Russia," he mumbled. "But by this one thing, I will redeem myself."

Nearby, Chioniya Guseva, disheveled and in beggar's rags rank with the stench of horse dung, rose from the street when she beheld the face of the man she had been ordered her to kill.

Houdini!

Bowing her head so that her face could not be seen, she approached her target and stuck out a dirty hand.

"Whatever you can spare, sir," she croaked.

Her "enemy" fished into his pocket for some coins. Then he looked up and recognized her.

"Chioniya?"

Before he could react, she whipped out the knife from beneath her tattered cloak and plunged it into his belly just above the groin. Then she thrust upward with all her strength.

"I have killed the deceiver!" she screamed, holding the bloody knife above her head triumphantly.

CHAPTER FORTY-EIGHT

Checkmate

Ripped open from navel to sternum, Rasputin staggered back, clutching his abdomen to keep his entrails from spilling out onto the street. Horrified onlookers tackled Chioniya.

"She's stabbed him! She's stabbed Rasputin!" cried one local.

While several residents of Pokrovskoe rushed to the aid of their native son, a mob converged on the assassin, kicking her and beating her mercilessly.

"Kill the murderess!"

As he was carried off by his neighbors, blood gushing from his wound, Rasputin now saw it all with perfect clarity. Chioniya had already been hypnotized when she came to him. Houdini had commanded her to see his own face when she looked at Rasputin. Knowing that when Rasputin heard that his enemy was coming to Russia, he would order her to kill him. Houdini had only to give a single newspaper interview on the other side of the world to strike at him without ever setting foot in Russia.

Such cunning. So, a false magician defeats a true one, Rasputin thought as his eyes closed and all went dark.

Big Ben chimed twelve, just as Bess caught up with Houdini. He turned from the newsstand, holding up a copy of the *Times of London*, so that she could see the cover. In large, bold print, the headline blared **"Heir to Austrian Throne Slain by Young Serb. Assassination Could Lead to War."**

"It's terrible," she said. "But you don't really think that the murder of one man could cause countries to go to war, do you?"

Houdini skimmed the text on the front page, his brow knitting.

"They seem to think so, Bess," he said. "You'd be surprised at how an action in one part of the world can affect something thousands of miles away."

***

The Great War that soon followed consumed Europe, with Austria-Hungary, Germany, Russia, France, England, Italy, the Ottoman Empire and other nations caught up in the conflagration.

As always in such dark times, the stage provided a distraction, and no performer commanded greater attention than Houdini.

On stage at the Lyceum Theater in 1916, Houdini transported the audience. They watched in wonder his mysteries and miracles, which climaxed with the Chinese Torture Cell. He took his final bow to a standing ovation. Afterward, in his dressing room, he and Bess discussed their plans for dinner.

"Let's go to Gargiulo's," she said, helping him off with his tuxedo jacket.

"Again? How about the Grand Central Oyster Bar?" Houdini suggested.

A stagehand knocked and told the magician he had backstage visitors.

"Show them in," he called.

Houdini's jaw dropped when the two women in black evening gowns entered: Militsa and her sister Stana. The Black Sisters bore a bouquet of white roses for Houdini and a box of chocolates for Bess, whom they embraced and kissed on both cheeks. He kissed each of their hands.

"A thrilling exhibition of your gifts," Stana said. "Your skills have only grown in the decade since I last saw you perform."

"I'm honored that I was able to entertain you and your sister once again," Houdini replied, trying to put aside his dislike for the witch-like pair.

Their discussion turned to the war, which was not going well for Russia. The Tsar himself had taken command of the army, without much success. His troops were suffering terrible casualties and morale had plummeted. Inevitably, the subject of Houdini's archenemy came up.

"You know that it took many months for Rasputin to survive that assassination attempt," Militsa told him. "As he languished in bed, his powers dissipated. The attack somehow sapped him of his unique psychic energy."

"Well, I wouldn't know anything about that," Houdini said. "I hear they say that crackpot Iliodor had something to do with it."

Militsa smiled. "Yes. But of course, he recovered and returned to the capital, and now he is far more powerful than ever before. With the Tsar at the front, it has been left to the Tsarina to rule Russia. And we both know what that means: Rasputin is ruling Russia. Poor boy, all your heroic efforts to stop Rasputin, all that you put your poor wife through, was for naught."

Houdini clenched his fists. "That won't last forever," he said with a scowl. "The people won't put up with it."

"Of course," Militsa concurred. "At home, the people have lost their faith in the Tsar. Some are convinced that Rasputin is betraying military secrets and that Alexandra, the 'German Woman,' is in league with the enemy. You can imagine how ill-equipped Nicholas is to run a military campaign. Soft, indecisive mouse."

"A debacle," Houdini said, shaking his head angrily. "Are you happy now that you introduced the Romanovs to that maniac?"

"You honestly don't see, do you?" Stana asked.

"No, I—" he paused. Then his eyes widened. "This is what you two wanted."

"To avoid outright revolt, the Duma will act," Stana explained. "Nicholas II will be forced to abdicate in favor of his son Alexei. And my husband the Grand Duke Nikolai Nikolaevich will be appointed regent and be the de facto ruler of the realm ..."

Militsa finished her sentence, "... but of course, the poor, sickly child will not last long. At the appropriate time, Nikolai will be crowned Tsar."

"With the pair of you the powers behind the throne," Houdini whispered, impressed in spite of himself at the wicked genius of it.

"Nikolai is big as an ox, and just as dense," Stana laughed, taking her sister's hand. "He will need our guidance."

"This is what you planned all along," Bess muttered. "From the moment you set eyes on Rasputin."

"There's an old saying," Militsa said. "Americans play checkers. We Russians are the masters of chess."

Bess objected, "But how could you see all the twists and turns ahead of time?"

Militsa's eyes shone with pride, as if she had just checkmated a grandmaster.

"My dear Bess, when one opens oneself up to psychic forces, the past, present and future are as one, laid out before you as plain as day," she boasted.

Houdini wanted to call stagehands to kick out these black cats on their keisters, but he maintained a gentlemanly air.

"I've seen plenty of mediums monkey with those crystal balls over the years," he told Militsa. "The trouble with crystal balls is that sometimes they show you what you want to see."

Epilogue

As it turned out, it was Prince Felix Yusupov who finally put an end to Rasputin, leading a band of conspirators that murdered him in that basement room of Yusupov's mansion after inviting him over for an evening's entertainment.

In March of 1917, Tsar Nicholas II was forced to abdicate amid widespread revolt and Russia was soon declared a republic. A short period of democratic rule ended that October with a Bolshevik coup led by Vladimir Lenin. By November, the communist government had banned the private ownership of property and issued its first censorship decree, abolishing "the bourgeois press."

The Imperial Couple and their children were imprisoned in their palace for months before being shipped to Tobolsk, in Siberia. They were never seen again. Rumors soon spread that they'd been murdered by the Bolsheviks.

Russia withdrew from the unpopular war, while the United States entered the fray. What later became known as the First World War ended with the defeat of Germany and the signing of the Armistice on November 11, 1918. Needless to say, the Black Sisters' scheme did not come to fruition precisely as they planned. Like many aristocrats, they were forced to flee the country, one step ahead of the Red Army. The White Russians who staged an unsuccessful counterrevolution actually did briefly name Grand Duke Nikolai Nikolaevich the Tsar when he was abroad. However, he never enjoyed a moment in power and died in exile on the French Riviera years later.

On the third anniversary of the Armistice in 1921, Houdini joined a circle of men gathered at the prestigious East India

Club in London. These included the military intelligence officer Robert Donatson, who had aided Houdini in Russia, the former ambassador Sir George Buchanan, and Sir Arthur Conan Doyle, author of the Sherlock Holmes stories. Enjoying cigars and brandy, the others listened intently to the magician's tale of his adventures in Russia and his deadly duel with the notorious Siberian mystic.

"Rasputin used every one of his nine lives," Donatson observed. "When poisoned cakes and wine failed to do him in, they shot him, stabbed him, beat him and threw his body in the river. Even then, he wasn't dead because when his body was found, the authorities saw that he'd been trying to free himself from the ropes. It was the water in his lungs that killed him."

"He always thought he would drown," Houdini said quietly.

"When all is said and done, Houdini, do you think he truly had supernatural abilities?" Conan Doyle asked as he lit a pipe.

"I honestly don't know," Houdini replied thoughtfully. "You know, I'm skeptical about those things. Yet he had something that made him different from ordinary men. If he'd never come to the capital and got mixed up in politics, if he'd stayed a peasant healer in Siberia, maybe he'd have been an okay guy."

"I have similar thoughts about the last Tsar," Sir George mused. "If Nicholas II had only been born an ordinary English country gentleman, he'd have had a very happy life. The sort of fellow who takes care of his dogs and his children and his garden, about whom his neighbors have nothing but kind words and who has nothing but kind words about others."

"He was a gentle soul," Houdini agreed. "Too gentle for that time and that place."

"Tragic what became of the family," said Donatson. "British intelligence has no doubt Lenin ordered their execution."

Houdini winced and looked sadly at the fire.

"You know, old boy, there is a rumor that Anastasia somehow escaped the fate of the others," Conan Doyle said. "And that she's out there somewhere, safe and sound."

Houdini smiled wryly. "I would like to believe that."

THE END

Afterward

Most of the major characters in this book are real. I adhered as closely as possible to the factual information about them I gleaned from history books. For example, Yusupov, Rasputin's assassin, really was a crossdresser. Many real events, such as the murder of Prime Minister Stolypin, are incorporated into the story. Wholly imaginary is the ballerina Natasha Stepanova, whose first name is a tip of the hat to the lady spy in the Rocky and Bullwinkle cartoons. The poet Illya, named after the cute young Russian agent Illya Kuryakin in TV's *Man From U.N.C.L.E.*, is likewise made up. My fictional Robert Donatson is based on the British spy sent to tsarist Russia in the film *Knight without Armor* ... starring the actor Robert Donat. The conniving Militsa existed, though I combined her schemes with those of the equally sinister Marie Pavlovna.

I frequently incorporated the exact words that Rasputin's contemporaries used to describe him into the dialogue. History books offer varied spellings of names such as Yusupov. I generally chose the simplest. I called Militsa's brother-in-law Nikolai instead of Nicholas to distinguish him from the Tsar.

It is true that Houdini toured Russia in 1903 and performed for the Tsar. In describing his tricks and escapes on that trip, I embellished upon the known facts. Houdini did boast that Tsar Nicholas offered him the job of spiritual advisor. Rasputin did arrive in St. Petersburg that year, but there is no evidence that the two larger-than-life figures ever crossed paths. Houdini did not, as far as we know, return to Russia in 1911, but this novel has as its premise "What if ...?"

About the Author

C. Michael Forsyth is a Yale graduate in English Literature with an MFA in film from New York University. He is a former senior writer for *Weekly World News*. He is also the author of

The Blood of Titans
Hour of the Beast
The Identity Thief
Sir Arthur Conan Doyle & Harry Houdini in The Adventure of the Spook House
Alphie the Albino Polar Bear
Bizarre News

Learn more about the author and his work at
http://freedomshammer.com

What Critics Say

"*Sir Arthur Conan Doyle & Harry Houdini in The Adventure of the Spook House* by C. Michael Forsyth is an adventure story with depth, full of atmosphere, suspense, ingenuity and a real feeling for place, period and personality. Mr. Forsyth brings the two men and their troubled friendship to life in this fictional investigation of murder in a haunted house. Intensive research, a good ear for the patterns and rhythms of speech, and an easy literate style make for a cracking good read."

— *The Sherlock Holmes Society of London*

"*The Blood of Titans* is jam-packed with adventure and non-stop drama. The author uses years of research as the gateway to allow the reader access into the golden years of African civilization, adorned with power and wealth ... Readers can hear the melodious sounds of African music that the royals listened to and taste the African food and the drinks that they consumed ... *The Blood of Titans* is worthy of an epic film."

— *The Final Call*

"*Hour of the Beast* is a fast-paced, rip-snorting, action-packed, sexy college romp."

— *Horror Fiction Review.*